THE FLOWERS OF EDO

A NOVEL

MICHAEL DANA KENNEDY

 VERTICAL.

Jacket image by De Agostini Picture Library / Getty Images

Published by Vertical, Inc., New York

ISBN 978-1-934287-80-4

Manufactured in the United States of America

First Edition

Vertical, Inc.
1185 Avenue of the Americas 32nd Floor
New York, NY 10036
www.vertical-inc.com

This book is dedicated to Japanese-American soldiers who fought and died for their country, the United States of America, during World War II while their families were incarcerated in "Relocation" camps.

A Note on Names

Japanese names are given surname first except for Japanese Americans identified as such. Diacritical marks for proper names (e.g., Tôkyô), etc., have been omitted in the dialog of non-Japanese speakers. The first name "Kyoko," however, is given without a diacritical mark throughout the text, reflecting a more intimate relationship.

プロローグ

PROLOGUE

August 3, 1945

Kobayashi Kenji stood before the *kamidana*, a small Shintô altar he had fashioned the night he boarded the battleship. He clapped his hands two times to summon the gods, then closed his eyes, bowed his head, and prayed silently. *Perhaps these will be my final prayers*, he reflected.

He felt odd praying to Japan's Shintô gods, not having done so since 1941, when he last stood on Japanese soil. He felt it wise to reacquaint himself with the ways of his ancestors before going back to Japan.

Resting on the *kamidana* was an *omamori*, a rectangular paper amulet given to him by his mother, Misaki. She had purchased it at a Shintô shrine two months before war broke out between Japan and America. When the war shattered the uneasy peace and Kenji later enlisted in the army she gave him the amulet for protection from harm.

In front of the *omamori* an ordinary candle flickered in a small crystal glass; on either side of the candle were photos of Kobayashi's parents, brother, and three sisters. At each of the two front corners of the shelf a small stick of burning incense released wispy, divergent trails of smoke, each dissipating throughout the small cabin.

The cabin, like most on the massive battleship, seemed drab and confining. His sole attempt to personalize it, the *kamidana*, was, he felt, inadequate.

His prayers to *Amaterasu-no-Ômikami*, the sun goddess and founder of Japan's Imperial line, were for the souls of his ancestors, the welfare of his family, and in particular the safety of his twin brother, Tomoyuki. Through his prayers he hoped to capture the serenity he felt certain his ancestors had found and to still the disturbing fears about his brother.

Tomoyuki's last letter to the Kobayashi family had arrived five weeks before the attack on America's naval base at Pearl Harbor. Somewhere in the shrinking empire of Japan Tomoyuki was still in the Imperial Japanese Army. Or he was dead.

As an afterthought Kenji also prayed to *Susa-no-O*, the storm god, beseeching him to protect his brother if he was still alive and if dead, to ferry his soul to the Yasukuni Shrine in Tôkyô, the final resting place of Japan's heroes.

Tomoyuki, my brother, are you alive? Will I see you again?

His prayers were clouded by a paradox. Unlike most Japanese, he did not truly worship the gods of his ancestors. Moreover, his four years at Tôkyô Imperial University peeled away any pretense that all of Japan's ruling class still genuinely embraced the intrinsic cultural mysticism of their heritage. He noticed, however, that the rulers, not being fools, accepted the fact that political reality often required them to invoke the gods during public religious ceremonies. By praying to the gods of the past, they ensured their secular future. Though he knew it was hypocritical, he too, while studying at the university, sometimes attended public ceremonies of worship. Curiously, he found it comforting to pray, not for his own soul, as in the Western tradition, but for his family.

At the conclusion of his prayers Kobayashi Kenji bowed toward the *kamidana* and stepped back. As he knelt to meditate, he loosened the *obi* wrapped around his *yukata*, a white and blue *kimono* made from soft, woven fabric. He found wearing it comfortable during meditation, especially in the oppressive heat of the confining cabin.

As he settled, he felt the ship's propellers increase their revolutions as the helmsman spun the wheel. He reflexively adjusted to the slight heeling motion of the ship as it changed course. It did this every few minutes, a process explained to him earlier as zigzagging, a precaution to avoid enemy submarines, the nemesis of surface ships.

Earlier in the evening, as he did every night, he had written a letter to his family. Then, settling back, he would compose poems. Before writing he would amend each phrase in his mind, perhaps a dozen times. Choosing just the right character would often take several seconds. Satisfied, he would dip the *fude*, a bamboo brush pen, in thick, black ink and make his strokes. Because he took pleasure from these occasions, this would sometimes last for hours. There was little else to do except exercise, meditate, read, eat, and sleep.

And go over in his mind his mission, again and again.

The constant throbbing of the powerful engines vibrating throughout the warship did not disturb him; now he was *samurai*, his mind and spirit impenetrable. He smiled as he considered how the Japanese were able to ignore intrusions during meditation. It was, he felt, a valuable trait non-Japanese never understood or developed.

No, not completely true, he thought. *The Chinese and Indians meditate, but not like the Japanese.*

He closed his eyes and summoned images of his family, evoking tender prewar memories. Composed, he placed his hands, palms down, on his thighs, preparing to descend to a deeper level, transcending his surroundings. But within a few moments, a loud knock at the door roused him from his meditation and he opened his eyes.

"Enter."

A sergeant opened the door. Stepping over the coaming

he entered the cabin and stood at attention, his eyes locked on Kobayashi's profile. The sergeant was a Marine guard, peculiar to the Western and Japanese navies. The Imperial Japanese Navy had acquired the practice of having Marines on their ships from the British, as had the American Navy. Their principal task was to provide security at the discretion of the ship's captain. And they had the captain's authority.

"Sir, excuse me. The captain has ordered me to escort you to the admiral's stateroom."

Kenji closed his eyes again and sighed, then stood and walked over to the table, looked at the clock, and nodded; 0200 hours. It was time.

The sergeant hadn't been in this cabin before, and he looked around fleetingly. His eyes paused at the *kamidana*. For reasons he didn't readily understand he didn't like this Army officer, this…outsider. He feared him, too. He ended his survey on Kobayashi's back, examining the *yukata*. *I don't like you, sir, but I don't know why. You fight with us, but you're an outsider and I don't trust you.*

Sensing the guard's uneasiness and without turning around, Kenji said, "Thank you, Sergeant. Please wait outside while I change."

"Yes, sir." The sergeant seemed eager to leave the room.

Kenji understood and accepted the captain's reasons for ordering the guard to escort him. He had boarded four nights ago and his movement about the battleship was limited to a section reserved for officers' cabins and the head across the passageway. A Marine guard was always posted outside his quarters. Kenji never left it, except to use the head and shower, and then only at nighttime and under escort. The guard made certain no one else entered the head while Kobayashi occupied it. Food was delivered to his quarters; the sentinel on duty would take it in only after the steward had left the passageway.

Five days earlier, while preparing to transfer to the battleship, he had received the admiral's terse orders instructing him to board in the middle of the night, to avoid arousing curiosity from the crew or other officers. When he had arrived, by an amphibious plane, the ship's captain himself had ushered Kobayashi to his quarters. Except for the admiral, the captain, the naval intelligence officer, and the ever-present Marine guards, who were ordered to secrecy, no one had seen him or knew he was on board.

The isolation provided a privilege every sailor and junior officer on a ship hungered for: a cabin to himself. He felt somewhat guilty occupying a cabin normally shared by two or three junior officers. He acknowledged, however, that an Army Intelligence officer, on a perilous mission, rated him the uncommon luxury.

Does this mission merit such luxury? Japanese are used to much less. Still, what I'm about to do, will it make a difference in the course of the war? Then an ominous, more chilling thought cloaked him: *Am I composing my death poem?*

He returned to the table and took a final look at the photographs. Every day, since his arrival, a mail plane had delivered a package for him. Each package contained numerous photographs of Miyakonojô, in southern Kyûshû. Each delivery showed minor changes. Each photograph was accompanied by written analysis. He put the photographs down. He had memorized the details.

He opened the wardrobe and reached for the Imperial Japanese Army uniform. In the corner, almost hidden by his uniform, stood his *katana*, a long-bladed, slightly-curved *samurai* sword. It had been hand-forged more than 350 years ago by the master sword maker, Umetada Myôju from Kyôto. Forward of the *tsuka*, the leather-wrapped hilt, was the *tsuba*, the hand guard between the blade and the hilt. It was behind this guard that the right index finger pressed against, offering balance for the sword and protection for the hands as well as ensuring that the hands did not slide forward over the blade. It was made of brass and richly decorated with a tiger and a dragon and stamped with the Kobayashi *mon*, the family crest.

The blade bore the sword maker's distinct stamp—Myôju on one side, Umetada on the other. On the other side of the blade was inscribed, "*Always one with the other.*" Near the *katana* stood its shorter twin, the *wakizashi*. Together they formed a *dai-shô*—large and small—a unified pair. His brother possessed a flawless duplicate *dai-shô*, with the same inscription.

On the bottom of the wardrobe lay his flight bag.

He laid the uniform on the bunk and removed the *katana* from the wardrobe. Gripping the *tsuka* in one hand and the *saya*—scabbard—in the other, he withdrew the blade a few inches. The light from the cabin's bare bulbs flashed off the blade, accentuating the unblemished surface. Whenever he held the sword he thought of Tomoyuki.

The duplicate sets of the Umetada swords, rare in Japan, remained unused for well over three hundred years, since the Battle of Sekigahara in 1600. In that battle another set of Kobayashi twins had fought for Tokugawa Ieyasu, and though Tokugawa Ieyasu triumphed and would later become *Shôgun*, both brothers died from wounds suffered near the end of the battle.

The swords had been solely treasured as family heirlooms, until Kenji's and Tomoyuki's father gave the swords to the twins in their youth. Kenji smiled at the memory of cherished childhood moments the sword evoked. He pushed the sword back into the *saya* and laid it on the bed, alongside his uniform.

He briskly untied the *obi*, removed his *yukata*, and placed them on the bed. He adjusted his *fundoshi*, a simple loincloth, then went back to the bed and picked up his uniform pants and pulled them on. After donning the shirt he sat on a chair and pulled on his leather boots. They had belonged to another Japanese officer, now dead. With the shortages of matériel in

Japan and lack of replacements in the occupied territories, it was not unusual to take another soldier's clothing or equipment, but only if the soldier was dead and no one witnessed the deed.

Before putting on his tunic he buckled on a fabric belt to which he would attach his *katana*. His Imperial Japanese Army tunic was replete with campaign ribbons, signifying several campaigns in service to *Tennô-Heika*. Attached to the lapels were rank badges of Major. The arm-of-service color on the left breast was dark brown, for combat engineers.

The tunic fit loosely over his compact, muscular frame. He buttoned the tunic and then buckled the leather tunic belt.

He walked back to the wardrobe and removed the *wakizashi*, smaller than the *katana*, used as a defensive dagger or a close combat weapon, especially if fighting two opponents simultaneously. After briefly examining it he replaced it. *No, if all goes well, I won't need you this time. If I complete my mission I'll come back for you.*

He buckled his holstered semiautomatic pistol, an 8 mm M94, around his waist and over his shoulder, then attached the *katana* to the fabric belt under his tunic. Finally, he pulled on his peaked officer's cap. A five-pointed star confirmed the rank of officer. He walked to the *kamidana*, wet his fingers with saliva, and snuffed out the incense sticks and candle.

He turned and looked in the mirror one last time and received a jolt. The loose-fitting uniform made him look gaunt. He adjusted his tunic but it didn't help. He wondered if his brother looked the same. A sense of sorrow enveloped him. Gripping harder the hilt of his *katana*, he shook off the image. Ready, he opened the cabin door and nodded to the guard. The sergeant caught his breath and then composed himself. It was fleeting but Kenji noted it. The sergeant turned and led Kenji down the passageway.

Most of the crew slept. Kenji's boot heels clacked loudly in the stillness. Neither man spoke, each occupied with his own thoughts. The sergeant led. He too wore a sidearm. Halfway down the passageway they turned right, passing through a doorway to a connecting passageway. They walked about ten feet forward, the sergeant alert for any crew members who might be walking about at the early hour. Abruptly, the ship changed course again and Kenji adjusted accordingly. He noticed his escort seemed to ignore the sudden movement.

Kenji followed closely, relying on the sergeant's knowledge of the ship. The soft red lights that lined the bulkheads, knee high, illuminated the corridors in a ghostly manner. At night the regular passageway lights were off. If the sleeping crew were suddenly called to battle stations, the red lights would preserve their night vision as they rushed to the deck.

When he first boarded the ship, Kenji noted above him countless cables, varying in size, running parallel and suspended in clusters from the overheads. All of them were exposed, ensuring repair crews immediate access in case of battle damage. A closer look revealed a tag dangling from each cable, identifying its purpose. Concealing the cables could delay repairs a few, sometimes fatal, seconds. To men who never served on a warship it looked confusing. To the crewmen who would have to make repairs during the fury of battle, it was as ordered as a blueprint.

Kenji followed the sergeant a few paces forward to a short ladder and, as he stepped on the first rung, admired the man's surefootedness in the ship's pitch and roll. At the bottom they circled halfway and proceeded down a second, continuing their angled descent. The Marine's practiced ease triggered Kenji's grudging respect. He wished he had more shipboard experience then realized he was being petty.

About to step off the top rung, Kenji flinched as the ship convulsed from several immense explosions. His first thought was that they were under attack. He steadied himself for a few seconds. At the bottom his guide stood and watched, waiting for him, apparently undisturbed by the explosions. Feeling foolish, Kenji continued, but his boot heel slipped off the edge of the rung. He tried to steady himself by grabbing the railings on either side, and as he pitched down the ladder his *katana*'s scabbard, no longer in his grip, slapped against some of the rungs. A chorus of clangs, wooden *saya* striking metal, echoed in the passageways above and below them.

The sergeant looked at Kobayashi's sword and then, raising his head, hard into his eyes. "Unloading through the muzzle, sir," he said softly.

Kenji looked perplexed.

"It's the only safe way to remove unfired projectiles rounds from the ship's guns, sir." He seemed embarrassed for Kobayashi.

"The ship seemed to move sideways. Or did I imagine that?"

"That's called 'crabbing,' sir. The ship supposedly moves sideways, like a crab, when all the guns are fired in a broadside at the same time. Or so the officers tell us. I don't know if it's true, sir."

Both fell silent, but Kenji, feeling inept, accepted the reproachful explanation and transferred his left hand from the railing to grasp the scabbard. His escort, satisfied, turned and continued.

The thick smell of heavy machine oil, mixed with the odor of burnt gunpowder from the ship's guns that had hammered the enemy's fortified shore positions earlier that day, permeated the passageways.

Each time they neared the bottom of a ladder his guide rapped the overhead with his knuckles as a warning to Kobayashi to duck. It was an unnecessary warning; Kenji was eight inches shorter. At the bottom of the final ladder they turned toward the main passageway. The sergeant paused.

His keen ears caught the sound of a doorknob being turned. He quickly surveyed the cabin doors and saw one open slowly and a drowsy ensign begin to emerge.

Whispering, he hastily instructed Kobayashi to back up a bit and stay still. Then he darted toward the ensign's door.

"Sorry, sir. Captain's orders," he said firmly as he blocked the doorway. "This section has to remain in quarters for the next thirty minutes."

"Damn it, I've got to use the toilet. And I didn't hear those orders," countered the ensign. He started to move out again and walked into the big treelike man. The sergeant tilted his head down and to the side and arched an inquisitive eyebrow. Though the ensign outranked him, the sergeant knew it didn't matter; he had the captain's authority.

Softly, almost deferentially, the large man repeated, "Sorry, sir. I can't let you use the passageway. Captain's orders, sir. Just thirty minutes. We don't want to disturb the captain, sir. Do we?"

The ensign seemed about to challenge the orders, but when he saw the cold, quiet determination in the man's eyes he backed into his cabin, allowing the guard to close the door.

"Thank you, sir. Just for half an hour." The Marine turned and gestured for Kobayashi to continue down the ladder.

As Kenji slowly descended he watched the sergeant keep his hand on the knob. It started to turn. With a mischievous grin the sergeant allowed it to turn completely. As the door started to open a fraction of an inch, his iron grip clamped on the knob and the door moved no further. After a moment, the door meekly closed.

"Sorry, sir. Captain's orders. Just a bit longer."

A sigh from behind the cabin door and release of the pressure on the knob signaled the ensign's capitulation.

"Thank you, sir. Good night, sir."

He proceeded confidently. The ensign would stay put. The

big Marine's quiet authority and sense of humor were evident. Then he saw Kobayashi looking at him and his smile disappeared, his face hardened again.

They walked toward the main passageway, entered it, and arrived just outside the amidships entrance to the wardroom. They stopped.

Drifting out from the wardroom, the mellow, touching melody of a Glenn Miller tune struck a familiar chord in Kenji. As he listened, he recalled Japan's love-hate passion for American culture. While a student at Tôkyô Imperial University he often found himself arguing against his brother and other classmates, and even some faculty members, about what they considered America's cultural intrusions, especially its music and movies. Kenji had defended what he called "America's enriching presence" in Japan, calling the movies and music a broadening experience. He was always in the minority.

Kenji and the large man exchanged glances. "Sir," the Marine said, and stood just outside the coaming, indicating Kobayashi should precede him. Kenji nodded once and, angling the scabbard back and upward, stepped over the coaming into the wardroom. His escort remained just outside.

Inside, several officers sat lounging around. Others stood, huddled in small groups. All of them were exhausted after a long, intense day and night of combat. The ship's mission, firing on enemy shore installations, had been threatened by attacking enemy aircraft. Though weary, the men were still tense; some enemy planes came too close with their bombs. None of the crew ever got used to that.

The wardroom's small galley, still open, served midnight rations and tea, coffee, or soft drinks. Some men played cards; several read letters. The thick drifting haze of cigarette smoke partially obscured Kenji's vision.

On Kenji's right, a few men sat at a table, laughing, describing the day's actions, and reviewing tactics. A lieutenant, chewing food and holding a cup in one hand, lifted his sandwich again with the other. Out of the corner of his eye, he saw Kenji standing in the doorway. Turning, his eyes widened and he yelled, "Wha' the hell…" spitting out food and dropping his cup, which shattered on the square ceramic tile.

Heads turned, conversation hushed in mid-sentence. Several men stood, amazement evident on their faces. Chair legs scraped the deck as they were pushed back. Surprise turned to anger, then to rage. A pilot grabbed an empty bottle, broke it on the edge of a table, and moved toward Kenji, the jagged neck pointing at him. Others followed, fists clenched, faces grim. At that point, the Marine entered the wardroom, pushed past Kenji, and lifted the flap of his holster.

Unexpectedly, from behind the knot of angry officers, a strong, commanding voice boomed, "ATTENTION ON DECK!"

Recognizing the voice, everyone froze, the response automatic. The battleship's captain walked across the wardroom and elbowed his way through his officers. When he stood a few feet before them he stopped, five feet in front of Kenji. Some of his officers moved in behind their captain, as if to reinforce him.

Hands on hips, the captain inspected the small-framed, muscular man before him. He took his time, his eyes carefully examining Kenji's black boots, pants, and his pistol. He noted Kobayashi's left hand holding the scabbard. The wrinkled loose-fitting jacket, with its campaign ribbons, also denoted the rank of major on the lapels. Each lapel held a red rectangle with one star imposed on three yellow parallel stripes. The embroidered badge of a pilot's wings was on his right chest. The captain nodded his approval.

Kenji's height, five feet eight inches, was tall for a Japanese man. The captain thought that he looked thin in the ill-fitting uniform. An angular face set off a firm jaw. His lips, full and bowed down slightly, displayed just a hint of arrogance. The ears were small and lay close to his head. His thick black hair, trimmed close, was in the style of the Imperial Japanese Army. His nostrils were slightly flared, the nasal bridge prominent. The captain was drawn to Kenji's eyes, dark brown and accentuated by the epicanthic folds. They were intense and impenetrable.

Kenji remained indifferent to the scrutiny. He looked straight ahead, appearing to ignore the captain.

The captain was impressed. A confident Imperial Japanese Army officer stood before him, oblivious to the tension he created in the wardroom. The captain turned to face his officers. The captain's earlier decision to have the wardroom occupied by his pilots worked; their response to seeing Kenji was visceral.

"As you were."

The wardroom erupted in a flurry of questions. Turning back and looking at Kenji, the captain, over his shoulder, declared, "I said as you were. Now, if you'll excuse us, the admiral is waiting. Sergeant, you're relieved. Kobayashi, come with me."

The captain turned around. He and Kobayashi walked straight ahead, through the semicircle of bewildered officers, some of whom refused to yield their shoulders to Kenji as he passed, barely controlling their confusion and anger.

They walked toward the port side wardroom door, diagonally opposite the door Kenji had first entered. Behind them, the mystified officers were left with their unanswered questions. Some pursued the Marine, hoping for answers.

Approaching the stateroom door, Kenji could see the admiral staring at him through a heavy cigarette haze. Though outwardly calm, Kenji was anxious. The admiral turned and withdrew deeper into his stateroom. Kenji and the captain entered the room as the admiral, taking his seat at a table, beckoned them with several impatient jerks of his fingers.

The admiral removed a cigarette package from his shirt pocket, pulled out a cigarette, and lit it. He inhaled fiercely then blew a column of smoke toward the overhead. Kenji breathed in the redolence. The admiral looked at the captain for a few seconds and then fixed his eyes on Kobayashi Kenji, staring from under bushy salt-and-pepper eyebrows with the intensity of a bird of prey. The captain saw that the admiral's emotions were barely under control.

Aboard the admiral's flagship, less than five feet from him, stood an Imperial Japanese Army officer. Without taking his eyes off Kenji, he violently crushed the cigarette in an ashtray.

"Gentlemen, take a seat," snapped Admiral William F. "Bull" Halsey, flying his flag aboard the battleship USS *Missouri* and commander of the United States Third Fleet, off the coast of Japan.

So, as you go into battle, remember your ancestors and remember your descendants.

—Tacitus

The United Nations War Objective is the Unconditional Surrender of the Axis Powers. The accomplishment of this Objective may require the invasion of Japan.

*Joint Chiefs of Staff Memorandum:
Strategic Plan for the Defeat of Japan
May 8 1943*

1

The Pasig River, replenished from a heavy rain before sunrise, meandered through the city of Manila. The morning sky glowed azure. At scattered points rainbows gave the illusion of multicolored bridges bowing across the river. A gentle breeze stroked the wildflowers that dotted the banks, and fishing boats plied the river. The Japanese were gone, routed by the Americans; normalcy was returning.

On the riverbank stood the Philippines' symbol of governmental authority, the Malacañan Palace, also called the Philippine White House. Outside the main entrance, American Army sentries stood at parade rest, their only activity snapping to attention and presenting arms when officers approached. This morning, the guards were presenting arms more often than usual. Allied officers from different countries were entering. The sentries exchanged glances, knowing something big was up.

Malacañan Palace, in its rococo opulence, was the focus of absolute power in the Philippines. Unlike most of Manila, it had escaped destruction during the American liberation of the city. In a final spasm of vindictive madness, retreating Japanese sailors and Imperial Marines destroyed most of Manila and indiscriminately murdered tens of thousands of Filipino children, women, and men.

Malacañan Palace was now the headquarters of General Douglas MacArthur, Supreme Allied Commander, South West Pacific Area. On entering, the Allied officers were awed by the grandness of the wide, ornate, red-carpeted halls. The dark paneling of the high-ceilinged walls was randomly highlighted by rousing oil paintings of Philippine history and mythic heroes.

Filipino workers were busy reinstalling the palace's enormous, ornate chandeliers, which had been removed for safekeeping when the Japanese invaded, right after Pearl Harbor. The workers, already used to the comings and goings of American officers, ignored the visitors.

After entering the palace the officers were ushered to a cavernous room that had served as the main conference room for senior Japanese officers. Now, Americans, Chinese, Australians, Dutch, British, French, and New Zealanders stood and talked in loosely formed groups.

"I'm serious," said an American in one group. He paused and dragged hard on a cigarette. "This is the very spot. Look at the stain on the rug." He pointed to a dark area under their shoes. "The Japs cleaned it as best they could. He stood right here, asking Yamashita for a quick lesson in geography while we were hitting the beach."

The American grinned as he related what he had been told. On October 10, 1944, shortly before the Americans invaded the Philippines, General Yamashita Tomoyuki, the "Tiger of Malaya," had arrived in Manila with orders to organize the Japanese defense in anticipation of an expected American invasion. Yamashita was one of Japan's ablest field com-manders, but his arrival was too late. On the same day the Americans invaded, Yamashita's new Chief of Staff, Lieutenant General Mutô Akira, flew in to the former—and future—Clark Field. A major informed him he was to be taken immediately to Yamashita's headquarters. As the small convoy reached the outskirts of Manila, American fighter planes strafed the open cars. General Mutô jumped headlong into a roadside ditch, not knowing it contained raw sewage.

"When he arrives here at Malacañan," continued the American, "he's immediately taken to Yamashita, who tells him that the Americans are landing at Leyte. Now picture this. Mutô, Yamashita's new Chief of Staff, apparently knows next to nothing about the Philippines. He's stinking something awful, covered with dripping shit. He looks at Yamashita and says, 'Very interesting, but where is Leyte?'"

An Australian, Colonel Jeremy Fitzhugh, looked down and grinned. "Roight here? On this very spot? Are you shittin' me, mate?" The rest broke out in laughter.

At the front of the room was a platform. At its rear two hard-looking Military Police sergeants stood at parade rest, their eyes occasionally sweeping the room. Each had a holstered .45-caliber sidearm. They flanked a set of large green drapes that were drawn together, a draw cord on either side. To the left of the drapes was a gray metal table holding forty or so notebooks. Each was sealed with a wide strip of red paper marked **TOP SECRET**. There was also, evidently at someone's insistence, a pitcher of water and several glasses and a wooden, rubber-tipped pointer, four feet long.

In the rear of the room a table had been set up with a large coffee percolator, cups, and donuts. Several men were appreciating them.

Cigarette smoke swirled upward, concentrating a few feet below the ceiling like high cumulus. A few of the men coughed or rubbed their eyes.

Standing by themselves at the rear, a handful of junior American Army and Navy officers grouped together. One of the American Army lieutenants, however, drew interest. A few of the new arrivals cast questioning or even icy glances his way, especially the Chinese. He was, they were sure, Japanese.

The chandeliers were turned on. Pale yellow beams etched through the surrounding blue haze. One of the British admirals wondered why the windows were being drawn at 0645 hours, which barred any breeze the tropics might mercifully offer. The humid air was already heavy.

In addition to being allies, these officers had two other things in common. They all spoke English fluently and they represented their respective nations' Theater Military Headquarters.

None knew precisely why he was in Manila. Their superiors, on short notice, had ordered them to fly, some with fighter escort, from Brisbane or Chunking or the Marianas to the Philippines for a meeting with MacArthur's staff. Most, however, had presaged the actual reason. After all, they had all been in the war a long time and knew how things went. And all were in intelligence.

Suddenly the doors at the rear of the room flew open and the two MPs snapped to attention. One yelled "TENNN-HUT!" Everyone stood to attention, facing front. Major General Charles Willoughby, MacArthur's Chief of Intelligence, briskly strode to the front of the room, his huge frame seeming to fill the center aisle. Trailing behind him was a portly colonel carrying a valise. As they reached the front row of chairs, the colonel moved to the right, standing in front of one.

Despite his bulk Willoughby bounded onto the platform, turned, and stood next to the table. He was enormous, a bear of a man. He towered over everyone in the room; his frame was wider than anyone else's. A native of Germany until the age of eighteen, he still spoke with a noticeable accent. Because of his German ancestry and accent as well as his aloof manner, always dressing in a custom-tailored general's uniform and at times wearing a monocle, he was sometimes called "Sir Charles" behind his back by some of his staff.

Willoughby cleared his throat. "Gentlemen, please be

seated."

Those not near seats found them, some crushing their cigarettes in the ashtrays they held. Those already at their chairs sat. Willoughby smiled and acknowledged some of the men he recognized.

"I'm glad you could attend this morning. As you know the Philippines are secured. Otherwise we might be meeting in the jungle instead of in this splendid palace. Iwo Jima is also secured and several air fields are already operational. Fighters from them are escorting our B-29s as they bomb Japan. Incidentally, we have had word that Japanese resistance on Okinawa is winding down. It is now estimated that the Okinawa campaign will be completed before the end of the month. Unfortunately, Army and Marine casualties so far have been quite high. Japanese suicide planes have also struck hard at the Navy, which is giving coverage to the invasion.

"Where we go from here is why you've been asked to come today. For the past few months a number of alternatives to ending the war have been put on the table, and they have been boiled down to three.

"The first is that we invade Japan, a plan favored by the Army.

"The Navy had proposed a second option. Rather than immediately invading Japan we would first isolate it from the Asian mainland and Formosa by invading Korea and the eastern coast of China. Some have suggested that Japan would then realize its complete isolation and offer to surrender.

"The third suggestion was not to invade but to encircle Japan completely and force them to surrender through blockade and bombardment, the latter by both the Navy and Army Air Forces.

"The Navy's argument, squeezing Japan into submission was, frankly, tempting on its face because, if it succeeded, we would win with little loss of Allied life. But that would take longer than the American people are prepared to wait.

"Washington wants this war to end as soon as possible. And General MacArthur wants to end it. This past April 3rd, the Joint Chiefs of Staff ordered General MacArthur to begin drafting preliminary plans for the invasion of Japan. More recently, May 25th, the Joint Chiefs completed and sent to General MacArthur, Admiral Nimitz, and General Carl Spaatz, commander of U.S. Strategic Air Forces in the Pacific, plans for the amphibious invasion of Japan's home islands. The Joint Chiefs expect President Truman to approve the plan within the next few days."

The room remained silent. Willoughby was not surprised.

"I'd like to explain why this decision was reached. First, if we follow the Navy's plan and invade Formosa, Korea, and the eastern coast of China, we disperse our forces and waste resources on partial and perhaps unnecessary objectives."

A Chinese general frowned, angered that the Americans regarded China as an "unnecessary objective." Willoughby noticed the response.

"Then, let me remind you, we would undoubtedly still have to invade Japan. We, or rather General MacArthur and the Joint Chiefs, felt that we might be paying twice the price for real estate that's already nearly in our grasp." Willoughby paused, then looked at the Chinese general. "Second, if we did invade China, we might become bogged down in a new front that will further delay the inevitable, including the liberation of China. Our objective is to end this war and liberate occupied nations, especially China. Japan is the key.

"As far as blockading and bombing is concerned, it might work but it will delay the outcome. Some have argued that such a delay will save Allied lives. This may be true. But we cannot forget that the longer this war goes on, the longer the Chinese people will continue to suffer disease, starvation, injury, and death from Japanese forces occupying their land." Willoughby, hoping he had deflected a possible contretemps, turned his attention to the rest of the gathering.

"We know that Allied POWs in the hands of the Japanese are suffering terribly. In addition, though admittedly not foremost in our concerns, Japanese civilians are suffering and will suffer even more with a protracted blockade and bombing. Our war is with the government and military forces of Japan. And we know the civilians are still being told that Japan is winning the war."

"Forgive me, General Willoughby," interrupted a British officer as he stood, "Japanese civilians are being injured and dying now with the bombing of their cities."

"Agreed. But we do drop leaflets letting them know which cities are going to be bombed."

"But, General, you don't always say when."

Willoughby looked at the British officer as if he were a grade-school student. "Colonel, there is a war on. We can't give them everything."

"Yes, quite. Point taken, sir."

"Therefore," continued Willoughby, "the Joint Chiefs and General MacArthur, in conjunction with Admiral Nimitz, have decided upon the invasion of Japan."

An American admiral leaned over to an aide and whispered, "'In conjunction with Admiral Nimitz' my ass."

"As you can see behind me there are several covered easels." General Willoughby nodded to one of the MPs. "Sergeant…"

The room became quieter as the sergeants began to remove the black covers. When the last cloth was removed there was complete silence. Revealed were several large poster boards, three feet above the floor, each containing a flow chart or map, the latter displaying the home islands of Japan. On the maps were symbols, arrows, and numbers. For several minutes, more than forty pairs of eyes, quickly at first, then slowly, darted from board to board, devouring details. A few of the officers caught their breath.

As if on cue, a low whistle from the back of the room shattered the reserve. Some officers stood, thinking they would get a better view. Others spoke softly, to no one in particular. There were many comments uttered aloud, in several tongues.

"Holy shit!"

"Gawd! Are there that many capital ships in the Pacific?"

"It's not possible to land that many men."

"Awh! Saang dee awh!"

"This makes the Normandy landing look like a cakewalk."

"It'll be Gawd awful. On both sides."

"Mon Dieu!"

Willoughby waited a few minutes, letting it sink in.

"I've asked one of my aides, Colonel Hanford, to give a detailed presentation of our plans for the invasion of Japan. Each of you will be given a detailed draft. You will study and return it by tomorrow morning. Of course, quarters will be provided for you while you are here. You will then report to your respective superiors and inform them. We think today's briefing and the blueprint you will read afterward will answer any questions you or your superiors may have. Now I will leave you in the capable hands of Colonel Hanford. Colonel?"

Colonel Hobart Hanford climbed the platform and walked to the table. "Thank you, sir." Turning and facing his audience he plunked his leather valise on the table. He looked up in time to watch General Willoughby leave the room. He checked his watch. 0700 hours.

Hanford, an unimposing, bookish man in his mid-forties, looked out of place in an army uniform. He was balding, with a close-cropped horseshoe fringe of hair, and his body was well into plumpness. He wore wire-rimmed glasses which he periodically removed to clean. His cheeks were red and flushed and his forehead beaded sweat.

When Hanford had joined MacArthur's staff in 1943, some of his fellow officers wondered about his slight effeminacy; others were more frank in their conclusions. Hanford knew about the comments but chose to ignore them. He was, in fact, asexual and lacked any desire for human intimacy. His work was his passion; without it Hanford would have been a lonely man, without purpose.

Many on MacArthur's staff wondered how he got such a coveted assignment, given his appearance and the assumptions about him. In time they ran up against Hanford's organizational skills, the very abilities for which General Willoughby had chosen him.

Before the war Hanford had been an attorney in Indianapolis. He had an extraordinary penchant for statistics and an encyclopedic mind for details. He abhorred litigation, because it placed him before the public and exposed him to the unpredictable. Instead, he chose to work for a decent-sized insurance company, preparing briefs and letting the other in-house attorneys bask in the public eye and quarrel before the bar.

He knew the United States would eventually enter the war, so in June of 1940 he joined the National Guard. Knowing his reluctance for things masculine, his relatives and coworkers wondered why. He admitted to himself that the military did not interest him, but he wanted to cast a new image. What organization, he surmised, embodied a more masculine image than the military?

Once in the Guard, he displayed his law-honed talents, though not in the Judge Advocates Corps. When his superiors recognized his skills, he was asked to put right the division's neglected records. For completing this formidable task he was promoted to the rank of first lieutenant and placed in charge of records for the division.

In late 1940 his Guard division was ordered into active federal service. He shipped out to Australia in 1942 and eventually angled a transfer to MacArthur's headquarters. By 1945 he was a full colonel. He knew he would not rise higher, but that did not matter to him for he also knew that when the war ended he could return with pride to civilian life, the snide comments of friends, coworkers and family effectively muted.

After assignment to General Willoughby's staff, everyone recognized Hanford's skills. He could briskly review the most impenetrable material, summarize it, and present it cogently, most of the time without consulting his notes. As time went on, Colonel Hanford assumed overall responsibility for preparing all briefings; occasionally he gave them.

As he looked out at the assembled officers with mild confidence, Hanford was aware of the importance of this particular briefing. As a calming ritual he reached for the water pitcher, poured some water, and slowly drank it. Then he took off his glasses, cleaned them, put them back on, removed some items from his valise and spread them on the table. Satisfied, he stepped to the center and stood in front of the boards. He was in his element.

"Good morning. Since some of you outrank me and others do not, unless there are objections, I shall address you as 'Gentlemen.' Is this acceptable?" No one objected.

"As General Willoughby stated, Japan is the next strategic target for invasion. After several months of planning, the Joint Chiefs have sent to General MacArthur their finalized plan."

He walked back to the table and held up one of the notebooks on the table, broke the seal, and opened the cover. He read aloud from the first page, "The Strategic Plan for Operations in the Japanese Archipelago. Code name: Operation Downfall."

He turned to the MP at his left. "Sergeant, both of you are to guard the doors from the outside. No one is to enter this room once you have closed the doors." When the guards exited he directed his attention to the rear of the room. "Lieutenants Kobayashi and Driscoll please step forward and distribute these notebooks to each individual."

Both Lt. Ken Kobayashi and Lt. Don Driscoll walked forward. As they did so, they were watched by the assembled, especially the Chinese. One of them smiled; he was right about the American Army officer being Japanese.

As the notebooks were passed out Hanford played with several three-by-five note cards he had taken from his valise. A couple of times he looked up, watching. When Kobayashi and Driscoll finished, Colonel Hanford thanked them both and instructed them to return to the rear. Hanford picked up the pointer from the table and proceeded to the first board. On it a large map displayed the Pacific Theater of War, labeled with detailed lettering, arrows, and numbers, identifying various military units.

"To begin, Operation Downfall has been divided into two stages, Operation Olympic and Operation Coronet. Let me preface this morning's presentation by pointing out that we can reasonably predict what to expect from the Japanese, in light of their defenses on Iwo Jima and particularly Okinawa, both of which were quite ferocious."

"Gawd," said Colonel Fitzhugh, "I've never 'erd 'ferocious' used so dramatically." Some of the officers near him snickered. Hanford looked at the Australian and raised an eyebrow, then sighed audibly while shaking his head. Inwardly he smiled, grateful for the well-known Australian irreverence for formality.

"Please work with me on this," he asked while casually moving to the table, sitting on the edge. "Some of you may have difficulty following these mundane albeit complicated concepts. But if you apply yourself and work hard, I'm certain you'll eventually grasp them."

Fitzhugh tossed Hanford an exaggerated salute and the

audience broke out in genial laughter. Then, like a chastened grade school student, Fitzhugh looked down at the **TOP SECRET** folder on his lap, concealing his grin.

"I'd first like to review the plans for Olympic, and then what we think we can expect from the Japanese." Hanford moved over to the second board. Japan's southernmost principal island, Kyûshû, was naked, exposed to implacable eyes. "X-Day is November 1, 1945."

Hanford brought his pointer down sharply on the map, the end landing on the southern tip of the island.

"It is estimated that over five million Allied soldiers, sailors, and airmen, as well as the largest concentration of ships and aircraft yet used in a single amphibious operation, will be involved in Operation Downfall.

"Before I proceed, let me point out that overall command of Downfall rests with General of the Army Douglas MacArthur, Supreme Allied Commander, Southwest Pacific.

"Let me offer a comparison of the size and scope of the operation. On June 6, 1944, in the Normandy invasion, about one hundred and seventy-five thousand men went ashore. For Operation Olympic, Admiral Spruance's Fifth Fleet will land, on November 1, over five hundred and fifty thousand soldiers and Marines, with an additional two hundred and fifty thousand reinforcements throughout November."

There was silence in the room as every man tried to imagine the logistics of landing, under enemy fire, over one-half million men from landing craft. To most, it was inconceivable.

"The goal of Olympic is to capture the lower seventy miles of Kyushu, to the Sendai-Tsuno line, which you can see here." With the pointer he traced a line across the southern end of Kyûshû, in a northeasterly direction, extending from the coastal city of Sendai in the southwest to the eastern coastal city of Tsuno.

"There are three primary objectives. The first is the obvious isolation of southern Kyushu. The second is to annihilate Japanese military forces and defensive installations there. The third is to seize and make operational airfields, bases, and naval facilities for the second phase of Downfall, Operation Coronet, including Kagoshima Bay and Ariake Bay. These in particular are crucial for anchorage of supply ships and warships. We know they will be heavily defended.

"The naval phase of the invasion will be carried out by the Fifth Fleet, as noted earlier, under the overall command of Admiral Spruance. These naval forces will be involved directly in the actual landings. For protection of the invading forces the Joint Chiefs have chosen Admiral Halsey and his Third Fleet, which will include a British Carrier Task Force under Admiral Rawling."

The British seemed pleased to see their military finally represented in the invasion.

"Admiral Halsey's Third Fleet will consist of seventeen fleet and light carriers, eight battleships, twenty cruisers, and seventy-five destroyers. In its entirety, the naval phase of Olympic will total over two thousand nine hundred ships and craft."

The room buzzed. Hanford stood silent for a moment, letting the numbers take effect. He spent the next ninety minutes giving a detailed overview of the naval phase of the invasion, describing each Task Force's involvement. Then he moved to the Army's involvement.

"The Sixth Army, to be landed by the Fifth Fleet, as previously noted, will be under the command of General Walter Krueger. It will consist of both Army and Marine divisions, the latter commanded by Major General Schmidt."

"At this juncture I'd like to give a brief overview of Olympic. After that I'll go into detail. On X-Day-minus-5, five days before the invasion of Kyushu, the 40th Infantry Division and the 158th Regimental Combat Team will land on offshore islands to establish emergency anchorages, radar installations, and seaplane bases."

During the next hour Hanford outlined the intricacies of Olympic's initial assault on Kyûshû.

"Now I'd like to go into the details of Olympic."

This phase of the briefing took ninety minutes. Concern with logistics shifted to sober thoughts and grim images of the land battles ahead.

Though Hanford was energized by his presentation he paused and scanned his audience. He could see that some were waning. *Too much detail*, he thought. He had seen it before. "Gentlemen, I think this is a good time to take a break. Fresh coffee and sandwiches will be brought in. We'll reconvene in, say, thirty minutes?"

The room erupted with conversation. Most drifted to the rear as fresh coffee and sandwiches were brought in. With food and coffee in hand many of the men gravitated to small groups, comparing notes on Hanford's briefing. Several British, Australians, and New Zealanders sought out American intelligence officers at the rear of the room, asking for details or bringing up matters not yet covered by Hanford. Though the conversations were friendly and sometimes sprinkled with genuine laughter, the Americans declined to respond with particulars, deferring instead to Colonel Hanford.

Colonel Fitzhugh saw the Japanese-American officer standing by himself in the back of the room. He walked over and offered his hand, hoping his affability and winning smile might get something not in the briefing but willing to settle for the story behind the odd sight of a Japanese in a Yank uniform, aloof from and maybe avoided by most of his fellow officers. "G'day, mate, I'm Jeremy Fitzhugh. Did you have anything to do with this?" He grinned and pointed his thumb over his shoulder toward the easels.

"Lieutenant Ken Kobayashi, sir. And no, I had nothing to

do with it. You can't get any lower on the totem pole than I am."

"I see. Do you work for Colonel Hanford then?"

"No, sir, I report to Colonel Mashbir. He's our senior Japanese translator. I was with Allied Translator and Interpreter Service but I've been temporarily assigned to the Central Bureau, General MacArthur's personal cryptanalytic outfit. That's where the intercept operators, mostly us Yanks and you Aussies, work. When they intercept Japanese messages I help translate them."

"I assume you're one of those splendid *Nisei* we in Intelligence keep hearing about."

"Yes, sir. But, actually I'm *Yonsei*, fourth-generation Japanese American. My family emigrated to America in 1869."

"Interesting. Have you seen any action?"

Ken grinned. "Yes, sir, I've been wounded twice sharpening pencils. And there have been several paper cuts. Actually, sir, I'm in the chairborne. When we get any enemy documents they're passed on to our group and we do the best translation we can. The closest I've come to the enemy is to question the few that were captured or surrendered."

Fitzhugh nodded and smiled. Attached to a desk, he too wanted combat experience.

"I must confess I've never encountered a living Japanese soldier. What's it like? I mean, talking to them?"

Ken grinned. "Well, I'm alive, last time I checked. You tell me what it's like."

Fitzhugh laughed. "C'mon, mate. You're not a Jap. You're a Yank. Seriously, have you questioned any Japanese officers?"

Ken immediately liked Fitzhugh. Not for a long time had a Caucasian called Ken an American. "No. Most die in combat or kill themselves. I've questioned a few noncoms and some enlistees. One time they brought in a wounded captain to a medical station. But before they could take care of him he grabbed a scalpel and slit his throat. The dogfaces seem to survive. Or maybe it's just that there are more of them. They seem the most vulnerable; a lot of them are from the farms. Most of them have little original thought. They believe what they're told by their superiors. Anyway, my boss, Colonel Mashbir, seems to feel that if Japanese Americans interrogate them, it might lower their resistance."

"Does it? Lower their resistance? After all, some of them looking at you might think you're a traitor to Japan."

"In some cases it doesn't. The wall is too high. Some convince themselves they're dead, and you can't talk to the dead. Some stop eating, hoping to starve themselves. A few, though, if you catch them at the right moment—some of the stories they tell about their basic training are hair-raising. It's amazing there are any officers left in the Japanese Army. You'd think all the recruits would want to kill them."

"What do you say to them?"

"I tell them some of my own prewar experiences about when I was in Japan. Some start to cry, some can't wait to tell me about their families. Some, ashamed, simply ask if I would kindly kill them."

Fitzhugh raised his eyebrows. "Is 'at roight, mate? I'm quite sure that's disturbing. And what kind of prewar stories can you tell them?"

"I spent four years in Japan, sir, studying at Tôkyô Imperial University. While there I did some traveling; Ôsaka, Kyôto, Nagoya, Nagasaki, Nara, other spots. I even did some skiing."

"Is 'at so? I've never been to Japan. I'd hoped to be going there right soon but it seems General MacArthur doesn't want that to happen too soon. Anyway, I've always had the impression it's pretty warm there. Where can you go skiing?"

"Actually, the winters can get pretty cold, sir. It even snows in Tôkyô. But as for skiing, Yuzawa is a good spot. That's in Niigata Prefecture, northwest of Tôkyô. We used to shake up the natives when we skied."

"'We'? You have friends there?"

Ken hesitated, feeling uncomfortable. He remembered skiing headlong, with utter abandon, down the slopes at Yuzawa with his brother, Tomoyuki, racing past the more inhibited Japanese skiers. They were always competing to see who would get to the base first. In a way, their competition had been lifelong. It culminated in a violent quarrel during their fourth year at Tôkyô Imperial University. He snapped out of his musings when Fitzhugh offered him a cigarette.

"Sorry? Oh, no thank you, sir."

"Yes, filthy habit. My wife won't come near me when I smoke. You were telling me about 'we,' Lieutenant. Anyone in particular?"

"Yes, sir. A girl I met while I was at the university."

"Ah! Splendid. Was it a close relationship?"

"I thought so, sir. I thought she did too. But we didn't date as you and I think of dating. It was pretty formal, even though she and her family had spent some time in the States when she was about twelve. She speaks fluent English and seemed pretty friendly with me. But her father wasn't. We broke it off just before I returned to the States."

"What was her name?"

"Kyoko." More memories. Their parting, difficult for both of them, was still painful to recall. When he returned to America, he dated several women in Los Angeles' Japanese-American community, even a few white women, but he felt nothing for them.

"When was the last time you heard from her?"

"Just before the war broke out I received a letter from her, sir."

"Kyoko… Does it mean anything? Her name?"

"Yes, sir. She's named for the city of Kyôto. That's a city we haven't bombed, yet, and I hope—"

"Gentlemen! Gentlemen!" Colonel Hanford called out

from the front of the room. "Can we resume please?"

Colonel Fitzhugh smiled and offered his hand to Ken. "Well Yank, maybe you can finish that story some other time. I'd like to hear it."

When everyone returned to their seats Colonel Hanford stepped over to the board that held the map of Kyûshû and resumed his presentation, more confident now than when he started, though he did pour himself another glass of water.

After another hour of detailing the Army Air Forces' role, Hanford completed his briefing and looked at the men in front of him.

"Are there any questions?"

Some murmured voices arose from the audience. Many sitting in the room continued to study the boards and went over in their minds the immensity of the American invasion plans. They pondered the implications of such a vast operation, never seen in the history of warfare. Finally, a member of the British contingent broke the silence.

"Yes. Colonel Hanford, General Merritt, British Army." The man stood. "First let me say your briefing was first-rate and I think I speak for everyone in this room. There. We've gotten the pleasantries out of the way."

That broke the tension and the room resonated with amiable laughter.

"I'd like to return to the ground operations. Except for the Royal Navy's contribution Olympic seems to be strictly an American show. Can you explain that? After all, we are your allies and, along with our Australian, New Zealand and Dutch counterparts here, we have had rather extensive experience in combat with the Japanese. Or to put it rather bluntly, we've had our fair share of this war. Oughtn't we too receive our fair share of the final operations?"

Hanford anticipated the question but hoped it would not be raised. He returned to the table and made a brief note. He knew that leaving the Allies out of the final campaign was tantamount to an insult.

"Let me preface by saying that America's allies were not purposefully excluded. The decision not to include Allied ground forces was made purely on the basis that the other Allied nations fighting in the Pacific Theater of Operations lack significant invasion fleet capability and do not have as much experience in amphibious landings in the Pacific Theater. In addition, it was felt that attempting to retrain Allied invasion forces and integrate them with American units would be too time-consuming and difficult, if not impossible, to accomplish."

General Merritt looked around the room, seeking support for his position, but found none. Although he acknowledged the Americans had borne the brunt of the offensive war in the Pacific against Japan he knew the British, Australians and New Zealanders had carried their share. He wanted to get in his protest. He sat down.

Hanford waited for more questions.

"Colonel, Major Alan Albridge, British Army, Airborne. I notice that there are no provisions for any airborne operations during Operation Olympic. At Normandy American and British airborne divisions landed behind the Germans and comported themselves rather well. In addition, other airborne operations were successfully carried out elsewhere in Europe. Why not here? Certainly you have the airlift capability and you do control the skies."

Colonel Hanford nodded and stood halfway between the table and the easels. "That's a fair question, Major. It was in fact considered and rejected. The conditions here are entirely different from Normandy as well as from other drop zones in Europe. When Allied airborne forces landed behind German lines, the civilian population, such as the French, were, for the most part anyway, friendly to the Allied effort and we could expect a positive reception, if not active cooperation. Obviously, dropping into Japan is a different matter. Japanese civilians, as tired of the war as they might be, will not regard us as liberators or respond passively to an airborne invasion of their homeland. General MacArthur's staff felt that the Japanese civilians, on the contrary, would try to kill Allied paratroopers as soon as they touched the ground. Facing that likelihood, airborne forces would probably have to shoot civilians as they came down and continue doing so after landing and securing their objectives. We do not want to engage in that type of war. Our goal is to destroy Japan's military and bring the war to as rapid an end as possible. Our war is with Japan's government and military, not its civilians. Does this answer your question, sir?"

"Yes," said Major Albridge. "Of course. Thank you, Colonel."

"Any other questions? Okay. Well, then I'd like to review with you what we think we can expect from the Japanese." Hanford turned and walked back to the first easel, showing all of Japan and southern Korea.

"We estimate that, in total, Japan has almost three million combat-ready men made up of about fifty-three infantry divisions and twenty-five brigades, two armored divisions and seven brigades, and four antiaircraft artillery divisions. This does not include the five infantry divisions on the island of Hokkaido. As best as we can determine, the Japanese military is backed up by over two million army workers, over a million navy workers and tens of thousands of garrison forces.

"For the defense of southern Kyushu we expect that there will be fewer than 300,000 Japanese soldiers, air ground troops, navy ground troops, and Imperial Army and Navy pilots in place.

"Finally, their radio broadcasts claim—and air reconnaissance seems to support this—that the Japanese military are training and equipping a civilian militia of over twenty-eight million in preparation of an invasion. There are about ten million civilians on Kyushu. We have to take that seriously and…"

There were numerous comments mixed with some profanities. Ken noted them in silence.

"Furthermore—gentlemen, please, your attention— furthermore, based on the experience of Okinawa, we expect the Japanese to utilize their suicide forces, especially *kamikaze* planes and watercraft against our naval forces.

"Though preliminary, the reports from Okinawa are alarming. So far about twenty ships have been sunk and more than two hundred have been damaged, including carriers, battleships and cruisers as well as destroyers.

"We believe the greatest danger to the assault force will come from the air. We have concluded, based on the limited number of Japanese interceptions of B-29s, that Japan is stockpiling its air forces for the invasion and will have around five thousand *kamikaze* planes and that, unlike Okinawa, the *kamikaze* will be used principally against troop transport ships.

"Let there be no mistake, gentlemen. They know we're coming. And they probably know just about where we're going to land. Reconnaissance photos taken over the past few months have shown the Japanese very active in preparing for the invasion, particularly on Kyushu and Honshu. Which brings me to the terrain of Kyushu. This map is based on photographs taken."

He walked to the easel that supported the large package marked **KYUSHU TERRAIN**, and tore off the paper covering.

"The Japanese have ably constructed railroads and roads that will be used for reinforcement once the invasion begins. Tunnels will undoubtedly be used to hide their planes. Bridges dot the landscape. The U.S. Army Air Forces will, of course, do their best to destroy all the aforementioned."

He continued for another hour or so then wrapped up.

"We expect the Japanese to throw everything into the battle for Kyushu, knowing full well that if we secure a beachhead there our next step will be Tokyo. And that brings us to stage two of Downfall, Operation Coronet. It will be concise as it is still in development and there will certainly be changes." He lifted the map of Japan and under it was an enlarged view of Japan's main island, Honshu.

"On or about March 1, 1946, Y-Day, depending on how soon the objectives on Kyushu are secured and made operational, the American First Army will land along the seaward side of the Kanto Plain, on Kujukuri Beach.

"The First Army consists of six Army infantry divisions and three Marine divisions. The First Army's principal objective is to seize and secure the Kujukuri beaches, along this line here, about fifty miles east of Tokyo." Hanford's pointer traced the path on the map. "We assume the Japanese will make their main stand there. The battles will be, as I mentioned earlier, ferocious." Hanford paused, looking directly at Colonel Fitzhugh. Fitzhugh's eyes drilled into Hanford's. The humor was gone, replaced by a grim, unspoken acknowledgment. Almost imperceptibly, Fitzhugh nodded. Hanford pushed on.

"Once securing the beaches the First Army will attack north and south to clear the eastern shores of Tokyo Bay. Simultaneously, one spearhead will drive straight for Tokyo.

"While the First Army is landing, the Eighth Army, with units from Europe, consisting of nine Army infantry divisions and two armored divisions, will land at Sagami Bay.

"The Eighth Army, after landing, will drive north and east to clear the western shore of Tokyo Bay and proceed to Yokohama.

"In reserve will be the Tenth Army, commanded by General Joseph W. Stilwell." Hanford caught the sneer on the face of one of the Chinese officers, and was not surprised. It was well known that "Vinegar Joe" had incurred the wrath of the

Nationalist Chinese by openly criticizing their corruptness and fecklessness. Hanford also knew that Stilwell's command of the Tenth Army was an acknowledgment of all his efforts in the China-Burma-India Theater and was certain that Stilwell would be pleased to know that he still irritated the Chinese.

"On or about Y-Day + 45 the Tenth Army, consisting of seven infantry divisions, one airborne division, and, in reserve, one armored division, will land. Air support will come from forty air groups that will be based on Kyushu, thus the importance of Kyushu as a staging area. In addition, air units of similar strength will lend support from fields in the Marianas, Iwo Jima and the Ryukyu Islands. The Army Air Forces, consisting of the Eighth and Twentieth Air Forces, will be commanded by General Carl Spaatz.

"Obviously, the Navy will be in the thick of it, both in landing troops and attacking and destroying enemy facilities and matériel. The Navy's total participation in Coronet will dwarf that of Olympic. Of course, Admiral Halsey's Third Fleet will be involved in offensive actions and the Seventh Fleet will be involved in amphibious operations.

"Furthermore, if required, preliminary plans call for an additional thirty divisions to be transferred from Europe to Japan if the battle continues. Once Tokyo falls and the Kanto Plain is secured, it will then be up to the Japanese Army either to surrender or continue the fight. If the latter, the Imperial Japanese Army will be annihilated."

Hanford placed another map on an easel. Like the plan for Operation Downfall, it covered the Pacific Theater.

"The total number of soldiers, sailors, Marines, and Army Air Forces involved in Operation Downfall will be in excess of five million men. Such numbers have never been seen in history and I pray to God that they are never seen again."

No one said a word. Every man in that room knew the amount of blood the United States had shed in fighting Germany and Italy as well as Japan. Now most grasped how many resources the United States had contributed to defeating the Axis Powers. For some, such as the Chinese, it was an unimaginable amount. For the British, envy rose to the surface, wondering how America could have provided so much war matériel, oil and food to the Allies and still support its own war effort.

Colonel Hanford returned to the table and picked up a notepad.

"Earlier, General Merritt asked a question about this being strictly an American effort, except for the British Royal Navy. General Merritt, I can tell you now that Commonwealth forces will be involved in the battle for the Kanto Plain. Three Commonwealth infantry divisions, the Third British Division, the Sixth Canadian Division, and the Tenth Australian Division, commanded by Lieutenant General Sir Charles F. Kneightley, will be involved in the latter stages. It's the consensus of General MacArthur's staff that New Zealand, as courageous as they have been throughout this war, cannot afford more losses."

General Merritt stood up. "Colonel Hanford, I believe you Yanks, when referring to 'latter stages,' actually mean 'mopping up' operations. Is that a fair interpretation?"

Hanford shrugged his shoulders and, for the first time, smiled. "Well, sir, I'm just the messenger. I'd prefer to call it a 'Subsidiary Allied Contribution.'"

General Merritt looked at the map for several seconds then sat down. Another British officer, sitting next to General Merritt, stood.

"Colonel Hanford, I'm Colonel Withers, British Army. I do not wish to, as you Yanks say, 'beat a dead horse' but, well, frankly, I think the British Army can make a significant contribution in the first phase, that is, in Olympic. Is there any possibility of modifying the plans? I think we can offer some suggestions that—"

"Colonel Withers," interrupted Hanford, "I sympathize, but I'm not here to entertain any proposed changes to Olympic. All I can say is that while plans for the second phase—Coronet—may be changed, those for the first phase are completed. I don't think they can be improved upon."

Withers pursed his lips and looked at his feet. "Are your plans as complete as were those for Tarawa, Colonel?"

The Americans in the back of the room stiffened and watched Hanford.

On November 20, 1943, the Second Marine Division stormed ashore on Tarawa, America's first seaborne assault against a heavily defended Japanese-occupied atoll. In spite of all the planning someone had overlooked the unmistakable importance of the tides. The Higgins boats—specially designed wooden landing boats with a front ramp made of metal—transported the Marines toward the coast but foundered on the coral reef, about 800 yards from the beach. The tide was out, stranding the first wave. The second wave stacked up behind the first. The third wave followed the second.

In spite of withering sheets of Japanese machine gunfire and unremitting artillery, the determined Marines, with nowhere else to go, jumped over the sides of the Higgins boats and struggled through the 800 yards of water, straight into the Japanese defenses. When it was over the Marines owned Tarawa, at a cost of 1,000 lives in 76 hours. The American public was horrified at the cost.

Colonel Hanford's response to Colonel Withers' comment came fast and hard. He strode to the front of the table and sharply put down his pointer, a cold grin playing at the corners of his lips. "Perhaps a bit better than Operation Market Garden. Wouldn't you agree, Colonel?"

Color drained from Colonel Withers' face.

Market Garden was a stratagem hatched by British Field Marshal Bernard Montgomery, an end-run through Holland around the northern boundary of the German Siegfried line. On September 17, 1944, three Allied airborne divisions, the American 82nd and the 101st, and the British 1st, were dropped into Holland. All three divisions were under Montgomery's command. Their orders were to capture bridges across rivers and canals as well as other objectives.

The American airborne divisions achieved their goals.

Unfortunately, the Germans captured the Allied battle plans for the entire operation from the British 1st Airborne. The British lost more than two thirds of their men. And Market Garden was a disaster.

Hanford let Withers hang there for a moment. "Colonel Withers, you're right. Tarawa was a bitter pill to swallow. We know that. And we learned from it. But I'm certain that Operation Downfall has been far better prepared than some British operations, such as Norway or Dieppe as well as Market Garden. Would you not agree? And let me remind you, Colonel, the Marines did take Tarawa, just as the American airborne divisions secured their objectives in Holland during Market Garden. We cannot say the same for the British, can we, Colonel? Market Garden was nothing to write home about. Nor were British and French failures in Norway. Have I adequately addressed your concerns?"

There was silence in the room. No one moved, waiting for the other shoe to drop.

The Americans at the back of the room were visibly astonished and acutely proud. It was a side of Hanford none of them had seen before. The room was as silent as a tomb. Everyone waited for Withers' response.

Withers was stung by the rebuke. Color slowly returned to his cheeks. His hands clenched and opened. Several men were prepared to physically intervene.

General Merritt's foot gently nudged Colonel Withers' ankle. Without looking up from the papers on his lap he said, *sotto voce*, "Sit down please, Colonel. Now." Withers hesitated. This time General Merritt kicked Withers' ankle. When Withers sat down, General Merritt continued. "Very good, Colonel. I think you've made our point splendidly. And Colonel Hanford has made his. As Prime Minister Churchill has often reminded us, though we sometimes find it difficult, we must remember the Yanks are our Allies. Let us graciously accept that this is their show."

An American Army officer at the rear of the room stood up, hoping to ease the tension by asking the question on everyone's mind.

"Sir, Lieutenant Driscoll. Are there any projections on casualties?"

Hanford dreaded the question, fair and anticipated though it was. The subject was disconcerting. Despite all his experience with actuarial tables and casualty lists, the Downfall estimates got to him. He stepped to the rear of the table and removed some papers from his valise. The pause before his answer, though momentary, was not unnoticed, contrasting as it did with his rapid responses heretofore. Hanford drank some water then spoke.

"Washington has offered several tentative estimates. Army Chief of Staff General Marshall suggested that in the first thirty days of Olympic we may lose about 31,000 men and that both Olympic and Coronet could cost anywhere from 250,000 to 1,000,000. Admiral King put the number at about 41,000, and Admiral Nimitz forecasts about 49,000. General MacArthur's staff predicts 50,800 casualties in the first 30 days, 27,150 more by day 60, and an additional 27,100 casualties by day 90." Hanford was annoyed that he had to drink more water.

"That totals to 105,050 killed and wounded for Olympic. The Joint War Plans Committee, a Joint Chiefs of Staff group, adding the cost of both Olympic and Coronet, determined the number at about 40,000 killed, 150,000 wounded, and 3,500 missing. That adds up to 193,500 casualties. I can also report that casualties on Iwo Jima and Okinawa have been thirty to thirty-five percent of the troops landed. We have several estimates, gentlemen. Take your pick."

Hanford paused and removed his glasses. For a moment he looked glumly at the casualty estimates sheets then, with a grimace, shoved them into his valise. He reached into his rear pocket for his handkerchief and wiped his forehead. He was fairly certain he had not betrayed any emotion.

"I don't know how sound these projections are. But perhaps what I say next will help all of you put it into perspective. I can tell you this. As of last night the Army and Navy confirmed that on Okinawa more than 8,000 Americans have been killed and thousands more wounded. And consider this: based on dead Japanese to date, they are projecting more than 80,000 Japanese will die before the campaign is over. We don't know how many civilians will die. Neither side is asking for or giving quarter.

"Finally, the U.S. Army Quartermaster has ordered 400,000 Purple Heart medals for Olympic. And the Navy has asked to borrow from the Army an additional 60,000 Purple Heart medals." Several heads turned and looked at the American naval officers, who tried to hide their chagrin. "For those of you not familiar, Purple Heart medals are given to those killed or wounded in action. From those numbers and facts you should be able to estimate casualties."

Everyone tried to comprehend the casualties, but none could. The only relevant comparisons that occurred to a few were to the figures for Verdun in World War I or the rumors about Stalingrad. For several moments no one spoke. No witticism or display of congeniality could be offered now.

General Merritt leaned close to Colonel Withers. "Still anxious to have the British Army join the Yanks and go ashore, Colonel?"

Withers looked at General Merritt for a painful moment and searched his soul. He looked at the folder labeled **OPERATION DOWNFALL** on his lap. Then, looking at Colonel Hanford and remembering Norway and Dieppe, he said, "Perhaps you're right, Sir." He opened and looked at the pages containing the casualty estimates and said nothing more.

Driscoll, shocked, sat down. He leaned over to Lieutenant Kobayashi and whispered, "Christ, you'd think we'd want to spread the glory around among our Allied friends, especially the damn Brits."

Ken frowned and whispered amid the sober hush, "Your Irish is up, Don. Glory? Not by a long shot. The only bastards who will see any glory in this are in Tôkyô, maybe some teenagers at Fort Benning and Paris Island still in training. But that'll change once they get to Japan. The Japanese cannot conceive surrendering, especially the Army leaders. Don't imagine for a moment that they think they can't win or even stop us at the beaches. I know them. I know how they think. They want to bleed us real bad before the end. Maybe even try to get better surrender terms. But there will be no glory here, just lots of good guys, a bunch of fanatics and innocent civilians dead. If only we knew their defense plans."

"Sure, the Japs will just mail them to MacArthur."

"No, I'm serious. Think about it. If we knew what their plans were, if we didn't have to base our strategy just on photos, speculations, radio intercepts, and especially their previous tactics, we'd save a lot of lives, American and—"

Driscoll cut him off: "Hell, why don't you just go to Tokyo... Ahhh, Hanford's wrapping up."

Lieutenant Kobayashi turned to look at Lieutenant Driscoll. "What? What did you say?"

"I said... Never mind. Hanford's wrapping up and he'll probably want us to grade him."

"Hell, that's degrading."

"Ken, give me a break, will ya?"

Hanford had resumed his briefing after regaining his crisp analytic self.

"Let me summarize. There is no easy way to end this war. But the Japanese won't end it themselves. We have to do it for them. Finally, let me remind you that tomorrow you must return the draft of the invasion plans. I'll be here at 0700 hours. If you have more questions I'll address them at that time. Thank you, gentlemen."

As the group filtered out, Lieutenant Kobayashi studied their faces. Clearly, though the size and scope of the American plans impressed them they were somber. He wondered if they were thinking what he was, the enormity of the dead and wounded.

Alone in the room, Ken walked to a chair and sat down. He looked at the maps and charts, studying each closely, imagining the carnage. He had seen War Department films of American soldiers in Europe handing out candy to kids and films of Americans caring for wounded Japanese soldiers and civilians on Okinawa. But he also knew that the American soldier and Marine could be fierce and deadly in battle.

Not surprisingly, he thought about the Japanese civilians on Kyûshû and Honshû forced into a militia. Americans would have to kill them as well, people who had no say in whether they wanted to fight.

His thoughts then drifted to his brother, Tom. Near the end of their last semester at Tôkyô Imperial University, *Tôdai*, the rift between them had widened to the point that they rarely spoke. Throughout their four years at *Tôdai*, Ken had been repulsed at the atrocities being committed by the Imperial Japanese Army in China, amply documented by the Western media, especially pictures in *Life* magazine. Tom, however, saw it otherwise; Japan was behaving no differently than the European countries when they had colonized Africa, and England

and Portugal took possession of Chinese territory, especially Hong Kong and Macao. As the years at *Tôdai* progressed, Ken saw Tom embrace Japan's militarism and aggressive foreign policy. Tom had come under the sway of Hiraizumi Kiyoshi, a professor of Japanese history and an ultranationalist. Hiraizumi had formulated a philosophy that the purest form of Shintô was to protect the Imperial Polity, or form of government. In short, whatever Japan's emperor ordered or was ordered in his name was unquestionable.

In April 1941, two weeks before Ken and Tom were to return to America, Tom said he was staying in Japan. Ken was stunned. For a week the brothers argued. But Tom's decision was fixed; he could not be dissuaded.

When Ken returned to California his parents were overcome with joy when they saw him but devastated when he told them of Tom's decision. Telephone calls to Tôkyô failed to sway him.

Then five weeks before Japan attacked Pearl Harbor, Ken received a letter from Tom that caused their mother, Misaki, to faint. Tom had joined the Imperial Japanese Army. Ken now wondered if his brother would be on Kyûshû or Honshû when the invasion began.

His thoughts were interrupted as he recalled Lieutenant Driscoll's suggestion: "Hell, why don't you just go to Tokyo…"

He lingered for several more minutes, looking at the map of Japan. He had of course done so many times before, while recalling his experiences there. Now he was pondering the bold strategic plans that often emanated from the minds of young lieutenants. And this time, new thoughts were beginning to form.

As he turned and left the room he asked himself, *Why not?*

2

Five days after arriving in Leyte, the Philippines, Admiral Halsey went to have lunch with General Douglas MacArthur. The two men liked each other and each considered the other a "fighting" commander.

Halsey had worked with MacArthur before. On April 15, 1943, they had met for three days to discuss strategy. Halsey wanted MacArthur's approval for an invasion of New Georgia. This in turn, Halsey argued, would be used as a jump off for a drive on Bougainville. MacArthur immediately agreed, having already drafted the same plans. Later he told him, "If you come with me, I'll make you a greater man than Nelson ever dreamed of being." After the meeting Halsey felt as if they were lifelong friends. That genuine mutual admiration, however, would be tested the next year.

On Friday morning, October 20, 1944, the largest concentration of warships and transport ships ever seen in the Pacific Theater assembled in the waters of Leyte Gulf. Over 700 U.S. Navy warships and transport vessels brought 200,000 American soldiers of General Walter Krueger's Sixth Army to Leyte Gulf. MacArthur's promised return to the Philippines had begun.

Halsey's Third Fleet was ordered to provide long-range offensive protection for the invasion by guarding the San

Bernardino Strait. The Seventh Fleet, commanded by Admiral Thomas Kinkaid, was charged with providing close-in protection. But Halsey was under the command of Fleet Admiral Chester W. Nimitz, who was in Honolulu. And Admiral Kinkaid was under the command of General MacArthur.

The Japanese Navy, anticipating the invasion, launched a major pre-planned counteroffensive, Plan *Sho-1*, "Decisive Battle in the Philippine Islands." Japan threw almost its entire naval might against the American invasion forces, again hoping for the long-sought decisive fleet battle. This time they would get it. The battle would last from October 23 to October 25, 1944.

Three Japanese fleets were assembled: Northern Force, Central Force, and Southern Force.

The Central Force, commanded by Admiral Kurita Takeo, consisted of five battleships, 12 cruisers, and 15 destroyers. Two of Kurita's battleships were the *Musashi* and *Yamato*, both displacing 64,000 tons, the largest and most powerful battleships ever built.

The Southern Force, led by Admiral Nishimura Shôji, included two battleships, four cruisers, and eight destroyers.

The Central and Southern Forces, coming from two different directions, planned to converge almost simultaneously, like two pincers, at Leyte Gulf at dawn on October 25, and lunge upon the American invasion fleet and soldiers, wreaking as much destruction as possible.

The Northern Force, under Admiral Ozawa Jisaburô, comprised four carriers, two battleships, three cruisers, and eight destroyers. But the Northern Force was a ruse; its four carriers carried just over 100 planes among them. The Northern Force's strategy was to lure Halsey's Third Fleet from Leyte and expose the Americans to the combined assault of the Central and Southern Forces.

Halsey, despising his support role of defending the landing, took the bait and turned his ships north, to search for and destroy Ozawa's Northern Force, giving Admirals Kurita and Nishimura the opportunity to close the pincers on the American invasion forces with their fleets.

While Halsey sailed north Kurita and Nishimura headed for the American beachheads. The battle had begun. With Halsey's ships gone the American Seventh Fleet had to deal with two Japanese fleets. Outgunned, they eventually radioed Halsey for assistance. But Halsey was too far away to render direct support. Besides, he had found Ozawa's Northern Force and was destroying it.

But the American Seventh Fleet, though outgunned, was resourceful. Through sheer courage, determination, and imaginative tactics the Seventh Fleet succeeded in destroying Nishimura's Southern Force and routing Kurita's Central Force, only some 40 miles from possibly destroying the American invasion forces at Leyte Gulf.

By the time Halsey's forces returned to Leyte the battles were over, the American Navy victorious. But Halsey had not been there to help.

The next evening, Thursday, MacArthur hosted a dinner for his staff officers. During the meal some of his officers criticized Halsey's conduct at Leyte, claiming his pursuit of Ozawa's fleet had exposed America's invasion force to destruction. MacArthur, angered, bunched his fist and slammed it down on the table. "That's enough! Leave the Bull alone! He's still a fighting admiral in my book."

MacArthur considered loyalty the finest military quality and he'd be damned if he'd allow his staff to show disloyalty to another American commander.

Now, eight months later, MacArthur was about to ask Halsey to reciprocate that support. When Halsey arrived for lunch MacArthur personally greeted him at the door and ushered him into the dining room.

"Bill, it's been a while. It's good to see you again. Come on in here. I've got lunch prepared. I bet it's been a long time since you've had decent land food."

Halsey, flattered, grinned. Near a large window a damask-covered table displayed two place settings of fine crystal, china, and silverware. On the table a roasted leg of lamb nestled amongst a pile of roasted potatoes. A fresh garden salad and a bowl of mixed vegetables added color. A warm loaf of bread, wrapped in a white cloth, gave off a savory aroma. A small dish of liver paté and crackers served as *hors d'oeuvres*. A bottle of wine completed the table. Halsey picked up the wine bottle, inspecting the label. He recognized the vineyard. It was a Cabernet Sauvignon, 1942, from the Beaulieu private reserve vineyards. Halsey decided he was hungry.

"Damn, I think I went to the wrong academy, General. I always thought the Navy laid out a better table."

"Sit down here, Bill. There's a nice view out that window. Incidentally, I heard about your problems with the Court of Inquiry."

Halsey winced, his shoulders sagging.

Five days earlier, on June 13, 1945, Admiral William F. "Bull" Halsey, Commander of the U.S. Third Fleet, had smiled with justifiable pride as his flagship, the battleship USS *Missouri*, received a hearty salute from other warships and their sailors and officers as she sailed into the Philippines' Leyte Gulf. The Okinawan campaign was almost over and Task Force 38, under his command, had sailed from Okinawan waters, victorious. One of Halsey's first acts after dropping anchor at Leyte was to give all the Filipino stewards leave to visit their families.

Soon after mooring, Halsey and three other admirals in Task Force 38 were bewildered when they were ordered to appear—in two days, on June 15—before a Court of Inquiry on board the USS *New Mexico*. The Navy charged that during combat operations off Okinawa, on June 5, some ships of Task Force 38 had sustained damage and loss of life due to a typhoon because Halsey, despite warnings by Navy meteorologists, failed to exercise sound judgment by not ordering his ships out of the storm's path.

The inquiry had been, at times, harsh. The presiding judge was Vice Admiral John J. Hoover, who had earned the ironic sobriquet "Genial John" owing to his severe temperament. Halsey, although deeply saddened at the loss of life, felt he had acted properly. After three days of testimony he was dismissed from the Court of Inquiry, to await their final decision.

"I don't know how the hell those desk-bound sailors could even think of judging an officer of your caliber. You'll beat them."

"General, they're all fine men, all line officers. And I'm not so sure they're not right. I know for certain that if I'm cleared and keep my command, whenever I get even a hint of a gust of wind, I'm going to hightail it the hell out."

MacArthur nodded sympathetically, pretending to be chastened. But he could see that Halsey was visibly pleased with his expression of support.

"Well, I'm certain you're right, Bill. Let's drop it. I've got some fine food here."

"Any good scotch, sir?"

"For you, Bill, only the best. I just received a shipment from Pearl."

MacArthur kept the conversation casual, the war temporarily put aside, the lunch a refuge from the struggle the Allies were winning throughout the Pacific. Halsey was enjoying himself. The two men spoke of their families and stateside gossip. The new man in the White House came up, but they both agreed that President Truman was just a new piece in an old political puzzle, unlikely to change Roosevelt's war policies.

But as the afternoon passed they again spoke of the Court

of Inquiry. It became evident to MacArthur that the Court of Inquiry troubled Halsey. His face reflected the stress of the last days. Slowly, MacArthur peeled away Halsey's patina of confidence and became acutely aware of how close Halsey felt he was to losing his command.

Halsey looked out the window. "For a while I felt like Patton. He slaps a dogface and loses his command. He never should have laid a hand on the kid; that was unforgivable. But to lose his command? I never understood Eisenhower's reasoning. Patton was one of his best field commanders." He paused and turned to his host. "I don't deny I should have paid serious attention to the warning about the typhoon, but I didn't think we'd get hit that hard. But I know I'll never forgive myself for the men and ships I lost. That was my mistake and I'll take it to my grave."

"Bill, you called it as you saw it. None of the Navy court members were there. If we paid homage only to our mistakes we'd be ineffective as commanders. Look at how many men Eisenhower lost during the Ardennes offensive. The Germans caught Ike sleeping. The press called it the Battle of the Bulge. It wasn't a bulge, it was an artery rupturing; Ike's army almost bled to death. Look at how many thousands of men he lost. And who saved his ass? One of them was Patton, the man he had fired."

Halsey brightened slightly. "Thank you, General. I appreciate that." Hesitating a moment he said, "This coffee's good, incidentally."

"Glad you enjoy it. Now, how about some of that scotch?"

"You'll get no arguments from me."

As the steward poured Halsey's scotch, MacArthur decided that now was the time to lay out a plan that had been presented to him. He sensed a weakness in Halsey he could exploit. Besides, he already knew that Halsey was not going to lose his command.

The steward walked to MacArthur's side and offered scotch.

"No, I'll just stay with the coffee." The steward poured more coffee for MacArthur. Then, at a discreet signal from the general, he left the room.

"Bill, I don't think you're going to lose your command. Only Japan would benefit from that. So I'm going to assume that the Third Fleet will be yours when this inquiry is over. In the meantime, there's something else I want to speak to you about.

"You know that our next move will be the invasion of Japan. That's no secret. Hell, even the Japanese know. Their radio traffic confirms it. Besides, there's little or nothing to stop us. And even though they're in full retreat and their cities and industry are being systematically destroyed with little or no opposition, it's their army, still intact on the home islands and the immediate threat to our invasion forces, which worries me. I'm not concerned about their navy. Who better than you knows the Japanese Navy no longer exists, especially with the loss of the *Yamato*. But their army is another matter."

Halsey smiled as he lifted the scotch glass, accepting the oblique compliment. He recalled what he'd heard about MacArthur's didactic social gatherings and wondered where this particular one was heading. He sipped his drink, enjoying the warmth that passed down his throat.

"Bill, you know about the plans for Operation Downfall. Washington has broken it up into two phases, Olympic and Coronet. If Japan's army fights as fiercely as it did on Iwo Jima and Okinawa, our casualties are going to be horrendous, certainly too high for the home front to accept. Iwo Jima and Okinawa were each won at too steep a price, and I'm sure Admiral Spruance felt a great deal of heat from Washington. I'm told that Secretary Stimson has estimated American casualties during Olympic and Coronet could easily approach a million."

Halsey, like almost everyone else in the Pacific, knew better than to interrupt MacArthur when he started to preach. He sat back, the glass of scotch in one hand and a freshly lit cigarette in the other.

"Recently, one of the members of my intelligence staff proposed a remarkable plan for getting hold of Japan's defense strategy."

Halsey's bushy eyebrows flexed upward. This was something new. He focused in, no longer concerned with MacArthur's social maneuvers. "Really? Go on, please."

"After going over it with members of my senior staff, including General Willoughby, I authorized the implementation of his plan. We're going to need all the help we can get on this one, Bill." MacArthur leaned forward and picked up his coffee cup. "Incidentally, I spoke with Admiral Nimitz and he told me that if the court clears you, you're going back to Japan, off Honshu."

"That's correct, sir. Admiral Nimitz told me he wants me to hit their coastal defenses with offshore shelling and to send in my planes to hit what's left of their industrial and military centers."

"Good. That should help end this war sooner. As I said, I'm going to need the Navy's help. I'm going to need your help."

"Anything I can do, sir."

"Good. I knew I could count on you." MacArthur leaned back in his chair and looked out as if gazing at students in a lecture hall.

"The concept of the plan is singular. It's based on the premise that the Japanese know we're going to have to invade their homeland. My intelligence people have gone over captured documents from Iwo Jima and Okinawa. Those papers confirm they were expecting us to attack those two key outposts. It's obvious that their intelligence is good. Good enough to predict where and when we'll probably strike next."

Halsey crushed his cigarette while he drank his scotch, then immediately lit another. "That's true, General. But besides Iwo and Okinawa there weren't that many strategic targets we could hit, except for China, Formosa, and Korea. They're smart but not that smart. It's just a process of elimination. I'm sure they're expecting us on Formosa or China's eastern coast as well."

MacArthur seemed annoyed but composed himself. "Okay, I'll concede that point. Nevertheless, the defenses on both islands were formidable; the actions of the Japanese soldiers were, frankly, stubbornly heroic. They're tenacious fighters, Bill, with damn few willing to surrender. Their code won't allow it. They stood their ground and stained it with their blood and the blood of our boys. It's a clear indication of what we can expect when we hit the beaches on their home islands. I don't want our boys to experience that again."

MacArthur paused and sipped his coffee. As he put down the cup, he noticed that coffee grounds had collected on the inside of the cup. He made a mental note to reprimand the steward later. He looked at his guest, speculating whether Halsey would be swayed by his eloquence, yet doubting that Halsey had even an inkling of where this conversation was going. How, he speculated, would Halsey react when he heard how the plan would be carried out? But he saw that his conjectures were unnecessary; Halsey was guileless. All MacArthur saw in that frank expression was a keen interest in a mission against Japan.

MacArthur continued. "Bill, Japan's beaten. Their military leaders have to know it. They just won't accept it yet. We've got to prove it to them. We can let the B-29s and your ships and planes pound away for the next two years. But until American soldiers stand on and occupy Japan's soil, the war won't be over as far as the Japs are concerned. We have to invade Japan, and American soldiers must occupy it. The plan I spoke of was proposed by a young man whose knowledge and understanding of the Japanese has been instrumental in modifying some of our tactics. He wants to ensure that the cost of our victories in Olympic and Coronet is not devastating."

Halsey, impatient, brushed some cigarette ashes off the table and inhaled deeply. He looked at MacArthur and smiled. "Sir, I'm anxious to hear it." *Get on with it, General,* he thought.

MacArthur grinned and nodded. "Not only am I going to share it with you, Bill, you're a major part of it. It can't work without you."

Halsey leaned back in his chair and exhaled smoke at the ceiling. He knew MacArthur was stroking him. His radar was on full. Was MacArthur, he wondered, about to pull out and light his corncob pipe? The pipe was a symbol every American recognized—MacArthur's attempt at homespun simplicity, an image constantly honed by the largest public relations staff of any theater commander in the war.

"As I said, General. Anything I can do. What *can* I do to help?"

MacArthur paused a moment then smiled broadly, ignoring Halsey's impatience. "Thanks, Bill. I told my staff I could depend on you and I'm grateful. Simply put, the plan requires my man to go into Japan. Once there he'll review their defense strategy, then bring the information back to us. We'll need your help in insertion and extraction. I don't have to—"

"Excuse me, sir." Halsey crushed his cigarette in the ashtray and leaned forward, elbows on the table. "Insert? Who the hell's going in?"

MacArthur expected this question, knowing it was the part to which Halsey would object.

"Bill, my man's been on my staff for well over a year. He knows the Japs better than anyone else on my staff. He lived and studied in Japan—"

"Sir, I don't want to be rude. I'm sure your man is competent. But if I'm going to go along I need to know who's going in. Certainly not a white man. With the Germans out of the war there would be no reason for the Japs to show their defense plans to a German. And they're not going to share them with the Russians."

MacArthur sagely nodded. "No, they're not."

Halsey smiled. "A Chinese? It won't work. I might have difficulty telling the difference but the Japs should be able to spot a Chink right away. Same with a Korean. Wait a minute... Japanese? You turned a Jap? General, I don't have to tell you, as soon as he gets there you've lost him. Or he'll turn again and give you false information. No, General, I can't go along with this. I won't have my ships take any part in this."

"Admiral. He's not Japanese."

Halsey froze, hearing the abrupt, impersonal formality in MacArthur's voice. He would have to back off, hear MacArthur out. "Then who the hell have you got? Sir."

"An American, Bill. A very brave and patriotic American. He's one of our *Nisei. Yonsei* actually, fourth-generation Japanese American."

Halsey started to rise.

"Now hold on Bill. Relax. His family's from California and they've been there since the late 1860s, before Edo became Tokyo. Hell, his great-grandfather had to get out in 1869 because he fought on the losing side in their civil war in 1868. He reads the Japs better than anyone on my staff. When we've captured documents his interpretations have not only been more exact than those of the other translators, including Colonel Sidney Mashbir, but he also catches nuances almost everyone else misses. Bill, his plan is audacious, it's remarkable."

Halsey stood and walked to the opposite side of the room. "General, he's a Jap. I don't care if his family came over on the *Mayflower*. I just don't trust the sons of bitches, including the

Nisei. You know that. This is a bad idea, General."

Halsey never hid his antipathy for the Japanese, especially after Japanese army pilots attacked and sank the American gunboat USS *Panay* and the three tankers she was escorting on China's Yangtze River, in early December 1937.

The tankers were evacuating Western nationals. When the *Panay* was abandoned and its lifeboats approached the shore, carrying survivors, Japanese planes returned and strafed them, killing three sailors and a civilian. What the Japanese Army did in China later only strengthened Halsey's hostility. Japan's attack on Pearl Harbor cemented that hatred. Halsey turned and walked to the window. MacArthur stood and joined him.

MacArthur closed his eyes and envisioned the carnage up close, the overwhelming spectacle of Americans being torn to pieces as they invaded Japan. He had always been critical of American commanders in Europe who sacrificed large numbers of soldiers. It reminded him of the Civil War, in which his father had fought, where thousands of Northern and Southern soldiers were slaughtered in mass formations in open fields. *What a stupid waste*, he thought. And though he welcomed the American combat soldiers that would soon arrive from Europe, as well as their tanks and planes and bombers and ships, he was not interested in any of the senior generals who commanded these troops and had not hesitated to inform Washington.

Halsey, a naval commander, rarely saw infantry up close, hadn't seen them dying on the beaches. His vision was solely of Pearl Harbor and the final reckoning he would bring to Japan, completely destroyed by his fleet and carrier-based planes, and Japan in hell, as he had promised on December 8, 1941.

MacArthur pulled a hand from his back pants pocket and rubbed the knotted muscles in his neck, trying to wipe from his mind the images of the inevitable slaughter. Yet, he understood Halsey's emotional objection.

MacArthur knew Halsey loved the Navy. Although Japan's

attack at Pearl Harbor was a brilliant tactical strike and Halsey might admire its audacity, he could not overcome his hatred of the Japanese race, even those members of it who owed their allegiance to America. But even Halsey, MacArthur decided, could not stand in the way of the greater need.

"Bill, I can't let American boys suffer an even greater bloodbath on Japan than they did on Okinawa. I've got to have that information. Just think what we could do with their defense plans. Imagine how many of our boys will go home alive and whole. If we don't get the plans, Bill, imagine instead how many American boys will be buried on Japanese soil. I don't want that, Bill, and I know you don't want it either."

MacArthur walked back to the table and poured more coffee. But it had cooled and he put the cup down. With his back to Halsey he said, "Bill, my man's proposal is exceptional and I'd like you to review it. His method of insertion is dramatic and it ought to convince the Japs he's one of theirs."

"General, you're asking me to put a Jap on one of my ships. I can't do that. I just can't."

MacArthur sighed with impatience. Halsey, he felt, was not seeing the implications and possible benefits of the mission.

Halsey's loathing for Japan, like most of his American and British peers, was based partly on racism. However, racism by itself played little in his hatred. His antipathy for Japan, before the outbreak of hostilities, stemmed from Japan's military aggression in China and elsewhere, coupled with his conviction that eventually America and Japan would be at war. With that conviction came distrust. Some who knew Halsey felt he hoped for war with Japan. Yet, to be fair, MacArthur knew that had Germany carried out a sneak attack on an American naval base on the east coast of the United States Halsey would have fought the Germans as viciously as he fought the Japanese.

MacArthur also understood some of the ghosts that haunted Halsey and drove his hatred of Japan. Guilt was one of them. When his beloved navy, and the men who served her, were under attack at Pearl Harbor and needed him most, he hadn't been there to help them repel the enemy.

MacArthur recalled the story. A few days before Japan attacked Pearl Harbor Halsey had met with Admiral Husband E. Kimmel, then the Commander-in-Chief of the United States Fleet at Pearl Harbor. Halsey received orders to deliver Grumman F4U fighter planes to Wake Island. Believing he might run into Japanese ships on the open sea, Halsey asked Kimmel, "How far do you want me to go?"

Kimmel, with typical candor, responded bluntly: "Goddammit, use your common sense!" Later Halsey commented, "I consider that as fine an order as a subordinate ever received."

During that same meeting Kimmel asked Halsey, "Do you want to take the battleships with you?" Like many admirals then, Kimmel felt that battleships were the most formidable weapons America had in the Pacific.

Tragically, Halsey declined. "Hell no! If I have to run I don't want anything to interfere with my running!" Halsey would take the carrier *Enterprise* to Wake Island but leave the battlewagons at Pearl Harbor. Kimmel understood, knowing none of the old battleships could sustain more than twenty knots while the other ships in the task force could exceed thirty. If Halsey were to attack the Japanese at sea he would need that extra speed.

At sunset on December 8, the day after the attack on Pearl Harbor, Halsey's task force returned from Wake Island. His ships steamed into Pearl, cutting through oil-coated water and floating debris. On the *Enterprise*'s bridge, he saw the devastation firsthand: smoking and twisted hulks of America's Pacific Fleet. Farther away, at airfields, navy and army planes lay smoking, twisted and shattered. Halsey could only imagine the number of casualties. Every man on the *Enterprise*, not occupied with duties, stood watching, mute. Near Hickam Field, along the shore, they saw exhausted soldiers wary at their anti-aircraft guns. One GI yelled out, "Where in hell were *you*?" Still another hollered, "You'd better get the hell out of here or the Japs will nail you, too." Both cries stung deeply. Halsey couldn't respond. He had no answer.

Halsey had the war he expected, and nothing would stop him from crushing the nation that had attacked the American fleet. Grim and defiant in the face of seemingly complete devastation, Halsey turned to an officer and said coldly, "Before we're through with 'em, the Japanese language will be spoken only in hell!"

Now, after more than three years of fighting a relentless and resourceful enemy, destroying his navy, Halsey had expunged most of the guilt. But not all. When his beloved navy was threatened at Leyte Gulf he was absent from there, too. And MacArthur knew he could exploit that as well. But in order to give Halsey a chance to save American lives, he was going to have to order him to take on board one of his ships a member of the hated Japanese race.

MacArthur turned. "Bill," he said bluntly, "Admiral Nimitz has approved the Navy's support. I'd prefer your cooperation, but if you want, I can ask Chester to cut you orders."

Halsey was boxed in. The approval of Fleet Admiral Chester Nimitz meant he would have to treat MacArthur's request as an order. Still, recalling MacArthur's support for him after the Leyte landing softened the blow. Now it was his turn.

"What can I do to assist, sir?"

*　　*　　*

On June 23, after eight days of hearings, the Naval Court of Inquiry recommended that Halsey be relieved of his command. When the court's opinion reached Washington the Secretary of the Navy wanted to retire Halsey. But others in

Washington, with more influence, felt that relieving Halsey of command would only lower America's morale and bolster Japan's. Halsey had been a national hero at the start of the war, a fearless combat commander throughout its course. The hearings were closed, and though Halsey received a verbal rebuke by the court he resumed command of the U.S. Third Fleet.

3

August 3, 1945

A moment after Lieutenant Kobayashi and Captain Murray entered Admiral Halsey's stateroom the Missouri's Naval Intelligence Officer, Commander Rutledge, joined the three men. As Rutledge walked to his chair he glanced at Admiral Halsey, who was sitting at one end of the rectangular conference table. Halsey fixed his gaze intently on Lieutenant Kobayashi, who sat stiffly with defiant grace across from him. As Rutledge sat down he looked across the table at Captain Murray, attempting to gauge everyone's mood. Murray raised his eyebrows, affecting a shrug. The three naval men, close comrades, were comfortable with one another. Rutledge easily perceived Kobayashi's sense of isolation.

Ken, still sitting erect, stared straight ahead, his hands resting on his thighs.

Halsey, still staring at Ken, lit another cigarette, then turned away and spat out a fragment of tobacco. Rutledge watched Halsey inhale on the cigarette several times. He seemed to be wrestling with a thought. At last, Halsey broke the tension, shaking his head and snorting. "Lieutenant Kobayashi, I think you're a brave but dumb son of a bitch for volunteering for this mission. I admire your courage but I can't say the same for your common sense. Incidentally, are we now required to call you 'Major' what with your recent promotion from Hirohito?"

Though Murray and Rutledge grinned, Ken answered firmly.

"Thank you, sir, no. 'Lieutenant' will do. It took an act of the American Congress to make me an officer. I value that more than a promotion from Hirohito. Infinitely more. And I didn't volunteer, sir. I proposed this mission."

Halsey raised his bushy eyebrows and stiffened a bit. Murray and Rutledge exchanged furtive looks, awaiting Halsey's wrath.

The intense setting Lieutenant Kenji Kobayashi found himself in was very different from his previous assignment. A week earlier he had been attached to General MacArthur's Intelligence Staff. His responsibilities included briefing MacArthur and General Willoughby as well as other officers. In the beginning it had been an uphill battle, a struggle, just to be accepted by the senior staff. Several resented Ken, seeing him as not American. Sensing this, he chose not to ingratiate himself with them. It turned out to be an astute decision. General Willoughby, aloof at first, eventually welcomed Ken, and the rest of MacArthur's staff soon fell in line. Willoughby warmed to Ken's wit and grew to respect his keen insight into Japanese thinking. As time passed, Willoughby started using Kenji's Americanized name, Ken.

Now, however, with these Navy men, Lieutenant Kenji Kobayashi was in hostile waters.

He faced Halsey, one of the most renowned and feared admirals in the American Navy, known throughout the Pacific for his unswerving hatred for anything Japanese. Like many in America, Ken was aware of one of Halsey's more famous dictums: "Kill Japs, Kill Japs, Kill More Japs!" Once, on a brief visit to Guam, Ken saw the quotation painted on a billboard in large block letters, greeting sailors as they sailed into the harbor. Now he recalled the remainder of the call to arms, which was not as commanding: "You will help to kill the yellow bastards if you do your job well."

Halsey spoke while exhaling cigarette smoke. "All right. Lieutenant, you've convinced me. Do you really think this plan of yours will work? Don't get me wrong, son. I'll admit you passed muster out there. I can't deny that. We all think you look like a Jap officer, don't we, gentlemen?" The others nodded. "Hell, if I didn't know better *I'd* have shot you.

"But let's think about this. I know you spent four years at Tokyo Imperial University. What if someone in Tokyo recognizes you? You've got to figure some of your former classmates are now in middle-level positions in the military, just about the rank you're wearing. If you're spotted and they recall you're an American and that you returned to the States after graduation, you're dead. But before they kill you they'll make you talk. They'll want to know what you're doing there at this stage of the game. They aren't stupid, they'll be able to put two and two together. You know about Olympic and Coronet. You spill that and a lot more Americans will die than you hope to save. Have you given thought to that?"

Ken, uneasy, shifted in his chair. General Willoughby had raised similar objections but without the personal animosity. He wondered if Halsey raised these objections for discussion, or was trying to scuttle the mission.

But he also knew Halsey was right. If captured by the Japanese, the only conclusion they could reach was that he was on an intelligence mission. The interrogation would be painful and protracted. Halsey's other argument also had merit. With his knowledge of America's invasion plans did he have the right to risk American lives by delivering those invasion plans to the Japanese? For the first time he began to question whether his plan could succeed. Halsey interrupted his thoughts.

"Relax, Lieutenant," said Halsey. "I'm not going to bite your head off. We decided to give you this opportunity to change your mind, but from the look of your new uniform I don't think you're going to do that. Am I correct?"

"Yes, sir. I've gone over those issues with General Willoughby and Colonel Mashbir several times. Though admitting the risks, they see the merit in this action. May I speak frankly, sir?"

Halsey nodded. "Lieutenant, if anyone aboard my ship doesn't speak frankly they'll find themselves on a garbage scow. Go ahead."

"I know you don't support this plan but when we hit the Japanese we've got to be sure we've done everything conceivable to reduce our casualties. I don't know any other way of finding out what they're going to do. Since it's their homeland that's going to be under attack, the Japs don't have to encode their plans and send them out over airwaves. They don't have to be transported by plane or ship. The plans won't leave the War Ministry. Someone's got to go in. That's me. That's the only way."

Halsey studied Kobayashi, still trying to separate the man from the Japanese uniform. Kobayashi, he noted, used the word "Japs" to describe the enemy. Halsey grasped the use was intentional, Kobayashi's attempt to convince them he was as loyal as any other American on board the *Missouri*. He knew from his conversations with Army staff that the *Nisei* did not use the term and felt certain it had been unpleasant for Kobayashi to use it.

Halsey had read Kobayashi's service record and was surprised that Kobayashi, even though imprisoned with his family in a relocation camp, had volunteered for duty in the Pacific. Then he recalled his surprise when he had heard, in 1943, that thousands of young Japanese-American men had done likewise. Most *Nisei*, however, were destined to fight in Europe, since the War Department was convinced their presence in large numbers in the Pacific might provoke hostilities from white soldiers.

Kenji Kobayashi was one of a handful of exceptions. Immediately upon entering the Army in 1943 he had been sent to Military Intelligence Service Language School in Minnesota, to study Japanese military terms. When General Willoughby found out Ken had graduated from Tôkyô Imperial University before the war he was assigned to MacArthur's intelligence staff upon graduation from the language school.

In Halsey's mind one certainty kept overriding everything else: In spite of what Ken Kobayashi and his family had undergone at Manzanar Relocation Camp he was prepared to risk his life for the United States, against his ancestral homeland. Halsey crushed out his cigarette, walked around the table, and placed his hand on Ken's shoulder.

"All right, son. I've read your plan. It's good. A bit theatrical, but that only shows how much General MacArthur has influenced you." Murray and Rutledge smiled. "Let's go over it one more time. If you've got the guts to try it, then the least we can do is help you get there."

Ken stood. "Thank you, sir."

Everyone walked over to the map table, and Commander Rutledge turned over the map lying on top. Ken rotated it to offer Halsey an optimal view. The three navy men leaned forward, resting on their elbows. Captain Murray motioned to Ken to take the lead.

"Sir, as you know I spent a day with several carrier pilots on leave and we've plotted the best approach. From Kyûshû I fly north-northeast and land at Atsugi Naval Air Base. No one there will recognize an Army pilot. And I'll be in an Army plane and uniform. The base is large enough for me to get lost in fairly quickly, and it's close enough to Tôkyô so I can probably get a lift or take a train there without questions being asked."

Halsey lit a fresh cigarette and studied the map for several seconds. He looked at Rutledge. "You satisfied with this approach?"

Rutledge glanced at Ken and then nodded. "Yes, sir. Lieutenant Kobayashi and I have gone over every aspect of it and I'm satisfied. There's no problem getting him in. It's getting him out that worries me. Obviously his exit can't be the same as his entrance. We can't improve on the exit plan that Colonel Mashbir's group put together. So we've agreed that Ken will radio us on a preassigned frequency, give us a predetermined pickup site and exit time and then grab a plane or boat. The radio message will have to be very brief. Once he gives us the information we'll have, if he's using a plane, carrier planes escort him to Iwo or, if by boat, a sub at the collection point as soon as possible, hopefully before he reaches it himself. But just in case, we'll have fighters overhead shadowing him, flying cover, as soon as he sets out."

Halsey squinted through the cigarette smoke, looked at Ken, and raised his bristly eyebrows. "You okay with this, Lieutenant? Because I'm not. I see two problems. First, you've never taken off from a carrier. Second, once you go in we can't help you. You understand that you'll be on your own?"

"Yes, sir. That's how I want it. Worrying about someone else backing me will only be a distraction. Besides, who else could follow me in? Commander Rutledge and I have discussed this and we agree; I go in alone. Lieutenant Burgess on the *Yorktown* agrees as well. As for not having taken off from a carrier I appreciate it's different from the ground but the pilots I've met with have done their best to coach me."

Halsey looked at Rutledge. "Who's Burgess?"

"William Burgess. He's a VF 88 division commander. He'll command the planes that force Ken down."

Halsey looked at Ken. "When do you take off from the *Yorktown*?"

Ken synchronized his wristwatch with the wall clock. "We already know that the Japanese officer from the army air base at Miyakonojô on Kyûshû I'm replacing is taking off sometime today. I take off from the *Yorktown* shortly after, sir. According to Sergeant Takayama—he's been translating radio traffic intercepts—the Japanese participants will radio the Imperial War Ministry with the time they are departing."

"How long to complete this mission, Lieutenant?"

"Colonel Mashbir and I've estimated about one week, sir."

"So you'll be out by the ninth?"

"Yes, sir. Give or take a day."

Halsey raised himself from the map table and yawned as he stretched his arms over his head. He was tired. Another cigarette appeared between his lips. He snapped the Zippo lighter shut. With the cigarette between his fingers, he absent-mindedly picked at a tooth with his thumbnail.

"You know, Lieutenant, it's one thing to convince a group of tired officers on the *Missouri* you're a Jap...Japanese, but can you do the same over there?" He pointed his thumb toward Japan. "What do you do if they catch on?"

Ken did not answer immediately. He felt certain it was the first time Halsey ever felt awkward using the word "Jap."

"I'll find out soon enough, sir. General Willoughby and I have an agreement. If I think they're on to me and I can't get out, I'll put a bullet in my head. I've accepted that."

"And if you don't have a gun?"

Ken's dark eyes flashed, looking into Halsey's, two determined men locking wills. "Japan is full of very sharp knives, sir. You have my word."

"Which reminds me. This message from General Willoughby came for you. Your eyes only."

Ken took the envelope and tore it open. The note was concise:

```
NEW ESTIMATES OF JAPANESE FORCES ON KYUSHU EX-
CEED HANFORD BRIEFING STOP ACCELERATED TRANSFER
OF JAPANESE REINFORCEMENTS TO SOUTHERN KYUSHU
STOP RATIO EXPECTED TO EXCEED ONE TO ONE STOP
```

IMPERATIVE YOU SECURE PROJECTED FORCE LEVELS
AND DEFENSIVE STRATEGY OF JAPANESE STOP WIL-
LOUGHBY

Halsey stared at the young man. Wisps of gray smoke separated them. He saw Ken's face reflect what was in Willoughby's
disturbing message. He wondered if he should ask then decided
not. He found Ken's matter-of-fact answer about killing himself
unsettling. He was familiar with the vicious method Japanese
officers employed to evade capture. He looked long and hard at
Ken, wondering if he would do it. His visceral guess was yes.
Though it was not easy to discern there was a new emotion in
the admiral's eyes. Something akin to concern.

"Okay, Lieutenant. What's your next step?"

Captain Murray finally spoke. "Sir, Lieutenant Kobayashi
will transfer from the *Missouri* to the *Gatling* on a Kingfisher.
We had one flown in for this mission. From the *Gatling* he'll
transfer to the *Yorktown*. *Ingersoll* will act as 'lifeguard,' cruising behind the *Yorktown* and *Gatling*. Both the *Ingersoll* and
Gatling have been temporarily reassigned to our Task Group,
38.4, for this mission.

"Designated code names for this mission are as follows: *Missouri* is designated Blackbird and the Kingfisher is
Blackbird One. *Yorktown* is Flatiron, *Gatling* is Fireside, and
Ingersoll is Hailstone. These call signs will be used during TBS
communication."

Halsey rotated the map to get a straight-on look. "Are the
people on *Yorktown* prepared, do they know what the lieutenant here expects from them?"

Rutledge focused on the map, studying it while collecting
his thoughts. "Admiral, Ken's going to fly a Nakajima *Shoki*.
The Japs call it the Devil Queller. The Army captured a few in
the Philippines, and they were in pretty good condition. On
orders from General Willoughby technicians were flown in
from the Technical Air Intelligence Center out of Anacostia.

They've flight-tested the *Shoki* and they're satisfied. Lieutenant Kobayashi has already logged about twenty hours in it. Not much but enough. The Anacostia people have made some changes. One of the guys from Tech Air, an engineer, even brought dental tools and scored some interior parts, just in case the Japs, uh, Japanese open her up. Twelve Hellcats, three divisions, will be involved in this operation. Division One will be armed with blanks. Divisions Two and Three will be fully armed. Finally, one of the Anacostia techs is still on the *Yorktown* to go over the details with Lieutenant Kobayashi. The only concern we have is that typhoon. It's about 400 miles northwest of us. Flying might be a bit bumpy but nothing that the pilots can't handle. We've been launching and landing with no problems."

Halsey crushed the barely-smoked cigarette while looking at the map. His officers knew not to intrude. He looked at Kobayashi, still a bit uncertain. He nodded his approval.

"Okay, Lieutenant. You're on."

For the first time Ken noticed the contradictory wrinkles around Halsey's eyes, lines etched by laughter, worry, and anger. Halsey was an unpretentious man. Those close to him called him Bill; his subordinates called him Admiral Bill. Above all else, Halsey was loved by his sailors. Stories about Halsey's affection and concern for his sailors and pilots were legion. Ken recalled two in particular.

During the Marshall Islands campaign, Halsey had ordered the *Enterprise* in closer to shore so his pilots would have extra fuel and could extend their attack yet still return to the carrier with an enhanced safety margin. It was a risky maneuver, exposing the carrier to potential shore batteries. Halsey was leaning over the port side of his open flag bridge, keeping an eye on flight operations. Unexpectedly, a Japanese fighter plane appeared, guns blazing, bearing down on the *Enterprise*'s island. Everyone on the bridge hit the deck. Several men threw themselves on Halsey, protecting him. No one was hit, and the enemy fighter veered off. When the men unpiled off Halsey, he was in a sitting position, attempting to recover his equilibrium and his dignity.

He heard then saw a yeoman laughing at his undignified collapse, unable to suppress his laughter. Pointing at the still-laughing yeoman, Halsey bellowed to the duty officer, "Who's that man?"

"That's Bowman, Admiral. Yeoman Ira Bowman," replied the ashen-faced lieutenant.

"*Chief* Yeoman Ira Bowman, you mean," growled Halsey. "Anybody who can laugh when my knees are shaking is somebody who deserves to be promoted."

Earlier, in April 1942, Halsey had taken his carriers, *Hornet* and *Enterprise*, on one of the most audacious air raids of the war. Colonel Jimmy Doolittle, with President Roosevelt's blessing, led 16 B-25s from the deck of the *Hornet*. Their target: Tôkyô and other sites. It was the first American strike against the Japanese homeland. Damage was minimal. But the morale of the American Navy and the home front rocketed. A few months later, on another mission, two sailors were speculating where Halsey was leading them.

"I don't care where we're going," said one. "I'd go to hell for that old s.o.b."

The sailor felt a tap on his shoulder and, turning, found himself face-to-face with a grinning Halsey. "Not so old, son. Not so old." Then Halsey walked away, still grinning.

Halsey noticed Kobayashi staring at him. "Anything else, Lieutenant?"

"No, no, sir. I'm all set. Thank you. I've got to go back to my cabin and get a few items. Then I'll take off for the *Yorktown*."

"Then let me add one final point, Lieutenant. I think you need to know this. Last week President Truman issued what's being called the 'Potsdam Proclamation.' Putting aside the diplomatic bullshit what it boils down to is, the United States, England, and China are demanding Japan's unconditional surrender. Otherwise, Japan faces 'prompt and utter destruction.' If I know the Japs, if anything, it'll stiffen their backs, especially their army brass. I don't know how this will affect your mission but I'm willing to bet it'll be pretty tense there. All right, Lieutenant. That's all. God speed and good hunting."

Ken stepped back two paces and pulled on his peaked officer's cap, the yellow star visibly offensive to Halsey. He stood at attention and snapped a salute. Halsey, transfixed, again wrestled with his emotions.

Captain Murray eyed Halsey, wondering how he would respond. Halsey did not have his campaign cap on. Navy tradition required wearing a hat when giving or returning a salute.

Admiral William F. "Bull" Halsey, Commander of the United States Third Fleet and implacable enemy of Japan, reached behind him and pulled his cap from his rear pocket, looked at it for a few seconds, then put it on. Then, looking resolutely into Ken's eyes, he slowly raised his right hand and returned the salute from an American Army lieutenant wearing an Imperial Japanese Army uniform.

Ken lowered his arm and, without another word, pivoted and started to walk out of the admiral's stateroom.

Halsey removed his hat and ran his hand through his gray hair, tension visibly etched on his face. "Lieutenant, one more thing."

Ken stopped and turned. "Sir?"

Halsey looked down at the map, tapped it several times with a finger, then looked up at Kobayashi. "Watch your back in there, son. The Japs don't play the game like we do. They're not like us...Americans."

Murray and Rutledge exchanged a quick glance.

Ken looked at Halsey, the implacable enemy of Japan. He saw an old man, worried about the young men he sent off to war, some to live, some to be broken and some to die. "Yes, sir," Ken said. "Thank you, sir."

As the others filed out of the stateroom, Halsey returned to the small conference table. He sat down and started to pull a cigarette from the pack but changed his mind, tossing the pack onto the table. He sat back, looking grim. Thoughtful and grim.

Halsey frowned, imagining Kobayashi putting a bullet in his head or cutting open his guts. The image angered and saddened him. *Too many brave American men are dying. When will it end? Will Kobayashi help end it?*

Unexpectedly, he felt responsible for Kenji Kobayashi, temporarily attached to his Third Fleet and now about to enter the belly of the beast. He knew once Kobayashi infiltrated Japan, not even the combined power of the Third Fleet could come to his aid.

Halsey, for reasons he could not explain, felt helpless. His overwhelming conviction was the same he experienced when he was told his son, a carrier pilot, was missing in action—he would never see the young man again alive.

4

Ken returned to his cabin. Entering, he instructed the Marine to wait outside; then he closed the door. He was surprised that he was so calm after his encounter with Halsey.

Allowing himself a few moments, he looked around the cabin. He walked to the makeshift *kamidana*, picked up the *omamori* and carefully placed it in his left shirt pocket. He went to the desk and opened the drawer. From it he removed his Japanese identity papers, paper money and ceramic coins. *No more metal for coins*, he thought, *just for bullets*. He then removed a package of Japanese cigarettes, a wristwatch, shaving kit, and, most important, his written orders to report to the Ministry of War at Ichigaya. Next, he walked to the wardrobe and gathered the spare shirt and pants, two pairs of white regulation socks, and a spare *fundoshi*.

Satisfied he had all that he needed he put on his wristwatch then got his flight bag. His flight helmet, goggles, and gloves were already in it. He packed his *yukata* and *obi*, clothing, and shaving kit. Done, he pocketed his cigarettes, money, and his orders. Then he sat on the edge of the bed and thought back on the events that had brought him to this point.

Can I really do this? Who the hell am I to think I can pull it off?

His mind drifted back to June 14, 1945, when the germ of the plan was first planted, during Colonel Hanford's invasion briefing at the Malacañan Palace. It had been Ken's first exposure to the invasion plans. As the details unfolded he, like most in the room, was overwhelmed by their scope and complexity.

But he was not surprised. This is what America had been fighting and dying for, only not on this scale. Still, for him as well as others at the briefing, one sobering element was paramount. The bulk of Japan's army, over two million disciplined and combat-ready soldiers, were on the home islands waiting for the Americans, knowing they were coming. American blood shed on Okinawa confirmed America's worst fears: the conquest of Japan would be not only America's but the costliest battle of any nation's in World War II.

The reality of hardened, fanatical Japanese soldiers, coupled with anticipated attacks on Allied ships by thousands of *kamikaze* and *kaiten*, manned suicide planes and torpedoes, had led Colonel Hobart Hanford, when asked, to speculate that the projected American casualties could approach one million men from the combined invasions. When these estimates were announced, Ken grasped the staggering cost to America. Then he caught himself as he realized he considered only American losses, not Japanese, though the invasion would certainly prove more costly to Japan.

And Ken knew that Colonel Hanford probably was right. He knew the Japanese and expected that they, both military and civilians, would fight to the death rather than allow the barbaric Americans to occupy their sacred soil.

He paused, wondering what Japanese word or phrase would best sum up this national suicide. Then he remembered: *Gyokusai*, what the West might call Armageddon. Yes, he thought, better *Gyokusai* or honorable death, than the humiliation of surrender.

It was toward the end of Colonel Hanford's briefing that the seed of a daring idea had taken root. After the June 14 briefing Ken had gone to General Willoughby's office.

*　　*　　*

"Sir, excuse me. I know this is highly unusual but I'd like to request an appointment with you."

Willoughby hesitated, wondering why the young man he had brought into his inner circle looked so uncharacteristically serious.

Willoughby liked Ken Kobayashi. Soon after Ken had joined MacArthur's intelligence staff Willoughby found out that Ken was fluent in German, Willoughby's native language.

Languages came easy to Ken. Growing up in San Gabriel, California he easily learned Spanish from the large Mexican-American population there. When he attended high school, his classmates were either Japanese Americans or Mexican Americans. Whites did not attend that school. It was natural for him to study Spanish. But he also studied German as Germany had been in the news. When he had entered high school in 1933 Adolf Hitler had already been named chancellor. To him it seemed logical to study the language.

Willoughby was delighted to speak German with Ken. One time, General Willoughby said to Ken in German, "Want to have some fun?" Uncertain, Ken said yes. Continuing in German, Willoughby said, "Good. Let's talk out loud, look at the junior officers over there and laugh." Ken smiled. They began speaking loudly; At one point Willoughby pointed to a captain and told Ken, "Just laugh." The captain's face reddened. The other officers laughed at him until Willoughby pointed at some of them and Ken and he spoke more German and continued laughing. Their smiles disappeared. Later, a few of the officers buttonholed Ken and tried to find out what he and Willoughby had said. Ken said it was confidential but that they could ask General Willoughby. They stopped asking and Ken's friendship with Willoughby was cemented.

"What's on your mind, Ken?"

"In the briefing this morning Colonel Hanford talked about how high American casualties might be. I think I know how we might be able to reduce that number. But I'm not sure. I'd like to talk with you about it."

General Willoughby smiled and raised his eyebrows. "Really? Interesting." He sat back, locking his hands behind his head. Ken stood at ease yet Willoughby felt he was as tense as a compressed spring.

"Okay. How much time do you think you'll need and when would you like to get together?"

"About an hour, sir, and as soon as possible. Tomorrow?"

Willoughby looked down at his desk calendar then picked up a pencil. "All right. Tomorrow's June 15. How about 0900 hours?"

"Thank you, sir."

The next morning, at 0900 hours, Ken returned to General Willoughby's sparsely furnished office. Besides a desk and chairs a sofa rubbed against a wall, an American flag tacked above it. A chipped wooden bookcase occupied a spot behind and to the right of his desk. On the bookcase a fan fought a losing battle with the humid air.

As Ken walked in Willoughby pointed him to the sofa. On Willoughby's desk a radio, tuned to the Armed Forces Radio Network, broadcast a woman's dulcet voice, strong and animated. She was singing "The Last Time I Saw Paris."

"Okay, Ken, what's up?"

"Sir, like I said yesterday. It's about yesterday's briefing and the projected casualties. Colonel Hanford tossed out some numbers ranging from over thirty thousand up to a million."

"I know, I read the reports. What's your mind?"

"Sir, over the last several days Central Bureau has picked up an increase in some coded traffic on the radio. More than usual. Three days ago Taka, Sergeant Takayama, showed me a translated message. It was about a big meeting at Japan's

Ministry of War at Ichigaya, for August fifth. Later that day he showed me the rest of the message. Chiefs of staff, intelligence officers, and combat engineering officers have been ordered to arrive by no later than August fourth. My guess is the Imperial General Staff is going to do a mirror image of what we just did yesterday."

"That's not surprising, Ken. If I were them I'd be making some plans too. Anything else?"

Ken wished he were anywhere but here; Willoughby could sometimes be intimidating. "We're not certain, sir, but Taka and I think these people have been ordered to Ichigaya to be briefed on Japan's preparations for Downfall."

For a moment Willoughby sat still. Then he reached over and turned off the radio and stood up. He walked to the front of his desk and sat on the edge, arms folded. The room seemed to shrink as his bulk filled it. Willoughby's eyes bored into Ken's.

"Interesting. Did Taka and you get a date?"

"Yes, sir. August fifth."

"No, no, you told me that. Did you get a date on when they think we're coming?"

"No, sir. But we did get three names."

"Three? Who are they?"

"The first one is a Major Hori Eizô. He's in Intelligence."

Willoughby turned his large frame around and picked up a pad and pencil from his desk. "Do we know him?"

"No, sir. His name's never come up before. But we do know his boss."

Willoughby stood and walked around his desk and sat down. He was curious. He felt he knew Ken Kobayashi better than most of the senior staff did, except perhaps for Colonel Sidney Mashbir, MacArthur's chief translator and Ken's immediate superior. So he was certain what he would hear. He leaned back in his chair, lifted his huge feet onto the desk and propped the pad on his lap. "I'm waiting, Ken. The second name."

"Yes, sir. Lieutenant General Arisue Seizô, Imperial Japanese Army Chief of Intelligence."

"No shit..." Willoughby said absent-mindedly while writing quickly, in German, which he did sometimes without even realizing it. "And the third?"

"Vice Minister of War, Lieutenant General Shibayama Kenshirô."

Willoughby paused for a moment. "Are these names Japanese or English form," he asked, knowing that family names in Japanese came first.

"Japanese form, sir."

"Okay, anything else?"

"Just that this Major Hori will give the Japanese intelligence estimate on what they think the American strategy will be."

Willoughby wrote a few more lines and looked up at Ken, a grin on his face. "Christ! The closer we get to them the more arrogant they seem to become. Imagine, sending that on the radio. All right. I think I know what's on your mind."

Ken was caught off guard. How could he have guessed? Then he shook off the reaction. He had often believed that the part of himself that was Japanese could hide his thoughts and feelings from *hakujin*, the whites.

"I don't think so, sir."

"Sure I do. You and Taka want more subs to monitor shipping and planes to increase photo recon. Right? It's a good idea. In fact it's a great idea. You and Taka earned your pay today. Tell me what you think you need and you've got it. Anything else?"

"Sir, those are good ideas and they should be done. But it's not what I was going to suggest."

"Oh? Well, what do you have in mind? Let me guess." Willoughby's face broke into a wide grin. "You want to attend the briefing at the War Ministry at Ichigaya. Right?"

Ken didn't smile. "Yes, sir."

General Willoughby's huge body started to fall backward in his chair. The pad and pencil left his hands and flew through the air as he reached for the desk. Ken leaped from the sofa and grabbed Willoughby's shoes, straining to upright Willoughby's massive body.

When Willoughby had recovered, his eyes widened and fixed on Ken. "Are you nuts? That's the most screwball idea I've heard since the war began! That's... That's..."

It was Ken's turn to grin. "No, sir, I'm not nuts. And I'm not so sure it's crazy. You said it yourself. The closer we get to them the more arrogant they seem to become. But I wouldn't say 'imprudent.' I'd say desperate. When you listen to their radio broadcasts to the nation they still talk about victory after victory. They broadcast to their people how they're drawing *us* closer and closer to *their* trap. They keep telling their people they want us to invade so they can wipe us out. They're desperate, sir."

"And you're nuts, Ken."

"Sir, it might work. If I can get in there somehow, get into the War Ministry, maybe I'll find the plans, review them then get out. Please remember, sir, I speak Japanese better than anyone else here, probably better than Colonel Mashbir. Damn it, sir, when I was at Camp Savage I ended up teaching Japanese to the Japanese language instructors before you had me transferred to Australia. Maybe it is crazy, sir. But I think I can do it."

Willoughby reached down and picked up his pad off the floor. When he spotted his pencil in the corner he got up and walked over to it but didn't pick it up. Instead, he said, "You're serious, aren't you? You really want to do it. Well, I can't let you do it, even if I did agree with it. No, it's out of the question. Forget it. I'm sorry, Ken, but my answer is no. You're too valuable here."

Ken stood. He wet his lips. For the first time he became angry at General Willoughby, the man who had brought him into MacArthur's inner circle and protected him from the occasional abuse of *hakujin* soldiers and officers.

When Ken had first come to the attention of General Willoughby he had been a corporal, and like most *Nisei*, bound to remain a noncom.

But Willoughby saw something, perhaps the cockiness of self-confidence, or perhaps just a hint of arrogance based on the knowledge that he knew the Japanese better than most everyone else on MacArthur's staff. And he was right, he did know the enemy better than the others, *hakujin* or *Nisei*.

Corporal Kobayashi had worked long hours, more than most, translating seemingly ambiguous or impenetrable documents the enemy had left behind during their retreats, arrogantly thinking the Americans could not translate them.

Of course when the Japanese retired from the battlefield they didn't call it a retreat. They called it *Tenshin*, a "Turned Advance." Even toward the end of the war they continued to lie to themselves.

Often late at night, while the *hakujin* were sleeping, Kenji Kobayashi, Tetsuo Takayama and other *Nisei* labored over captured enemy documents, what they derisively called *Tenshin-no Senrihin*, "Spoils of a Turned Advance," intelligence trophies that had been collected from battlefields.

Before Ken arrived at MacArthur's headquarters the morale of the *Nisei* was low. In spite of their invaluable work on behalf of a nation that still held their families imprisoned, they were taunted by some white soldiers. Then Ken arrived. When provoked by the white noncoms he would fight back, mostly verbally, but sometimes physically. He lost some fights, but he won most. Word quickly spread; Corporal Kenji Kobayashi was one tough *Nisei* who wouldn't take shit from anyone.

If an officer antagonized him he used his wit. Subtle

insults, though in English, often went unappreciated by the offending officer. But the *Nisei* understood what was said and what was not. Soon their morale shot up. So did the quantity and quality of the work.

General Willoughby was pleasantly surprised and made inquiries. Initially, some of his staff officers tried to claim responsibility for the *Nisei*'s increased output. Willoughby didn't buy it. One day he sent for Corporal Takayama. At first, Taka denied any knowledge about anything. But Willoughby wouldn't drop it. Taka finally opened up, his anger and humiliation replaced by pride. For Willoughby it all fell into place. Some white officers were transferred. When Colonel Mashbir complained, Willoughby told him the work was more important than a few jerks. And what the *Nisei* were doing, he reminded Mashbir, was saving American lives, white Americans. That silenced Mashbir.

Soon, Ken rose in rank, eventually to master sergeant. The promotions had come faster than was normal and some of the white noncoms resented it. Willoughby brought his enormous hand down like a sledgehammer and quashed the protests. Recognizing the work of Corporal Takayama, Willoughby promoted him to tech sergeant.

In February 1945, during the battle for Manila, Master Sergeant Kenji Kobayashi received a commission to Second Lieutenant. There was some grumbling, some white lieutenants pointing out that Ken had not attended Officers Candidate School. Willoughby pointed out that the stars on his own shoulders made it all right. Besides, he added, Kobayashi had a university degree in engineering, "just like the smart boys from West Point." Near the end of June Ken was promoted again, to First Lieutenant.

But now General Willoughby, who had protected and guided Ken, was blocking his way.

"General, I can't accept that answer. I've been sitting at a desk too long. Every time I ask for a transfer to interpret for a combat outfit you tell me that I'm too valuable here. And so far I've bought it. But the war's going to end soon. I can feel it. I want a crack at them. They're my enemy too, sir. I've seen the casualty figures for Iwo Jima and Okinawa. What I'm proposing might reduce the casualty numbers for Downfall. Sir, if you refuse this request I'll go to General Sutherland. I've never asked anything from you. And I know what you've done for me. But I want to do something *before* and not *after* a battle. I won't be in that much danger, sir. I'm not going into battle. No one will be shooting at me—"

Willoughby slammed his pad on the desk. His eyes were angry, threatening. Ken swallowed hard, knowing he had gone too far.

"You're damn right, Lieutenant. No one will shoot at you. They'll just cut off your damn head. And right now I need your head where it belongs, on your shoulders. And right here, in my headquarters. Is that understood, Lieutenant Kobayashi?"

For the first time in almost a year Willoughby was addressing Ken by rank. A boundary had been crossed, their mentor-protégé relationship damaged, perhaps irreparably. But Ken would not turn back.

"General, I appreciate your concern for my head. I really do. I like it where it is, too. But I think this could help us. If I can get in that building and figure out what they plan to do when we invade, it might save a hell of a lot of American lives. Isn't that more important than my life?"

Willoughby's shoulders drooped a bit. "You know, you are one tough s.o.b. I used to think the only person in this whole damn army who wasn't afraid of me was General MacArthur. Now you show up. So, you'll go to General Sutherland? Ken, that inflated asswiper doesn't know you exist."

Willoughby stopped himself. It was wrong to insult a fellow senior officer, especially in front of a subordinate. He wondered how he could dissuade Ken from what he judged as a foolhardy and suicidal mission. Long ago he had come to regard Ken as his most valuable intelligence asset as translator and interrogator. Then he looked into Ken's eyes and knew he could forget it.

"You're determined, aren't you?"

"Yes, sir."

Willoughby returned to his desk chair and sat down heavily. "Sit down, Ken."

"Thank you, sir."

"You're just going to march in there? Just how do you propose to get in?"

"Frankly, sir, I haven't thought it that far through yet. I wanted to touch base with you first. I have some ideas. The one I've been thinking about most is to go in by submarine at night to within a few hundred yards off the coast, transfer to a rubber raft, and when I near the shore, sink the raft and swim in the rest of the way. I'll have civilian clothing with me, and papers, inside a rubber bag, and once on shore I change. From there I make my way to Tôkyô. I guess from there I wing it."

"Wing it, huh? To abuse your simile, it'll never fly. However, it's clear to me you want to go ahead with this. So let me think about it for a day or so. In the meantime I'm going to order increased monitoring of the traffic Central Bureau's been picking up. I'll get back to you shortly. Thank you for coming by, Lieutenant."

The following afternoon General Willoughby summoned Ken to his office.

"Well, Ken, you can knock me over with a feather. Sit down. I spoke with General MacArthur last night. He told me to give you a green light."

Without looking, Ken staggered back the few feet to the sofa. Instinctively his hand groped for the armrest. Instead of sitting he seemed to fold into the sofa.

"What's the matter, Lieutenant? Were you hoping we'd turn you down," Willoughby asked with a wicked grin. "It seems the general actually likes your plan, even though it's a bit rough around the edges. That's what General MacArthur said. I told him in fact your plan has no edges. Nor a top or bottom, for that matter. But I take orders too. And so will you. He agrees with you. Right now we can only surmise what the Japs have in mind for us. So I suppose if you can find out you'll be the biggest hero around these parts.

"As to your orders, at 0700 hours tomorrow you will meet with Colonel Mashbir. Right now he's putting together a group to give this idea of yours some edges." General Willoughby saw the light in Ken's eyes fade a little. "Relax, Ken. Colonel Mashbir is going to chair the group but he knows it's your baby. He'll defer to you but don't try to do an end run on him. He'll box your ears. He's already submitted the names of the group and I've approved them. Some are here and a couple more are on their way and should arrive by late tonight. Obviously, of those being assembled, only Colonel Mashbir is acquainted with your plan. Incidentally, in case you want to know, he disapproves. Let me add he also thinks that you're crazy.

"Hopefully all of you, working together, will come up with a credible way to get you in. Incidentally, you never mentioned how you intend to get back. So they'll probably help you with that, too. Is that understood? Lieutenant?"

"Uh, yes, sir. Thank you, sir."

"Good. I'm glad you're pleased. Dismissed."

As Ken opened the door Willoughby called to him.

"Ken, one more thing. I'm not happy about this. But I think I know how you feel. Therefore, let me remind you of a poem that is, in this case, appropriate. It goes something like, 'If you can keep your head when all about you are losing theirs...' Remember it?"

Ken smiled. "Yes, sir."

"Then please keep that line in mind and keep your head. God speed."

But as Ken started to leave Willoughby stopped him once again. "Ken, one question. Have you and Taka been talking about anything else lately?"

Ken hesitated. He and Taka spoke almost every day, sometimes several times a day. "Sir, I don't understand. Taka and I talk all the time. Can you narrow it down for me?"

Willoughby looked at Ken for several seconds, wondering if he was being disingenuous. "Well, I mean, about any upcoming operations. Any intelligence missions?"

Ken stepped back into the room and closed the door. "No, sir. Should I know about any?"

Willoughby studied Ken's face for a moment. "No, no. It was just a thought. Dismissed."

After Ken left, General Willoughby interlaced his fingers behind his head, leaned back, and studied the ceiling for a few moments. In a desk drawer was a copy of a proposal from the Office of Strategic Services, the OSS. Though MacArthur distrusted the OSS and had banned any OSS operations in the South West Pacific Theater Willoughby often monitored any OSS operations in the Pacific Theater. He opened the drawer with his foot and rested it on the edge, as though afraid to acknowledge its existence. After a few moments he removed his foot, leaned over and pulled out the OSS file.

Like MacArthur's staff, the OSS had been carefully following what was happening in Tôkyô. The relentless American bombing campaign, coupled with the blockade of Japan by the U.S. Navy, especially by American submarines, was inexorably disintegrating Japanese society. In Tôkyô, few homes still stood. Hundreds of thousands of civilians were living in makeshift shelters made from scraps of wood and corrugated sheet metal. Except for the military and civilian leadership, most Tôkyôites barely existed on a subsistence diet.

The OSS had hatched a plan to contact Japanese leaders who might be able to convince Emperor Hirohito to end the war. To accomplish this mission the OSS had asked for *Nisei* volunteers from the Army's Military Intelligence Service.

Twelve *Nisei* had immediately volunteered. Each one knew it would probably be a one-way mission, ending in their deaths. Of these twelve three would be chosen to carry out the mission. These three *Nisei* volunteers would parachute into Japan, at night, each one into a different wooded area on the outskirts of Tôkyô, then make their way to the capital. They would be dressed as soldiers or workers. Whoever survived, upon arrival in the city, would approach 14 pre-selected leaders of Japan, believed to be in favor of ending the war regardless of the cost.

The purpose of the mission would be to convince Japanese leaders of several points. The first assurance was that the Allied demands of "unconditional surrender," as reported in the Western press, would in fact be less harsh than most Japanese believed. The second guarantee was that only the American Army would actually occupy Japan, thus keeping the Russians, Chinese and British off Japanese soil. The third commitment was that American occupation forces would be limited in number and under strict military discipline. The fourth promise was that the Americans did not intend to turn Japan into a "political vacuum"; the fifth, that any future Japanese government would be chosen by the Japanese people. The sixth and last pledge, related to the fifth, was that the United States was not interested in "disturbing" the emperor.

Taka, Technical Sergeant Tetsuo Takayama, was one of the volunteers.

When General Willoughby finished reading the OSS document he thought about why the *Nisei*, in spite of how shamefully America had treated them, were still willing to die for America. He had no answer. Certainly, thought Willoughby, other Americans throughout the war had risked their lives without hesitation. But their families had not had their rights, homes, and way of life taken from them, had not been forced into prison camps. He remembered his reaction when he had found out that some German Americans had been sent to "relocation" camps in early 1942, as had some Italian Americans. But most of those had had some relation to Nazi Germany, such as being members of the German *Bund*. Yet there were others who were innocent. But they did not lose their homes or businesses like Japanese Americans. If his family had been interned would he and other German Americans have been so willing to fight and die for their country? Would General Eisenhower, of German-Swiss descent? Again, he didn't have an answer and was ashamed.

And yet here was another Japanese American, volunteering to go on a hazardous mission. Willoughby shook his head and wondered where America found such men.

*   *   *

The following morning, at 0700 hours, Colonel Sidney Mashbir, commander of General MacArthur's Japanese translation section, entered a small conference room. Six people were already there. One of them, a corporal, stood and called, "Ten-hut!" Everyone in the room stood as Colonel Mashbir walked to the head of the conference table, a bound set of papers under his arm.

Mashbir's dark face was angular. His eyes drooped, as if trying to overtake the bags under them. His hair and eyebrows were black and thick and his mustache was neatly groomed. What was most noticeable were his large ears, which stuck out. Someone once joked he looked just like Clark Gable if you only looked at his mustache and ears.

Colonel Mashbir was a remarkable student of the Japanese. In addition to his responsibilities supervising translators, mostly *Nisei*, he made weekly radio broadcasts from Manila to Japan, in fluent Japanese, telling the Japanese the true status of the war.

Long before the war, in the 1920s, he had worked in Tôkyô as Assistant Military Attaché and as a spy for the United States. An Army captain at the time, he had tried to develop a spy ring in Japan. Ironically he met with resistance, not from the Japanese but from American Army bureaucrats, who felt a spy ring was unnecessary during peacetime.

In 1923, frustrated, he resigned his commission and tried to maintain his clandestine efforts, trying to organize what he called Japanese "true patriots." He had not been successful.

Mashbir was now Chief, Allied Translator and Interpreter Service, attached to Willoughby's G-2.

Standing at the head of the conference table, he put his papers down.

"Good morning. Please sit down. For those who don't know me, let me introduce myself. I'm Colonel Sidney Mashbir. You've been asked to come here because of an intelligence mission recently approved by General Willoughby. Most of you don't know one another, but you were ordered to come here because each of you has skills and backgrounds well suited to offer advice on this mission. I'll just go around the table; as I call your name please, for the benefit of the others, identify yourself by raising your hand and I'll briefly review your background.

"First is Captain Roger Paschal, U.S. Army." Paschal nodded at Mashbir. "Born in Tôkyô, 1914. Captain Paschal's father was an American consular official in Japan. In 1932 Captain Paschal returned to the United States and took his B.A. in Far Eastern History at Harvard University in 1936 and a Ph.D. in 1940, same area of study, same school. His dissertation was *The Japanese Mind: Importing Foreign Industry, Excluding Foreign Culture*. Later that year he published a book, *Wind from Asia: A Study of the Mongol Attempts to Invade Japan*. Captain Paschal is fluent in Japanese and Chinese, both Mandarin and Cantonese, and has recently been assigned to this command."

Throughout Colonel Mashbir's summary Captain Roger Paschal, woefully thin, looked down at the table. Though a brilliant scholar he was painfully shy, made worse by a stutter. Ironically, he stuttered only when he spoke English.

Once, when asked by his Ph.D. thesis advisor to prepare some lectures for undergraduate students, he fainted in the advisor's office. The professor was sympathetic and withdrew the request. Resigned to his stutter and his fear of speaking in public, Roger Paschal chose to devote his life to conducting research and writing journal articles and books rather than accept offers of a faculty appointment from Harvard, Princeton, Stanford, and Yale.

Though the stuttering earned him a draft deferment, one week after Japan attacked Pearl Harbor he tried to join the army. At first he was rejected, his stutter apparent. But when he started to swear profusely at the recruiting officer in Japanese, and then Chinese, both without stuttering, he was hastily inducted.

However, one personality quirk stood conspicuously in contrast to his shyness. Roger Paschal loved to box and was the army's Officers Featherweight boxing champion in the Pacific Theater. In the ring Roger Paschal didn't have to say a word. His analytically swift mind would quickly evaluate his opponent's tactics, then his gloved fists did his talking for him, frequently before the end of the second round.

"Thank you, Captain. Master Sergeant George Tall Bear Bliss, U.S. Army. Born in Seattle, Washington, 1903. In case you're wondering, Sergeant Bliss is an Indian. He served with distinction during World War I in France, having signed up at the age of 15. Before he turned 16 he was awarded two Purple Hearts. Later on, Sergeant Bliss displayed an affinity for guerrilla warfare. During the mid-thirties Sergeant Bliss served in

China with Colonel Carlson, studying the tactics of the Chinese Communist leader Mao Tse-tung. As some of you know Colonel Carlson had led Carlson's Raiders. While in China Sergeant Bliss observed Mao Tse-tung's methods of inserting and extracting agents in and out of enemy territory. For the last eighteen months he has been attached to the Sixth Army's Special Reconnaissance Unit, the Alamo Scouts. He has led several commando units on intelligence missions into Japanese-held territories. Insertion and extraction are familiar to him."

Lieutenant Kobayashi looked at Sergeant Bliss and thought that his name, Tall Bear, was incongruous. Sergeant Bliss was just five feet four. But his wide frame bristled with corded muscles. A lifetime in the sun had left a patchwork of parched gullies wending their way across his face. His eyes pierced anything they looked at. His lips were bent downward, like a taut bow. Ken wondered if that mouth had ever smiled. He noted that Bliss' nose had been broken at least once. He turned his attention to Bliss' hands—they were enormous, fingers comparable to thick tree roots. Ken imagined Bliss could easily crush a man's face in one of those powerful hands. Earlier, when Sergeant Bliss first walked into the conference room, Ken had noticed a bulge below Bliss' knee, under the pant leg. He guessed a very large knife caused it. Though a concealed knife was technically illegal, if anyone had noticed it no one had objected.

"Thank you, Sergeant. Corporal Edna Collucci, U.S. Army. Born in New York City. We don't know when Corporal Collucci was born. She won't tell us. And I'm not about to demand that information. I am, after all, a gentleman. Corporal Collucci is attached to the OSS. Her specialty is designing and sewing enemy uniforms and insignia and, as warranted, enemy civilian clothing. Before the war she designed and sewed costumes in Hollywood."

When Ken first saw her he wondered what her role would

be. While Collucci listened to Colonel Mashbir her eyes, dark brown and cold, were examining Kobayashi's frame, estimating measurements. Ken wondered if they were for clothes or a pine box.

"Thank you, Corporal. Lieutenant Michael Elgin, U.S. Navy. Born in Memphis, Tennessee, 1922. Took his B.S. in geography and geology at Illinois Institute of Technology at eighteen years of age. Two years later took his Ph.D. in geography. Upon entering the Navy he was assigned to Air Reconnaissance Intelligence, specializing in photo analysis. Thank you, Lieutenant.

"Next is Technical Sergeant Tetsuo Takayama. U.S. Army. Taka, as we fondly call him here, was born 1925 in California. In 1943 he enlisted." What was not said was that Taka, like so many *Nisei*, enlisted while in a relocation camp. "He is a graduate of the Military Intelligence Service Language School at Fort Snelling. He was attached to Allied Translator and Interpreter Service, ATIS. However, due to the sheer volume of deciphered Japanese Army messages he has been temporarily assigned to Central Bureau, General MacArthur's cryptanalytic agency, where his translating skills have been needed.

"He has a solid grasp of the Japanese language and recently reported about an upcoming meeting at the Imperial War Ministry. That's why we're here today. He works closely with our final member."

Colonel Mashbir looked down the length of the conference table, to Lieutenant Kobayashi. "The last member of our group is Lieutenant Kenji Kobayashi, U.S. Army. Born in California, 1919. In 1937 he was admitted to Tôkyô Imperial University, where he studied engineering. In 1941 he was awarded a B.S. degree. Subsequently Lieutenant Kobayashi returned to the States.

"In 1943 Lieutenant Kobayashi enlisted in the Army. Because of Lieutenant Kobayashi's unique experiences in Japan

General Willoughby had him transferred to General MacArthur's command. Like Sergeant Takayama he was attached to ATIS but he too was needed at Central Bureau. He has distinguished himself to date. He now works directly for me. Any questions? Okay.

"We're here to discuss a plan proposed by Lieutenant Kobayashi. As a preface I'm authorized to tell you that in a few months we will invade Japan. That's not a big secret, even to the Japanese. Lieutenant Kobayashi's plan, if successful, could save thousands of American lives, possibly tens of thousands. Frankly, it might work. On the other hand it might not. Namely, because he might be captured and killed.

"First, the background. A few days ago Sergeant Takayama translated a radio message that the Japanese are convening a meeting in Tôkyô to review their defense strategy for the impending American invasion. With that information Lieutenant Kobayashi proposed to General Willoughby that he enter Japan, make his way to the Imperial War Ministry, somehow get a look at their defense plans and get the hell out. Obviously, if we got hold of that information it might radically alter our invasion blueprint.

"Let me be candid at this point. Though Lieutenant Kobayashi's proposal is tempting I oppose this plan. The reason is simple. He knows our invasion plans. If he does not get back, we'll assume he's been captured and interrogated, and even if he doesn't divulge what he knows, we will have to assume that, under torture, he spilled his guts. The invasion will, if not be delayed, require modification. But General Willoughby and General MacArthur are willing to take the risk. Although I must admit the only one presently taking a risk is Lieutenant Kobayashi. So let's move along.

"I've thought about his plan and I think there are a few weak points. Paramount is that there are no points to Lieutenant Kobayashi's plan. Consequently he is at risk. We're here to see he gets in safely, acquires the necessary information, and gets out. Before we begin let me suggest that this is an informal group. So don't be afraid to speak your mind. There's just one rank in here today, mine. So let's begin. Ken, why don't you take it from here and summarize your proposal."

Everyone turned to Ken. He stood and walked toward the center of the wall opposite the conference table. A map of Japan was nailed to the wall. Below it, on the floor, the latest air reconnaissance photographs, taken yesterday, leaned against the wall. Ken turned, facing the conference table.

"Thank you, sir. I need not repeat any of what Colonel Mashbir told you. So let me start by reviewing with you my proposed method of insertion. To me that's the second most difficult part of this plan. I suggest that a sub transport me, late at night, close to shore, about two miles. At that point I transfer to a rubber raft. I'll be wearing swim trunks. I'll have Japanese clothing and a towel in a watertight bag. A few hundred yards from shore I sink the raft and swim the rest of the way. Once on shore I dry off and change into the Japanese clothing and bury the bag, towel and trunks. From there I make my way to Tôkyô."

Sergeant Bliss had been looking out the window. He was recovering from a party the previous night at a bar in Manila that had been interrupted by Military Police. Though Bliss had been drunk it required four MPs over twenty minutes to convince him to enter the back of their truck. Getting Bliss off the truck took another ten minutes. Bliss had a few bruises and cuts. Two of the MPs went to a hospital, one to have his jaw wired and one to have a broken arm set. Colonel Mashbir had to personally intervene to get him out of the stockade. Bliss was tired and caustic. "It's not going to work," he grumbled

Ken was caught short. "I beg your pardon, Sergeant?"

"With all due respect, Lieutenant, it's dumb. It's something Hollywood would think up. Sorry, Collucci."

Collucci, looking like a fierce stepmother from Hollywood typecasting, smiled malevolently, her yellowed teeth proclaiming her heavy smoking habit. Her voice growled, sounding like a dull buzz saw grinding through thick oak. "Don't let it worry you, dear. I agree."

Colonel Mashbir stood and walked to the wall opposite Ken, turned and leaned against it, tenting his fingers horizontally in front of him as he spoke. "People, by this evening we've got to have a way to get Lieutenant Kobayashi into Japan. Let's keep on track. Bliss, what's your objection?"

"Colonel, it's too weak. The Japs still have significant coastal defenses. Surfacing a sub two miles off shore is risky. Lieutenant, you go in on a raft and some guy on a fishing boat might spot you. You swim in and a shark might, *might* get you. Or you might drown. If you do get to shore you might be spotted. Imagine the questions: Why are you in swimming trunks? Why are you swimming with Japanese clothing in an American bag? Or the next morning the raft washes up on shore which sets off alarms up and down the coast. It's too loose. You come from nowhere. The Japs aren't stupid. I don't like it."

Captain Paschal looked at the pencil he nervously twirled in his fingers. "I agree with Sergeant B-B-Bliss, Lieutenant. I respect your p-p-prior experience in Tôkyô. However, I think I understand the J-J-J-Japanese mind." Everyone in the room stared at Captain Roger Paschal. He saw them staring at him and the pencil spun faster as he spoke.

"R-R-R-R-R-Right n-n-now the Japanese p-people know that we're g-g-g-going t-t-to invade and are t-t-terrified. I b-b-believe that any stranger, including a Japanese, swimming ashore at n-n-night is g-g-g-going t-t-to set off alarms. No, we've g-got t-t-to g-g-get you into Tôkyô by a different yet b-believable way. Sorry, C-C-C-...sir."

Mashbir felt that to accept the apology would call attention to Paschal's stuttering, so he ignored it. "Fine. I've got three negatives. Give me some suggestions. Come on, Sergeant Bliss. This is why you're here. Give me something."

Bliss shrugged. "His appearance in Tokyo has to be, uhhh... legitimate? Yeah, legitimate. He plans to get into their army HQ and look at their defense plans? Not as a civilian he ain't. I doubt if even the *Kempeitai* can just waltz into the War Ministry at Ichigaya and look at the defense plans. No, he's got to go in as military. And he can't just appear out of the blue. He's got to have a reason to be there and a place to come from. *We* know his reason. But what's his *Japanese* reason for going in? Assuming you accept that and that he's got to go in as military, then also assume someone in Tokyo's going to ask him where he's from and what his unit is and why he's not with that unit. And what's he doing at Ichigaya?"

Lieutenant Elgin stood. He was groomed to perfection and his uniform was pressed despite the humidity of Manila. Collucci, wise to the ways of Hollywood, wondered. "Lieutenant Kobayashi, as Sergeant Bliss noted, we know why you're going in but we don't know the plan in detail. What do you intend to tell the Japanese your reason is for looking at their defense plans?"

Ken was silent. He suddenly realized that he had not thought this through. What could he tell the Japanese?

Colonel Mashbir started to walk around the conference room, hands clasped in front, as if in prayer. "As I mentioned earlier, Lieutenant Kobayashi's plan calls for him to get to the War Ministry. The question just raised is valid. So what does he tell the Japanese about where he came from and his reason for looking at their plans?"

Mashbir looked at them individually, his pencil-thin mustache bunching as he pursed his lips. He felt like he was in a classroom, a teacher asking ill-prepared students a question that no one was going to answer, not wanting to appear obtuse.

Captain Paschal got up and walked to the map of Japan. Facing it he spoke, to no one in particular. "When is the m-m-meeting t-to b-be held?"

"August five, sir," said Sergeant Takayama.

"And the p-p-p-p-pur—"

"Damn it," muttered an impatient Bliss, tired from lack of sleep. "Write the fucking word out. I don't have all day for this shit."

Everyone heard him. The room froze. Mashbir glared at Bliss then exploded. "Sergeant Bliss! You in fact do have all day for this and, if necessary, you will sit in that goddamn chair for a fucking week if I deem it necessary. Is that understood, Sergeant?"

Bliss had not intended his remark to be heard. He knew he was in trouble with Mashbir. Startled by Mashbir's outburst, he was speechless. He nodded once.

Ken had seen someone else do what Bliss had just done. While interned at Manzanar he had met another internee, a teenage boy, who stuttered. The more he talked the worse it got. A couple of the army guards poked fun at him, which only served to increase his anxiety and humiliation. One guard, a corporal, was particularly vicious. While looking at Bliss Ken fiendishly remembered the tannic acid incident at Manzanar.

*   *   *

One day in early December 1942, two hours before sunrise, the corporal was on guard duty, patrolling the outer southeast perimeter of the camp, a duty he hated. The cloudy desert night was cold and his Army-issued greatcoat did little to keep the frigid winds at bay. Moreover, the wind blew desert sand in his eyes and nostrils and his anger toward the dirty little Japs in the Manzanar Relocation Camp only deepened. On more than one occasion he thought of how better it would be serving in the Pacific, killing Japs rather than babysitting them. The sole outlet for his anger was ridiculing a Japanese-American teenage boy who stuttered.

When the corporal had day duty he would occasionally see teenage boys playing baseball or football. The kid who stuttered excelled in both sports, eliciting admiring comments from several soldiers. But that didn't matter to the corporal. What mattered was that he could ridicule the boy when he spoke, struggling to form sentences.

No one else made fun of the kid and he didn't care about the tears that would occasionally flow from the boy's eyes.

Others, however, saw the tears. One was Ken Kobayashi and one day he had had enough. He gathered four friends and told them of his idea. No one disagreed or expressed fear. One, referred to as "the Chemist" by his friends, said simply, "Okay, let's do it, tonight." The rest nodded.

Later that evening the "chemist" walked toward the camp's hospital, near Guard Tower #3, northwest corner. It was natural that he would go to the hospital; he had studied chemistry in college and now worked in the hospital. No one paid him any mind. And no one noticed that he took three small stoppered glass bottles from a shelf and put them in his pants pockets. He smiled and nodded to one of the nurses as he left.

Around midnight the five gathered inside one of the garages, between Guard Towers #5 and #6, on the southeast perimeter. One of them lit a lantern. They were cold but they ignored it. Four went to sleep while one stayed awake. Two hours later one of the sleepers was awoken and his companion went to sleep. At around 4:00 A.M. the four others were aroused. There was no grousing about how cold it was. One showed the pieces of rope he had collected. Another showed the masks each would wear. The Chemist showed the three bottles he had; the third one was empty. They looked at each other then put on their masks. One lifted his mask and blew out the lantern. They exited the garage.

They dropped to the ground and crawled toward the barb-wire fence. Just before the searchlight from Guard Tower #5 swept over them, they froze; then they resumed their way to the shallowest point of Bairs Creek, which flowed in and out of the camp. They partially stood and jumped over. Then they hugged the ground again and waited for the searchlight to pass. They crawled to the barbwire fence and slithered under the bottom row, something they and others often had done, just for the hell of it, sometimes for the romance of it.

They crawled westerly toward the Chicken Ranch, consisting of two warehouses connected at one end, eight brooder houses, and six laying houses. The warehouse and office building was of a tipped-over U-type construction. There they waited, their unpracticed stealth offset by their determination.

As the corporal walked in an easterly direction toward them the searchlight in Guard Tower #5 at the southwest corner of the camp washed over him. In a few minutes it passed over him again, heading back toward the inside of the camp. Other than the corporal the guard in the tower did not see any movement, inside or out. Besides, he was cold and tired and he knew the Japs were asleep on their Army-issued cots, huddled under their brown Army blankets.

Kenji and his four companions heard the corporal approach and froze. In moments their patience was rewarded.

Quietly Kenji stood, and then rushed the corporal, knocking him to the ground and the wind out of his lungs. The other four quickly joined the two wrestling men. One hastily jammed a rag in the corporal's mouth. Another tied the corporal's wrists together behind his back and still another tied his ankles together. Another covered his eyes then picked up his M-1 rifle. They held the corporal in place, insuring his attempted movements did not arouse the Guard Tower's interest. They froze as the searchlight approached and waited until it swept back into the camp.

They stood hunched over and carried the corporal into the ranch's office building. A kerosene lantern was lit. The blindfold was removed and the corporal blinked several times then looked around. At first he was angry then became frightened. The men wore masks. But he could see their eyes, Japanese eyes.

Ken Kobayashi bent down on one knee and said, "Corporal, you've been a bad boy, picking on one of our friends just because of the way he talks."

The corporal uttered muffled sounds which were unintelligible.

"This," said Ken, "can't go on. So we're going to help you understand how difficult it is to be misunderstood."

Ken turned and nodded to the Chemist who took a bottle from his pocket. Near the lantern he read the label: Tannic Acid, an astringent chemical. Then he almost filled the empty bottle with water from a sink.

The corporal, lying on his side, anxiously watched as the man unplugged the tannic acid bottle and poured some into the bottle of water. "This won't be exact," he said as he poured. "It should be about a five-percent solution but I can't be certain. We might end up poisoning him."

The corporal struggled but the men who held him down were strong. And they were enjoying themselves. They knew the man mixing the tannic acid with water had graduated from U.C.L.A. with a degree in chemistry, *summa cum laude*.

Ken looked at his watch. "Corporal, relax. This won't hurt us a bit. Besides, in a short while it'll be reveille and it will be all over. Everything's gonna be all right. Let's all just relax."

The Chemist shook the bottle several times, insuring a perfect mixture of water and tannic acid. He knew that it was exactly a five-percent solution. They waited; they wanted the corporal to experience dread. As time passed they were rewarded. Soon, the corporal shut his eyes, certain he would be poisoned. Ken looked at his watch. Twenty minutes before reveille.

Ken turned his head and nodded. The Chemist poured the mixture over a rag then squeezed the excess fluid out of the rag. The corporal's eyes opened due to the movement. Ken and the other three held the corporal still as the Chemist approached the corporal, who was now struggling violently. One of the men removed his helmet, grabbed his hair and pulled tight. The rag in the corporal's mouth was pulled out, but before he could scream or shut his mouth the Chemist shoved the tannic acid solution-laced rag in the corporal's mouth, held it tight in his mouth as his body was rolled over, facing the ground, making certain none of the solution flowed down his throat. Ken looked at his watch. The corporal waited to die but he did not.

He had stopped breathing for a moment, fearing that he might inhale poisonous fumes, but when he inhaled he smelled nothing. Then he tasted something sour or bitter and, fearing poison, he retched but the rag was held in his mouth. Ken looked at the minute hand of his watch; it circled slowly under the crystal.

The corporal's eyes widened. Something was happening to his mouth and he panicked. Almost ten minutes; the sun would soon rise. A bugle sounded reveille. The night guard would be replaced by the day guard. The corporal and the other night guards were expected to report to their assembly point, to be replaced by the day guards.

The Chemist removed the third bottle and looked at the label: Chloroform. Carefully, he poured some over another rag and approached the corporal. He placed it over the corporal's nose for five seconds. In a minute the lights went out.

One of the men holding the corporal let go and cut the ropes binding his ankles and wrists. The rag in his mouth was removed. Ken and his companions pocketed their masks and one by one they exited the building, crawling on the ground toward and under the barbwire fence. Once inside the camp each stood, waited for the searchlight to pass and walked in different directions.

In a few minutes the corporal came around, groggy and confused. It took him a few more minutes to figure out where he was. He stood and steadied himself. Then he picked up his helmet and put it on and grabbed his rifle. He stumbled toward the door and steadied himself. He opened the door and made his way to the assembly point. To his chagrin he saw that the other night guards were already assembled and at attention, their lieutenant getting redder in the face as he waited for the corporal to join his fellow guards.

When the corporal joined the guards he was drooling, saliva covering his chin and shirt. At that point the lieutenant took one look at his corporal and exploded.

"Corporal! What the fuck is this? Have you been drinking while on duty?"

The corporal tried to stand to attention. "Noooo, Thiiir!" He tried again. "Thiiiir!"

The words weren't coming out right. He tried to spit but drooled instead. Then he realized that his tongue wasn't working right. In fact, his whole mouth wasn't working right. The other guards struggled to maintain composure.

The tannic acid solution had constricted the mucous tissue of his entire mouth, including his tongue. He tried again. He wanted to say "But" but said instead, "Puh!" showering the lieutenant with saliva.

"Sergeant!" yelled the lieutenant.

"Sir!" replied a sergeant as he stepped forward.

"Place this man, this private, under arrest and escort him to the guardhouse!"

"Sir!"

While being escorted to the Military Police Housing near Guard Tower #7 the now-private saw some young Japanese-

American men inside the camp watching him. They were smiling. The private tried to urge the sergeant to arrest them but only meaningless utterances were heard. Then, before he entered the Military Police H.Q. he saw the young Japanese-American boy who stuttered. He understood.

* * *

Ken was not going to let Paschal become a target of Bliss' cruelty. Deliberately looking directly at Bliss, he said slowly, "Captain Paschal, would you please repeat your question? And take your time."

Paschal slowly turned and looked around the room. He saw complete support in the faces of everyone except Sergeant Bliss. When he looked at Bliss he saw guilt and regret.

"Sergeant T-T-Takayama, is the p-p-purpose of the m-m-meeting solely t-t-to review their defense p-p-plans?"

"Best guess, yes, sir," said Taka. "All the traffic we've gotten so far is that they're calling in their tactical, intelligence, and engineering people, from all the home islands and, if they can make it, from occupied territories, such as China, Korea, and Formosa."

Paschal turned again and looked hard at the map. His hands, gripped behind him, turned whiter. A chair scraped the floor as Lieutenant Elgin stood and joined Paschal. Both stared at the map for several moments, deep in thought. Then Elgin crouched and casually flipped through the photos at his feet, seemingly distracted.

Paschal watched Elgin for a moment. "Sergeant B-B-Bliss is right, C-C-Colonel. L-L-Lieutenant Kobayashi c-c-can't just appear from n-n-n-nowhere. He's g-got t-t-to c-c-come from somewhere. And he has t-t-to have a r-r-r-reason why he left wherever it is t-t-to c-come t-t-to Tôkyô. Somehow we've g-g-got t-t-to tie t-t-together these l-l-loose ends."

Ken had been listening to Paschal and noted that when he started a word with a "t" he often stuttered. But when he said "Tôkyô" or his name he never once stuttered. He found it interesting.

While Paschal spoke Elgin continued to flip through the photos. Occasionally he looked up at the map of Japan. He lifted one of the photos and showed it to Paschal. "What do you think?"

Caught off guard, Mashbir refocused. "What?"

Paschal looked at Elgin and grinned as he nodded. "Are you th-th-thinking wh-wh-wh-what I'm th-th-th-thinking?"

"Probably," Elgin replied.

Mashbir, feeling left out, briskly walked to his chair and sat. "Would you gentlemen care to share your thoughts?"

The color drained from Captain Paschal's face. Both he and Elgin turned to look at the others. "If I w-w-w-were J-J-Japanese Intelligence I w-w-w-would expect the Americans t-t-to invade Kyûshû first. It b-b-brings us c-c-closer t-t-to Honshû. That's b-b-been our s-s-s-s-strategy t-t-t-t-to d-d-d-d-date. S-S-Sorry, s-s-sir."

Paschal's insight surprised Mashbir. In the room, only he and Kobayashi knew about Operation Downfall. "I'm not following you, Captain."

"Sir, all the islands w-w-w-w-we've invaded have b-b-been for a r-r-reason, t-t-to use them as s-s-s-support or springboard f-f-f-for our n-n-next assault. Each one g-gets us c-c-closer to J-J-J-Japan. It seems l-l-l-logical that we w-w-w-w-would n-n-n-next invade Kyûshû, use it for a f-f-f-final assault on Yokohama and Tôkyô."

Mashbir said nothing. Elgin, looking at the others, guessed that he and Paschal were a few steps ahead of the rest. "What Captain Paschal is getting at, sir, is that it makes sense to get Lieutenant Kobayashi in from Kyushu. And just as Sergeant Bliss suggested, as a Japanese Army officer."

Mashbir stood slowly. "Go on, Lieutenant."

Paschal, grateful, looked at Elgin and nodded his permission.

"It's like this, sir," said Elgin. "I think Captain Paschal is right, that Kyushu is the next objective. If the Japanese are assembling their intelligence, engineering, and tactical people, as Sergeant Takayama says, then it makes sense that Lieutenant Kobayashi go in as an officer. He just might get lost in the crowd. Like the others, he'll be expected. He has a degree in engineering. So he attends the briefing as an engineering officer from an army base on Kyushu. Rather than going in as an army officer from an army base on Honshu, where someone *might* recognize him or might *not* and start to question him, let's situate him from some place far away. Let's have him come from Kyushu.

"No one in Tokyo can be expected to necessarily recognize someone from Kyushu." Elgin looked at Ken. "Besides, Lieutenant, Kyushu has its own distinct accent. Being posted there would have sullied your fine Tokyo accent. If someone from Boston went to Dallas he'd stick out like a sore thumb just based on his accent. No one will suspect if they think you're from the countryside, even if they ask. So you're left alone in the crowd. You get a look-see at the plan and maybe even make a contribution about—"

"What would I have to contribute?" asked Ken, unconvinced.

"Take a close look at the photos of Kyushu. They clearly show the Japs are hastily building pillboxes, tank traps, revetments, ditches, even trenches and other obstacles. You can see artillery and mortar positions and hundreds of machine gun emplacements. If asked, and let me emphasize that point, *if* asked, you give a progress report on the efforts at Kyushu. Maybe you won't have to. Maybe the purpose of this meeting is just to keep the outlying command informed, sort of a morale booster. But if you have to say something then these photos, and others that we can have taken as we get closer to the time you go in, and your engineering background, will allow you to speak with some authority."

"That's absurd. They'll know who's attending the meeting and who's coming from Kyûshû," rebutted Ken.

"And so will we, Ken. Uh, sorry, sir. Lieutenant."

Everyone turned and looked at Taka, a wide grin lighting his youthful round face.

Mashbir, exasperated, scowled down the table at Taka. "All right, Sergeant. Obviously you know something the rest of us do not. Care to share it?"

Taka's face became businesslike. "Uh, sir, last evening Central Bureau intercepted a message from Japan's Eleventh Area Army, headquartered at Sendai. That's on the eastern coast of Kyûshû. They radioed to the Imperial War Ministry the name of their guy who's going to attend the August fifth meeting. On the day he's traveling he's supposed to radio the Ministry and give the time he's leaving and how he's traveling."

Mashbir slowly shook his head for a few seconds. "Why didn't you tell us this little bit of information earlier, Sergeant?"

Taka swallowed and looked at Kobayashi for support. Ken simply grinned and shrugged his shoulders. "The subject didn't come up before, sir," said Taka. "I didn't think it was important...just the usual traffic..."

"Not important..." Mashbir drummed his fingers. "Anything else, Sergeant?"

Taka quickly pulled a piece of paper from his shirt pocket and unfolded it. He was becoming a little flustered. "Yes, sir. Late last night Central Bureau intercepted a second message. This one came from the Sixteenth Area Army. They're in Korea—"

"Thank you, Taka. I know where the Sixteenth Area Army

is situated. The message, please?"

"Uh, yes, sir. The Sixteenth Area Army transmitted the name of their guy. They received the same instructions, to radio in on the day he departs and how he's traveling."

"Any others in that magical pocket of yours?"

"Yes, sir. And each one who is traveling to the War Ministry is apparently going to be bringing information about their local defense preparations. Things like charts and so forth. That's what we have so far. Each headquarters will probably send in the name of its representatives over the next several days or weeks."

"Thank you for your cogent analysis, Taka," said Mashbir. "Next time don't hesitate to volunteer information. Oh, and guess what you're doing until August fifth? After this meeting you're living with the folks in Central Bureau. Any messages that come in about this meeting you translate immediately. Understood? I want more names and dates."

Taka shrunk in his chair, an unhappy young man. The others started to laugh.

Lieutenant Elgin jumped in. "Colonel, what Sergeant Takayama has told us dovetails with what Captain Paschal and I were suggesting. If we know the names of individual representatives from each headquarters, it stands to reason we'll get the name of the Kyushu representative."

Ken Kobayashi looked around the table. "Wait. Slow down a bit. This is going too fast. How do we know they'll do what we expect? Can we assume that everyone is going to check in and confirm their departure?"

No one spoke. Colonel Mashbir nodded silently. He knew they were in fact assuming quite a lot. They were guessing and in turn risking Ken's life. Then Taka raised his hand and cleared his throat. Every head turned in his direction.

Mashbir sighed and slowly sank back in his chair. "Go ahead, Taka."

"Sir, they've already done just that."

Mashbir's eyebrows flew up. "What? Did what?"

"This past April, sir. The Imperial General Staff sent out coded messages that they had completed an outline for their defense plans. They called it *Ketsu-Gô*, 'Decisive Struggle.' The Japanese bigwigs ordered that all homeland area armies send their chiefs of staff, intelligence officers, or engineering officers to review the plans at Imperial Army HQ in Tôkyô. After that order went out everyone who was to go checked in and confirmed their attendance. Only it wasn't a formal shindig like I suspect this one coming up is. I guess by now they've fixed their plans. So I guess we can predict that, like before, everyone will check in with their schedule. Sir."

Mashbir got out of his chair and slowly walked over to Taka. Everyone else, not wanting to raise the wrath of Colonel Mashbir, struggled hard not to laugh. Corporal Collucci covered her mouth with her hand. Mashbir stopped two feet from Taka and scowled for several seconds. Taka, not knowing what Mashbir expected, sat perfectly still, looking straight ahead.

"Sergeant? Last April, you say?"

"Yes, sir," chirped Taka.

"Sergeant, is there any reason why I wasn't told about this?"

Taka, not moving his head, rolled his eyes upward, looking in Mashbir's direction. "Sir, you were. Indirectly, that is. I wrote up a report and gave it to Lieutenant Lewis. I guess he forgot to give it to you, sir."

Mashbir allowed this fact to sink in while returning to his chair. He sat down and looked at Taka. Lieutenant Lewis was white. Let the Nip take the heat for not delivering the message to me, Mashbir imagined Lewis' thinking. Lewis had done it before but this time, Mashbir knew, what Lewis did was too serious to disregard. Taka was off the hook. Mashbir made a mental note to speak with *Private* Lewis later.

"Okay," said Mashbir. "Ken goes in as a Japanese Army officer. How?" They were silent again. "What I mean is, how does he get into Japan?"

Everyone exchanged glances. No one had an answer. Sergeant Bliss leaned back in his chair, his fingers interlocked at the back of his head. He focused on a spot on the ceiling. "I think we all agree the sub is a bad idea, Colonel. Lieutenant, you ever parachuted from a plane?"

"Sergeant, I haven't jumped from a plane period."

"Well, maybe you could jump into Kyushu then go by boat across the Shimonoseki Strait. Cross over, land on Honshu, and hitch a ride to Tokyo."

Lieutenant Elgin raised a hand. "It won't work, sergeant."

"Why not? Sir?"

Elgin heard the sarcasm in Bliss' voice. He knew he was talking to a man who had always operated on his own and did not like officers.

"How's he going to cross the strait? Rowboat? If we drop him into Kyushu someone will have to ferry him across. He's too close to his alleged base. Someone on Kyushu just might call that base. Obviously he can't get the Japs to ferry him across. He's got to go in alone. And even though he's supposed to come from Kyushu he in fact cannot arrive in Tokyo *from* Kyushu. It looks like we're back to the submarine."

Bliss leaned further back in the chair, delicately balancing on its rear legs. Collucci wondered whether Bliss would lose his balance and fall and if anyone in the room would bother to help him up. Or would dare laugh. She knew she would.

A small, hesitant voice piped in. "Lieutenant Kobayashi can pilot a plane."

Colonel Mashbir sighed and slowly shook his head. "Sergeant Takayama, would you care to take over this meeting?"

Again, everyone laughed and looked at Taka. He seemed to shrink even lower in his chair.

"Lieutenant," said Mashbir. "*Can* you pilot a plane?"

"Yes, as a matter of fact I can. At home my father owns... My father used to own a large farm. Both my brother and I flew crop dusters. No white pilot would fly for my family, so my brother and I learned to fly. We also did some barnstorming to make money."

Mashbir seemed pleased. He even managed to wink at Taka. "Okay, so far we have Ken going in as a Japanese officer and we know he can pilot a plane. Where do we go from here? Anyone? Sergeant Bliss? Insertion is your bailiwick. Any ideas?"

"Well, he could fly an American plane. Wait, wait; hear me out. Let's stay with the concept that he's a Jap officer. Say he was captured on Okinawa and eventually escapes. Or he was never captured but hid out and finally sees his chance. He grabs a plane at night and flies it to Japan. We get him a Jap uniform, tear it up a bit, and dirty him up a bit before he takes off."

Corporal Collucci smiled and exhaled cigarette smoke. "Sure, I can give him a uniform that will make him look like he had been hiding out for weeks. Even make him look like he's half-starved. Just give me the name of the unit he's supposed to be attached to and I'll do the rest."

Lieutenant Elgin hesitated, and then contradicted Bliss again. "That won't work either, Sergeant. Our scenario is he's coming from a friendly location with a purpose. That being the case, why would he have to pilot an American plane?"

Bliss nodded, conceding the point. He felt foolish. He knew he was tired.

Lieutenant Elgin walked toward Bliss. "I'm not completely rejecting what you said, Sergeant. Lieutenant Kobayashi, you said you can pilot a plane. Any plane?"

"Not a bomber or a seaplane. I have experience in a single-engine plane. Why?"

"Before coming to the Pacific I was briefly assigned to the

Air Technical Intelligence Unit at Anacostia. While there I saw photos of some captured Jap planes on Guam. Colonel, what if Lieutenant Kobayashi flew a *Jap* plane into Japan?"

"From Guam?" asked Mashbir, confused.

"No, not Guam, Colonel. Someone is bound to ask how the hell he flew a fighter from Guam to Tokyo. That's over two thousand miles. With that he becomes the center of attention. We're trying to avoid that. How about from a carrier?"

"Lieutenant Elgin, the Japs don't have any operational carriers left. The Navy sank or damaged them all. Remember?"

"Not a Japanese carrier, Colonel. One of ours."

"Jesus, what the hell do you... Interesting... Kobayashi flies a Jap plane off one of our carriers and lands in Japan?"

"Yes, sir," said Elgin. "And where he lands is crucial. A large air base. I believe the best one is Atsugi. It's Japan's largest air base. Plus it's a naval air base and he's going in as a Japanese Army officer. No one is going to know him and he should be able to get lost in the crowd fairly quickly. Lieutenant Kobayashi takes off from one of our carriers southeast of Kyushu. Once over Kyushu he then vectors in a northerly direction, as if coming from the south, from his base on Kyushu."

Ken stepped in. "Let me ask two questions, Lieutenant. Why did I choose to *fly* from Kyûshû to Honshû? Our planes control the skies over Japan. Why take the risk that I'd get shot out of the sky? Might not someone ask why I didn't take a *train* from my base to the northern coast of Kyûshû and transfer to a ferry, cross the Shimonoseki strait and then make my way north by train or a car?"

"Let me answer this way," said Elgin. "As we agreed earlier, you can't just appear out of nowhere, either on Kyushu or Honshu. Besides, how do you get to the train? It's still an issue of getting you in. No, it's got to be a plane. It's best that we, here and now, choose your method of entry. With a plane we have some control. On a train you're a sitting duck. What do you do if a passenger strikes up a conversation? Or someone from the *Kempeitai* sits next to you and wonders why you aren't at your base? And your second question?"

Ken paused, looking at Elgin and Paschal. "What's the reason for my landing at Atsugi? I'm supposed to be Army."

Captain Paschal raised his hand. "G-G-Good q-q-question. How about if w-w-w-we f-f-force you d-d-down? We have s-s-s-some American f-f-fighters chase Lieutenant Kobayashi into Atsugi. Shoot up the sky a b-b-bit. There w-w-will be l-l-l-lots of c-c-c-confusion, l-l-l-lots of f-f-fireworks. No one's g-g-going to q-q-question a p-p-pilot who almost g-got his ass shot off b-b-by American f-f-f-fighters and l-l-l-lives to t-tell about it."

Colonel Mashbir nodded. "I agree. I like the idea of a plane."

Corporal Collucci crushed a cigarette. "Sweetheart, uh, Colonel, I'm not as smart as you boys, I'm just a girl who sews clothing. And I don't want to rain on your parade, but all someone at Atsugi or Tokyo has to do is call Keyushu. The folks at Keyushu won't know the lieutenant from Adam."

"That's Kyûshû, Corporal."

"Colonel?"

"You said 'Keyushu.' It's not key. It's K-y-u. Sort of like queuing, you know, standing in a line in London… Kyûshû…"

Collucci frowned as she dug out a cigarette from a pack. "Thanks, sir. I'll try to remember that the next time I'm in a line in London."

Sergeant Bliss' shoulders shook with quiet laughter. He made a mental note to buy Collucci a drink later. "Colonel," he said, "she's right. I think Lieutenant Elgin's idea that Lieutenant Kobayashi land at Atsugi is a good one. But what base on Kyushu is he supposed to be coming from? And more important, what air base is he *supposed* to be flying *to*?"

Mashbir nodded. "Lieutenant Elgin?"

Elgin walked back to the photos and flipped them again.

He picked up one that showed the Tôkyô area in detail and carried it back to the table. He held it up and pointed to a spot.

"Here is good," said Elgin. "Chofu Army Air Base. It's a perfect fit. He's Japanese Army and so is Chofu. It's about 16 nautical miles northeast of Atsugi. It's ideal, just about 12 nautical miles west of Tokyo. In order to get to Chofu he has to fly near or over Atsugi. As far as what base Lieutenant Kobayashi is supposed to be coming from, Sergeant Takayama will tell us that."

"I will?"

"Sure," said Captain Paschal. "You t-t-told us earlier that everyone w-w-who is attending the m-m-meeting on August f-f-f-five will c-c-c-call in. We wait for that c-c-call. Then we'll k-k-know."

"Of course," jumped in Elgin. "Once we know the name of the base and the time the real Kyushu officer is leaving it, his mode of travel, and his destination, Lieutenant Kobayashi can take off from the carrier."

"Just t-t-two f-f-f-final p-p-points. Sergeant T-T-Takayama m-m-m-must give us the n-n-name and r-r-r-rank of the m-m-man who is supposed to c-c-come from Kyûshû and w-w-w-when and how he's g-g-going to t-t-travel t-t-to his d-d-d-destination in or n-n-near Tôkyô. We m-m-m-m-must have this information."

Colonel Mashbir was curious. "Why?"

"T-T-T-Two r-r-r-reasons. Once we know how and when he's t-t-t-traveling, whether b-b-b-by p-p-p-plane, t-t-t-train or b-b-b-boat, we k-k-k-k-k-kill him. We launch c-c-carrier-b-b-based fighters to attack whatever he's t-t-traveling in. R-R-R-Right after we k-k-k-kill him we b-b-bomb the b-b-b-base he c-c-came f-f-f-from, especially its c-c-communications f-f-facilities. Then, in a f-f-f-few hours we send *our* signal to the Imperial War Ministry. We only g-give them L-L-Lieutenant Kobayashi's l-l-last n-n-name and rank. We t-t-tell the M-M-

M-Ministry that the original officer was k-k-k-killed and that an officer n-n-named Kobayashi is a su-su-su-substitute. Then, when Lieutenant Kobayashi l-l-l-lands at Atsugi, he c-c-can explain, if n-n-necessary, that he's t-t-taken that m-m-man's place. Second, if anyone asks, L-L-Lieutenant Kobayashi should k-k-know the n-n-name of the m-m-man whose p-p-p-place he's t-t-t-taking."

Everyone was silent, surprised that Captain Paschal could discuss killing someone so matter-of-factly.

"Why do we need to know his destination," asked Mashbir.

"L-L-Lieutenant Kobayashi is a s-s-substitute. So he has t-t-t-to choose his own d-d-destination. F-F-F-For him, everything is l-l-l-last m-m-m-minute."

Bliss was on track again. "Besides hitting that base you could have fighters bomb other bases, on Kyushu and across the strait. Keep it random. We occasionally did that when we inserted an agent or coast watcher, as a diversion. Only in this case, instead of creating a diversion, the fighters, being more accurate, actually knock out the base's communications capability at Kyushu. And this is important. The fighters also bomb Chofu, especially their communications capability. This has to include telephone facilities. This should be done every other day at first then ramp it up to every day as we get closer to August five. By the time the Japs at Atsugi get to calling Kyushu or Chofu the bases' communications should be knocked out. But hit that particular Kyushu base and adjacent ones every other day or so, insuring they don't get back on the air. The same with Chofu."

Mashbir was quiet for several minutes, collating all he had heard so far. "Lieutenant Elgin, would the Navy be interested in something like this?"

"Colonel, whatever General MacArthur requests the Navy will gladly comply with. One other thing. Let's promote Lieutenant Kobayashi to say...Major? He's got to have the rank for this meeting. A lieutenant showing up won't cut it."

"Agreed," said Mashbir. "Captain Paschal. You said you had two points. What's the other?"

"Sir, Sergeant T-T-Takayama has t-t-to f-f-f-find out when and how the other p-p-p-participants will b-b-b-be c-c-c-c-coming in. We have to k-k-k-kill a f-f-f-few other p-p-p-participants so L-L-L-Lieutenant Kobayashi does not stand out. His n-n-name should n-n-not b-b-b-be the only one on a s-s-s-substitute l-l-list."

Colonel Mashbir was silent for several minutes. He looked at everyone. "Let me summarize. 'Major' Kobayashi flies a captured Japanese plane from one of our carriers, allegedly from a base on *Keyyûshû*. Right, Corporal Collucci? He lands at Atsugi, and gives those guys a song and dance about having been ordered to report to the War Ministry. Do I have it right so far?" Several heads nodded. "Good. Then Atsugi calls Kyûshû but no one's answering the phone or the radio because there isn't one. Same with Chôfu. So no one at Atsugi can confirm his story. But, no one can refute it either. For the time being, thanks to a few American fighters chasing him, Ken's story holds water. Then he travels to Ichigaya, tells them he's there to listen to the final defense plans for Kyûshû. Maybe Tôkyô calls the base at Kyûshû and again no one is answering the phone. But for how long does his story hold up? Someone in Tôkyô will start to ask questions, namely who is this guy and what are his *bona fides*? Where are his service records?"

"Why, sir?" asked Paschal. "F-F-First, he's g-g-g-going to be there for just a f-f-few d-d-d-days, m-m-m-maybe a week at the m-m-m-most. He's Japanese. L-L-Look at him. P-P-Picture him in a Japanese uniform. He's a hero, fighting off American p-p-p-planes. Besides, I suspect the Japanese are n-n-not in the m-m-m-mood t-t-to l-l-look at r-r-records. B-B-Bombs are d-d-d-dropping on their heads d-d-day and n-n-night. No, I

d-d-don't agree with you, C-C-Colonel. Also, sir, and this is
s-s-s-s-something you should c-c-consider, L-L-Lieutenant
Kobayashi. The J-J-Japan that Lieutenant Kobayashi and I
k-k-knew in the late thirties is changed. J-J-Just about all the
cities have been d-d-d-destroyed, the p-p-p-population has b-
b-b-been d-d-d-displaced, with m-m-most having g-g-g-gone
to the c-c-countryside. Those who r-r-remain in the cities are
p-p-probably half-starved and lethargic. In other words, C-
C-C-...sir, the J-J-Japan that was sharp and on its t-t-t-toes no
l-l-l-longer exists. They will accept his story. In f-f-fact they'll
want to b-b-believe his story. He's there to help d-d-d-defend
the empire. We will n-n-need the skills of C-C-Corporal C-C-
Collucci to make 'M-M-Major' Kobayashi fit in, look as if he too
has endured a p-p-p-poor diet. N-N-N-Not t-t-t-t-too m-m-m-
much, though. I suspect that, as m-m-m-mentioned earlier, the
m-m-m-m-military and civilian l-l-l-leadership have f-f-f-fared
b-b-b-better than the general p-p-population."

Colonel Mashbir was speechless. Before today Captain
Paschal had always responded with as few words as possible,
sometimes just nodding or shaking his head. Now he spoke
more than the rest. Mashbir, pleased, ignored his stuttering.

Ken too had been watching Captain Paschal. Now he
understood why Colonel Mashbir valued Paschal's insight into
Japan. It was another point Ken had not considered when he
submitted his proposal to General Willoughby. He realized that
he had not thought about what he would encounter when he
went into Tôkyô. He was going to enter a city that he would no
longer recognize. He wondered how he would respond to that,
how he would feel when he saw, first hand, how his ancestral
homeland has suffered at the hands of his adoptive homeland.
It was a disturbing thought and he tried to discard it.

Sergeant Bliss' voice and demeanor had earnestness to it
now. "Colonel. If I may?"

"Go on, Sergeant."

"Just this. When we radio the Japs in Tokyo that Lieutenant Kobayashi is taking the place of the Kyushu officer we give them only his rank and last name, like Captain Paschal said. Nothing else. If they ask for more we kick in static and cut the transmission. That way they can't go to their files."

"Sir," said Taka. "Just one point. We can't radio the Japanese in Tôkyô."

Mashbir frowned. "Why not?"

"Well, I'm not an expert but the Japanese have a complicated encoding system. They'd spot a phony message right away."

"Can you elaborate on that, Sergeant," asked Lieutenant Elgin. "I'm navy and not familiar with your Central Bureau."

Taka looked at Mashbir, who nodded his assent.

"Sir, the Japanese use a two-part code. Without putting everyone to sleep, for encoding they use Chinese ideographs or *kanji* and Japanese *kana*. It's based on the *I*, *Ro* and *Ha* system of the Japanese alphabet. When they decode they use 10,000 four-digit groups numbered from 0000 to 9999. This gives them 9,500 possible meanings. That leaves them 500 groups deliberately blank as a security measure. It also allows them to insert new meanings into their code system. In short, all Imperial Japanese Army messages carry a routine and consecutive serial number. If we duplicate a serial number then we, uh, Lieutenant Kobayashi is dead in the water, so to speak."

Everyone was quiet; a sense of pessimism encompassed the room. Several minutes passed. Drumming fingers only aggravated the silence.

Captain Paschal dropped his pencil on the table. Everyone heard it. "Sergeant T-T-T-Takayama, how about a v-v-v-voice m-m-m-message?"

"You mean an open message, sir," asked Taka.

"Y-Y-Yes. W-W-We c-c-could b-b-b-broadcast an open m-m-m-message, g-g-g-garble some of it as well as the s-ssender's n-n-n-name and s-s-s-s-serial n-n-n-number. When d-d-done ask them t-t-to r-r-repeat what you t-t-told them. I'm g-g-g-guessing they w-w-w-will. Then, if they ask you t-t-to r-r-r-repeat who you are you b-b-b-break off."

"Sure," jumped in Bliss. "We do the broadcast while the base of origin is being attacked by our planes. On an open mike they'll hear the explosions."

Colonel Mashbir wanted to accept the plan, knowing that everyone in the room had already done so. Bliss' last comment nailed it down.

"Any of you have any objections to this scenario? Any other suggestions? None? Are we all agreed that this is the best method of entry?"

Except for Ken, everyone nodded.

"I agree. I want to finish this tonight. By tomorrow morning I want to hand in a detailed report to General Willoughby. Let's fill in the blanks."

Ken looked at them. They were convinced but he wasn't. "Sir, I'm assuming that the others who will attend this meeting will have prepared documents, maps, figures and so forth. My hands are going to be empty. How do I explain that?"

"That's the beauty of it, Lieutenant," said Elgin. "You won't have to worry about it. You tell them the documents that were going to be presented were with the guy who was on the plane or train that was destroyed by the Americans. You're the last-minute substitute and there was no time to prepare more documents. You're there more to listen and comment on what you've heard than to contribute to this briefing. But if someone does ask questions you should be able to bluff your way through with the information we feed you. Does this make sense? We listen very carefully to all the traffic from Kyushu and any information having to do with their defenses and we feed it to you. Plus we'll have air reconnaissance photos taken every day. That way your ass is covered."

No one objected to Elgin's reasoning. But Ken was still uncertain.

"I have a question," said Ken. "After I land, where am I going to stay? This mission is going to take a few days. At Chôfu? I'll stand out like a pimple on a nose."

There was silence for several minutes. Everyone's face was blank. Ken surveyed all of them. Then he saw Paschal start to smile.

"There is one section of Tôkyô that has n-n-n-not b-b-b-been t-t-t-t-touched by our b-b-b-b-b-bombers or c-c-c-c-carrier-b-b-b-b-based p-p-p-planes. Tsukiji. L-L-L-Lieutenant Kobayashi, I'm sure you're familiar with that section of Tôkyô."

"As a matter of fact, I am. When I lived in Tôkyô I visited Tsukiji quite often."

Bliss sat down. "What's so special about... How do you say it?"

"I can field this one," said Colonel Mashbir. "I lived in Tôkyô for a few years and I'm quite familiar with Tsukiji, Sergeant Bliss, just like it's spelled." He wrote Tsukiji on a piece of paper and passed it down the table. Everyone who needed to looked at the paper.

"And it's special because it was a government-mandated settlement in eastern Tôkyô for foreigners. It means 'reclaimed land' or 'built-up land.' It's less than two miles southeast of the Imperial Palace. It was a low marshy section on the bay with no use or value. But by the mid-eighteenth century, Edo, what we now call Tôkyô, was becoming overcrowded. More land was needed. So Tsukiji was created to ease the crowding. Just like Boston did during the middle of the last century. They filled in a marshy area and built on it. It's called the Back Bay and it's a ritzy section of Boston.

"And like the Back Bay, Tsukiji wasn't given to the poor and homeless. Instead, it was given to the feudal lords who, after all, paid for it in the first place.

"One hundred years later, Tôkyô was changing. The first foreigners were coming, and the government decreed that all foreigners should be segregated in a single district, the better to keep an eye on them, I guess. Ironically, or perhaps poetic justice, since Tsukiji had been taken from the sea, the Meiji government took it from the feudal lords."

Mashbir paused to see if anyone was listening. To his delight he saw that everyone was absorbed. *Finally*, he thought, *my cultural education is paying off.* He went on, enjoying having an audience not held captive.

"The foreign resident quarters included a massive hotel, and a huge government sponsored brothel. It's said there were more than seventeen hundred courtesans. Much to the government's surprise, neither venture succeeded because the foreigners seemed uninterested in sex. At least with Japanese women.

"Anyway, Tsukiji was, for many years, a center of foreign influence. One example is Saint Luke's Hospital, the largest hospital in Tôkyô, started around 1902. By the way, legend has it that Japan's first fork and spoon were used in Tsukiji. It's an interesting section of Tôkyô. And it'd be perfect for you, Lieutenant Kobayashi; it's safe. It's off limits to our planes because Americans and Europeans once lived there. Furthermore, there seems to be little Japanese military activity there. It's predominately residential. Besides, when we take Tôkyô that hospital is going to be needed. Anyway, I recall that there were some inns there. And if you can't find an inn I'm sure you could rent a room in a house. Lieutenant, you'll have plenty of money to spare and I'm certain someone in Tsukiji could use extra cash. What do you think, Lieutenant?"

Ken nodded his agreement. He remembered Tsukiji and was impressed with Mashbir's knowledge and had to agree that Tsukiji would be a perfect place to stay.

"I have a question, Colonel," said Bliss. "How the hell does the Lieutenant get out?"

"That's easy, Sergeant," said Lieutenant Elgin. "The Navy gives Lieutenant Kobayashi a frequency the Japs aren't using and the Navy will keep it monitored just for him. He also gets a set of numbers. Each set specifies a method, date, time, and where he'll be when he leaves. Depending on the first number we will know whether he is flying—and carrier planes will escort him to Okinawa or Iwo Jima. If by boat, carrier planes will escort him out of Tokyo Bay until a raft from a sub can pick him up. In either case we will know how, when, and where he will be leaving and the Navy will pick him up. We'll have his frequency monitored around the clock, by Sergeant Takayama, here." Everyone laughed, except for Taka. "When Lieutenant Kobayashi is ready to exit he transmits the numbers to the Navy. The intercept zone could be any of a dozen prearranged points. Obviously, he chooses whichever is best at the moment. We'll have subs patrolling all those points but out of range of offshore batteries. If he uses a boat then figure it'll take him at least thirty minutes to get to the pick-up area. As soon as we get the call and he tells us it's by boat, and the date, time, and location, the sub goes in to meet him and the Navy orders in fighters to escort him from the coast. All the lieutenant has to do is steal a boat, any kind of a boat. As soon as he leaves shore we cover him from the air. We'll get him out." Elgin paused for a moment. "If he can get out. Sorry, Lieutenant. I'm new at this but it seems to me that you're going into the tiger's cave and everyone there but you has a set of teeth."

Mashbir watched as the others looked at Ken. He had seen the expression before. *People looking at a dead man*, he thought. He interrupted the mood. "All right, people. Let's flesh this out."

Everyone added details. By 1900 hours, 7:00 PM, Colonel Mashbir had a completed plan. Eventually even Ken was satisfied, certain the group had produced a more realistic and convincing method of insertion and justification for his seeing Japan's defense plans than had existed in the morning.

Before they broke up Corporal Collucci raised her hand.

"Corporal?" asked Colonel Mashbir.

"Lieutenant Kobayashi," she said. "One week before you leave for Japan make sure you get a haircut. You look like a Hollywood star with that much hair." The group laughed.

As they exited Ken asked Colonel Mashbir if he could speak with him, privately. "Sir, I'm going to need one item to bring with me."

"What's that, Lieutenant?"

"A sword, sir. A *katana*."

"That shouldn't be a problem. There are plenty available."

"Pardon me, sir. It has to be special, not a standard issue made in a factory."

"What have you got in mind, Lieutenant?"

"Mine, sir."

"I've never seen you with a *katana*."

"Correct, sir. But there is one in California. My father buried it on our farm. It's an Umetada *katana*."

Mashbir pursed his lips and whistled. "Your family has an Umetada?"

"Yes, sir."

"And you feel you'll need it?"

"It may open doors, sir."

"Okay. Draw me a map and it will be here in a few days. Anything else?"

"Yes, sir. It's in a case. Ask whoever digs it up not to open the case. Just keep it in the oilcloth wrapping during transport."

"I understand. Consider it done, Lieutenant."

*   *   *

Ken picked up his flight bag and neared the door of his

cabin then turned, making a final sweep of his quarters. His eyes temporarily focused on the wardrobe, wondering if he would return for the *wakizashi*, and shrugged. Then he remembered. The red string under his pillow. It was a gift from Kyoko.

By 1941 they were deeply in love. He had to return to America and her parents had rejected their getting married, which would have meant her leaving Japan to live in America. They were both devastated. The last time they were together there hadn't been much time for all the words that needed to be said; the ship was preparing to leave. As he turned to walk up the gangway she reached out and touched his hand and with her other hand gave him a small gift, wrapped in blue paper. Gold-like string held the paper together.

Curious, he accepted it and looked into her eyes. He said, "*Dômo arigatô*." He carefully untied the knotted string and peeled back the paper, careful not to tear it. Inside, a small red string lay on white paper. When he looked at her, puzzled, she smiled through tears.

"In Japan we say, 'You are tied by an invisible red string to your future husband even before you are born.'" Her eyes welled up. "Please keep this next to your heart and remember me."

He turned over the pillow and tenderly picked up the wrapped paper containing the red string. Dropping his bag, he removed the string from the wrapping and looked at it, waves of painful memories washing over him. He put the string back in the wrapping and put it in his shirt pocket with the *omamori*, and rebuttoned the pocket.

He grabbed his bag, turned, and walked out, closing the door behind him. As before, the sergeant was waiting to escort him back to the wardroom.

5

Commander Rutledge was waiting in the wardroom for Ken. He ignored the confused officers still clustered in small groups. Word about Ken had spread and the wardroom's complement of officers more than tripled. Some sailors loitered outside the wardroom door, not daring to trespass into "officers' country." In turn, none of the officers inside the wardroom risked questioning Rutledge; his expression didn't encourage inquiry.

As Ken and the Marine sergeant approached the wardroom door the curious sailors parted. The sergeant, as before, was in the lead. As Ken entered the wardroom, the Marine sergeant fell in behind him. Rutledge walked over to them. "Thank you, Sergeant, why don't you get some coffee?"

"Yes, sir," he replied. He seemed relieved

Rutledge studied Ken for a few seconds. Then, "You ready, Lieutenant? You have everything you need?"

Ken's eyes darted about. He nodded. "Yes, sir. I think we ought to get this show on the road."

They passed through the portside door of the wardroom and stepped onto the weather deck. They turned aft, toward the stern of the ship. They picked up an escort, bracketed by four Marines, two in front and two bringing up the rear. The weather deck walkway was a little wider than ten feet. Winds from the receding typhoon farther northwest caught Ken by surprise, and he raised his hand to hold onto his officer's cap. Droplets of mist, carried by the winds, occasionally sprayed them. As they walked they passed beneath the barrels of the five-inch batteries and then under the 40 mm quad guns. Rutledge's and the Marines' lower pants snapped about their ankles, like tiny flags in the wind. Ken's lower pants were tucked inside his boots.

Rutledge slowed their pace. He wanted to talk to Ken but wasn't sure how to start. He was certain Kobayashi was nervous, going over every detail of the mission in his mind. Rutledge began to pull a pack of cigarettes from his shirt pocket then stopped. In the darkness even a lighted cigarette might be visible to a Japanese sub's periscope.

Ken shifted his gaze again. As they continued to walk he looked out at the ocean and watched the waves giving off phosphorescent flashes.

In fact Ken was not reviewing his plans. He was thinking about his family, still quartered at the Manzanar Relocation Camp in California.

He looked up and compared the Pacific night sky with the night skies of California. Tonight, the sky was overcast, not a star in sight. Some nights, when he was at a California shore, the skies were crystal clear, filled with thousands of twinkling lights. Sometimes meteors arcing across the sky briefly eclipsed the stars. Now, above him, fast-moving clouds, urged on by the receding typhoon, blotted out the moon as well.

He wondered what his parents would say if they knew what he was doing. In the past, whenever he wrote them, he told them he was safe, assuring them his duties involved mostly paperwork. He never mentioned that he interrogated captured enemy soldiers, not knowing how his family would be treated if word got out in the camp. When he left Manzanar in 1943 there was still a vocal minority of Japanese Americans who were angry with the American government. They felt that to help America in the war effort was also an endorsement of their imprisonment. Ken worried that if word spread in the internment camp that he was on MacArthur's staff, interrogating Japanese prisoners, the handful of bitter camp members might harass his family. Or worse, cause them to be ostracized. With a slight smile, he tried to imagine what they would say if they knew about his mission.

As they neared main battery turret three Rutledge asked, "You doing okay? Anything else you need?"

Preoccupied, Ken again hesitated before answering. "No, I'm fine, sir. Thanks."

"You know, Admiral Halsey's not a bad guy. I know you feel he gave you a rough time back there. Sometimes he can intimidate people."

"It's not that, sir. I'm used to senior officers. Try briefing General Willoughby. It was the way Admiral Halsey looked at me when I first walked in, like he wanted to rip my guts out and tear them to pieces."

Rutledge smiled in the darkness. "Can you blame him? Look in a mirror, Lieutenant. What you're wearing is not standard U.S. Army issue."

"I know that, sir. But, when I was in Manzanar… You familiar with Manzanar?"

"Only by name, Lieutenant, not by reputation."

"No, I suppose not. When I was there I used to see that look from some of the guards. Not all, just a few. But those few were enough. They made it rough on me after they found out I went to college in Tôkyô before the war. That in turn made it rough on my family, not the cracks toward them so much but having to see how I was being treated.

"My father told me under no circumstances ever to be out in the evening alone, to have at least two other guys with me in case some guards wanted to sneak into the camp and jump me. I never saw the guards go after anyone, but he didn't want me to take a chance."

Ken felt an emotional tug and looked over the horizon toward Japan. With his mentioning college, the memories of his four years there came rushing over him like warm water over naked flesh. The image of a beautiful woman stirred emotions he thought were long suppressed. *Kyoko*, he thought. He never loved anyone like that before or since. When he returned home in 1941 it was apparent to everyone that he had matured, become more cosmopolitan. *Nisei* women sought him out because of his four years in Japan. He possessed fresh ideas and entertained them with stories of his experiences there. They especially wanted to know about the women of Tôkyô.

White women, too, were interested in him, finding him handsome and exotic. They too wanted to know about the women of Tôkyô. Both *Nisei* and white women wanted to be told they were better than Japanese women. He found their attempts to elicit these comparisons tiring and puerile. Later, at Manzanar, he was the focus of interest from young *Nisei* women. He dated some, but none excited him like Kyoko had.

Rutledge stopped too, trying to look at Ken. An unexpected wave crashed against the hull. As it broke over the deck it sprayed them. Rutledge sensed Ken's mood, the eternal pull of land. He saw that yearning look in many landsmen.

Rutledge, like most lifelong sailors, always felt the pull of the ocean and chafed at being on land for even a short time. He wondered whether Kobayashi's longing for land was for Japan or America. Was there perhaps someone special in Japan?

"Let me guess, Lieutenant. You got a girlfriend there?"

Ken was surprised. "Yeah... I mean, yes, sir. But I don't even know if she's alive. We've been pounding Tôkyô pretty hard, and she was living there when she last wrote to me in November forty-one."

"You feeling ambivalent about going in, Lieutenant? I can understand. My lineage is Irish. I wonder how I'd feel if we were doing to Ireland what we're doing to Japan."

"It's not that, sir. Back in forty-one, when I heard about Pearl, I ran home to talk with my father. He was pacing in his den, yelling and swearing at Tôjô and Hirohito. I'd never seen him like that; angry, upset. He was always a levelheaded guy." Ken was silent a moment. "The irony was that he wasn't swearing at them because of what might happen to his family or friends in America. Most of us never dreamed our government would do to us what it did. He didn't think of us as Japanese or even as Japanese Americans. He always told us to be proud that we were Americans. Period. His anger was directed toward Japan. Our country, America, had been attacked by Japan and he didn't like it one bit."

Ken's eyes focused on another time and place. His memories continued to pour out. "My father was born in America, he grew up in America. He thinks like any other American and used to live like one. Quietly, perhaps, which is his nature. And segregated, though not by choice. But as an American, nevertheless. He never thought of himself as anything else. He was a prosperous man, traveling to Europe and South America. Sure, he went to Japan. But just once, in the mid-thirties, and for about three months. He wanted to make investments. But he also wanted to see and feel the ancestral homeland. What's funny is that while he was there he felt remote, distant from the Japanese. That's because the Japanese made him feel that way. When he returned home he told his family that America *was* his home and he *was* an American.

"Unfortunately, most white Americans didn't see him like that. Just a few tried to get to know him. Most just saw his face. People looked at him and immediately concluded he was from somewhere else, a foreigner. So what? Isn't everyone in America originally from somewhere else? You say your family came from Ireland.

"When Pearl was attacked, in spite of his age, he tried to

join the Army, offering to translate documents, share what he knew about Japan from his trip there. The Army sergeant chased him out of the recruiting station. Later on my family was one of the first rounded up and arrested. Not in his wildest dreams did he think his country would arrest us and other Japanese Americans because of Pearl. He's a patriot, Commander. He was angry because Japan attacked America, *his* country. On the train ride to Manzanar he kept our spirits up, telling us that the government would soon see its mistake and let us return home. But after we arrived and were locked up I saw my father cry for the first time, not understanding why his country was doing this to us. He was a broken man. And that broke my mother's heart.

"No, Commander, I'm not ambivalent about going in. Even though America has treated us like dirt, America is still my home, my country."

Rutledge remained silent. Like almost all Americans he supported America's visceral response to Pearl Harbor. To him and millions of others, arresting Japanese Americans and sending them to the relocation camps had been the right thing to do. But as time passed he occasionally questioned the fairness of the internment. He remembered the German American *Bund* movement, made up of German Americans and German immigrants in America, who organized to support Nazi Germany before the war broke out between America and Germany. The *Bund* was a greater threat to America's internal security. Yet, except for some leaders, few were arrested. At the outbreak of the war with Germany there were no mass arrests of German Americans. Rutledge did not know how to respond to Ken.

They continued walking. Then Rutledge asked a question that dogged him for days. "Lieutenant, I have to be honest with you. I agree with Admiral Halsey. I don't think you'll get out alive. I know you'll do everything to ensure the Japanese don't get wind of our plans. But the enemy's not stupid. He's tough and he's capable. He's proven that. So why are you doing this? Why are you risking your life?"

Ken stopped and glared up at Rutledge, who towered over him. "I thought I told you, sir, I'm an American who happens to love his country, despite what my country has done to us. I want America to win this damn war as soon as possible so I can get back home and get my family together again."

Rutledge remained silent, letting Kobayashi release his coiled anger.

"I don't want to see Americans slaughtered invading an island fortress, because that's what will happen. I've heard that the Japanese-American Regimental Combat team in Europe, the Four Forty Second, might be shifted for the invasion. That means Japanese Americans are going to die invading their ancestral homeland. Or should I say, what's left of the Four Forty Second. My guess is the Japanese are hoping to bleed us so bad we'll have to pull off the beaches and continue to bomb or negotiate a conditional surrender. So long as no American soldier occupies their soil, in their minds, they're winning, or at least not losing.

"You have to know your enemy, Commander. As far as the Japanese are concerned they've never been conquered. They've had their civil wars but no external conqueror has succeeded in twenty-six hundred years; that's a hell of a record. They're proud of that and want to keep it that way. Right now some Japanese priest or monk is praying for another Divine Wind, a *kamikaze*, to destroy any invasion fleet, just like before when the Mongols tried to invade.

"I want us to break that record and I want to get home, just like a few million other guys. Commander, I've seen our invasion plans and as it stands we'll probably lose tens of thousands of men. You understand that, sir? Tens of thousands. You have to figure the Japanese know that. They're banking on it. If I don't at least try to get their defense plans, I'll always wonder. It seems to me I'm the only one, right now, able to do it."

About 15 feet away, in front and behind them, the four Marine escorts were willing them to proceed so they could get some coffee instead of standing there being sprayed with seawater.

Rutledge decided to probe further. In a soft voice he asked, "Lieutenant, what about your brother?"

Ken, surprised, assumed a defiant stance. "What about him, sir? I haven't heard from him since late forty-one. I don't even know if he's alive."

Rutledge backed off. "Calm down, Ken. No one questions your loyalty. Not even Admiral Halsey. What I mean is, are you doing this to atone for what he did?"

Ken loosened up, releasing his clenched fists. Rutledge turned and started to walk aft again. Ken walked with him. Both were silent for a bit. Then Ken spoke.

"I don't know, sir. I'd be lying to you if I said I never thought about it, wondering if that's one reason. But my gut tells me no. What I'm doing reflects my obligation to my country, not a response to my brother's actions. What he did he chose to do, and I can't be held responsible. And my family should not be held accountable either. But they are. When my father found out my brother had joined the Japanese Army he refused to speak his name, forbade any of us to say his name or speak about him. It broke my mother's heart but she honored my father's injunction. What I'm doing *I* choose to do."

They stopped just short of the portside Kingfisher launch area.

"Let me offer a thought, Lieutenant. Family ties are, at best, tenuous, especially during these times. At worst they can smother or even destroy us. And one of the saddest feelings of all is guilt. Is that what you've got, Lieutenant?"

Before Ken could answer, a short man in flight clothes sauntered toward them. "Commander?"

Rutledge was disturbed by Kobayashi's earlier emotional outburst and wished he hadn't broached the subject; he was grateful for the interruption.

"Ah, Basque. Lieutenant Kobayashi, this is Lieutenant Gregory Basque. He'll get you to the *Yorktown*. Basque, Lieutenant Kenji Kobayashi. You two get acquainted. I'm going to check in with the skipper on the bridge."

Basque looked up and down at Ken's uniform and a wide grin broke out on his face as they shook hands. "Lieutenant Kobayashi, a pleasure. I know Halloween ain't due for a few months, but I'll tell you it's one hell of a way of gettin' someone's attention. Or gettin' yourself shot. Around here, at least."

Ken grinned and nodded, identifying the unmistakable Texas twang.

"Lieutenant Basque, you from Brooklyn?"

"That anywhere near Houston?"

"Just a bit northeast of it."

"Anyway, been on a Kingfisher before?" Basque asked, tilting his head in the direction of a plane perched on a metal monorail, high above the deck.

Ken looked up at the peculiar plane, mounted atop a large center pontoon, which in turn rested on a small wheeled car whose wheels rolled along a long, narrow metal rail. Suspended below each wing was a smaller version of the center pontoon. A single propeller powered the Kingfisher. He thought the cockpit canopy looked like a greenhouse. Ken felt it was an ugly little plane.

"No, I've never been on one before, Lieutenant. Does it actually fly?"

The length of metal rail on which everything rested was about sixty feet long. Ken, an experienced pilot, wondered how the plane would take off from such a limited platform.

He faced Basque, who, grinning, nodded. Ken immediately liked Basque, a man his size, who wore a white scarf around his neck like a rakish World War I ace.

Greg had heard the question before. Each time his skin grew thicker, more impervious than the Kingfisher's thin aluminum membrane. The *Missouri*'s wardroom often resounded with humorous comments about the *Missouri*'s "small" aviation detachment. Greg was never sure whether the men were joking about the Kingfisher or his short stature.

"She'll get you to wherever you're going, Lieutenant, as long as we wind the rubber band on the prop real tight."

His sense of humor aside, Greg Basque was a fearless and decorated fighter pilot, able to get the job done no matter the circumstances. Greg was now attached to the *Yorktown*'s VF-88 fighter squadron, flying an F6F Hellcat.

But in 1944, during the Battle of Leyte Gulf, Basque was attached to Halsey's flagship, the USS *New Jersey*, ferrying confidential guard mail from the *New Jersey* to American warships at Leyte Gulf, just before the Imperial Japanese Navy attacked. When the battle had erupted Halsey had already been lured away by a Japanese Carrier Task Force commanded by Admiral Ozawa Jisaburô.

Basque flew smack into a sky ripped with flak, exploding antiaircraft fire from American ships trying to beat off a *kamikaze* attack. To avoid the exploding flak he rapidly descended, preparing to land next to a cruiser. At just over 4,000 feet he chanced to look up and saw a *kamikaze*, at about 7,000 feet, heading toward a carrier. Under its belly loomed a large bomb.

The *kamikaze* blew through the carrier's fighters and eluded the withering flak from the ships. Then, certain of his target, he started his dive, making certain he would strike the carrier.

Greg Basque was about 2,000 yards from the carrier. Without warning, he banked his plane, putting his Kingfisher on an intercept course with the *kamikaze*. His rear-seat observer, Frank Kowalski, was yelling over the intercom, wanting to know what the hell Greg was doing. Greg ignored him.

The *kamikaze* pilot took a quick look at his instruments. When he looked at the carrier he caught sight of the Kingfisher, several hundred yards in front of and to his left. He turned his head to see better. Noting the center pontoon under the Kingfisher, he knew it was not a fighter. He smiled, thinking the stupid American was going to try to intercept him. But he knew the American plane was not fast enough so he didn't bother to alter his course.

Greg knew his plane was no match for the Japanese fighter. But he didn't alter his course either. It was a gamble based on a dicey calculation.

Gunners on the carriers and destroyers watched, transfixed. Some of them also thought the Kingfisher's pilot was going to try to ram the *kamikaze*. But they continued to fire, willing to risk destroying the Kingfisher in order to destroy the *kamikaze*.

But that wasn't Greg's plan. His Kingfisher's fixed nose machinegun held 500 rounds but he would have, at most, a split second to fire at the *kamikaze* as it flew by in front of him. As the two planes closed Greg readied his machine gun. Flying straight ahead, he watched the *kamikaze* approach his flight path from the right. With the *kamikaze* about 200 yards from the point of intercept Greg turned to port, into the *kamikaze*'s direction. Then he started to fire his machine gun.

Bullets and red-hot tracers from the .30 caliber machine gun filled the sky in front of the *kamikaze*, at a 45° angle. The Japanese pilot's eyes went wide with horror, realizing what the American was trying to do. If he changed course he would expose his plane's side or belly to the withering antiaircraft fire coming from the picket destroyers; if he stayed on course the bullets coming from this impudent plane might hit his fighter. It was too late to do anything. Stoically, he held his course.

He flew directly through a stream of bullets and tracers; they stitched the *kamikaze* from nose to tail. Several punctured the engine; bullets and tracers tore into the rear of the left wing, penetrating the fuel tank. Just as the *kamikaze* flew past Greg's still-turning Kingfisher an immense explosion rocked it. For a split second fire and smoke enveloped the Kingfisher; pieces of metal peppered the plane. Greg and Kowalski screamed, both lacerated by jagged pieces of hot metal that had ripped through the Kingfisher's thin skin and canopies. Blood pulsed from a gashed artery in Kowalski's neck. Greg was bleeding from wounds in his right cheek, arm, side and thigh. Their plane started to break up. He yelled into his radio for Kowalski to bail out but got no response from him. Greg turned and looked over his seat and saw blood spurting from below Kowalski's right ear. His eyes were rolled back in his head. Basque saw the right side of Kowalski's canopy had a fractured hole.

The Kingfisher, damaged beyond control, started to plunge. Greg hollered several times at Kowalski and finally roused him. He watched anxiously as Kowalski, struggling, slid open his canopy. When Kowalski looked like he was strong enough to climb out Greg opened his own splintered canopy. "NOW!" yelled Greg. He watched as Kowalski, weak from loss of blood, barely crawled onto the edge of the cockpit. Then he stopped, no longer able to move. Greg banked the plane, rolling Kowalski out, then immediately jumped out. After clearing their now-flaming plane Greg shouted at Kowalski to release his chute. Greg guided his own chute as best as possible to land near Kowalski. They splashed down not more than a hundred feet apart and Greg, ignoring the pain exploding through his shoulder, side, and leg, ditched his chute and swam over to the now-unconscious Kowalski. When he reached him he stripped off his chute and inflated Kowalski's Mae West, then inflated his own. Seeing blood still spurting from Kowalski's neck Greg applied pressure on the ugly wound with his hand. In minutes a destroyer steamed to their position and a whaleboat was put into the water. Basque ordered the sailors to pull Kowalski on board first. While two sailors hoisted Kowalski Greg tried to maintain his hand pressure against Kowalski's neck wound. One of the sailors brushed Greg's hand away and pressed a towel to the wound. Then Greg was hauled in like a large game fish and both men were quickly taken aboard the destroyer. Soon after, they were transferred to a hospital ship. Kowalski survived his wound and was eventually sent back home.

Ten days later, back on the *New Jersey*, Ensign Gregory Basque was ordered to the bridge. His limp was noticeable and his right arm was in a sling. A bandage covered his still-swollen right cheek.

Admiral Halsey stood ramrod straight, his hard eyes probing Basque.

Greg saluted with his left hand. "Ensign Basque reporting as ordered, sir." Greg, not knowing what to expect, remained at attention.

Halsey returned the salute then walked to within two feet of Greg. "So, Ensign, thought you'd be a hotshot pilot and bag a Zeke with your little put-put, huh? You flamed him but you also lost your plane and almost lost a good observer. Well? What do you have to say for yourself, mister?"

"Sir, I—"

"You're at attention, mister! Now hear this, Ensign. There are no hot-dog pilots in my Task Force. Just smart, capable pilots. You're being transferred off the *New Jersey*. Your orders, Ensign." Halsey slapped a manila envelope onto Greg's chest. Greg grabbed it as it started to slide down. "Pack your gear and get off my ship as soon as possible. A Kingfisher is waiting for you. But this time you're a passenger on this trip. Dismissed!"

Greg was confused. He had risked his life saving a carrier and Halsey was kicking him off the *New Jersey*. He swallowed hard, slid the manila envelope in his sling, and saluted. Halsey returned the salute then abruptly left the bridge.

As Greg started to leave the bridge the captain of the *New Jersey* stopped him. "Just a moment, Basque. You're with me."

Greg followed the captain out and down to the main deck. There, Admiral Halsey was standing in front of a row of officers. Behind them was a row of Petty Officers and behind them were several ranks of sailors. Greg, confused, thought Halsey was going to break him in rank or, worse, cashier him out of the Navy, on the spot. Greg followed the captain to stand between Halsey and the row of officers. They turned and faced Halsey. The *New Jersey*'s captain then stepped forward and took his place behind Halsey.

The *New Jersey*'s XO yelled, "Ship's company! TENN-HUT!"

A single crack of men coming smartly to attention snapped across the deck.

Halsey turned and stepped forward to stand in front of Greg. He unfolded a sheet of paper and read from it.

"For conspicuous gallantry and daring at the risk of his life above and beyond the call of duty while serving aboard the USS *New Jersey*. During operations off the Philippines Ensign Gregory Basque, with utter disregard to personal safety and ignoring antiaircraft fire…"

Greg was confused.

"…at close range and with devastating effect on the enemy…"

Greg, dazed, dared not make eye contact with Halsey.

"…his unparalleled personal heroism and initiative saved countless American lives and a United States Navy ship and reflected great credit upon himself and the United States Naval Service. Therefore, I take great pride in presenting the Navy Cross to Ensign Gregory Basque, United States Naval Reserve."

Greg was numb as Admiral Halsey pinned the Navy's second-highest decoration to his chest, stepped back, and saluted him.

The *New Jersey*'s captain ordered, "Ship's company, SALUTE!"

On autopilot, Greg returned the salute.

Halsey's wrinkled face broke out in a huge smile. "Perhaps you'd better read your orders now. Lieutenant."

Greg, confused, hesitated. He was an ensign, not a lieutenant. Then he recalled that he held the envelope in his sling. His hands trembling slightly, he opened it and removed his orders. As he read he was puzzled, then astonished. Quickly, however, these emotions were replaced by disbelief, then elation.

Newly-promoted Lieutenant (jg) Gregory Basque was ordered to Pensacola where he would train to be a carrier-based fighter pilot. Already an experienced pilot, Greg would enroll in Flight Operations training which would include gunnery tactics, glide bombing, Field Carrier Landing Practice, with final Carrier Qualifications landings at the naval air base. After graduation he would transfer to a fighter squadron to complete his training.

Greg looked at Halsey. "Sir, I don't know what to say."

"Like I said, Lieutenant, 'just smart, capable pilots' serve on my carriers. When you graduate from Pensacola you're to return to Third Fleet." Halsey extended his hand. "Good luck, son. And hurry back."

"Thank you, sir. Thank you."

Greg completed the course in six weeks and was assigned to the *Yorktown*, attached to VF-88 fighter squadron. His plane was an F6F fighter. His plane crew had already painted on the plane's nose a large sewing needle tearing through the Japanese flag. Below it was the word "Stitcher," Greg's new call sign.

Now, at Halsey's request, he had stepped back to the familiar role of Kingfisher pilot.

With Ken trailing him, Greg walked around the plane while he made a final inspection. The crewmen preparing the plane for flight couldn't help but notice Ken, but they carried out their duties without comment. It was approaching 0400 hours.

Ken's eyes flitted from the clouds to the choppy sea, then back to the Kingfisher. "Lieutenant, can we fly in this weather? For that matter can we fly in this plane?"

"It's a snap, Lieutenant. I've flown in stuff worse than this and I've never lost any cargo. Don't worry, Lieutenant, I'll get you there."

"What's under the wheeled car?"

"You've never been on a battleship before, Lieutenant?"

"No. I'm Army."

"That's a launch platform, Lieutenant."

Before Ken could ask what a launch platform was, Rutledge rejoined them. "Lieutenant, the *Gatling*'s ready to receive you. The admiral told me to ask you if you wanted to change your mind. He knows you won't, but he's giving you one last chance."

"Please thank the admiral for me, sir. I'm going in."

They shook hands. "That's what he thought. Lieutenant, one more thing. Admiral Halsey has just sent a radio message to Admiral Nimitz. It's about your family."

Ken stiffened. "Sir?"

"Admiral Halsey has requested that your family be released from internment as soon as possible and safely escorted home by train."

"I don't know what to say, sir."

"Don't bother. That's Admiral Halsey. Good luck, Lieutenant. You'll be in our prayers."

"Thanks, Commander. With any luck, I'll be back within a week."

Lieutenant Basque spotted a seaman giving him a thumbs up. He turned to Ken.

"Lieutenant, we're all set to take off. I don't know what's going on but over there is a Japanese flight suit. Also, a Japanese helmet, goggles and gloves you'll need on this flight. I guess you better put them on." He pointed in the direction of one of the 40 mm quad gun mounts on the port side.

Ken walked over to the stern AA gun, unhooked his *katana*, leaned it against the gun's circular shield, and pulled on the two-piece summer flight suit. His rank insignia was on the left breast. After tucking his officer's cap under the flight tunic he fastened it. He pulled on the leather Japanese flight helmet and gloves and adjusted the goggles just above his forehead. He recovered his sword and walked back toward Greg.

"I'm all set, Lieutenant."

"Everyone calls me Greg, Lieutenant," he said, checking Ken's flight suit.

"OK, Greg. I'm all set. And call me Ken."

Greg led Ken to the Kingfisher's launch platform, climbed up on it, then up the main float support. With practiced ease, he lifted himself onto the forward edge of the wing. He extended a hand to Ken, steadying him as Ken, holding his sword, climbed up to the wing as well.

Ken did not know why but he turned and saw in the darkness the orange-red glow of a cigarette. He smiled; smoking on the deck at night was strictly forbidden. He knew it was Halsey, a chain smoker, dragging on a smoke. Ken saluted the otherwise darkness then turned back.

Greg slid open the rear canopy for his passenger. Ken, following Greg's instructions, climbed into the rear cockpit. Facing forward in the observer's seat he secured the *katana* inside the cockpit, avoiding the rudder cables.

Greg grabbed the two shoulder straps and pulled them over Ken's shoulders while Ken pulled the waist belt. Ken then seized the ends of the shoulder straps, locking them and the waist belt into a circular fitting equipped with a one-hit emergency release. The .30 caliber machine gun in the rear cockpit had been removed since Ken had no experience with it. A sailor handed Ken's flight bag to Greg. Greg placed it on the rear cockpit floor.

Ken's flight helmet contained removable earphones and a cord running from the helmet. Greg plugged the end of the cord into the Radio Interphone System jack box and turned the switch to INTER so Ken and he could communicate with each other.

Greg climbed into the forward seat, locked his straps, and gave the deck crew a thumbs up.

As the engine kicked over, Greg switched the selector on his Radio Interphone System jack box to INTER.

"Ken, this is Greg. Do you copy? Over."

"Roger, Greg. I read you. Over."

"These quarters are somewhat close. It's usually best to keep communication less formal. We can drop the 'overs.' OK?"

"OK by me. Ov—"

Greg smiled. "OK. After my engine reaches maximum RPMs we launch. It's going to be a bit different from taking off from a runway. Ever take off from a carrier?"

"No, but I saw it once in a film."

"OK, it's like a carrier launch, a piece of cake."

"The launch platform's kind of short, Greg. How do we clear it?"

"Well, a carrier uses a hydraulic propulsion system to launch their planes. We do the same." Then, softly, "Kinda. Our catapult is the launch platform we're sitting on."

Ken's eyes widened. "Say again, I didn't copy that. Over."

Ken felt the plane shift as the catapult rotated 30° outboard, the front end now over the water, and another thought occurred to him. "Greg, what about our canopy? Shouldn't we close it?"

"Uh, negative. If, after the launch, we crash we have to get out real fast. The canopy stays open until we're safely airborne."

Greg tilted his head forward a bit, listening to the engine as he increased the RPMs, while checking the magnetos. He looked out and spotted one of the aviation detachment members, the launch seaman, wearing a chest mike and earphones— a "talker." During a day launch the launch seaman would also have a green flag, but in the pre-dawn sky the flag would have been superfluous. The launch seaman radioed the bridge and spoke to another talker, who relayed information to Captain Murray. The captain would give the order to launch.

Greg continued to ratchet up the Kingfisher's RPMs. Ken found the vibrations unnerving. He looked down and wondered why the launch crew was standing around while the Kingfisher seemed to be shaking apart.

After the launch seaman radioed the bridge, the captain ordered the ship turned into the wind and increased the ship's speed. The *Missouri*'s bow rose and fell as it turned. Some of the men started to move away from the catapult. So did the launch seaman, looking at and listening to the Kingfisher's engine while marking the ship's rise and fall with the horizon.

Just as the *Missouri*'s bow reached its apex the Kingfisher's tail section seemed to explode. Ken was first thrown upward then instantly slammed against the rear seat, the air knocked out of his lungs. He felt as if he were being blown from a cannon. He tried to rotate his head to see if there was any damage to the tail section but couldn't move. He tried to raise his hand to smack the circular strap lock release, to escape, but he could not move his arm. He rotated his eyes right to see if flames were engulfing them or if there were any injuries on the deck. But the deck was gone, replaced by the black surface of the ocean.

They were airborne.

Unknown to Ken, the Navy's Kingfisher utilized a black powder charge to explosively propel the plane forward and off its catapult like a rocket. The force pressing against him was about five times the pressure of normal gravity. After a couple of seconds the pressure relaxed just as quickly. The Kingfisher's single propeller now powered them.

"Uh, Greg, thanks for the warning."

"Copy that. Now you're baptized and a true Kingfisher."

Ken looked down at the ocean but could see nothing except the occasional flashing of the phosphorescent algae. He swiveled in his seat and peered over his right shoulder, watching the *Missouri* recede.

"That's the strangest takeoff I have ever had, Greg."

Greg chuckled. "That's OK. You're the strangest sack of mail I've ever hauled."

"What's our ETA?"

"Uh, the *Gatling* is waiting for us. She's about a hundred and fifty miles south-southeast and with the tail wind, compliments of the typhoon, it should take us about forty-five minutes. Uh, you can close your canopy now. Looks like we're not gonna crash."

Ken slid the canopy closed and settled back, just another piece of cargo, as the Kingfisher climbed to 6,000 feet. With nothing to do as a passenger he let his mind wander. Not surprisingly he thought about Kyoko.

✳   ✳   ✳

When Ken and Tom arrived in Tôkyô they knew adapting would be difficult. During their first term beginning in April they buckled down and studied hard, harder than Japanese students. They knew that everyone, fellow students and faculty, were waiting for them to falter but they didn't. At the end of the term their grades were solid, in the top five percent of their class. Before the next term began both knew they had to have some fun. And the best place for that, they heard, was the Ginza.

The Ginza, often compared to New York's Fifth Avenue, was first developed in the early 1870s, with two- and three-story Georgian-style brick buildings with a major shopping promenade, all of which delighted the Japanese.

Tragically, the Great Kantô Earthquake of 1923 struck. No one was certain but it lasted between four and ten minutes, destroying Tôkyô, Yokohama and most of the Kantô region. Perhaps as many as 140,000 people died. Trolley lines running down the Ginza were ruptured and twisted. And most of the brick buildings were destroyed. Throughout the Kantô region steel bridges buckled. Railroad stations collapsed; train tracks were horribly twisted. Traditional homes and building made of wood and paper were consumed by the fires. Over 30,000 people in the Honjô and Fukagawa districts of Tôkyô, taking safe haven in open spaces, were surrounded by raging infernos and incinerated. Even most of the modern brick and concrete buildings failed to survive.

But the Japanese rebuilt. In the Ginza the new buildings were even larger, offering a center of upscale department stores, large, open and inviting, with glass cases displaying Western consumer goods so the shopper didn't have to wait for something to be taken from a back room. But there were other attractions to delight the Japanese, including cafés, coffeehouses, restaurants and dancehalls.

Both Ken and Tom had heard upperclassmen talk about the Ginza in awe, especially the prices. But their father had given them a generous allowance so they went one Saturday night accompanied by several fellow students. The whole area was illuminated. People were walking along the sidewalks, often stopping to window-shop. Down the main strip, trolleys dropped off or picked up passengers. There was a charged energy unlike anything they had experienced since they arrived in Japan. Both agreed that this was what Manhattan must look like. They soon came across the Chicago Café and hearing American music decided to go in.

They were struck by the gaiety, the lights and décor, all of it American. The floor was made up of large black and white tiles. Glass-topped tables seated two for intimacy or up to ten. And tables could be drawn together for larger parties. The music was right out of New York. There were several murals displaying Chicago gangsters, some carrying Thompson submachine guns, and all with cigarettes dangling from their mouths. And there were the *mobo* and *moga*, modern boys and modern girls. Ken's and Tom's jaws dropped.

The young men and women wore American-style clothing, dressing like the fashion plates of major American cities. The men wore sharp suits with slacks that flared out at the bottom. Their hair was combed straight back with no part, held in place by hair tonic. They held cigarettes like Americans seen in movies. But it was the girls that caught Ken's and Tom's attention.

Though they had been disciplined students during their first term they occasionally toured the university's neighboring area. What they saw were men mostly dressed in Western clothing and women in traditional *kimono*. But not these girls. They wore short skirts ending just below their knees, silk hosiery and high heels. Their hair was short and some had perms, with their ears and the back of their necks exposed. They wore makeup like Hollywood starlets. And they smoked cigarettes.

Then both Tom and Ken realized something. While they wore their school uniforms their fellow students were dressed in American suits. They thought it would be proper to wear uniforms but now grasped that they stuck out like a pimple on a nose. The *moga* noticed too.

One came up to Ken, smiled and winked. Ken froze. No woman in Tôkyô had ever approached him, never mind smiled or winked. "*Tôdai, neh?*" Tôkyô Imperial University, no?

It was so informal, almost rude, that, "*Hai,*" was all he could say.

She circled him, looking him up and down. Then she faced him again and shocked him even more. "And you are American, right?" she said in English, American English.

In the background Ken heard Benny Goodman's "Sing, Sing, Sing" playing on a phonograph and saw couples dancing to it. *So uncharacteristic of the Japanese*, he thought.

He swallowed and nodded once. She laughed.

"Relax, Cowboy. I used to live in New York City a few years ago. You've got the accent. I'm told that when I speak English I have a funny accent too. Where are you from?"

He turned and looked at the other students, including Tom, a plea for help in his eyes. Except for Tom they were smiling and some even laughing. Tom could not believe what was happening.

"Um, do you want me to speak English or Japanese," he asked in Japanese.

"Oh, I think I'd like to practice my English. So, let's have it. Tell me in English."

He heard Gene Krupa playing drums in the background. "Tell you what?"

"Where are you from, silly? And in English."

"I'm from California, San Gabriel. It's near Los Angeles."

"So what's a nice American *Tôdai* boy doing here? Trying to impress the girls with your school uniform?"

Ken began to relax, enjoying the unexpected repartee. "Did it work?"

She smiled. "We'll see. What's your name, Cowboy?"

"Kenji. But my friends call me Ken. Want to be my friend?"

"You're fast, Cowboy. Maybe."

"What's yours," he asked.

"Kyoko. And who are these other boys?" She looked at Tom. "Oh! A mirror with two legs."

"Him? He's my brother," said Ken.

Kyoko looked back at Ken. "Really? I can't tell."

Ken was getting a bit jealous. "He's the ugly one in the family."

"You *are* fast, Cowboy."

She walked toward Tom.

As she walked toward Tom and the other *Tôdai* students Ken thought that she was the most beautiful girl he had ever seen. She was taller than most Japanese girls and had shapely calves, accentuated by the high heels. Her eyes were large and wide apart. Her nose was not as flared as other Japanese girls' and had a pronounced bridge. Her hair was cut short. Her lips were full, accentuated by the deep red lipstick. And her body was curvaceous; he watched her hips as she walked to Tom.

"Are you a cowboy, too, or a mirror," she asked Tom in Japanese.

"No, Ma'am. But I do fly planes!"

"You're such a cute boy," she said. The upperclassmen laughed.

"And who are these boys with you? Your friends?"

The upperclassmen tried to stand a bit taller because she was tall. "Relax, boys, someday you will all grow up."

Ken and Tom laughed. Their classmates did not. While looking at her talk to Tom, Ken could not help but think of Mae West. *Wow! Just like her*, he thought. He knew he was going to marry her.

✳   ✳   ✳

The flight got bumpier and Ken was roused from his reverie.

Though Lt. Basque could no longer see the ocean's surface, he guessed the waves to be up to ten feet, since the sea was rough. After making a notation in his plotting board Greg settled in for the flight. After a passage of time he returned his attention to the plane's instruments, making slight course adjustments when rough winds pushed the small plane off course.

Twenty minutes later Greg looked at his watch, noted the time on his plotter, and started to scan the horizon. Off in the distance he saw several planes approaching out of the breaking dawn. He did not change course or try to evade them. "Uh, Ken, we got company. Eleven o'clock high."

Ken looked up and a bit to the left and saw the shapes approaching. He began to wish the .30 caliber machine gun had not been removed. "You know them?"

"My guess is they're from the *Yorktown*, compliments, no doubt, of Admiral Halsey."

In two minutes the planes raced over and on either side of them. Ken tried to count them: eight possible fighters. He was right. The fighters were F6Fs, Hellcats. Two minutes later a larger plane, a twin engine, rumbled overhead. It was a Martin PBM-5 Mariner, an amphibious rescue plane ordered from Okinawa, in case the Kingfisher went down in rough weather. The Hellcats, flying at about ten thousand feet, were for protection against Japanese planes. It was then that Ken realized how well organized the Navy was and how much Halsey wanted to protect the mission. Or was Halsey protecting him? Either way, Ken was impressed and grateful. Greg flashed his running lights on and off.

The Hellcats, having passed the Kingfisher, banked sharply and began a weaving pattern above and behind. The PBM Mariner came about and followed along behind as well.

Greg switched his jack box to COMMAND and told Ken

to do likewise. The Hellcat's flight leader called in.

"Blackbird One, this is Flatiron One. Do you copy? Over."

"Uh, roger, Flatiron One. On my way to collect that beer you owe me. Over."

"Ah, copy. Understand you got some special mail in your bag. Over."

"Roger. A Sears and Roebuck catalog with the latest fashions. Over."

Ken laughed.

"Roger. Maintain present heading and altitude. Squawk if you need an assist. Over."

"Appreciate that, but this should be a milk run. Over."

"Uh, roger that. Haven't seen any bandits in the past few days. Guess the yellow Japs can't get their birds in the air or don't want to. Over."

"Shit," Greg said softly and winced.

"Blackbird One, say again. Over."

"Uh, negative, Flatiron One. I'll collect that beer later. Out."

Greg felt ill at ease. He switched the jack box to INTER after telling Ken to do the same.

"Sorry, Ken. I guess you're still a secret, just a VIP. Sorry."

Ken shrugged it off. "Don't worry about it, Lieutenant. I'm used to it." Greg noticed the lapse to formality. Ken realized it too and immediately regretted it. They flew in silence as the sun continued its long climb over the horizon.

As the formation approached the *Gatling*, the destroyer had them on radar. Greg returned the communications jack box to COMMAND. In a moment the silence on the Kingfisher ended.

"Blackbird One, this is Fireside. Do you copy? Over."

"Roger, Fireside, I copy. Over."

The *Gatling*'s radar operator needed to be certain he had a proper fix on the formation. "Roger that, Blackbird One. Come to course zero nine zero degrees. Over."

Greg adjusted his course, knowing the *Gatling*'s radar operator would be watching his screen, confirming the formation's new heading. A moment later the radar operator issued new instructions.

"Blackbird One, resume heading one five five degrees." A moment passed. "Uh, Blackbird One, I have you at angels six, bearing one five five degrees. Range twenty-five miles. Over."

"Roger, Fireside, confirm altitude, six thousand feet and bearing one five five degrees. Range twenty-five miles. Over."

Greg again checked his watch and plotter. He knew that even before the *Gatling*'s radar operator had contacted him, his plane's transceiver had been queried. Ships had special radar that electronically probed incoming planes, initiating a response, an Identification, Friend or Foe answer. The answer appeared on the ship's radar screen. If the incoming plane was an enemy, fighters could be vectored to intercept. Or the ship's antiaircraft guns could open up.

Ten minutes later Greg received instructions to start his descent. He started to bank, heading for the *Gatling*, which was now in visual range. He was going to try to land about an eighth of a mile from the destroyer.

In the meantime the *Gatling*'s crew prepared to receive its special package. Three sailors manned a 26-foot motor whaleboat just before it swung over the starboard side on its davits. The captain then ordered the helmsman to create a slick.

The *Gatling* was on the tail end of the typhoon and the ocean's surface was still choppy. Whenever a battleship or cruiser, each far larger than a destroyer, prepared to receive a seaplane it would first create as smooth a water surface as possible. To create a "slick" the battleship or cruiser would come about and cut an arc through the water, blocking the wind. With the wind blocked briefly the chop would settle, leaving a calmer surface.

Since a destroyer customarily did not carry a seaplane, she was not required to perform this maneuver. But the helmsman knew what to do. The captain ordered him to turn his wheel to starboard. The helmsman did so and waited for the second change-course order. Satisfied, the captain ordered the helmsman to again change course, heading to port. He then ordered the engine room to reduce speed to five knots. With the wind temporarily blocked by the *Gatling*, the surface chop settled down.

As Greg made his approach, he expected the surface would still be a bit rough. The Kingfisher smacked down and bounced several times, but Greg was a good pilot who knew his plane and controlled it. As the Kingfisher came to a stop he estimated he was less than an eighth of a mile away. The *Gatling*'s captain then ordered the whaleboat swung out and lowered into the water. Greg could see the whaleboat approaching. He left his engine running; he was still in a combat area.

In a few moments the whaleboat bumped against the plane's pontoon. Inside the whaleboat were three men. The first, the bowhook, stood balanced in the bow. His task was to extend a six-foot pole with a hook on the working end and snag whatever needed to be. He extended his pole and hooked one of the pontoon's support struts, keeping the two vessels together. In the middle of the whaleboat sat the engineer, maintaining the engine. The coxswain, who was in charge, stood at the stern, tiller in hand. They waited patiently for the two men on the Kingfisher.

Greg climbed out of his cockpit, stepped on the wing, slid open the rear cockpit canopy and reached for Ken's flight bag and tossed it to the bowhook who threw it behind him. Greg then took hold of Ken's *katana*, worried that Ken might lose his balance on the wing and drop the valued sword. Ken, a quick learner, needed no assistance as he climbed out of the rear cockpit onto the wing.

Ken extended his hand and shouted over the engine's roar, "Good flight, Greg. Bouncy, but good. Thanks for getting me here in one piece."

"My pleasure, Ken. Sorry about Flatiron One's comments. He's lost a lot of friends."

Ken nodded. "Me too, Greg. I know how it is. My best to Commander Rutledge when you get back. Take care of yourself."

"I don't know what you're up to, Ken, but I have an idea. Be careful. Real careful." Greg snapped a salute, which Ken returned. He climbed from the wing onto the pontoon and stepped into the whaleboat. He turned and Greg handed him the *katana*.

The bowhook looked up, puzzled to see a sword. Ken passed the bowhook and headed toward the center of the boat. Sitting down he faced the stern of the whaleboat and lifted his goggles. The engineer and cox'n got their first good look at Ken and their eyes shot wide. The cox'n, spotting the collar of Ken's uniform, gripped the tiller even tighter and locked his eyes on Ken.

Ken returned the hard stare. "Any questions, sailor?"

The cox'n shook his head. "No, sir. Our orders are to get you aboard and to keep our mouths shut no matter what we see or hear."

"Then carry on, sailor."

"Aye aye, sir," said the cox'n. "All right, you heard the... the... Sir, what the hell are you? Your rank?"

Ken laughed softly. "Right now, in this uniform, I'm a major."

"Yes, sir. All right, you heard the major. Let's shove off."

The bowhook released the hook from the strut and used his pole to push the whaleboat away from the Kingfisher.

As Ken settled in, he stood the *katana* between his legs and noted the flinty glances of the whaleboat crew.

As they headed for the *Gatling* Ken turned and watched Greg's stubby Kingfisher prepare to take off. Above, the Mariner lumbered off, back to Okinawa. Higher up, the Hellcats orbited once and headed toward the *Yorktown*. Ken stared intensely at the lead Hellcat, wondering what Flatiron One looked like.

As the whaleboat approached the destroyer, the *Gatling*'s crew lowered a Jacobs ladder and a rope. The whaleboat pulled alongside. The bowhook threw his bowline to the men on the *Gatling*'s deck; the cox'n in turn threw his stern line.

With the whaleboat secured, Ken, holding his *katana* in one hand, ascended the Jacobs ladder. The bowhook tied the rope to Ken's flight bag. On deck, at the top of the ladder, the *Gatling*'s executive officer stood waiting. As Ken stepped on the deck the two men exchanged salutes.

"Welcome aboard, Lieutenant," the executive officer said while offering a handshake which Ken gladly accepted. "I'm Lieutenant Commander Tony Casella, ship's Executive Officer. The captain asked me to convey his respects."

"Thank you, Commander. I'm Lieutenant Kenji Kobayashi."

"If you'll follow me to the wardroom, Lieutenant, we'll be getting underway as soon as the whaleboat is stowed away. One of the sailors will take care of your bag. And call me Tony."

"Thanks. And I'm Ken."

Ken appreciated the friendly greeting. He knew that destroyer crews were seasoned, proud sailors, not easily rattled. Several sailors passed them as they made their way to the wardroom but made no comments.

As they entered the wardroom Ken looked at his watch. It was 0540 hours, just about on schedule. He looked around. The wardroom on the *Gatling* was far smaller than the *Missouri*'s but just as neat. It spoke volumes about Halsey's Third Fleet.

The *Gatling* was a fast-moving ship, designated a fighter direction ship, responsible for vectoring carrier-borne fighters toward incoming Japanese planes.

"Coffee, Ken? It's fresh. And if you're hungry we've got a good cook on board. At least no one's died from food poisoning yet. You might want to get out of that flight suit. You might get a bit uncomfortable."

"Thanks, Commander. Coffee sounds good right now. Black, no sugar." Ken removed his flight goggles and helmet, pulled the officer's cap from inside the flight suit tunic and removed the flight suit and placed everything on a chair.

Casella came back with two mugs of steaming coffee. "How was your flight?"

"Except for the bumps, nothing remarkable."

"Basque your ferry, right?" Ken nodded. "Let me guess, 'Carrier hydraulic launch,' right? He likes to 'baptize' innocent officers, Navy or Army."

"I almost baptized my pants."

"Incidentally, we, uh, were monitoring your radio. Sorry about Stanton. He's a good pilot but sometimes a bit aggressive." Casella stared at his coffee and stirred it more than was necessary.

"You lost me, Tony. Who's Stanton?"

"Oh, right. Bob Stanton. You sort of met him already. Flatiron One?"

"Right. Don't worry about it, Tony. I've already met a hundred Stantons. I'm almost getting used to it."

Ken, though grateful for Greg and Casella's sensitivity, was weary of the double takes and apologies and changed the subject.

"When did you first know I'd be coming aboard?"

"We knew two days ago to expect you. But just that you were a VIP. About six hours ago we got a flash, direct from the *Missouri*. You come with very influential references, Ken. The captain seriously considered piping you aboard, the whole ball of wax."

Ken sipped his coffee then said, "I'm supposed to be kept under wraps, Tony."

"Oh, don't worry. The skipper laid down the law. As soon as you transfer to the *Yorktown* you were never here."

When Casella had brought the coffee, he had taken a long look at Ken. Ken noticed the inspection and knew Casella was barely controlling his interest.

"I'm curious. Your flight bag is not standard issue. What's in it?"

"The usual. An extra uniform, *fundoshi*, identity papers, money, shaving kit."

"Okay, I'll bite. What's a fun…uh, what's that?"

"Japanese underwear. Very simple and practical."

"And the sword? Did you get it off an officer?"

"Sorry, no exciting war tales. General Willoughby won't let his intelligence people get near an armed enemy soldier. He claims we're too valuable. My father gave it to me. It's been in the family for over three hundred years."

"Uh, Ken, I've got to ask. What's the scoop? That uniform is not seen on an American warship every day. Nor is that flight bag, and never mind the sword. I'm not supposed to ask and, like I said, after you transfer you were never here. Look around you. We're the only ones here. The skipper put the wardroom off limits to everyone except you and me. But you can bet the entire crew knows you're here and when you're gone I'll be buttonholed by the skipper. Can you fill me in?"

Ken appreciated Casella's candor and agreed with his assessment. He knew the captain would badger Casella for answers and wouldn't accept any explanation but the truth. And captains were known for making their XO's lives miserable if thwarted. Knowing the *Gatling* would remain at sea, he was confident he could reveal his mission to Casella without risking disclosure to the enemy. He could not have risked that with Greg because the Japanese were monitoring open channel communications just as the Americans were monitoring Japanese frequencies. And there was the possibility, though slight, of Greg's unwittingly telling Flatiron One about his passenger or, less remote, ditching, and being pulled from the water by the Japanese. Better, Ken felt, that Greg did not know.

"Fair enough. Here it is. I'm going into Tôkyô. I'm going to try to get a look at Japan's defense plans. They know we're coming and they're getting ready. They don't look at surrender like we do or even like the Germans did. Not the Japanese. I know them and I know they'll fight to the last drop of blood, ours as well as theirs. If we don't get a handle on what their defense strategy is, we're going to run into a bloodbath, worse than Okinawa and Iwo Jima. I'll try to find out how they're going to greet us. Then I get out."

Casella breathed heavily then sipped his coffee. After putting the mug on the table he raised his eyebrows and whistled. "That simple, huh?"

"Yeah, simple as that."

"I don't think so. Too risky. Plenty of coast watchers were inserted into enemy-held islands and a lot didn't come out. I know. We were assigned to pick up a few when they were supposed to exit. Some just never showed up. I think you know the odds are stacked against you. It's one thing to go to an island with a jungle between you and the enemy. Tokyo's a city—you're going to be in the middle of a major metropolitan area. And that means all their intelligence resources can be brought to bear. So it's not so simple."

Ken knew Casella was right. While at Tôkyô Imperial University, he experienced Japan's secret police, the *Kempeitai*, or Thought Police. Occasionally, like many Japanese-American students, or *kibei*, he was "asked" to appear at the police station for questioning when the American press wrote negative articles about Japan.

"You aren't the first to raise that issue. But I'm depending on a couple of things being in my favor. For one thing, Japan's been blockaded by the Navy for quite a while and desperately-needed food and oil aren't getting through. Starve a man and he slows down, and that includes his thought processes. But there's another thing in my favor. We've been bombing Tôkyô for months. Drop bombs on a guy for months and he has other, more important issues to cope with, like living. Right now I'm willing to bet that the Japanese are experiencing a national lethargy, sort of a malaise of the collective mind. These aren't the same folks as in forty-two. They were winning then. But I'm not dismissing your arguments. I'll deal with it if it comes up."

Casella picked up his mug of coffee and swallowed more of the hot beverage. "I'm curious. How'd you get the go-ahead for the mission?"

"I'm on General Willoughby's intelligence staff. In that capacity I attended a briefing on our invasion plans for Japan. During the briefing it occurred to me that when we go in, we go in blind. On the other hand, if we could get hold of their defense plans our casualties might be lowered. That's when it hit me that I'm the best man for the job.

"Besides, this is my chance to contribute to the war something more than just translating captured documents or an enemy radio transmission or interrogating a prisoner. If I go in and get the information we need, that will be my contribution without having fired a shot. Like you said, 'That simple.'"

"Any chance they'll catch on to you?"

"Sure. There's a chance. The Japanese are smart, but we're smarter. That's all the edge I need."

Casella smiled and nodded. He looked at his watch. When Ken had boarded, the *Gatling* was about 75 nautical miles from the *Yorktown*, about 30 minutes sailing time at their current speed of 20 knots. The *Yorktown* was traveling toward them at the same speed.

"Ken, we better get ready. We should be coming into visual range of the *Yorktown* in a few minutes. Ever been highlined?"

Ken quickly swallowed the rest of his coffee then put down the mug and groaned. "Remember, I'm Army. All this is new to me."

"Don't worry. It's a snap."

"You know, that's what Greg Basque promised me."

"You better grab that flight suit. It'll keep your uniform from getting soaked. It's still a bit choppy out there."

Ken put on his officer's cap. He picked up the suit and flight helmet and goggles then followed Commander Casella as they made their way to the main deck, port side. Crewmen looked at Ken but did not openly stare. When they arrived on the main deck a sailor with a chest phone approached them.

"Commander, bridge reports the *Yorktown* two thousand yards off the port beam."

6

The *I-402* submarine moved ominously through the Pacific's waters, the hull enveloped in the inky darkness. The *I-402* was submerged at 30 meters, one-third her maximum depth. Her brooding presence stood in stark contrast to the agitated denizens of the ocean darting from her.

In the control room Leading Seaman, First Class, Koyama Tsutomu rotated the hydrophone knob for the sixth time while watching the sonar bearing indicator screen. He was using the K type hydrophone which could detect battleships, carriers and cruisers from over 35 kilometers distance, more than 19 kilometers for destroyers, and beyond nine kilometers for merchant vessels. Koyama Heichô, ever thorough, allowed each rotation of 360° to take about two minutes. *No haste. This is too important, always important,* he told himself.

He started to narrow his sweeps until he was within a 20° range. His earphones tightly gripped his skull; he ignored the discomfort. From habit he closed his eyes for a few seconds, listening. He tilted his head forward and a little to the left as if this would help him hear better. He opened his eyes and looked at the clock located just above the sonar screen. While listening to and counting the revolutions of the contact's screws in his earphones he watched the second hand of the clock for 15 seconds then multiplied the count by four, trying to estimate the speed of the contact from the contact's revolutions per minute.

Three consecutive sweeps of the bearing indicator, now narrowed to a 10° spread, confirmed his initial assumption. He turned his head to the right then lifted the earphone from his right ear.

With him in the control room, a meter away, Lieutenant Watanabe Shigeharu watched and waited silently. Finally, Koyama spoke to Lieutenant Watanabe.

"Tai-i! I have a single contact, bearing right ahead. Speed approximately twelve knots. Tai-i! It's on an intercept course!" At 12 knots the contact was making more than one kilometer in three minutes.

Though his voice was restrained Koyama couldn't mask his excitement.

The *I-402* had left Yokosuka in the darkness of night, more than 48 hours ago, on August second. When the *I-402* left port she had immediately submerged and had remained under the surface, avoiding American warships that skillfully hunted throughout the waters off Japan. Within minutes of leaving port the *I-402* had encountered and cautiously threaded through scores of the thousands of mines that had been dropped into Japan's coastal waters by American planes and ships. When the *I-402* was 40 kilometers out at sea she changed course and headed south. She would soon change course again, heading south-southwest. She was on a resupply mission, transporting desperately needed provisions to Japanese forces on Formosa, more than 1,900 kilometers from Yokosuka. Now, at about 55 kilometers out of Yokosuka the *I-402* was still deep in enemy territory, so completely did the American Navy control the Pacific Ocean.

The *I-402*'s top speed, submerged, was 6.5 knots, powered by batteries. Top surface speed was 18.5 knots, using diesel engines. Surfaced, the cruising range was over 55,000 kilometers at 16 knots or almost 70,000 kilometers at 14 knots. Submerged, range on the batteries was 111 kilometers at three knots, the boat's current speed.

At night the *I-402*, like any submarine, would customarily surface and open the hatches to run on diesel engines and recharge the batteries. Opening the hatches would also sweep out the stale air in the boat, something the crew gravely needed. There were over 140 sailors and officers on board the *I-402*, each man aware of the risks of carbon dioxide poisoning.

But due to the reality of prowling American warships, surfacing had not been possible. Instead, the *I-402* had remained submerged. When clear of the mine fields her rudimentary schnorchel, technology the Japanese navy acquired from the German navy, was occasionally run up. It acted as an air intake and exhaust, admitting limited air into the *I-402*'s engine room, permitting her to use the auxiliary diesel engines. None of the air, however, benefited the crew, just the voracious diesel engines. Those engines provided propulsion as well as recharging the batteries while the sub was submerged and underway. When extended, the schnorchel's head valve needed to be just above the water's surface, which meant the *I-402* had to come perilously close to the surface. With the batteries recharged the schnorchel was lowered and the submarine went deep.

The *I-402* was launched in 1944 and completed its shakedown cruise. Before acceptance for service, however, the boat went through extensive modifications to serve as a submarine tanker, to transport oil from the East Indies to Japan and other Japanese-held territories. It was a last-ditch attempt to elude the ever-tightening American naval blockade of Japan's empire. But Japan was running out of quality matériel and many of the modifications to the *I-402* were made with shoddy jury-rigged or cannibalized equipment. The boat was accepted for service in July 1945.

Mounted on the forward main deck, slightly offset to starboard, was an ingenious steel aircraft hangar, over 30 meters long, fully one quarter the length of the submarine, which measured 122 meters, making the *I-400*-class longer in length and more than twice as heavy as American destroyers. Except for the flat base the steel aircraft hangar was cylindrical in shape internally and externally and had a diameter of over 3.6 meters. Its internal volume was over 322 cubic meters. The enormous hangar, sealed at the forward end by a massive, watertight bulbous door, was designed to shelter three assembled and one reserve (disassembled) single-engine reconnaissance floatplanes, the Aichi M6A1 *Seiran* bomber. In addition, three 798-kilogram bombs and twelve 250-kilogram bombs, which could be carried by the planes, were also stored in the hangar. The Aichi M6A1 *Seiran* floatplane, a revolutionary addition to a submarine, was constructed with a single wing, collapsible at both ends, and armed with 7.7 mm machine guns. However, its primary mission was to act as reconnaissance and to search for distant targets for the *I-402*'s torpedoes.

Above the hangar were three 3-barrel 25 mm guns and one 1-barrel 25 mm gun. Aft of the hangar, on the main deck, was one 140 mm cannon. Inside the hangar, on the floor, were two parallel rails used to transport the planes out of the hangar. While submerged, the inside of the hangar could be pre-warmed through an ingenious system of circulating heated lubricating oil through metal coils. Forward of the hangar door, on the foredeck, was a 25 meter-long catapult, cambering upward as it approached the bow. The catapult could launch a plane at 68 knots and launch another within four minutes. A large crane, lying parallel to the catapult and folded flush into the deck, recovered the returning floatplanes when they landed on the water. When the *I-400*-class subs were first photographed, American air reconnaissance officers thought the crane was a "disappearing 16-inch gun."

The *I-402*'s conning tower and periscopes adjoined the hangar, on the port side, keeping the hangar free of any obstructions.

Coupled with its deck hangar, the *I-400*-class, submerged, displaced over 6,665 metric tons and was the world's largest submarine class built during the war.

Oddly, the *I-400*-class only had forward torpedo tubes, eight in all. Submarines customarily had aft torpedo tubes as well. Twenty torpedoes were stored in the forward torpedo room.

The *I-400*-class submarines were originally designed on orders of Admiral Yamamoto Isoroku for one mission: to bomb Washington, D.C. and New York City. They were called STo Type or *Sen-Toku*, "Special Submarines." That plan was discarded but when it became apparent that war would break out the *I-400*-class was given a new mission: to bomb and destroy the locks at the Panama Canal. They never carried out that mission either.

Later on, as America's B-29 bombers were incinerating Japan's cities, another mission was given to the *I-400*-class submarines. Plans were devised to deliver the floatplanes just off the west coast of America in order to drop bombs on major coastal cities. This was the only reply Japan could devise in response to the American B-29 onslaught.

When the plan for bombing America's coastal cities was proposed, Vice Admiral Ozawa Jisaburô, Vice Chief of the Naval General Staff, suggested another, more sinister use for the *I-400* submarines: PX Operation. Admiral Ozawa proposed the *I-400s*' floatplanes drop on America's coastal cities not bombs but rats, laden with fleas carrying bubonic plague, as well as other vermin carrying cholera and typhus bacteria. General Umezu Yoshijirô, Chief of the Army General Staff, was convinced that germ warfare would escalate against all humanity and he suppressed the plan in March 1945, in spite of the objections of powerful supporters.

For the I-402's present mission, however, the cylindrical hangar housed not floatplanes but over 1,300 metal barrels totaling more than 320,000 liters of scarce aviation fuel for Japanese planes stationed on Formosa. Additionally, stored throughout the I-402 in every available space were over 1,200 metric tons of supplies, including spare parts for planes, tanks, and vehicles, medicine, including quinine and opium (for morphine), unarmed artillery and tank shells and metal boxes laden with ammunition.

Since there were no planes in the hangar, four equally-weighted cylindrical watertight steel tubes, each filled with valuable aviation fuel, were mounted forward of the hangar on the main deck, port and starboard to maintain trim.

And there was something new, not designed for the I-400-class submarine, added two days before they left port. For this mission two *kaiten*, manned suicide torpedoes, were mounted on the main deck, aft of the conning tower. Normally, *kaiten* were affixed only to attack submarines, mounted directly over hatches which would give a *kaiten* pilot immediate access, and able to be launched while the submarine was submerged.

Because there were no hatches on the I-402 leading to the *kaiten* they were not mounted flush to the deck. Rather, each was mounted and chained on two hastily-improvised, six-foot wooden platforms, each with a U-shaped groove in the middle to hold a *kaiten* in place. A steel bolt six and one-half feet long and two inches in diameter ran through either side of each platform, anchoring each to the deck. The bolts were secured with two one-inch nuts and a one-quarter-inch brass washer, flush to the engine room overhead. The platforms offered enough room for the pilot to crawl into the *kaiten* from underneath. However, to launch the *kaiten* the I-402 would first have to surface, allowing the crewman to go on deck to enter it. Other crewmen would have to unchain them and the

I-402 would then have to submerge so the *kaiten* could float off. Everyone on board knew the maneuver would expose the boat to detection. With such a risk to the submarine none of the officers expected the *kaiten* to be employed.

Like most Japanese submarines, the *I-402* had never been effectively utilized during the war. Unlike American submarines, which had attacked Japan's lines of communications, sinking merchant marine ships as well as warships and disrupting resupply, the Imperial Japanese Navy had directed their submarines to concentrate most of their attacks on America's warships. Ironically, while American submarines were inexorably choking Japan's lifeline, America was able to transport supplies by merchant marine ships across the Pacific. America's merchant marine fleets went out in large convoys and were protected by warships and submarines and suffered far fewer attacks by Japanese submarines.

Despite these deficiencies and the transformation of the *I-402* from a warship to a supply ship the officers and sailors were highly motivated. And, like their American, British, and German counterparts, considered themselves an elite branch of the Imperial Japanese Navy. They also knew, however, that the Imperial Japanese Navy High Command never forgot that Japanese submarines were ineffectual in the attack on Pearl Harbor. When Japan's fleet returned from the attack only the submarines and their crews were not honored. As the American Navy closed in on Japan's home islands many Japanese submarines were relegated to supply duties. Sometimes, the submarines transported small amounts of troops who were needed on other islands, in anticipation of an American invasion. Ironically, the Americans in Admiral Nimitz's island-hopping strategy toward Tôkyô bypassed many of these islands. The Japanese submariners were demoralized. But they were still proud and determined to give their all, including their lives, for *Tennô-Heika*, His Imperial Majesty.

Leading Seaman Koyama Tsutomu had initially heard the contact at about 35 kilometers, bearing green 03°, the *I-402*'s starboard bow, but the bearing was an estimate. He had been tracking it since. There was a very slight bearing drift. At 30 kilometers the contact's bearing changed to green 02°. Koyama reasoned the contact was on a near-intercept course with the *I-402*. At an estimated 25 kilometers the contact's bearing was green 01°.

The crew of the *I-402* was in an enclosed world, and as such unconcerned with conventional points of a compass. Whatever bearing the bow of a submarine pointed was relative 00°. Bearing green was to starboard, bearing red was to port, the same system used by Britain's Royal Navy, from which Japan had derived most of its naval practices.

Lieutenant Watanabe leaned over the shoulder of Koyama and picked up the spare earphones, listening while Koyama rotated the sonar bearing indicator. After listening for several minutes Watanabe closed his eyes briefly, then he nodded and replaced the spare earphones and stepped back. He picked up the voice-powered phone and pressed the button for the conning tower where the *I-402*'s Executive Officer, Lieutenant Commander Mori Hiroshi, had the watch. When the phone started to buzz Mori Shôsa grabbed it. "Mori!" snapped his resonant voice through the phone.

"Shôsa! Watanabe Tai-i! Sonar reports a contact, bearing green zero one degrees. Shôsa! It's on an intercept course!"

"Watanabe Tai-i! Does Koyama Heichô have a range estimate?"

Lieutenant Watanabe paused. The only way to get an accurate fix on the range of a known contact was to go from passive sonar to active sonar. That meant sending out a pinging signal, bouncing it off the contact and waiting for it to return to the submarine. Measuring the time from sending the ping to receiving it gave an accurate range. Of course this also informed the contact of your presence because his sonar operator would hear the ping. This, in turn, opened the submarine to attack by the contact. By their very nature submarines did not want to give away their presence.

Mori, Watanabe and Koyama knew passive detection never gave an exact range, which was why Mori Shôsa asked Watanabe if Koyama had an estimate of range.

With passive detection, range was estimated by experience, equipment, condition of the water, and the nature of sound itself. Did it sound far away and therefore mushy or could the sonar operator hear the rumble of propulsive machinery? If the propulsion was machinery, was it steam, piston, turbine or diesel engine?

Koyama's estimated range of 25 kilometers meant that the sounds, though no longer mushy, were muffled. But that closure of ten kilometers had given Koyama an opportunity to listen to and study sounds the contact made. As the range between the *I-402* and the contact closed the noises became more distinctive. Whooosh-whooosh-whooosh became zish-zish-zish. The propulsion machinery became more discernible. Soon Koyama was able to identify the number of screws. Earlier, when the contact had reached 30 kilometers, each of the four screws started to reveal individual sounds. Screws operated synchronously but, with long-term operation and poor maintenance, occasionally fell out of synchronization, sometimes by just tenths or hundredths of a second. But that was enough for someone like Koyama; as for most sonarmen it was experience and seat-of-pants insight.

"Koyama Heichô! Do you have an estimate?"

Koyama looked at Watanabe. "Tai-i! I estimate range is about twenty-five kilometers! Course change! Bearing right ahead!"

Watanabe nodded. Experience taught him never to doubt Koyama's estimates. He knew most sonar operators hesitated to make range estimates. But Koyama was different. Not yet 18 years of age he was considered one of the best sonar operators in the Imperial Japanese Navy Submarine Service.

Koyama, a prodigy, had studied the violin and piano from the age of three and his sense of pitch was almost flawless. His ability for differentiating sounds was, some felt, limitless. Watanabe knew better than to second-guess Koyama.

Watanabe spoke into the phone. "Shôsa! Sonar estimates range at about twenty-five kilometers! Bearing right ahead!"

"I'm coming down!" Lieutenant Commander Mori replaced the phone, mounted the ladder, and slid down the parallel vertical poles, ignoring the rungs. He brushed past Watanabe and stood behind Koyama and picked up the spare earphones, holding one against his ear, then nodded once to Koyama. Mori watched Koyama rotate the sonar bearing indicator. He heard the faint, rapid rotation of screws but the sounds were too mushy for him. Like Watanabe, Lieutenant Commander Mori was not as able as Koyama to confirm the number of screws or ships or distance. He admired Koyama. Mori put down the earphones.

"Koyama Heichô! What do you think? Merchant or warship?"

Koyama turned to face the XO. "Shôsa! I count four screws. I conclude it's a warship!"

Lieutenant Commander Mori nodded slowly several times, weighing Koyama's evaluation. Japan had few merchant ships and even fewer warships left that could challenge the American task forces that roamed the Pacific. Besides, merchant ships of all nations had only one screw and destroyers and submarines two. The contact, with four screws, could only be a cruiser, battleship, or, that most desirable of targets, a carrier.

"And you are certain of just one contact?"

Koyama, in fact uncertain, hesitated. "Shôsa! The distance is great. There might be other contacts out there but the present contact might be masking their presence. So sorry, sir!"

Mori could not fault Koyama's logic. "Koyama Heichô! Maintain a sharp listen on the contact. For now designate it Contact Number One. Watanabe, maintain present speed and heading!" Mori turned and quickly climbed up the conning tower ladder.

Back at his station Mori Shôsa reviewed the captain's Night Orders: the captain was to be informed of any contact less than 25 kilometers if he was not on the bridge, conning tower, or control room. Though the contact was now about 25 kilometers, given that the distance was closing and the bearing was right ahead and steady, and therefore on an intercept course, Mori knew that unless the *I-402* or the contact changed course they would eventually converge. Mori, knowing the captain had been awake for more than forty hours guiding the *I-402*, first through the mines then American warships, hesitated to wake him. But the captain's Night Orders were explicit. Besides, a warship with four screws would be an irresistible prize. The captain, Mori concluded, had to be informed. He picked up the voice-powered phone and pressed the control room button. Watanabe picked it up.

"Watanabe Tai-i! Inform the captain!"

"*Ha!*" Yes!

Mori smiled at Watanabe's use of the forceful "Ha!" instead of the normal "Hai." Watanabe, though junior in rank to Mori, was seven years older. Sometimes, Mori felt uncomfortable that a more experienced officer was his junior. But he knew the reason why.

Though Watanabe Tai-i had graduated from Eta Jima, Japan's naval academy, Mori Shôsa had graduated from Tôkyô Imperial University, *Tôdai*, having studied Japan's Tokugawa period.

He was cultured where Watanabe was unpolished. Mori's family had influence with Japan's Foreign Ministry and they tried to convince Mori to enter the government but he refused. The lure of war pulled at him. The warriors he had studied had inspired him. There could be no greater calling than to fight and, if necessary, to die for *Tennô-Heika*, His Imperial Majesty, and Imperial Japan. And though educated at *Tôdai*, known for producing Japan's governmental leadership, at age 24 he displayed notable military skills and leadership qualities. The Imperial Japanese Navy desperately needed men like Mori Shôsa. With sadness, his family acquiesced when he joined in 1943.

As Watanabe made his way forward to the captain's quarters, he saw a rat that had torn open a rice sack and was feeding on the spilled contents. Watanabe tried to kick it but the rat dodged his foot. What was frustrating to Watanabe was that the rat did not scurry away and hide but just waited for Watanabe to leave, its eyes continually shifting from Watanabe to the rice. Like most Japanese submarines, the *I-402* suffered from free-roaming rats and other vermin that fed on food, stored or spilled. Fleas and body lice plagued the crew, many of whom shaved their body hair, including pubic hair. The rats shared with the crew every habitable compartment of the submarine. They were bold enough to rip open the rice sacks and eat under the tired eyes of the crew. Watanabe, disheartened, quietly swore and continued forward. He arrived at the captain's quarters and knocked.

An irritated voice responded, "What? Who is it?"

"Chûsa! Watanabe Tai-i reporting! Mori Shôsa ordered me to inform you that sonar reports a contact, bearing right ahead at twenty-five kilometers! Koyama Heichô reports it's a warship!"

The captain, who had been trying to sleep, swung his legs to the deck, sat up and frowned. "Watanabe! Come in! Were you able to confirm it?"

Lieutenant Watanabe entered the captain's cabin and stood at attention. Like everywhere on the *I-402* the air was musty; the odor of stale cigarette smoke mingled with sweat, diesel oil and battery acid permeated everything. "Chûsa! Just the presence of a contact, sir! I heard what Koyama heard but I cannot confirm what it is I heard! Koyama is certain it's a warship!"

Commander Iwata grinned at Watanabe's report. "Watanabe Tai-i! Relax. There are no admirals present."

Watanabe smiled. The two had served together since 1942.

"Sit, Watanabe. What do you think?"

Watanabe relaxed and looked for a place to sit. "You know Koyama Heichô, sir. He is Koyama. If he thinks it's a warship then it is, Chûsa."

Chûsa, or Commander, Iwata Kantarô, was captain of the *I-402*. He scratched his closely cropped scalp then rubbed his meager beard. Watanabe was the ablest control room officer to have served with him and Iwata appreciated his candor. Iwata knew Watanabe had twice declined a promotion which would have led to his own command. He understood further that Watanabe did not want the responsibility of ordering men to their deaths.

Iwata put on his shoes and stood. He was offended at the odor of his shirt as he pulled it on. He wore his uniform shorts while sleeping. While he was dressing Watanabe looked at him and thought how old his Chûsa looked. In 1942 he looked his age. Now, he thought, his captain looked 45 years old. Iwata was 31.

He followed Watanabe to the control room, no longer inspecting his submarine as he had in times past. He didn't have to; he knew its condition. As he made his way aft he considered using the lavatory but changed his mind. Before they left port his supply officer was unable to acquire sufficient *washi*, or rice-straw paper for the single toilet. Japan was running short of everything.

Iwata's crew was exhausted, existing on reduced rations. On this mission he had seen hunger in their eyes as they looked at the decreased sacks of rice. While in port, none of the crew had been allowed leave nor given rest, forced instead to make crude repairs after the deck modifications. Much of the equipment they replaced was jury-rigged or cannibalized from other submarines unable to serve.

Standing just outside the coaming of the control room he looked at the sweat coating the bodies of his crew, most dressed only in *fundoshi*, gray-white loincloths. A few wore white *hachimaki* around their heads, lettered with *kanji* characters *Shichi Sho Ho Koku*, "Seven Lives to Serve Country." In Japanese the phrase meant "Born seven times to serve the homeland." It helped to keep the sweat from their eyes.

Having remained submerged for over forty-eight hours, the air in the *I-402* was hot, fetid and heavy with the odor of machine oil, diesel fuel and sweat. The crew longed for fresh air. The lone relief for the crew was the fans that circulated the foul air in each of the cramped compartments of the submarine. Yet in spite of their fatigue and hunger they maintained, Iwata noted, excellent discipline and dedication. He was never more proud of a crew than this one.

Since leaving port the *I-402* had avoided the fast-moving American destroyers by utilizing the ocean's thermoclines, distinct layers which separated warm and cold water. Cold water, denser and containing less oxygen, would sometimes absorb or diffuse sonar pings before they reached their intended target. A crewmember constantly measured the outer water temperature using the *I-402*'s new bathythermograph. It was a cat-and-mouse game both sides played, and Commander Iwata was an expert.

His first opportunity to prove his tactical skills in wartime was when he helped his captain avoid American destroyers outside Pearl Harbor. Iwata stepped over the coaming and entered the control room just as Mori descended to the control room.

"Mori Shôsa! I was dreaming of beautiful *geisha*! What does Koyama Heichô have for me?"

"Chûsa! Single contact, bearing right ahead, range about twenty kilometers. Koyama Heichô reports four screws. Still faint."

Commander Iwata noticed that Mori did not claim that he made the distinction of number of screws but had instead given credit to Koyama.

"Koyama Heichô! Report!"

"Chûsa! Bearing is still right ahead! Single contact! Four heavy screws! Perhaps eight turns per knot!"

Iwata took the spare earphones from Mori, put them on, and stood behind his sonarman, slightly hunched over. Koyama continued to rotate the sonar bearing indicator then fixed his hydrophone toward the bow. Iwata heard the unmistakable zish-zish-zish-zish cavitations of screws. Iwata was almost as good as Koyama. He closed his eyes, blocking out any extraneous motion around him. He knew that the four screws of heavy warships rotated seven to nine times per knot and destroyers and submarines, with just two screws, rotated ten to twelve times per knot. He counted the turns of the heavy screws. Iwata made a quick mental calculation. It was possible the contact was making twelve knots. He removed the earphones, inhaled deeply, and stood straight.

"Koyama Heichô! Has the contact been zigzagging?"

"No, Chûsa! Straight heading, course unchanged."

Iwata Chûsa looked at Mori, clearly puzzled.

"Koyama Heichô! Are there any other ships in the immediate area?"

"I can't be certain, Chûsa! But so far I'm not acquiring anything else."

"Mori Shôsa! Koyama Heichô is correct! Single contact, either a battleship, carrier, or cruiser." He placed a hand on the sonar operator's shoulder and squeezed it. "Very good work, Koyama Heichô! Very good! Mori Shôsa, you have designated the contact as Contact Number One?"

"Ha!" replied Mori.

Leading Seaman Koyama Tsutomu, one month shy of 18 years, kept an intense watch on the sonar bearing indicator. Inside he swelled with pride that others had heard Commander Iwata praise his performance.

Iwata turned and walked to an isolated niche of the control room, followed by Lieutenant Commander Mori. He turned and faced his XO.

"What do you make of it, Mori-san? Single contact, four screws, and not zigzagging? And no destroyer screen? Something is not right. The Americans are too intelligent to be so arrogant. What do you think?"

"Chûsa! It is an excellent opportunity to sink them! A blow to honor Tennô-Heika! We have an obligation to Tennô-Heika!"

Iwata hardened. "We also have an obligation to our heroic soldiers on Formosa! I know our duty is to destroy enemy ships but our brave soldiers and pilots on Formosa need our cargo. As much as Tennô-Heika needs victories we need to get to Formosa. If we try to sink this contact and we fail what then? That contact has a destroyer screen; Koyama has not located it yet. But that destroyer screen will locate us, move very quickly and maybe sink us instead."

Mori was embarrassed. "I apologize, sir! I only thought of the moment! It was selfish of me!"

"I understand. What do you think the Americans are doing?"

"Single contact and not zigzagging? Its rudder could be damaged, perhaps taking on supplies, or they might be transferring injured personnel."

"Possibly. Still, I want to take a look. Maybe I can catch sight of a destroyer screen. Mori Shôsa, back to your station! Rise to periscope depth! All hands to action stations!"

Both Mori and Iwata climbed the ladder to the conning tower. Iwata walked over to the periscope station.

Mori issued orders. "Make depth twenty meters!"

The order "action stations" passed quickly throughout the *I-402*. Crewmembers, not already on duty, raced to their stations. Metal doors between compartments were sealed tight, insuring that if an exploding depth charge damaged a portion of the sub, water rushing into a compartment would not rush to others.

The *I-402* assumed an up angle and reached periscope depth. Iwata could feel the energy level change in the conning tower. The crew was now at action stations, waiting for orders.

A telephone talker, earphones on his head and a microphone resting on his chest, stood behind Iwata, waiting to relay orders from the captain or receive information from any compartment in the submarine. Unlike the phone system, the telephone talkers were on an open circuit and were located in every compartment of the ship. What a telephone talker in one compartment said was heard by the telephone talkers in the other compartments.

Petty Officer, Second Class, Yamada Ichirô stood ready to raise the periscope.

The telephone talker relayed Mori's report, "All stations manned and ready."

The captain nodded once and looked at the telephone talker. "Control room! What is your bubble?"

The telephone talker relayed the question to his counterpart in the control room who in turn relayed it to Lieutenant

Watanabe, who in turn reported, "Zero bubble!" This was relayed back to the captain, letting him know the *I-402* was no longer at an angle but level under the surface.

Again, the captain faced the telephone talker. "Sonar! Have any other ships arrived in the area?"

Koyama rotated the bearing indicator away from the 00° heading, making a full sweep of the area. "Chûsa! None in the immediate area! Nor have I detected any submarines!"

Iwata, hearing the response, smiled, pleased that Koyama anticipated his next question.

"Yamada Nitô heisô! Raise Number Two periscope!"

Petty Officer, Second Class, Yamada Ichirô pulled the Number Two periscope lever. Number Two periscope was for search, Number One for attack.

As Number Two periscope rose into position Commander Iwata wiped the sweat from his forehead with the back of his forearm. He put on earphones, lowered and gripped the periscope's textured brass handles then angled up the lens 45° and quickly swept the sky, looking for planes. Finding none he then lowered the lens and swept the horizon 360°, insuring there were no ships in proximity, before stopping at 00°. The eye of the periscope was about 1.2 meters above the waterline, giving him a visual range of only 3.5 kilometers, to the horizon. He saw nothing. He had not expected to. He remembered his submarine school instructor drumming the equation into their heads: "The distance to the horizon is proportional to the square root of the height of the periscope—above the water." The contact, about 20 kilometers, was over the horizon.

He slowly fanned 45° red and green but still saw nothing. Then he swept 360° slowly, again looking for enemy planes off the horizon. Still nothing. The waters were still agitated by the receding storm. Waves, though tapering, were still close to two meters, thwarting his view, and haze hung over the water.

"Mori! Make your depth ten meters! I want to try to get a better look. I'm curious why an American ship does not zigzag in Japanese waters."

Mori ignored the irony and issued the orders: "Make depth ten meters!"

The crew became excited as high-pressure air flushed out more water from the main ballast tanks. In a moment the *I-402*'s bridge breached the choppy surface of the Pacific, offering the captain enhanced periscope visual range.

Suddenly, Koyama's head snapped up. He brought both his hands up to the earphones, as if the sounds emanating from them were puncturing his eardrums. His eyes shot up, to the overhead. "Chûsa! Chûsa!" he screamed,

In the conning tower Iwata fairly leaped to the ladder and leaned over. "Koyama Heichô! Report!"

"Chûsa! I have just picked up new sounds, irregular banging noises—"

Iwata interrupted him. "Bearing!"

"Chûsa! Directly overhead!"

Iwata looked up to the hatch, his eyes widening. "Damn! The deck plates!"

Two days before they left port the *kaiten* platforms had been installed on the deck, under the supervision of Ensign Oda Shûichi. The day before leaving port it was discovered that some of the deck plates had to be replaced. Mori had put Oda in charge of the minor operation, to be carried out by the weary navy yard workers at Yokosuka. Iwata guessed that Ensign Oda had not properly supervised the deck plate repairs. His blunder could give away their position and possibly sink them. Iwata had no alternative.

"Sonar! Range of the contact?"

"Chûsa! Range of Contact Number One is less than twenty kilometers!" Iwata knew that at that distance his boat and the contact were still out of visual range, but the Americans had radar. He would have to risk it.

"Mori! Surface! Open the hatches! Lookouts topside! Order maneuvering and engine room to remain on batteries!"

Even before his orders were relayed fully Iwata cracked the conning tower hatch and made his way to the bridge. Behind him two lookouts scurried up the ladder, trying to keep up with their captain. As soon as they reached the bridge they stationed themselves red and green. Mounted on the bridge were five pairs of large 20x watertight binoculars. The lookouts immediately began to scan the horizon, fore and aft. They encountered the same haze and saw nothing but water and clouds.

Iwata looked down on the aft deck and instantly saw the cause of the noise. The latches on two deck plates had come loose, and as the *I-402* approached the surface, rough waters moving over the deck had repeatedly lifted the deck plates while their hinges slapped them down. Each deck plate was made of wood with a metal sleeve surrounding it. Each was one meter long, five centimeters wide and one and a quarter centimeters thick; many plates were hinged, allowing access to hatches or other fixtures underneath them. If the contact's sonar operator was any good, Iwata knew, the *I-402*'s position might have already been betrayed. He grabbed the voice-powered bridge phone, removed the rubber coverings, and buzzed the control room.

"Control room! Mori!"

"Mori! Fans to high speed! Have Oda Shô-i report to the bridge with a wooden mallet and crowbar! Quick time!"

With the hatches open fresh air swept in and the fans circulated it quickly throughout the *I-402*. Within two minutes Ensign Oda Shûichi appeared on the deck. With a confused look on his face Oda Shô-i stood at attention, tools in hand. An angry Iwata confronted him and Oda Shûichi knew he was in trouble but not why.

"Chûsa!"

Iwata crossed his arms in front of his chest. "Look at the aft deck, Oda Shô-i! Tell me if you see anything amiss!"

"Chûsa?"

"Shô-i! Look down at the aft deck! Now!"

Ensign Oda turned and looked down at the deck and paled. He immediately bowed at the waist. "Chûsa! I present myself for punishment! Please allow me to commit *seppuku*!"

"*Bakayarô*! Would you like to perform the ceremony on the deck, in its entirety? Do you wish to put on *kimono*? Should I order *sake* to purify your *wakizashi*? Who would you like as your second to cut off your foolish head?"

The two lookouts were appalled. Oda's mouth quivered, unable to respond to the blatant sarcasm or to look at his captain. *Bakayarô* was an insult with which a man could be put down as an idiot, a stupid boy, and worse.

"Oda Shô-i! Make repairs now!"

"*Ha!*" Yes! Ensign Oda looked at one of the lookouts, both of who saw and heard the humiliation of Oda. "You! Kowa Ittô hei! Come here!"

Able Seaman Kowa, carrying out his all-important duties as lookout, grimaced at Commander Iwata, visibly torn.

Iwata, enraged, did something he had not done in his entire career. He slapped Oda across the face. "Kowa Ittô hei has his duties to perform! You were responsible for these repairs while we were in port in Yokosuka! Do it yourself!"

"*Ha!* Chûsa! What do you wish me to do?"

Iwata struggled to regain his control. He was horrified that he had struck a man under his command. "You can either spend the next hour repairing them or rip them off and toss them overboard. There is an enemy ship in this area. Time is of the essence. What do you suggest?"

Ensign Oda immediately climbed down to the deck and made his way aft to the *kaiten*. He dropped to his knees and worked the crowbar under a deck plate, struggled to sever it from its latch and hinge, then grabbed the deck plate and rocked it back and forth until it tore free. He tossed it overboard and started to work on the other plate.

While Oda was thus involved Iwata went to one of the binoculars on red and scanned the horizon. He saw nothing due to the haze and started to turn to green. As he did so he caught both lookouts glancing at Oda, a superior officer on his knees, making repairs. Iwata knew the lookouts felt it was work they should be doing, but he was furious. As an officer it was Oda's right to delegate work but it was also his responsibility to make certain the repairs had been done correctly while in port. That he had not done so did not surprise Iwata. Oda had other priorities.

Oda was assigned to the *I-402* as senior *kaiten* officer three days before the *I-402* left Yokosuka. Before reporting to Yokosuka a proud Ensign Oda had said goodbye to his family in Hiroshima, a young wife of 19 and two small children, the younger three months old. Oda, like Iwata, had attended Eta Jima and upon graduating had applied for submarine service. Early in the war an ensign had to wait until reaching the rank of lieutenant, junior grade, before applying for submarine service. However, by 1945 standards had changed. And, concluded Iwata, so had the standards of some of the Imperial Japanese Navy's officers. Iwata knew Oda had a young family and the fact that Oda had volunteered for duty on *kaiten* angered Iwata. At this late stage of the war Iwata knew Japan was defeated but men like Oda refused to acknowledge that brutal reality as they rushed headlong to their, in Iwata's mind, pointless deaths.

As a counterpart to the *kamikaze* the Imperial Japanese Navy created the *kaiten*, by elongating and retrofitting torpedoes. With the mid-section elongated to create a cockpit, the pilot sat in a canvas chair practically on the deck of the *kaiten*, his legs straight out in front. A rudimentary periscope hung directly in front of him, and the necessary controls close to hand in the cramped cockpit enabled him to pilot the *kaiten* to the target.

The *kaiten* was a treacherous weapon at best; fast, difficult to control, subject to uncontrollable dives and broaching and other accidents. Furthermore, it suffered from a number of mechanical problems, including saltwater leakage into the control space when the mother sub was submerged, and a tendency to catch fire from oil leaks. Owing to these pitfalls, its usefulness as a weapon was of dubious value especially when compared to the normal Type-93 torpedo. However, the *kaiten* did have the asset of being able to make multiple runs at a target; a pilot who missed once could reacquire his target and attack repeatedly until he ran out of fuel, and then he would simply sink to the bottom of the ocean.

The *kaiten* weighed over 8,000 kilograms, was almost 15 meters long and had a diameter of one meter, just enough room for a man to sit with his legs straight out and look through a periscope. It had a range of about 25 kilometers at 30 knots or, incredibly, almost 80 kilometers at 12 knots. It carried a massive 1,542-kilogram warhead. Like the *kamikaze*, the *kaiten*, which meant "Turning of the Heavens," a euphemism for a desired change in Japan's military condition, was a suicide weapon. Yet thousands of Japan's best young men were prepared to die for *Tennô-Heika* on these suicide missions. Iwata, though devoted to the emperor, thought it was a stupid, tragic waste.

Iwata didn't personally dislike Oda but rather what he represented: Japan's fanatic refusal to see that the war was lost and that further loss of life was unnecessary. It was, ironically, a concept he had once defended.

Eleven months before World War II began Iwata and several other Japanese navy officers had visited San Diego, California and met with their American counterparts. Everyone was polite and skirted the issues of the American gunboat *Panay* and Japan's war in China. But both sides knew that if Japan and America didn't settle their differences diplomatically they would be at war. During a luncheon aboard an American cruiser the Japanese and American officers got into a polite discussion about the code of *Bushidô* and death. At the conclusion Iwata left with the clear impression that the Americans, if ordered by their leaders, would fight unrelentingly, even to death, but they did not believe in simply dying for the honor of dying.

One American captain told him, "If we lose a battle there's a brief period of anger or shame. But at least we're still alive and if we escape then we get back on a new ship and go after the enemy again. And again. Until we destroy him. But if you're dead you're no good to your country. So what's the purpose of dying simply for the sake of dying honorably?"

Iwata, as hard as he tried, could not explain *Bushidô* to the American captain. And the American couldn't explain why it was all right to live after defeat, that the ultimate goal was to win the war.

Iwata was an experienced, shrewd submarine commander, a veteran of six years of conflict, first off the coast of China, then, as the war widened, against the British and Americans. Like his grandfather, he was devoted to the Imperial Japanese Navy and had graduated near the top of his class at the Naval Academy on Eta Jima, a small island adjacent to the Kure naval base.

Rather than please his grandfather, Iwata had volunteered for submarine service. At first his grandfather, a captain of a cruiser during the Russo-Japanese War, had objected to his grandson's choice. He wanted Iwata to serve on a surface ship, a battleship, cruiser, or carrier. After the disasters at Midway and Leyte Iwata's grandfather, a pragmatic man, was grateful his grandson had chosen not to accede to his wishes.

Iwata, unlike his fellow graduates who had chosen duty on the more glamorous surface ships, was less formal and doctrinaire. His crew was composed yet maintained a high level of proficiency. Though he maintained a disciplined boat up until today he had never had to exercise his right to strike those serving under him, a common practice in the Imperial Japanese Army. He felt that the close confines of a submarine did not require a harsh attitude. He was satisfied with the fact that after each mission he had brought his boat and crew safely home while Japan's surface fleet as well as other submarines disappeared.

Abruptly the bridge phone rang. Iwata grabbed it. Lieutenant Commander Mori's metallic voice leaped out of the phone.

"Chûsa! Sonar reports multiple contacts! Range approximately fifteen kilometers, bearing from red zero eight zero degrees to green zero seven five degrees! Contact Number One now at nineteen kilometers!"

Iwata reflexively shifted the binoculars and squinted as he looked through the powerful Zeiss lenses, quickly sweeping the horizon left to right off the *I-402*'s bow. He barely saw a plume of smoke.

"Mori! How many new contacts?"

"Chûsa! Koyama Heichô reports four contacts, two screws each, fifteen knots. Two inner contacts maintaining distance of about three point five kilometers forward of Number One Contact and three point five kilometers between them. Two outer contacts maintaining four point five kilometers distance red and green of Number One Contact! Chûsa, the new contacts are zigzagging! Effective speed is twelve knots!"

"Damn! That is the destroyer screen protecting Contact Number One! Mori! Designate them Contacts Two through Five! Seal hatches! Prepare to dive!" He turned and yelled, "Oda! Lookouts! Below! Clear the bridge! Mori! Dive! Dive!"

The harsh "ah-oooo-gah, ah-oooo-gah" of the diving alarm tore throughout the boat. Immediately all other hatches were closed. The lookouts scrambled to reach the open bridge hatch. They had to move quickly. The *I-402*, despite her enormous size, could crash dive to periscope depth in less than one minute. As he watched the lookouts dash Iwata's mind pictured two destroyers forward of Number One Contact and two more destroyers, one on either side; an arc of steel protection, prowling for enemy submarines. He knew that when an escorting ship zigzagged it maintained a faster speed than one traveling on a straight path. Yet the constant course changes kept the distance traveled equal to the slower ship following on a straight path. The destroyer screen zigzagging was standard, preventing a submarine from acquiring a bearing for a torpedo bowshot.

Iwata looked through the binoculars one last time, frustration spreading over his face, then sealed the lenses and placed the rubber coverings on the phone.

Ensign Oda climbed back up the bridge, his feet slipping off some rungs. He reached the bridge and started toward the hatch but stopped, waiting for the captain to precede him. Iwata angrily shoved Oda to go first, knowing he had never secured a hatch during an emergency dive. Oda, clumsy with confusion and humiliation, stumbled down the rungs. Even before Iwata entered the hatch the boat's main ballast tank vents opened to purge their captured air and allow seawater in.

Fast behind Oda, Iwata, ignoring the rungs, placed his hands and shoes on the outsides of the ladder poles and skidded down the bridge ladder. He slid two meters before stopping to reach up and grab the lanyard and pull the hatch closed. On the other side of the ladder remained one of the lookouts, supported by one arm and one foot on rungs, leaving one arm free. Iwata let go of the lanyard and slid down the ladder as the lookout reached up and spun the hatch handle to dog the hatch tight.

Iwata hurtled down the final three meters of the ladder to the control room below. Located at the bottom of the ladder a canvas cushion, a meter thick, softened landings during a crash dive. As his shoes hit the cushion the waters of the unforgiving Pacific enveloped the main deck of the *I-402*.

7

Ken Kobayashi shifted his sight to port and saw the *Yorktown*. Even at 2,000 yards Ken appreciated the carrier's enormity.

The carrier dwarfed the destroyer. The *Yorktown* was an *Essex*-class carrier, an enlarged and improved version of the *Enterprise*-class carriers. She was eight hundred and seventy two feet long, a sixth of a mile in length. On her deck were fighter planes, torpedo planes, and fighter-bombers, some with wings folded up, others with wings spread, ready to take off and pounce on the enemy. F6F Hellcats were flying CAP over the ships. Within ten minutes the two ships closed the distance. The *Gatling* came about, paralleling the *Yorktown*'s course, about 75 feet apart. Both ships then decreased speed to 12 knots, with the *Gatling* on the *Yorktown*'s starboard side, adjacent to the carrier's superstructure.

A crewman on the *Yorktown*, using a shoulder-fired line-throwing gun, sighted from the carrier's starboard hangar deck bay opening. Satisfied, he fired the leader for a 5-inch manila highline to the *Gatling*'s main deck, about ten yards lower than the carrier's hangar deck. The sailors on the destroyer, after retrieving the line, attached their heavier lines to the lighter one and the *Yorktown*'s pulley crew pulled them back to the carrier. The ends of the heavy lines were then attached to each ship's highline pulley arrangement. Ken Kobayashi watched with keen curiosity, an interested observer. Commander Casella had seen it before and decided to join him.

"Relax, Ken. We do this all the time. Besides, you're the second shipment. We've got some supplies coming over. You can watch how it's done."

"How long does it take?"

"If nothing goes wrong, typically fifteen to twenty minutes."

The *Yorktown*'s sailors attached the lines to a skip box already loaded with supplies.

On each ship two teams of men, fifteen to twenty men per team, faced each other. On the *Yorktown*, the delivery ship, one team held an inhaul line. The opposite team of men held the highline. The same arrangement was in place on the *Gatling*, the receiving ship, except that the *Gatling*'s crew controlled an outhaul line. Those men holding the highline on both ships would hold it tight, maintaining stability of the skip box as each ship individually responded to the ocean's rolling. The men on the *Yorktown* would pay out the inhaul line, while the men on the *Gatling* would pull the outhaul line, bearing the skip box toward the destroyer.

With the lines secured, the *Yorktown*'s sailors began transferring the skip box to the *Gatling*.

As each ship moved up and down with the ocean's swells, the skip box rose and fell in exaggerated response to first one ship, then the other. The sailors controlling the highline on both ships tightened their grip. Kobayashi followed the movements with apprehension. Casella watched him with an ever-widening grin.

"See? Piece of cake."

"What's coming over?"

"A couple of things of real importance that the men haven't had in a while. New movies, fresh food, and, thanks to you, lots of ice cream. And some mail for us that's been flown in."

"Why am I responsible for the ice cream?"

"Every time a destroyer rescues a pilot the crew gets twenty-five gallons of ice cream. The big guys on the flattops consider the ice cream a gift to us little guys on the tin cans. Though we didn't rescue you we are sending over a pilot. I guess they feel obligated. Or they're needling us."

The skip box was hoisted over the railing and one of the *Gatling*'s crewmembers grabbed the retrieving line that hung from its base. The skip box set down on the *Gatling*'s deck with a soft bump. Several men hurriedly unloaded it. Ken was surprised to see a sailor place his flight bag in the skip box, which was returned to the *Yorktown*.

This time Ken watched as a transfer-at-sea chair, otherwise known as a bosun's chair, was sent over to the *Gatling*. He was not happy with what he saw.

The bosun's chair, constructed of metal piping, looked like a vertical one-man ski gondola. Like the skip box the bosun's chair was hoisted over the railing and one of the *Gatling*'s crewmembers grabbed the wet retrieving line that hung from its base. The bosun's chair settled on the *Gatling*'s deck with a metallic clang. Both operations took twenty minutes.

"See? Like I said, piece of cake," said Casella.

"Somehow I think I'm going to get my pants wet after all. Just don't tell Basque," Ken said as he put on the flight suit. He inserted his flight helmet and goggles in a large pocket that was on the front of his pants. The pocket bulged a bit but he was able to button the pocket flap. Seeing sailors clothed only in shirts he left his flight tunic open.

Just then a sailor came forward, carrying a Kapok floatation vest. "Excuse me, sir. But I thought you might need this."

"Thanks, sailor. I think you're right." Kobayashi quickly put on the vest, then, noting the wind gusts, pulled his officer's cap on tighter. The sailor showed him how to inflate the Kapok life vest, just in case.

Kobayashi turned to Casella and they shook hands. "Tony, thanks for your hospitality. Good luck with your skipper. When you tell him my mission he won't believe you, so you'd better create something more credible, otherwise your life will be miserable."

Casella laughed. "Good luck, Ken. Listen, if...*when* you get back, maybe you can tell me the history of your sword. I think it has an interesting one. Keep your head down. God speed."

Ken Kobayashi settled into the bosun's chair and positioned his *katana* vertically between his knees. His flight boots rested on an angled platform. A burly chief petty officer named Wheeler, with forearms the size of hams covered with a thick blanket of dark, curly hair, buckled the safety harness. After securing the harness he instructed Ken how, in an emergency, to unlock it. "Just in case, sir. Though I ain't never seen it happen before."

After Ken settled in, ready for the transfer, Wheeler paused, looked around, and saw several sailors looking at Ken. Gripping the uprights of the bosun's chair he leaned in. His face was barely a foot from Ken's. He spoke barely above a whisper. "Sir, I really don't know whatcha doin' but I think I got an idea. Good luck. I think you're gonna need it."

8

After landing on the meter-thick cushion Commander Iwata rushed up to the conning tower. In that compartment were also the Torpedo Firing Control Solution area and the periscope station. Iwata turned to his Executive Officer. He was still angry and a bit agitated.

"Mori Shôsa! What is the status of Contact Number One?"

"Chûsa! Koyama Heichô places the range of Contact Number One at eighteen kilometers, bearing right ahead! Speed twelve knots! Contact One is not zigzagging! The four new contacts maintain their distance from Contact Number One! The four new contacts are zigzagging! Range on the new contacts, fourteen kilometers, still bearing red zero eight zero to green zero seven five degrees, effective speed twelve knots! Sonar reports Contacts Two through Five are using active sonar!"

"That is not surprising, Mori." For the first time since he awoke he lit a cigarette. Not for the first time memories of the aroma of American cigarettes drifted up with the smoke around him. "What's our status?"

"Chûsa! The crew is still at action stations. Current depth is fifty meters. Zero bubble! Speed is three knots, course unchanged. What are your orders?"

"Obviously Contact One not zigzagging indicates it is taking on supplies or making a personnel transfer. Maintain present speed and heading. Evidently, the noise from Contact One masked the destroyer screen from us. Now is the time to see if our German technology really works. Let us employ it. Ready torpedo tubes one through six!"

Mori's head snapped around. He knew once torpedo tubes were loaded the enemy ships were no longer contacts but targets.

"*Ha!*" Mori walked over to the Torpedo Fire Control Solution area. "Sakamoto Hei sôchô! Designate Contact Number One as Target Number One! Designate Contacts Two through Five as Targets Two through Five!"

Immediately, the crew was electrified. The *I-402* was finally going into battle.

"*Ha!*" responded Chief Warrant Officer Sakamoto Hideaki.

Mori then relayed the same information to Koyama. Lastly, he picked up the phone and called the torpedo room.

"Forward torpedo room! Sasaki Jôtô heisô!" responded Chief Petty Officer Sasaki Sadamitsu.

"Sasaki Jôtô heisô! Ready tubes one through six!"

"*Ha!*" responded Sasaki. "Ready torpedo tubes one through six!"

While Germany was still in the war they shared with Japan what was thought to be a method of concealment from sonar. After the *I-402* was accepted into service the exterior of the boat was coated with a two-to-three-millimeter thick anti-sonar reflecting substance made up of a compound of synthetic rubber and silica sand powder. A thin coat of plastic in turn covered this. Characteristically, the Japanese modified the formula somewhat, which helped it to adhere better. Still, Iwata was uncertain if it protected his boat from sonar, but he was willing to take the risk.

Iwata leaned against the targeting table and rubbed his whiskers, driving the fatigue from his face. Cigarette ashes fell on the table. He blew them off. He was tired but excited.

"Sonar! Range on the targets!"

"Chûsa! Target One is seventeen kilometers; bearing, zero zero degrees true! Speed, twelve knots! Targets Two through Five are thirteen kilometers, bearing red eight zero to green seven five degrees. Speed, fifteen knots; still zigzagging, sir!"

Tension throughout the *I-402* heightened. And so did the level of anticipation, but no one panicked and no one ignored his duties.

While Iwata and Mori discussed strategy Ensign Oda stood transfixed, not knowing what to do. Iwata had seen it before. No matter the amount of training, first combat sometimes froze men into inaction. Iwata approached the periscope station then stopped and faced Oda. "Oda Shô-i! Prepare for *kaiten* action!"

Ensign Oda, eyes excited, nodded once and turned, leaving the conning tower. He headed forward to alert the *kaiten* crewmembers, and would choose the two who would have the honor of dying for *Tennô-Heika*, His Imperial Majesty. Lieutenant Watanabe followed him.

Lieutenant Commander Mori looked at Iwata closely, baffled. The captain's attitude seemed to be a complete sea change from their discussion before Iwata went topside. If his actions were driven by a desire to strike one final blow at the enemy, Mori wondered, then did the captain forget his mission to Formosa?

Mori approached Commander Iwata, intent on slowing him down. "Chûsa! We have been lucky so far. Possibly, thanks to our German friends, Targets Two through Five have not yet located us with their sonar. We cannot surface to launch *kaiten*."

"Don't worry, no *kaiten* will be launched. I needed to get

Oda Shô-i occupied and away from here. Also, I am curious. I remember my father telling me an old proverb: 'A man does not worry about a fire across the road when flames are licking at his own home.' Formosa's across the road but Targets Two through Five are near my home. I want to see what the Americans are up to, that is all. Nevertheless, I am not a fool. I have ordered the torpedo tubes ready only in case we are acquired. If we were to attempt to sink Target Number One then the destroyer screen will try to sink us. If we sink one of the destroyers first, Target Number One will be alerted and escape while the other destroyers hunt us down and sink us. We will maintain our speed and heading, approach the targets, then determine what our course of action will be when we are about eight kilometers distance from the screen."

"So close? Is that not dangerous?"

"Desperate circumstances require foolish actions. However, we will be prudent. We will use torpedoes only in defense."

Mori lowered his voice. They were friends, the kind that only war makes. "Iwata-*san*, forgive me. Koyama Heichô is the best sonar operator I have known. I know he blames himself for not locating the destroyer screen sooner. The screws of Target Number One masked the destroyers even though they were closer. He was ordered by you to use passive sonar at the start of this mission. That he did eventually locate the destroyer screen is characteristic of his abilities. May I ask that you speak with him?"

Iwata looked at Mori and smiled. This was not the first time his XO's good sense prevailed when the captain was annoyed or distracted. If Japan had more submarines Iwata was convinced Mori would have had his own command by now. Iwata smiled and rubbed his sparse whiskers. "You're right, of course."

Iwata walked to the ladder and descended to the control room. He walked over to Koyama then stopped, one meter from the young sailor. He noted Koyama's hunched shoulders. Iwata knew Koyama blamed himself and knew he had to restore Koyama's dignity.

"Koyama Heichô!"

Koyama promptly stood, turned and bowed. "Chûsa!" I...I was in error! I should have done better! Chûsa! I request punishment!"

Iwata was proud of the young man's immediate acceptance of responsibility. Purposefully, he spoke loudly, insuring others heard him. "Koyama Heichô! There is no fault! The initial contact masked the destroyer screen. Continue to monitor the targets."

"*Ha!*"

Lieutenant Watanabe returned to the control room. "Chûsa! Ensign Oda has assigned Okada Shô-i kôhosei and himself! They expressed their gratitude to you for this honor! They have prepared themselves for *kaiten* action! They await your orders!"

Iwata sighed and thought of the young age of Midshipman Okada, 17, and of Ensign Oda's children. "Thank you, Watanabe."

"*Ha!*"

Iwata, his shoulders heavy, slowly returned to the conning tower and walked to the map table. He told Mori of Oda's choices for the *kaiten*.

"Japan has too many dead heroes, Mori-*san*, and more waiting to die. I'm certain Targets Two through Five have not yet discovered us just as Koyama did not initially detect them. Everyone, the second target group and we, seems focused on the first target. Why? I want to find out.

"Mori Shôsa! Bring us to periscope depth! I want to have a look. Something is happening and we should know!" He turned to his telephone talker. "Sonar! Range on Targets Two through Five!"

9

Before Ken Kobayashi could respond to Chief Petty Officer Wheeler the bosun's chair abruptly leaped off the deck, tugged up by the sailors pulling on the outhaul line on the *Yorktown* and guided over the destroyer's railing by the *Gatling*'s crewmen holding tight onto the inhaul line. Attached to a pelican hook on both ships was the highline which supported the bosun's chair itself. As the chair cleared the railing it immediately dropped several feet toward the water, then rebounded like a whipsaw, as the transfer crews of both ships quickly pulled firmly on their lines. Kobayashi felt the spray hitting his hands and face. A large wave crashed against the side of the *Gatling* and sprayed his flight suit pants, soaking them. He quickly appreciated the potential need of the Kapok flotation vest and silently thanked CPO Wheeler.

The *Yorktown* and *Gatling* maintained their parallel course, separated by about thirty yards. Because of the importance of Kobayashi the two ships maintained a reduced speed of twelve knots. The speed reduction was a compromise. A slower speed would make them a tempting target for any submarines Japan might still have at sea. Anything over twelve knots might break one of the lines, putting Kobayashi at risk of falling into the ocean.

With each pull Ken bounced and slowly increased distance from the water's surface, going "uphill," while approaching the hangar deck of the immense carrier.

Because he was facing the rear of the ships Kobayashi did not see the periscope just rising above the surface behind him.

Neither did the lookouts of the destroyer screen, forward and aside the *Yorktown*.

10

"Chûsa! Sonar reports range of Targets Two through Five is now less than twelve kilometers, still bearing green eight zero to red seven five degrees!" Lieutenant Commander Mori wished he could read his captain's mind.

"Helm! Maintain speed and course! Mori Shôsa! Implement ultra quiet!"

Mori relayed Commander Iwata's order to the entire crew. Everywhere in the boat each crewmember weighed his movements.

Iwata and Mori watched the clock, both calculating the closing speed. The *I-402*'s speed was still three knots. The speed of the destroyer screen was 15 knots but since they still zigzagged the effective speed was 12 knots. Their combined closing speed was 15 knots. If speed and course were maintained they would close those twelve kilometers in about 25 minutes.

"Yamada Nitô heisô! Raise Number Two periscope!"

"*Ha!*" said Petty Officer, Second Class, Yamada Ichirô as he pulled the Number Two periscope lever.

Commander Iwata lowered and gripped the brass periscope handles and quickly swept the horizon 360°. Only at 00° did he see what he knew he would: several plumes of smoke from the targets. The choppy waters still obscured his view but... There! A break in the waves! That most prized of targets! A carrier!

He stood back. "Lower periscope!" He looked at Mori, who, nodding, confirmed Iwata was under ten seconds. Japanese doctrine required that on approach to targets the periscope not be above water more than ten seconds. Iwata watched the clock for two minutes. "Raise periscope!" He fanned 90° red and green. There! The destroyer screen... He watched briefly as they zigzagged. Another wave hit his lens. "Lower periscope!" Mori nodded again. Iwata waited over a minute.

"Raise periscope!" He elevated the lens up 45° and swept 360°, searching for enemy planes. This time he saw them. They were flying CAP. He estimated their altitude at about five kilometers and perhaps four kilometers distance but he could not be exact. He knew that at that altitude and distance and with the conditions of the sea his boat was almost invisible to the planes. He also knew they were looking for Japanese planes or surface ships and that the destroyers were looking for Japanese submarines. "Yamada Nitô heisô! Lower Number Two periscope!" Iwata stepped back and faced his XO.

"Mori! Target Number One is a carrier. Targets Two through Five are destroyers. Planes flying Air Patrol!" Mori observed his captain and waited, saying nothing. There was nothing else to do. The crew was at action station, torpedo tubes one through six were loaded and their destructive payload ready to be launched. Midshipman Okada and Ensign Oda waited for orders to launch the *kaiten*. Everyone carried out his tasks and waited. Iwata went to the targeting table and played with a pencil. He occasionally looked at his crew. He caught some looking at him. No one spoke. The silence was alien to him. The engines' vibrations, usually unnoticed, were now palpable.

Mori walked over to the other side of the targeting table. Never before, he thought, had Iwata so recklessly risked his boat. And the lives of his crew. Everyone on board knew the danger of one American destroyer. They knew the Americans were relentless when they located a Japanese sub. He wondered what his captain was thinking.

Six minutes passed. Now, little more than eight kilometers separated *I-402* from Targets Two through Five.

Iwata looked at Mori.

"Right now I wish I had an American cigarette. Damn this war! It has taken away one of the pleasures in my life!"

Mori, eyes wide, stared at his captain. "Chûsa?"

Iwata looked at Mori. First Iwata then Mori started to laugh, the absurdity striking them. The crewmen in the conning tower, not knowing the reason for the laughter, nevertheless started laughing as tension drained from their bodies.

Iwata looked at the clock. Two more minutes passed. He looked at Mori. Mori nodded. "Sonar! Range and bearing on Targets Two through Five!"

"Shôsa! Range on Targets Three and Four is seven kilometers! Targets Two and Five are further out!"

"Yamada Nitô heisô! Raise Number Two periscope!"

As Yamada turned to raise Number Two periscope he knocked a glass ashtray off the targeting table. It shattered on the deck. The crew in the conning tower froze, horror etched on their faces, knowing that sound traveled through water. Any sound, this close to an enemy ship, could give away their position.

Iwata sprang to Yamada, their faces inches apart. "*Bakayarô!*" he whispered fiercely. "I ordered absolute silence! We are too close to the enemy to have any noise give away our position!"

"Sorry, sir!"

"No rations except water for the next two days!"

"*Ha!* Thank you, sir!" Yamada bowed quickly then raised Number Two periscope.

Iwata stepped to the periscope and lowered the handles. He hastily swept the horizon 360°. He was tense and immediately regretted reprimanding Yamada. He made a mental note to reduce the punishment to one day. Satisfied no other ships were within view he focused the periscope on the bearing of the targets. At bearing 00°, seven kilometers distance, the American destroyer screen continued to bear down on the *I-402*. However, their actions did not indicate that they had located his sub. Perhaps the Germans were right about the anti-sonar coating, Iwata thought. "Yamada Nitô heisô! Lower Number Two periscope."

Time crawled. With the ashtray striking the deck tension had returned. No one spoke. Iwata watched the clock. Two minutes later and six kilometers from the destroyer screen Iwata broke the silence.

"Yamada Nitô heisô! Raise Number One periscope!"

Carefully, Yamada reached for the Number One periscope lever, the attack periscope. As it rose Mori watched it. Iwata's telephone talker, who would relay the orders to launch torpedoes, looked first at Mori then Iwata. It was an exercise they had performed hundreds of times. Now it was different. There were American destroyers scant minutes away.

Iwata peered through the Zeiss lenses of Number One periscope, sweeping green 80° to red 75° then back to boat's head. He caught his breath and gripped the handles tightly. Mori saw Iwata's fingers whiten as he adjusted the focus.

"Mori! That bearing! Another destroyer! Running parallel to the carrier! Designate it Target Number Six!"

Iwata, ignoring the immediate threat of the destroyer screen, increased magnification to take a closer look at the destroyers. He wished he could see the destroyers' sterns, where depth charge crews operated. Then he took a closer look at the newly-discovered destroyer, noting that its bow was aft of the carrier's. He caught a glimpse of a transfer under way although he did not see a bosun's chair, just a resupply container.

He turned to the carrier, a tempting target. None of the targets, he noted, gave any indication they had located his sub.

"Mori Shôsa! They still have not located us! Yamada Nitô heisô! Lower Number One periscope! Mori! Make your depth twenty meters!"

Mori relayed the order then went to a bookshelf and picked up the *SHIPS IDENTIFICATION* book and opened it to the pages displaying known American warships. Iwata shook his head. He had seen only the carrier's bow and not her profile. Mori understood and returned the book.

The *I-402* was less than six kilometers from the destroyer screen, 12 minutes apart. It was possibly too late to turn away. If a course change was ordered the *I-402*'s entire hull would be exposed to the enemy's sonar.

Mori knew exactly what his captain intended. By maintaining what was in effect a collision course the *I-402* exposed only the bow aspect to the destroyer screen. This limited the area available to reflect the destroyer's active sonar and cloaked the *I-402*'s propulsion and propeller noises behind its stern.

Some crewmembers turned briefly to look at their captain. Tension had returned to the conning tower. Sweat was rolling down their chests and backs, collecting on their *fundoshi*, their loincloths. The air in the control room, though recently refreshed when the sub had surfaced, was now suffused with the scent of excitement coupled with fear. The captain had never approached an enemy ship so closely. Eight months ago they had closed to within eight kilometers of an American cargo ship before firing torpedoes. Now he was approaching the target ships, only a bit more than five kilometers distance, ten minutes closing at 15 knots.

"Chûsa! Orders?"

Iwata was weighing his options. "Mori Shôsa! Come to periscope depth! Yamada Nitô heisô! Raise Number One periscope!"

With Number One periscope raised Iwata carefully studied the destroyer screen, then the carrier and the new destroyer beside it. Then his vision was again obscured by waves but he had seen enough. "Yamada Nitô heisô! Lower Number One periscope! Mori Shôsa! Make your depth sixty meters! Watanabe Tai-i! Monitor the bathythermograph for thermoclines! Koyama Heichô! Range on Contacts Two through Five!"

"Chûsa! Range is now four kilometers!"

He went to the targeting table and gestured for Mori to join him. "Mori-*san*, we're now about eight minutes from the targets. It is too late to come about. But there is enough space between the lead destroyers for us to pass below and between them. We have practiced this maneuver many times with our own destroyers. If the Germans were right about their coating then we will be safe. If not... Besides, I was thinking of a maneuver that would position our torpedo tubes where we would need them."

"Chûsa? What maneuver?"

Iwata stared at his XO. "I was thinking that we could turn at rest, what the American Navy calls 'walking the stern.'"

"Chûsa! A boat this size? It has never been done! We could become unstable! We would be safer if we just dove to maximum depth and hid under a thermocline!"

"Mori-*san*, I want a closer look at the transfer. Who knows, it might not be supplies; it might be Halsey Taishô." Iwata smiled grimly. Mori knew what Iwata was thinking.

On April 14, 1943, the U.S. Navy's Pacific Fleet Radio Unit intercepted and decoded a Japanese naval message detailing an inspection by Admiral Yamamoto Isoroku to the Japanese base on Bougainville. The decoded message went to Admiral Chester W. Nimitz, Commander-in-Chief of the Pacific Fleet, who in turn forwarded it to Washington. The United States was given an opportunity to, in one stroke, eliminate Japan's most brilliant naval strategist and strike a major blow against Imperial Japan.

However, that meant assassinating a senior military commander, something the United States had not yet done during the war. Even senior ranking American military commanders felt that to give the order to assassinate an enemy commander exceeded their authority. Eventually Admiral Nimitz issued the authorization, with good reason. More than once Nimitz had told his staff that Yamamoto was the greatest danger the American Navy faced. Besides, Yamamoto, Commander-in-Chief of Japan's naval forces, was in overall command of the Japanese attack on Pearl Harbor. Admiral Nimitz turned over planning of the attack to Admiral Halsey, who had operational command of the Central Solomons area.

On April 18, 1943, exactly one year after Doolittle's bombing of Tôkyô, 18 American P-38s from the 13th Army Air Force flew 500 nautical miles from Henderson Field on Guadalcanal to Bougainville, intercepted Yamamoto's flight and shot down his plane, killing him. The P-38s then returned to Henderson Field, a total of 1,000 miles. Japan never recovered from the loss of their ablest naval commander.

Many Japanese naval commanders fantasized avenging Yamamoto's death by striking an equal blow at the Americans. Japan regarded Halsey Taishô as America's ablest naval commander. It was a dream which Mori Shôsa dismissed.

"Mori-*san*, if we pass between the destroyer screen and under the carrier, at this bearing we are vulnerable to aft attack. We do not have aft torpedo tubes. If we turn at rest after passing the destroyer screen we protect ourselves from detection and can launch torpedoes if necessary."

"Chûsa! The boat is too large! There is the risk of broaching or losing buoyancy!"

"I agree. Therefore, as we approach the destroyer screen, we stay at sixty meters, maintain course and ultra quiet, slow to two knots, and rely upon our German friends' hull coating."

Mori Shôsa noted Iwata's pointed sarcasm at his last comment. In fact, the Japan-German Axis was anything but friendly. The Japanese regarded the Germans as arrogant.

Mori momentarily weighed his captain's strategy, nodded once then issued the orders. The *I-402* responded. Additional tons of water entered the negative tank forward of the boat's center of buoyancy while two powerful screws exerted downward pressure on the boat. Next, Mori ordered negative tank blown to the mark—the normal submerged water level in the tank—and then vented in case it would need to be flooded again. Men opened their mouths to equalize pressure in their ears and, those who could, watched the depth gauge as the needle inched toward the 60 meters mark.

"Chûsa! Thermocline at fifty meters!" reported Watanabe Tai-i as they descended.

In less than two minutes the *I-402* leveled off at 60 meters.

Iwata felt the anxiety, but was proud to note every crewman was efficiently performing his task. He watched Watanabe make notes from the bathythermograph, collecting data on thermoclines. He knew Koyama was listening closely for any sonar pings hitting the hull. He felt the heat and imagined how much hotter it was in the engine room, the men rubbing oily sweat from their faces and hands. He wondered how Oda and Okada were preparing themselves for their possible deaths in the *kaiten*.

The passage of time became interminable. Everyone was concerned with the closing distance to the American destroyer screen. The *I-402* no longer had the time or speed for maneuvering. Their safety lay in keeping the bow aspect towards the destroyers, exposing as little of the hull surface to reflect active sonar pings.

A bead of sweat fell off Iwata's chin and landed on the targeting table. He watched it, wondering if his blood would look the same when striking the deck.

"Sonar! Report!"

Koyama knew what his captain needed, factual brevity. "Chûsa! Range to Targets Two through Five now three kilometers. No changes in speed or bearing or zigzagging. Maintaining long range pinging." Six minutes apart.

"Sonar! Make all future sonar reports relative to the two lead targets!"

"*Ha!*"

As long as the Americans continued using long-range sonar they were still searching for something they had not yet located. Once they went to short range it meant they had located a target and were acquiring an exact fix on its location.

Iwata was convinced the Americans had not located his boat. *Let me make it as difficult as possible*, he thought. *We will stay below the thermocline.* However, this was a weakness in Iwata's strategy and he knew it. Thermoclines could remain stable for kilometers, offering excellent coverage. They were also sometimes weather dependent; a calm sea helped to maintain the stability of a thermocline. Iwata knew they were at the tail end of a typhoon. At any moment the thermocline could disappear or develop a large opening, exposing the *I-402* to American sonar. Besides the skill of Iwata their lives depended on untested German technology.

The *I-402* continued closing toward the destroyer screen. Iwata turned to his telephone talker.

"Sonar! Range!"

"Chûsa! Range to lead targets is two kilometers!" The *I-402* and the two lead screen destroyers, closing at 15 knots, were now four minutes apart.

Iwata wished he could get a last look at the lead destroyers, one final check of their status. Now, due to their depth, Koyama Heichô was his eyes as well as ears. The safety of the crew and boat depended on a 17-year-old boy.

Mori Shôsa looked around the control room. He too could feel the tension and worried about the crew. He wondered if anyone would crack as they closed with the targets. He had seen it before, while a lieutenant on another boat. That captain was not like Iwata. He had treated his crew harshly; personal honor was his sole goal. The more enemy boats he sank the greater his chance of promotion. He took chances, as did Iwata, but was reckless. On Mori's last mission with that captain a year ago, off the Philippines, an American destroyer had damaged the boat with depth charges. It had been a relentless 35-hour game of hide-and-seek. For five hours the American captain ignored the usual attempts at feigned destruction: discharged oil and flotsam. Every five minutes the Americans launched depth charges, one of them damaging the sail and later another explosion flooding the forward torpedo room. Finally, they lay quiet on the bottom for 30 hours. After ten hours one of the men cracked under the pressure. Others subdued him but the rest of the crew was shaken. Seven hours later another man, in the aft torpedo room, simply bent over and started to wail. He too was subdued but several more crewmembers were becoming agitated. But the captain could do nothing except keep his boat on the bottom. Then, unexpectedly, it stopped. Either the Americans felt they had sunk the sub or broke off the hunt. When they returned to Japan Mori requested a transfer and it was granted. His next assignment was the *I-402*, at the request of Iwata.

"Sonar! Range!"

"Chûsa! Range to lead targets is one kilometer! They are maintaining long range pinging." Two minutes apart.

Everyone in the control room waited to hear from Koyama. Both Iwata and Mori were painfully conscious of the fact that the German coating had never been tested under combat conditions.

Neither was certain if it was the hull coating, the thermocline, or the distance of three and one-half kilometers between the two lead destroyers that shielded them from detection. One short sonar ping and they were probably dead. They might escape from one destroyer but two, or worse, four, sealed their fate.

"Sonar! Range!"

"Chûsa! Range to lead targets is five hundred meters! Maintaining long range pinging! One minute before we pass through the screen!" Iwata steeled himself for the short ping.

"Sonar! Range!"

"Chûsa! Range to lead targets is two five zero meters! Maintaining long range pinging! Forty-five seconds to lead targets."

"Sonar! Call out range every fifty meters!"

"Chûsa! Range two zero zero meters!" Thirty seconds.

"Chûsa! Range one five zero meters!" Twenty seconds.

"Chûsa! Range one zero zero meters!" Ten seconds.

"Chûsa! Range fifty meters!" Five seconds.

"Mori Shôsa! Make your depth thirty meters!"

"Chûsa?"

"Carry out my orders, Shôsa!"

"*Ha!* Helm! Make depth thirty meters!"

Just as the *I-402*'s bow went between the bows of the leading destroyers the sub started to ascend. When the *I-402* reached 30 meters depth she was 50 meters aft of the lead destroyers.

Now! thought Iwata. "Helm! Green full rudder! Red ahead standard! Green back two thirds!"

Gradually, the giant submarine shuddered as it began pivoting, to turn at rest.

Abruptly, with buoyancy compromised, the bow started to rise. Mori knew this could happen; he had warned his captain.

Now Iwata was in a box. Forward momentum had come to a stop but the stern was still pivoting. If he did not regain control the *I-402* might surface, surrounded by the enemy. Yet he could not emergency flood the negative tank; the noise, so close to the enemy, might alert them. And he could not stop the turning of the boat; that would aggravate the situation. Iwata had one tactic open to him.

"Watanabe Tai-i! Order all nonessential personnel forward to the torpedo room!"

Watanabe, trusting his captain, relayed the order immediately. Over 60 men, almost half the crew, raced forward, jamming in the forward torpedo room. Every possible space was occupied. Men climbed on torpedoes, crawled into spaces at the overheads and into gaps on the deck, under torpedoes and shelving and, where possible, on top of one another. The majority, however, could not fit and crowded together immediately outside the compartment. Still they pressed inward, as if willing that more space would open up. Those being squeezed did not complain but instead exhaled, trying to make themselves thinner. With the weight redistributed the *I-402* slowly started to level off. Iwata looked at Mori and grinned; Mori brushed the sweat off his upper lip.

At 30 meters depth the *I-402* continued to pivot while remaining level. Strangely, Iwata was calm. He should have been worried that as his boat turned his hull would be exposed to enemy sonar, from the forward destroyers or the carrier. But he wasn't concerned; he trusted in the forward destroyers' baffles. A destroyer's sonar search is ineffective 30° on either side of the stern, for a total of 60°. The *I-402* was safely hidden in the baffles, the noise of the two lead destroyer's engines and the wake in the water created by their screws. The *I-402* would be hidden from the other ships' sonar for the same reason.

He leaned against the targeting table, crossed one leg behind the other, lit a cigarette and looked at the gyrocompass which gave him his true heading and the bubble. There was nothing else to do except watch these two indicators and wait for Koyama's warning of discovery.

While keeping watch on the stable bubble Iwata ordered the men outside the torpedo room to return to their stations in groups of five. Cautiously, more men inside the forward room were also ordered to return. Iwata watched the gyrocompass and the bubble. He looked at the clock.

"Sonar! Range on the lead destroyers!"

"Chûsa! Range is two kilometers! Bearing zero zero zero degrees relative!"

"Mori Shôsa! Red full rudder! Red back two thirds! Green ahead two thirds!" Iwata smoked his cigarette as he watched the gyrocompass.

Six minutes had passed. The *I-402* had turned 180°, its bow pointed in the same direction as Target Number One, the carrier.

"Mori Shôsa! All stop!" The boat's engines stopped. Iwata felt the *I-402* struggling to obey his will. He waited several seconds. "Mori Shôsa! *Now!* All-ahead full!"

Like a lumbering giant still groggy from sleep the *I-402* started to make its way forward, struggling to reach 6.5 knots.

"Sonar! Range on Target Number One!"

"Chûsa! Range is one point five kilometers! Bearing green astern! Speed twelve knots!"

Now the *I-402* and the destroyer screen around the carrier were on the same heading. And Target Number One, the carrier, was four minutes behind the *I-402*, steaming at 12 knots, and the *I-402* had just started to move forward.

"Chûsa! Orders?" asked Mori.

"We wait, Mori-*san*. Target Number One will overtake us in about four minutes."

"Chûsa! This will be quite close."

"Yes, Mori-*san*. Do you know what the Americans call it?" Mori shook his head.

"They call it 'a close shave.' I like that." Iwata closed his eyes and rubbed his face. "Yes, Mori-*san*, it is a close shave."

Both men watched the clock. One minute passed.

"Sonar! Range on Target One!"

"Chûsa! Range is one kilometer!"

Mori Shôsa was baffled. In all his training he had never heard of anyone putting his boat in this position. He admitted to himself that for the first time he had doubted his captain. But that was all he could do, simply doubt. And admire his daring.

"Sonar! Range on Target One!"

"Chûsa! Range is point seven five kilometer!"

Iwata saw Mori's expression. "Mori-*san*, are you worried?"

"Chûsa! Yes! I am your Number One but you do not share your thoughts with me. Yes, I am worried. We cannot forget our mission. I fear you have jeopardized it."

"I appreciate your candor, Mori Shôsa. Now watch and learn! Sonar! Range on Target One!"

"Chûsa! Range is point three five kilometer!"

The *I-402* was 350 meters from the bow of the carrier. In the conning tower and control room men strained to look at Koyama, waiting for the dreadful news that they were located and trapped by a force they could not escape from.

300 meters. No one spoke.

200 meters. Iwata and Mori looked at each other.

100 meters. The clock's second hand moved like a snail.

50 meters. The helmsman gripped his steering mechanism tighter, wishing he were somewhere else. He was not a coward; he was, like everyone else around him, simply scared.

25 meters. The crew in the engine room, closest to the carrier, felt turbulence as the gap closed. The bow of the carrier was creating large swells as she cleaved through the water.

Zero meters. The *I-402* was below and to the left of the carrier's bow and would pass between the carrier and the destroyer alongside her. Everyone in the conning tower stopped working.

Iwata was exhilarated, never before so close to the enemy.

"Sonar! Call off bearings every five seconds to the first target's screws!"

The telephone talker relayed the orders. He heard "*Ha!*" and nodded to Iwata.

For Koyama geometry, in relation to the *I-402* and the carrier, the first target, and the destroyer came into play. He drew an imaginary line from the stern of the *I-402* to the carrier's screws. Every five seconds Koyama measured the angle of the line from the *I-402* to the carrier's screws. As the stern approached the carrier's screws the more obtuse the angle became.

"Chûsa! Bearing...six degrees... Eight degrees... Fourteen degrees... Twenty degrees... Thirty-one degrees!" They passed the destroyer's screws. Seconds passed. "Chûsa! Bearing changing fast!"

A terrible, deafening roaring thundered throughout the submarine. Kathrum! Kathrum! Kathrum! Kathrum! Kathrum! Kathrum!

The screws of the carrier were passing over the *I-402*.

While instinctively looking up, the crew in the engine room, never having heard it before, literally recoiled as if trying to duck below it. In the torpedo room some looked to the torpedoes, hoping they would not fall from their racks.

The noise was deep, incessant and deafening, penetrating the sub's hull, pounding into the very bones of the crew. Throughout the boat some men cringed and covered their ears. One, in the control room, grimaced and moaned loudly.

The diving officer looked at his captain and Iwata read the question in his eyes: Could the giant propellers come so close as to shred the *I-402* to pieces?

Iwata quickly turned to observe the rest of his crew and saw some men had tightened their buttocks, squeezing their anuses. *Puckering*, he thought. No one wanted to mess in his *fundoshi*.

Iwata's telephone talker sprang to life. "Chûsa! Sonar reports bearing ninety degrees!"

Iwata smiled and nodded to Mori. Koyama's latest bearing told him the screws of the carrier were just passing the *I-402*.

"Mori Shôsa! Come to periscope depth!"

To the crew it had seemed an eternity. Mori nodded but said nothing, his breathing shallow.

The vibrations and noise slowly receded. Puckering relaxed. Crewmen again looked solely to their stations. Iwata made a final cursory survey. No brown or yellow stains. He smiled.

"Yamada Nitô heisô! Raise Number One periscope!"

The *I-402* rose to periscope depth 50 meters astern the carrier. Iwata lowered the levers of the Number One periscope and, before looking through the lenses, immediately rotated it to 00°, the bow of the *I-402*. It was Iwata's first mistake and it would cost lives.

Caught in the cavitations of the *Yorktown*, the seas were rough. But the *I-402*, displacing over 6,665 metric tons, was not easily thrown about.

Water splashed against the periscope lens. Iwata, patient, took a few seconds to look at both ships. Then, falling further behind the *Yorktown*'s cavitations, he saw what he expected.

"Interesting... Mori Shôsa! They are transferring someone from one ship to the other! Mori Shôsa! All-ahead flank! I want to stay with this..."

The *I-402* vibrated heavily as the motors ramped up to the full submerged speed of 6.5 knots. The American ships were still traveling at 12 knots. Mori knew, however, the *I-402*'s speed would soon be reduced to three knots due to the drain on the batteries powering the engines. He could keep the transfer in periscope range for only a brief period.

A few crewmen in the control room again looked at Mori, dread returning. Their XO was approachable, the direct conduit between crew and captain. Mori felt the fear within the confines of the cramped and oppressively hot control room. Yet he had to admire the daring of his captain. So long as they were directly aft of the carrier they were safe. The carrier's roiling screws created too much disturbance for the carrier's sonar operator to filter out. Again, geometry came into play. As long as Iwata kept the *I-402* within 30° of either side of the carrier's outer screws they were safely masked astern of the targets.

Mori was still concerned with Commander Iwata's decisions. At any moment, the two outer destroyers that were screening the carrier might locate them. He knew American destroyers were fast and deadly. Many of Japan's submarines lay at the bottom of the ocean because of them.

Iwata gripped the brass periscope levers and adjusted to maximum magnification. Then everything within the *I-402* changed forever.

All that Iwata had held true in his world collapsed. He slowly pulled away from the periscope, numb, confused. Mori was puzzled. He had never seen the captain show his feeling so visibly. Iwata's face had sagged and lost color. His eyes, unfocused, saw nothing. His body was trembling, his hands opening and closing.

His voice was hoarse, hesitant. "Mori... Come... Look... Look..."

Mori Shôsa vaulted to the Number One periscope and grabbed the levers. It took him just a second to focus on what Iwata had seen. In the center of the cross hairs of the lens he saw the face of an Imperial Japanese Army officer sitting in a transfer chair, his officer's cap pulled on tightly. He held his *katana*! The *tsuka*, the leather-wrapped hilt, bore the distinctive design of an ancient sword.

Mori Shôsa could not determine the rank on his jacket, hidden by the Japanese Army flight suit. He was being pulled toward the carrier. His hands were unbound. *Impossible!* He was smiling! *There!* He gave a salute to the Americans on the destroyer! His face showed no fear! He was *not* a prisoner!

"Chûsa! *Impossible!* This cannot be! He is a Japanese officer! He is not bound! He holds his *katana*! We must sink the carrier! Even if the destroyers sink us, we must kill this Badoglio!"

11

Seaman First Class Pat Murphy was bored. He was the port bridge lookout on the USS *Ingersoll*. He had awoken two hours earlier, famished and eager for breakfast, when he was ordered instead to report immediately to the bridge. He was given a pair of binoculars and told to watch the waters aft of the *Yorktown* and *Gatling*. His eyes hurt; the sun had finally broken through the clouds and reflected off the water.

The *Ingersoll* was at General Quarters, Dawn Alert. She was designated "lifeguard," trailing 1,500 yards behind the *Yorktown* and *Gatling*, both at Condition Three, a lower level of alert.

Murphy knew should the VIP, whoever he was, fall into the drink, the *Ingersoll* was to race forward, pull the poor slob out of the Pacific, dry him off and then convince him he should get back into a bosun's chair and risk it again.

"Officers," Pat Murphy muttered. Still, he took his job seriously and swept the waters off the port bow. He started to yawn but his jaw froze while open.

"Holy shit," he muttered. "They ain't supposed to be no sub behind them or in front of us."

He turned and faced the open doorway of the bridge, ignoring the bridge phone. "Mister Maher! Periscope in *Yorktown*'s wake!"

The OOD, Officer of the Deck, Ensign Tom Maher, was young but levelheaded and not prone to hasty judgments. He was new to the *Ingersoll* and being OOD was an important assignment. With him was Commander Francis Blouin, captain of the *Ingersoll*. On a mission of this importance it was standard practice for the skipper to be on the bridge as well. Blouin nodded to Maher.

Maher picked up the phone and buzzed the port wing bridge lookout. When Murphy picked up the phone Maher asked, "Murphy, you're sure it's not a swab handle?"

It was a fair question and Murphy knew it. Sometimes mops were lost or tossed overboard. A wooden mop handle would float and the weight of the wet mop would keep the handle upright. Swab handles had been mistaken for a periscope hundreds of times.

"Don't think so, sir. This one's got a feather."

"Damn," growled Maher, slamming down the phone. "Captain, Murphy says it's got a feather."

"Check it out Tom." Maher ran to Murphy's position, looked through his binoculars and muttered, "Good work, Murphy. Son of a bitch! It does have a wake. Son of a bitch!" Ensign Maher ran back to the bridge. "Captain, it's a feather."

Blouin picked up the phone. He knew that if the sub took a stern shot at the *Yorktown* a torpedo could cripple one of the carrier's screws or rudder, allowing the sub to pick her off at her leisure. "Sonar, bridge! This is the captain. We got a pigboat dead ahead. Ping that son of a bitch! Let them know we spotted her!" Then he picked up the TBS—Talk Between Ships—radio and contacted the *Yorktown*.

"Flatiron, this is Hailstone. Periscope in your wake. Repeat, periscope in your wake. Sonar is pinging her! Over."

The *Yorktown*'s bridge radio speaker crackled with Blouin's calm voice. The *Yorktown*'s OOD picked up the phone. "Acknowledged, Hailstone." The OOD looked at the captain for orders.

Captain W. Frederick Boone, skipper of the *Yorktown* since April 1945, was about to drink his second cup of coffee when the bridge radio had squawked. He had been leaning out the window of the lighthouse, in the superstructure, following every step of the highline transfer closely. With his seniority he was designated OTC, Officer in Tactical Command, for the transfer.

He quickly stuck his head out the window again to gauge the progress of the transfer. He guessed in another minute it would be completed. But now his ship might be in immediate danger. He could order the *Yorktown* hard to port, ripping the transfer lines apart and smashing the bosun's chair, and Lieutenant Kobayashi, against the carrier's hull. Or he could wait to complete the transfer, putting his ship and crew at risk for one man.

Boone pulled his head back in. He removed his glasses and rubbed his eyes. "Order *Ingersoll* to engage and sink the bastard!"

The OOD nodded. "Hailstone, this is Flatiron. Your orders are to engage and sink the contact. Over."

12

Koyama was aware of the activities around him, both in the submarine and on the surface. Since the carrier overtook the *I-402* he had been carefully shifting his passive sonar bearing indicator red and green rather than a full 360°. It was a mistake. He had become concerned about the destroyers protecting the two targets on either flank. They had stopped zigzagging and had altered course, heading in towards Target Number One, the carrier.

Unexpectedly, a new sound burst through his earphones. *Impossible! Multiple short range sonar pings! Behind us!*

"Chûsa! New contact! Bearing, one eight zero degrees. Range, over one kilometer and closing rapidly! I believe they have detected us!"

13

When the *Ingersoll* radioed the *Yorktown* on the TBS she also automatically radioed the *Gatling*. *Gatling*'s captain did two things. First, he looked at his XO, Tony Casella, and said one word: "Go!" Casella bolted. Next, *Gatling*'s skipper picked up the TBS radio mike.

"Flatiron, Fireside. What are your orders? Over."

"Fireside, Flatiron. Maintain present speed and heading. When the transfer is complete conduct an emergency break-away then form an aft screen at one thousand yards and follow my movements. Over."

"Wilco. Out."

When Casella arrived at the aft port transfer station on the main deck he quickly assessed the progress then joined in and grabbed the end of the delivery inhaul line.

"*Ingersoll* just reported a sub astern," he yelled to no one in particular. "*Yorktown*'s going to get him moving!"

In front of Casella, maintaining tension on the delivery inhaul line for all he was worth, was CPO Wheeler, who earlier had wished Ken luck. His massive arms were already straining and the thick black hair on his forearms lay flat against his skin, weighted down with sweat and spray from the ocean. If they let loose of the delivery inhaul line Ken might fall into the water. Their counterparts on the *Yorktown* had been informed and were already feverishly pulling the outhaul line. Casella looked at the bosun's chair and gauged its distance from the *Yorktown.*

"Wheeler! Grab the axe!"

Wheeler spun his head around, uncertainty on his face, not wanting to release his grip on the inhaul line.

"Now," yelled Casella. "Just in case the pelican hook jams, damn it! *Now!*"

In the bosun's chair Ken felt the abrupt increase in movement and, in blissful ignorance, was grateful that the junket would end a bit sooner. He was grateful he had his cap on; the sun was becoming intense. Besides watching the transfer crews on each ship he occasionally glanced at the *Ingersoll.* He had surmised her purpose and wondered how long it would take her to get to him should he fall into the water and if the metal bosun's chair would pull him under before he could release the safety harness.

He looked at the carrier again, feeling ever more insignificant as he neared her, and estimated he was now less than 30 feet away. He turned to the *Gatling* and now had to look down. He saw Tony Casella lending a hand on the highline. Ken smiled and tossed a parting salute to him. Turning back to the *Yorktown,* he gauged the distance. He looked back to Casella and his eyes went wide. Standing at the railing was the sailor who earlier had wished him luck, holding a menacing red-tipped axe above his head, while gravely looking at the delivery highline attached to the pelican hook.

Without warning, Ken's ears were lashed by a piercing clamor rushing toward him. Reeling and confused, he turned and saw the *Ingersoll* sailing fast toward him, blaring WHOOOP WHOOOOOP WHOOOOOOOOOP, WHOOOP WHOOOOOP WHOOOOOOOOOP. He looked toward the carrier's hangar deck and saw a pair of anxious eyes looking at him, less than ten feet away.

He looked to his right again, wishing Casella could help him understand. He saw but did not hear Casella's barked orders. Transfixed, he saw the vicious axe in Wheeler's hands arc down and sever the delivery highline, the pelican hook ignored. The highline anchored to the *Gatling* caught the rush of air and fluttered toward him, flaccid in the wind. Ken started to plummet down, toward the waters.

As he lowered his eyes to the water he saw the sun reflect off a moving pole in the water.

14

Iwata's eyes shot wide open. Fairly flying, he grabbed the levers of Number One periscope and quickly spun it to 180° relative, to stern. In his lens he saw the nightmare of every sub commander: a destroyer bearing down on him, thick, black smoke erupting from her stacks. Without even thinking, Iwata knew that more fuel was rapidly flowing into the destroyer's engines, her speed increasing. He watched the bow waves increase in size and curling back, beating against the destroyer's hull. He estimated the destroyer was making over twenty knots and was headed right toward his stern. It was going to ram his boat.

"Yamada! Down scope! Mori! It's a destroyer! Red full rudder! All-ahead full! Flood negative! Emergency deep! Make depth eighty meters! Ten degrees down bubble! Secure for depth charge!" *This destroyer captain, as the Americans say, has a bone in his teeth!* he told himself.

15

On the *Yorktown*, the last few seconds of the transfer were frenzied; the bosun's chair lurched toward the hangar deck with each galvanized haul of the *Yorktown*'s transfer crew. Then the line went slack. The carrier's transfer crew knew *Gatling*'s highline was detached. With a furious pull on their outhaul line the bosun's chair rammed against the edge of the hangar deck, then jumped up. Another fierce pull and the base of the bosun's chair rammed against the hangar deck's edge, vaulted up again and at last swung onto the hangar deck with a bone-jarring thud.

A sailor on the *Yorktown* reached to unlatch the safety harness but jumped back when he saw Ken's uniform and face. An officer, embarrassed at the unprofessional behavior of one of his sailors, roughly brushed past him, unlatched the safety harness and extended his hand as Ken stepped out and stood.

Just then the *Yorktown* tilted as she turned hard to port, breaking away from the *Gatling*. Ken tried to adjust just as the carrier's speed increased, causing him to stagger. The officer grabbed Ken's arm.

"Welcome aboard the *Yorktown*, Lieutenant Kobayashi. I'm Lieutenant Bill Patterson. When you get out of the flight suit we'll get you some hot java." He turned to the confused sailor and said, "Sailor, report to your DO. Tell him I've put you on report."

"One moment, sailor." Kobayashi sighed. He handed his *katana* to Lieutenant Patterson then removed his officer's cap and wiped the droplets off the bill. He removed the Kapok flotation vest and the flight suit and handed them to the confused sailor who, without thinking, took them. The sailor's eyes widened with confusion when he saw Ken's Imperial Japanese Army uniform and holstered sidearm.

Ken Kobayashi was tired of people reacting with surprise or hostility whenever they saw him but this time he understood and did not want the sailor in trouble. He knew the procedure. After the sailor reported to his Division Officer, the DO would go to the XO, ask about the sailor's infraction, then carry out the XO's punishment.

"Sir, a word?" As they stepped away from the transfer station Ken put on his cap. Although both had the rank of lieutenant, the Navy's rank of lieutenant was equal to an Army captain. Ken gestured and Patterson returned the sword.

"Lieutenant Patterson, here's the lowdown. I'm here on orders of General MacArthur and Admiral Halsey. But once I leave this ship I was never here. Both of us know that's bullshit but that's the way clandestine operations work. I think you know that. If you punish this man you'll have to include your reason for punishing him. What explanation will you use? That he behaved unprofessionally when caught off guard by the unexpected appearance of a Japanese officer, with sword and sidearm, on an American warship? My guess is your captain didn't take all his officers into his confidence. This sailor didn't know what to expect. If I were in his shoes I'd probably have reacted the same way. I'm sure Admiral Halsey would see it that way. And can you have my suit dried?"

Patterson smiled. "You play poker, Lieutenant? Point taken." They returned to the transfer station. "Sailor, take that flight suit to the laundry and have it dried. Then return to your station. Dismissed."

Before the sailor could carry out the orders Ken stopped him. "Sailor, there's a flight helmet and pair of goggles in the right pants pocket. Make sure they're removed before the suit is dried. Okay?"

"Aye aye, sir," he replied and, though confused, nodded once to Kobayashi as he walked past him. Patterson, grinning, watched the bewildered sailor head for the laundry, increasing his pace as he withdrew.

"Sir, just before I came aboard I saw what I think was a periscope in the water and that destroyer behind us coming on fast. By any chance is the sub one of ours?"

"Afraid not, Lieutenant. It's a Jap sub."

"What happens next?"

"To the sub? That destroyer tailing us has been ordered to sink her."

"What about the *Gatling*?"

"She stays with us, screening our stern, taking a position between the sub and us. We have other destroyers but they'll stay forward of us rather than go after the sub. Seems you're just about as valuable as the *Yorktown* herself."

"Will the *Ingersoll* sink the sub?"

"That's what they've been ordered to do." Patterson was uneasy. "Does that trouble you, Lieutenant?"

"No, sir. Like you said, they're Japs. It's just a lousy way to die, at the bottom of the ocean."

"Lieutenant Kobayashi, first, I'm Bill. This 'Lieutenant' to 'Lieutenant' stuff will get a bit redundant. Okay? We got off to a rough start. If it will make you feel any better, that sub was aft of us. The *Ingersoll* spotted her pipe just in time. You have to figure they spotted you. If she survives she'll radio Tokyo about a Jap officer on a U.S. warship. Might it throw a monkey wrench into your mission?"

"I'm not sure but as you said, Lieutenant, point taken."

"Try Bill. Besides, I know of only one good way to die. In bed with a bottle of scotch on one side and a beautiful dame on the other."

Ken turned to look at the sailor who had jumped away from him, now leaving the hangar deck, and wondered what would have happened if he had had a gun. Patterson followed his gaze.

"Come on. You may not exist after today but for now, in that sailor's eyes, a Japanese officer just saved his ass from his XO and became a hero. No one will believe him."

"Where to, sir?"

Patterson was exasperated. He knew Kobayashi was keeping his distance. "First, I'm going to call you Ken and you'll call me Bill. That's an order. Let Admiral Nimitz and General MacArthur continue this fight. We on the same page?"

Ken looked down at the deck and smiled. "Okay, Bill. Where are we headed?"

Patterson was relieved. "Wardroom for some hot java. We have some good cooks on board as well. Hungry?"

Kobayashi pulled on his cap. Then, while buckling his *katana*, he noticed scores of men milling about, staring at him. "Bill, if it's all right with you, I'd like to take a look at the *Shôki*."

"That's fine. However, we have a briefing scheduled shortly with the flight crews."

"I just want to get a quick look to see what shape she's in. I'm as anxious to meet the flight crews and go over the mission."

"Ok. It's further aft. Let's walk and give the crew a good look at you."

As they walked Ken was silent, visualizing Japanese sailors dying under a torrent of depth charges dropped by the *Ingersoll*. He pictured their faces as they died slowly, their crippled sub unable to surface, the crew's lungs poisoned with lethal carbon dioxide. Or abruptly, as their sub broke up, their lungs filling with cold water or being crushed by the weight of the water rushing in to envelop them, a grave no one would visit. He wondered what type of men willingly entombed themselves in a sub, no avenue of escape available to them while submerged. He looked at Patterson for a moment, thinking about the man's indifference toward Japanese sailors who were about to die, men who looked like himself. Patterson, Ken thought, displayed the same emotion talking about Japanese sailors dying as talking about the weather at the beach.

As they walked aft, all around them, men stopped their work to stare openly; confusion was boundless.

A recurrent argument played through Ken's mind. He was torn whether he had any right to judge Patterson, or Admiral Halsey, remembering Halsey's initial response to him on the *Missouri*, or anyone else who risked his life every day while Ken sat behind a desk, insulated from the killing—and the dying. Patterson and the others, he admitted, had a right to hate the enemy, just as the Japanese hated men like Patterson. And, Ken conceded, he looked liked the enemy and dressed like him. He spoke the same language and preferred the company of other Japanese Americans to white Americans. Of course, he reminded himself, white Americans were not breaking down his door to be his best buddy.

What was it, he wondered, America hated? Was it an enemy at war, or a race of people so obviously different from themselves, racially and culturally?

During the last two years he wondered why so many white Americans reacted to him so viscerally, hatred and fear issuing from their eyes, even when he wore an American Army uniform. He had to remind himself that they'd been fighting and killing Japanese for almost four years. Not because they were Japanese, but because of the war. The Japanese were doing the same; not only to the Americans, but to the Chinese, Koreans,

Dutch, Australians, British, Indians, Burmese, Vietnamese, New Zealanders, Filipinos, and so many other peoples in Asia and the Pacific, military and civilians. But, he reminded himself, American planes were bombing Japanese cities and killing civilians.

Then came the admission that he had kept to himself, not daring to share it with others, that he hated some white Americans, at least some.

As long as he could remember, whites had taunted his family. School was especially cruel, particularly when white teachers would not stop the other students' taunting or when a handful of white boys attacked his brother and him or when white girls attacked his sisters. Perhaps, he had reasoned, that was why, after completing their studies at Tôkyô Imperial University, his brother Tom had stayed while Ken had returned home.

Only once, while at the Manzanar Relocation Camp, did he wonder if his brother had made the right decision. Tom wasn't the only Japanese American who had remained in Japan after graduation. And when Ken had returned home and Japan attacked Pearl Harbor, he and his family, and over 110,000 other Americans of Japanese ancestry and Japanese immigrants, had been imprisoned, by Presidential Executive Order 9066 in February, 1942 because of their family name, their faces, their race.

But that wasn't the case for Americans of European descent. America didn't hate the Germans or Italians like they hated Japanese, not during the war. Indeed, there was often grudging respect between the combatants. Only after Allied troops had liberated the Nazi concentration camps, and Allied POW camps, and the American and British press had exposed Nazi crimes, did America as a nation feel revulsion at what Germany had done. Now Germany was collectively despised for its crimes against millions of murdered European civilians, prisoners of war and the inmates in the concentration camps. Until that time, Ken knew, America focused its hatred on Japan. He also knew that the hatred for the Japanese was more than hatred of an enemy of war; it was hatred of a race, hatred, he thought, based on what we look like. *We?* he wondered. He wondered what the American Army and Marines would do when they invaded Japan. He thought about Kyoko. He wished he could protect her from the invasion. Then he drudged up that most awful of thoughts: Was she still alive?

As Ken and Bill Patterson walked aft, sailors, flight crews and pilots stopped what they were doing and stared. At this point Ken began to enjoy the show he was giving them. After a few minutes of striding down the center of the hangar deck Kobayashi sighted the *Shôki*, the Devil Queller, parked alone.

Her tail section was toward the bow. In front of her a Marine, with a holstered .45 on his hip, stood at parade rest. As Lieutenant Patterson approached, the Marine snapped to attention. When he looked at Ken his hand started to inch toward his sidearm.

"As you were, Corporal," he said. "He's one of us."

From behind, Ken heard a familiar voice, vigorous, commanding.

"*Shôsa! Koketsu ni ittekureruka?*"

"*Ha! Tai-i!*" replied Ken. "*Kaigun-ga haha-tora o koroshite kuresa-e shite itadakereba!*"

Both Ken and Patterson turned around. Ken faced a grinning Roger Paschal, the Army captain who had helped plan Ken's mission into Tôkyô. Ken, perplexed, stopped grinning.

Paschal understood and smiled. "The d-d-docs c-c-can't f-f-f-figure it out, either. F-F-For some strange r-r-reason I s-s-s-s-stutter just in English. Once, when I sang 'Happy B-B-Birthday' at a p-p-p-p-party, I did okay then too. M-M-Maybe it's the *sake*."

Patterson felt left out. "Well, is anyone going to tell me what the hell you two said about me?"

"R-R-R-Relax, L-L-Lieutenant. I'm j-j-just k-k-keeping L-L-Lieutenant Kobayashi here s-s-sharp."

Ken looked at Patterson while speaking to Paschal. "Do we tell him now or make him sweat a while?"

"G-G-Go ahead. L-L-Let's see if m-m-m-my Japanese is r-r-rusty."

"Captain Paschal asked, 'Major, are you ready to enter the cave of the tiger?'"

"And? Are you?"

"That's up to you, Bill. You see I told Captain Paschal, 'Yes! Captain! But only if the Navy has slain the mother tiger!'"

"K-K-K-Ken, there's s-s-someone here I w-w-want you t-t-t-to m-meet. This is Jim R-R-R-Reichheld. He's from the Air T-T-T-Technical Intelligence Unit at Anacostia."

A very tall, lanky man sauntered over to them and extended his hand. Ken took the proffered hand and noticed how delicate it was, how long and tapered the fingers were. He was struck by how young looking Reichheld was.

"Pleased to meet ya, Lieutenant. Heard a lot about ya. Even know what you're up to," Reichheld said and winked. He brushed past Ken and Paschal and walked over to the *Shôki*. "Got some right nice surprises for ya, Lieutenant. Think you'll be mighty pleased. Come on over and take a look-see."

The three men followed Reichheld toward the *Shôki*. Ken and Roger Paschal exchanged grins. "Where'd you find him," Ken whispered to Paschal.

"I didn't. He c-c-came with the p-p-plane. He l-l-loves his w-w-work. B-b-b-but d-d-don't let that b-b-backwoods m-m-manner fool you. There's n-n-n-n-no one b-b-b-better."

16

The *I-402* turned hard to red, to port, immediately hiding in the baffles of the *Yorktown*, cloaking the sub from the *Ingersoll*'s sonar. Negative tank was emergency flooded allowing the rapid inflow of tons of water, increasing the boat's weight.

The sub's bow plunged downward. The *I-402* was at 15° down bubble. The stern was too high and for just a few seconds the screws were out of the water even though Iwata had ordered 10° down bubble. Fortunately, the weight of the negative tank pulled the sub down. When the screws bit again the sub shot downward, still hidden by the *Yorktown*'s cavitations. Watanabe, in the control room near Koyama, saw that everyone carried out his duties at his station.

Iwata knew the carrier's screws had a ten-meter draft and that the screw's turbulence would go down about twenty-five meters. Once clear of the turbulence the *I-402* would be exposed to the destroyer's sonar. Now his skills would succeed or he, his crew, and his boat would die. If the other destroyer engaged they would, he knew, definitely be sunk.

"Watanabe Tai-i! Chart thermoclines!"

"*Ha!*"

Now, more than ever, sound was the *I-402*'s enemy, sounds made while diving and probing sound from the enemy sonar. Iwata signaled Mori to join him. "Mori-*san*, instruct the crew to rig for ultra quiet." Mori Shôsa gave the order to the telephone talker who nodded and relayed it to his counterparts throughout the boat.

Koyama Heichô listened closely at his sonar station. He was still searching but more than that he was waiting.

17

"Status, Mr. Maher," asked Commander Blouin.

"Sir, sonar's been pinging her. Halfkenny thinks he had her briefly then lost her. As soon as we located her she turned hard to port and went under. Sonar lost her when she went into *Yorktown*'s cavitations but reacquired her screws briefly. Halfkenny thinks she's found a thermocline."

Commander Blouin focused his binoculars on the waters off the port beam, scanning the wake of the *Yorktown*. "Okay, this guy's experienced. All-ahead full. Let's go to ASW Condition One."

With his tinny pipe a bosun's mate blew a piercing whistle into the ship's PA system and then relayed the captain's orders. "Set ASW Condition One. All hands man your battle stations." He then toggled a switch below the microphone and the destroyer resonated with the familiar klaxon, calling men to battle. The *Ingersoll* went to anti-submarine warfare status. Sailors sleeping or not on duty rushed to their stations, climbing up or down ladders and running along passageways. At each compartment within the ship the last sailor entering or exiting stopped and closed the door and turned a levered metal wheel tight, sealing his area from other sections in the ship, protecting his compartment from potential flooding. On deck men put on life jackets and metal helmets and manned their guns. Others ran to their stern, port, and starboard depth charge stations and readied the depth charge launchers.

Animated voices rapidly reported to the bridge.

"Skipper, all repair parties manned and readied! Condition Able set!"

"Captain, Quartermaster First Keegan at the helm, sir!"

"Bridge! Quartermaster Second Falcone on the enunciator!"

"Bridge, engineering spaces manned and ready! All boilers on line! Maximum speed available thirty-one knots!"

"Captain, Halfkenny! Sonar manned and ready!"

"Bridge! Magazines manned and ready."

"Captain, all guns manned and ready, sir."

Every man was in his assigned station in less than two minutes. The captain was satisfied with the response time.

"Very well. Mister Maher, ring up flank speed. Heading, last known position."

Maher went to the helm voice tube and passed on Blouin's orders. Helmsman Keegan turned his wheel to port, heading for the *I-402*'s last known position.

Ingersoll's XO entered the CIC, the Combat Information Center. Already in the CIC were plotters. If the bridge was damaged or destroyed and the captain killed or disabled the XO would carry out ASW operations from there.

The sonar operator, Seaman 1/C Pete Halfkenny, was waiting to pass through the *Yorktown*'s turbulence. He was not worried. He knew the game; the sub had cover for about a minute, maybe two, then he would reacquire her.

Like his counterpart on the *I-402*, Halfkenny was just a kid, age 19. He was born and raised in Wyoming and never saw the ocean—except for pictures—until he joined the navy. His blond hair was cut just a bit too long to suit the captain but he was never reprimanded for it; just a slight frown from the skipper and Halfkenny would take the hint. But it seemed to grow fast and he was always brushing it away from his eyes. Once, while in a bar, another sailor, larger than Halfkenny, kidded him about his cute "bangs" over his eyes and being a "ping jockey." Though outweighed by 50 pounds, with one right cross he broke the man's jaw. Teasing from the crew about his hair never came up again. But the captain still occasionally frowned.

Commander Blouin saw or knew that everyone was in position. "Tom, let's think like him. If you were him, what would you do?"

"Sir, just what he did. I'd turn into the *Yorktown*'s wake, and go deep. Then I'd head straight for a while. Put as much distance between him and us. He knew where and how to hide; that gives him a couple of minutes. Then he's exposed. He knows we'll come after him. He'll go deep and try to hole up, probably in a thermocline."

"I agree. This guy knows what he's doing. He didn't panic and dive first. Crossing the *Yorktown*'s wake gave him a few minutes cover. I doubt very much whether he'll try for a run at the *Yorktown* but let's make certain he doesn't want to."

A talker approached the captain. "Sir, CIC reports we're over the last known datum."

"Tom, let's roll one off the fantail; we'll let him know we're looking for him. Set depth to one five zero feet."

At the stern of the *Ingersoll*, 200 yards beyond the *Yorktown*'s wake, a depth charge, set to detonate at 150 feet, rolled off the fantail. Twenty seconds later a massive eruption of water gushed to the surface quickly followed by a deafening "brr-roomp."

*   *   *

At 45 meters the explosion jolted the *I-402*. The depth was almost equal to the *I-402* but the distance was too far forward to do any damage. In fact the *Ingersoll* had overshot the *I-402*. Iwata waited for the next three explosions, knowing destroyers fired off depth charges in groups of four, one from the stern, one each from red and green, and a final from the stern, a diamond pattern. Silence. He smiled. The hunt was on.

"Mori Shôsa! The American captain is letting us know he is knocking on our door. He is very polite. Watanabe Tai-i! Depth!"

"Chûsa! Depth is fifty meters! Level bubble!"

"Mori Shôsa! Let us not make this easy! Helm! All-ahead two thirds! Green standard rudder! Steady on course zero nine zero!"

Increasing speed to five knots Iwata was heading straight into where the depth charge had just exploded, knowing that while in or near the agitated waters the destroyer's sonar could not locate his boat for several minutes.

"Mori Shôsa! Order Sasaki Jôtô heisô to load a pill!"

"*Ha!*" Mori Shôsa picked up a voice-powered phone. "Forward torpedo room! Conning!"

"Conning! Forward torpedo room! Sasaki Jôtô heisô!"

"Sasaki Jôtô heisô! Load one Pillenwerfer!"

"*Ha!*" Chief Petty Officer Sasaki Sadamitsu unpacked a Pillenwerfer and placed it into the signal ejector, a small tube-like mechanism which could launch small diameter flares, signals, and evasion devices.

"Conning! Forward torpedo room! One pill loaded!"

Iwata turned to Watanabe Tai-i. "How long since the depth charge?"

"Chûsa! Three minutes!"

"The next knock will come soon, Mori Shôsa!"

*　　*　　*

Blouin leaned toward the voice tube. "Sonar. Bridge. This is the captain. Any contact?"

"Bridge. Sonar. Negative, sir."

Blouin sipped from a cup of coffee. He didn't really expect a finding. After a depth charge explodes at 150 feet sonar loses any contact for a few minutes; five to ten minutes if the charge had detonated at 250 to 500 feet.

"We overshot him, Tom. He dove while we went after him at full speed. Right full rudder, steady on course, 210°."

The *Ingersoll* changed course 180°, heading back to the last known position of the *I-402*.

"Depth Charge party, Bridge. Fire medium pattern, set depth to one five zero feet." Blouin had a feeling it would be a long hunt.

800 yards from the first depth charge the *Ingersoll*'s two port and two starboard K guns fired one depth charge each. Seconds later the water's surface was ripped by four massive explosions. 100 more yards and another depth charge rolled off the fantail, completing the diamond pattern. Another explosion ruptured the surface.

"Okay, Tom, he knows we mean business. Let's initiate a box search."

After the *Ingersoll* rolled the fourth depth charge Ensign Maher ordered an Expanding Box Search. The search was a standard pattern laid out on 90° turns, port or starboard. The destroyer would proceed on a straight course, based on information supplied by the CIC or sonar reports, then after an intentional distance turn 90°. This pattern would be repeated, expanding out ever further. All the while Halfkenny, the sonar operator, would constantly listen for screws or other noise, hoping to locate the sub. If Halfkenny picked up the contact Commander Blouin would immediately alter course toward the contact and start a diamond depth charge pattern.

"Sonar. Captain. Commence underwater search. Short range scale. Pipe it through to the bridge speaker."

"Aye, aye, sir."

A telephone talker listened for a moment. "Sonar searching beam to beam, Captain."

Halfkenny, following Blouin's orders, pinged every three seconds.

*   *   *

Koyama listened for a moment. "Chûsa! Short range pinging!"

Iwata had the moment he needed. He knew the tactics of American destroyers. This captain was looking in all directions. He pictured his American counterpart, on his bridge, scanning the surface of the water, looking for that elusive trophy every destroyer captain wanted. Iwata nodded, understanding. But, he thought, not today. At their increased speed, the *I-402* had left the temporary shelter of the agitated waters created by the first depth charge. "Forward torpedo room! Conning!"

"Conning! Forward torpedo room! Sasaki Jôtô heisô!"

"Sasaki Jôtô heisô! Launch the pill!"

The Pillenwerfer, a German innovation, was a metal cylinder containing lithium hydride. When launched from the ejector tube it remained at a stationary depth. As water entered and reacted with the packed chemical compound an enormous mass of bubbles was discharged. When those bubbles were hit by a sonar ping the sound that came back was similar to a submarine. The bubble mass slowly surfaced while the *I-402* headed for the fourth depth charge.

*   *   *

Seaman 1/C Pete Halfkenny continued to ping every three seconds but nothing came back. Halfkenny liked his job. He imagined every ping sent out as a magic rubber bullet, and if one of those rubber bullets hit the contact and bounced back he learned two things: time and line of travel. Time told him the distance to the target which in turn gave him the range. The line of travel gave him the bearing. Put them together and you have the position of the sub. He rotated the hand wheel, turning the echo ranging gear, and thought he heard something. This time it came back, a loud and clear sharp sonar echo similar to the outline of a submarine's beam. His brows furrowed. Something was wrong.

"Bridge. Sonar."

Blouin moved to the voice tube. "Sonar. Bridge."

"Captain, I got a return but something's not right."

"Spell it out, Pete."

"Sir, it's too sharp and I got zero Doppler."

The Doppler Effect was well-known to sonar operators. During sonar training students were told to imagine a train approaching a station and blowing its whistle. It always had a high tone or frequency. As the train passed the station the whistle's frequency dropped and became a long, languid, drawn-out sound. In the case of a sonar ping the frequency is high when sent out but when it returns from a moving object the frequency drops.

"Pete, ping it again." Blouin leaned toward the bridge speaker, listening. He heard the return frequency; it had not changed. "Damn!" he muttered. Halfkenny was right. The Doppler was zero. "Pete, it's a pill. Ping again to make certain."

Halfkenny, rotating the hydrophone knob, listened for the sub's screws but heard nothing. He sent out another ping. Nothing. He shifted the hydrophone back to the previous position, listened and pinged. The ping returned. He pinged again. It came back loud and clear. He waited a moment and pinged again. It came back loud and clear. Still zero Doppler.

"Bridge. Sonar."

"Bridge."

"Sir, I've lost contact on the sub. All I have is this station-ary object."

"I know, I've been listening on the speaker. Forget it, Pete. Go to long-range active scale." Blouin looked at Maher. "Let's continue the box search, Tom. And let's continue to let her know we're on top of her with depth charges. If we can't find her we can at least keep her down. If we're lucky we'll put her there permanently."

18

"Not much to look at, is she? Kinda ugly, in fact. At least when you compare her to a P-51 or the Hellcat or a Corsair. Any of ya know much about it?" Jim Reichheld asked with a grin.

The three men accompanying him shook their heads. In fact, Ken did know about the *Shôki* but wanted to listen to Reichheld.

Reichheld was quite tall, over six feet, seven inches and, to Ken Kobayashi, as thin as a rail. Ken wondered if he were yet twenty. His dark hair was slicked straight back with a part in the middle. Ken thought Reichheld looked like a 1930s movie gangster. In spite of the oppressive heat on the *Yorktown*'s lower decks Reichheld wore a white shirt and tie. His shirt pocket, blemished with several small ink stains, held several pens. There were oil stains on his sleeves. Oddly, for pants, he wore blue dungarees.

Reichheld touched the nacelle with what looked like affection. The *Shôki* was a bland-looking interceptor, with a fat nacelle, a cockpit just forward of the middle and a body that tapered to the rear. But Reichheld saw something in the plane that an experienced pilot or an aeronautical engineer could appreciate. It was a feeling that Ken had experienced when he had flown the plane in preparation for the mission.

"Well, for starters, if you was a B-29 crew you'd wanna stay clear of her. Let me tell you a bit about her. Could raise your hair a mite, though."

Reichheld's lanky frame moved toward the right wing. The others followed, compliant students anxious to learn.

"First off, the Japs call her the *Shoki*, the Demon or Devil Queller. Demon I can understand. This Devil Queller stuff I'm not sure I understand. Are they tellin' us that it silences devils or are they callin' us devils and they're gonna quell us? I just don't understand them folks. But they don't pay me to so I guess it don't matter. Anyways, here's what we got here. We call her 'Tojo.' She's probably one of the fastest-climbing interceptors in the Jap air force. She's got a Nakajima Ha-145 eighteen-cylinder air-cooled radial engine. At takeoff she's rated at 2,000 horsepower, 1,880 horsepower at 6,560 feet, and 1,450 horsepower when she's over 26,000 feet. You can see, unlike earlier models, she's got a four-blade prop and she carries a set of thrust-augmentation exhaust stacks. Based on earlier models of the *Shoki* the wing area has been increased and the tail surfaces have been made larger.

"In short, she can move and she can climb. But I'm sure, Lieutenant Kobayashi, you know that."

Ken did know, having flight-tested her for about one hundred hours.

"She's got good performance, too. We pushed her. Maximum speed is over 375 mph at 17,000 feet. We got her up to 16,500 feet in less than four minutes. Her service ceiling seems to be over 36,000 feet, and the maximum range, depending on what she's carrying, is over 1,000 miles.

"She comes equipped with two 20 mm cannon in the fuselage and two 37 mm cannon in the wings. That's a lot of firepower. We know they're capable planes. So, Lieutenant Kobayashi, you got yourself a tough bird.

"We first got wind of the *Shoki* in China, Burma, and

Malaya. We also know these planes were given the chore of defending them oil fields at Palembang on Sumatra. Then, when the B-29s started to fly over the Jap home islands things got a bit thick. There ain't that many other Jap fighters able to climb high enough and still be a bother to the B-29s. But these babies can do the job.

"Not that there ain't problems. Here's the lowdown. At high speeds she really loads up and it takes both arms on the stick to roll her. At lower speeds it ain't too bad. So you gotta watch for that, but I suspect you already know this, Lieutenant. But back to the good stuff for you at least, Lieutenant. She's got good pilot armor protection and self-sealing tanks, but that in turn makes her kinda heavy, so maybe that's why she's got maneuvering problems. But that armor is pretty ineffective against .50 caliber rounds. They just go right through. So a lot of them, being able to climb so high, don't bother to try to shoot down the B-29s, they just ram into them.

"But that's not your mission. So let me go over what we did for you. We were told you gotta have a forced landing at Atsugi and that the Navy here is gonna help you do that, make it look like you gotta land there fast. And it's gotta look real. I had to think of a way to get you down without the Japs on the ground asking questions. So after talking with the flyboys here and what they're thinking of doing I worked out something that just might do the trick. The flyboys are gonna give you the details on what they're gonna do but right now *I'm* gonna tell you what you're gonna do. So here goes. The flyboys are gonna attack you as you approach Atsugi. You're gonna mix it up a bit and they're gonna tear into your ass. You're gonna lose. Follow me."

Mesmerized by Reichheld's presentation they obediently followed around to the side of the *Shôki*.

"This plane ain't got all its original parts. The Japs have been cannibalizing parts from other planes. So you can see the paint job's not the best when it came to matching up. So the changes we made ain't gonna matter much either. First off, I put several bullet holes in the fuselage. Of course, they tore right through. But I was careful that nothing important inside was damaged. You gotta fly this bird. Some exit holes are large; they reflect a tumbling .50 caliber tearing through. I went inside and did some damage like rounds do before coming through. None of this will affect your flying but it looks real. You know that some rounds are tracers so I took a torch and left a lot of scorch marks and blistered some inside surfaces. I suspect you might think it's overkill but if the Japs go lookin' inside to make repairs they'll see the damage. Their mechanics ain't dumb, Lieutenant. Ya gotta figure they're gonna go in and have a look-see before they make repairs. I did the same thing on the other side of the fuselage, entrance and exit holes. Now I put just a few into the tail section. Again, it won't really disturb your flying either but because of the size of some of the exit holes you'll feel it a bit when you make turns. So keep that in mind. Same damage to the wings but I avoided the fuel tanks. In short, you're gonna take hits everywhere but the canopy, cockpit, and rudder.

"But none of this is enough to get you down. So let's go to the engine. I put three holes in the engine. But on the other side is just one exit hole. What we did was to shoot some .50 caliber rounds from one of our planes into a junk engine and recover them. They're bent up some. I sort of jammed them in your engine, just like a round would end up. They won't affect the engine's operation but when the Jap mechanics go in to fix her up they'll be sure to find them, except for one that did exit. But not from the engine. We'll get back to that in a minute. Now let's go back to the forward edge of the right wing. I think you're gonna like this."

Captivated, they followed Reichheld as he guided them through the maze in his mind. As Ken walked he thought about Reichheld and was struck at how at ease he was using "Japs" rather than Japanese. It was, he thought, as if Reichheld didn't see him as Japanese, in spite of the uniform or how he looked. He was surprised at how relaxed Reichheld was with him. He felt, for the first time, that someone saw him as an American, period.

"Lieutenant Kobayashi, how we get you down real fast took some thinking. If you was to stay up there the Japs on the ground watching are gonna know you're gonna get chewed up. The *Shoki* can't match a Hellcat and definitely not a division. First, let's look at the forward edge of the wing here. See anything?"

Patterson, Ken, and Paschal stepped close and examined the forward edge of the right wing. They saw nothing but Reichheld's thin hand.

"That's good. Real good. You see, we had to open this wing right here then weld it shut. Lieutenant Patterson, your welders and painters here did a right good job. You'd never know she was opened up. Inside we put a four-gallon metal container, shaped to fit real comfy. It's welded real tight to the inside of the wing so it won't jiggle. Inside the container is four gallons of paraffin oil. You know, the kind that's used to coat concrete forms so the concrete don't stick to the forms? Anyway, the oil is real light in viscosity. And that's gonna be important in a moment. Now let's go back to the engine cowling. Remember that third round, the one that's got an exit hole? Well, that third one went into the engine's cowling then into the collector area and it grazed the exhaust collector and finally ricocheted out the opposite side of the engine cowling. At least that's what the Jap mechanics will think when they go in and make repairs. You with me so far?"

The three novitiates nodded, totally at a loss. But Ken was beginning to see where Reichheld was going and began to appreciate his thinking.

"Okay. Now, in the right wing I've also installed a small electric pressure pump. Don't worry; it'll make sense in a minute. The pump sucks the paraffin oil out of the tank in the wing. It then pressurizes the oil and propels it to the tube injectors located under the exhaust collectors. That way if the Japs look inside, which ain't likely, they won't be visible from above. Being pressurized the paraffin oil is gonna squirt right into the ejectors located in the exhaust collector which is situated right close to the engine cylinder. The oil, as I said, being light in viscosity, is gonna get real hot real fast. It'll vaporize into smoke. You get it? The Japs on the ground will see smoke coming from your engine. You're gonna have to come down, real quick like. What I did was to make small holes in the collector to allow smoke in the collector to escape out around the cowling rather than the exhaust outlet collector. This way we make certain the smoke coming out doesn't block Lieutenant Kobayashi's canopy visibility. I bet you're wondering how you get the smoke to come out, ain't you, Lieutenant? Let's go to the cockpit."

Reichheld and Patterson pushed a wheeled ladder to one side of the cockpit. Paschal and Ken did the same on the other side. Two men per ladder climbed up to look inside the cockpit, three of them mystified. Except for the Japanese characters on the instruments, which both Ken and Paschal could read, it looked like any other fighter plane that had seen service. The seat was worn in several places and paint was coming off the sides of the cockpit.

"I think you're gonna like this. What I've done is wire the smoke ejection system into the cockpit light switch, here. It ain't gonna turn on the cockpit light. But that's okay 'cause it's gonna be daylight while you're over Atsugi. When you think the time is right you just toggle the light switch and presto! Smoke! But you gotta remember this. You only have four minutes' worth of oil to burn. So you gotta be on the ground real quick like. And that brings me to another point. It's real important. You ain't gonna be able to time this what with all the shootin' you're gonna be doin'. So, just in case you can't land in that time frame, I added a reserve oil tank. It holds two gallons and this oil is more viscous so it's gonna burn darker, so to speak. When the first tank is almost empty the second one will kick in. And that's your cue. When you see darker smoke you got about two minutes to get on the ground. With the darker smoke the Japs are gonna think you're really in trouble. And this you gotta time, Lieutenant, shootin' or no shootin'. When you land and if you're still smokin' you gotta taxi some to drain it empty. As soon as the smoke starts to thin out toggle the light switch closed then cut your engine. Otherwise, if any of the oil is still in the reserve tank and the engine is turned on and the switch ain't toggled off any remaining oil is gonna be pumped and smoke is gonna come out. That happens, someone is gonna start monkeyin' around in there to make more repairs than we want. We don't want anyone looking at anything that's gonna raise a stink."

Ken and Roger Paschal looked at each other, amazed and bemused. When the "Kobayashi Group," as they later called themselves, put together Ken's insertion plan the one issue they had not ironed out was his pretext for landing at Atsugi. They had agreed that having Navy fighters shooting at him made a convincing argument that he had to land or be shot down. However, it was pointed out that he could try to elude the Hellcats and fly to his designated destination, the Imperial Japanese Army Air Base at Chôfu, northeast of Atsugi. So they agreed to table it, hoping the Navy might help. Now this engineer from Anacostia had put together a method that was so outlandish that both Ken and Captain Roger Paschal believed it would work. Reichheld stood at the top of the ladder, grinning. *My work*, he told himself, *is done. Time to get some more coffee.*

Ken looked across the cockpit. "Okay, Jim, I'll buy it. Will it work?"

Reichheld's smile disappeared. "On this one, Lieutenant, you gotta believe me. I've tested it thirteen times. That's my lucky number, see? Every time it's worked. It being in flight ain't gonna make no difference. But just in case, before she was transferred to the *Yorktown* one of the pilots took her up three times and it worked smooth. Afterwards, I took it apart, cleaned it, and put it together. I supervised the wing welding and painting here on the *Yorktown*. I ain't gonna send you up there with just a joystick to keep you alive. Nope, it's gonna work. Your life's depending on it. And so's my word. Everything else is up to you. I ain't leaving the *Yorktown* for a while so I've been briefed on your mission. Anything I can do in the time left just let me know."

With nothing more to say, the four men climbed down the ladders. Ken walked around the *Shôki* to Jim Reichheld and offered his hand. Reichheld grinned and enthusiastically took Ken's hand.

Just then a navy pilot came up to Lieutenant Patterson.

"Bill, they're waiting for you in Ready Room Three."

"Thanks, Bob. Oh, this is Lieutenant Kobayashi. I believe you two met."

Ken shook his head. "No, I don't think so."

"Sure we did, Lieutenant. Well, indirectly, at least. I'm Bob Stanton. Flatiron One. My squadron escorted you to the *Gatling*." Stanton extended his hand.

Ken hesitated, wrestling with his emotions. Swallowing hard he took Stanton's hand. It was a lifeless handshake and Stanton felt it.

Patterson could feel the tension from Ken. "Captain Paschal, how about if you take Lieutenant Kobayashi to Ready Room Three. I'll be there in a second."

As Paschal and Ken walked away Stanton approached Patterson.

"What gives, Bill?"

"I got a message from Lieutenant Greg Basque. He's the Kingfisher pilot you escorted. He told me that Lieutenant Kobayashi heard your comments about 'yellow Japs.'"

"Shit! I didn't mean it about him. I know what he's doing. Hell, I have to tell him."

"Leave it alone, Bob. If I get a chance I'll square it with him. I have to go."

*　　　*　　　*

Leaving Reichheld with the *Shôki* Ken and Paschal made their way to Ready Room Three, directly under the *Yorktown*'s flight deck. In a moment Patterson caught up. When Ken walked into the low-ceilinged white-walled steel room every head turned and conversations ceased but there was neither surprise nor hostility in anyone's expression. Instead, several of the pilots nearest the entrance, men with grim intent and experience etched on their faces, stood and walked over to Ken and shook his hand and introduced themselves. After brief exchanges they returned to their seats. Ken was caught off guard. Some of these men had been killing Japanese for at least three years. Others looked less than 20 years old.

"Lieutenant Kobayashi, Lieutenant Patterson, Captain Paschal." An authoritative voice from the front of the room interrupted the unexpected conviviality. "Up front here, please."

As the three men moved to the front Ken noted the metal-framed chairs with cushioned black leather and leather-covered arm rests.

There were eleven pilots sitting in the chairs. Some pilots nodded at Ken as he passed and he returned the acknowledgment. Others were playing cards or acey-deucy. A thick haze of smoke from Camels and Lucky Strikes blanketed the room. Some pilots took two or three puffs from their cigarettes then put them out and immediately lit another. The room was tense; Ken sensed it.

Standing at the front of the room was Commander John W. Brady, Executive Officer of the *Yorktown*. Seated in front were Commander Robert A. Macpherson, Air Officer, and Lieutenant William Burgess, a VF-88 division commander. Behind them was a large chalkboard, covered with numbers.

Up front three empty seats were waiting. Commander Brady beckoned to Patterson and pointed at the seats. Ken and Paschal followed Patterson to the front and sat down.

"Okay, everybody. Settle down. We have work to do. We know why we're here today so we need not waste time. Lieutenant Burgess has chosen you men for this mission because of your experience and good judgment. Lieutenant Kobayashi's mission is dangerous and, on a personal note, extremely courageous. In order that he carry out this mission he needs our help and we gladly extend whatever cooperation he needs. Lieutenant Burgess?"

Lieutenant William Burgess, a ready smile on his young craggy face, stood and searched the faces of the eleven pilots under his command. Then he looked at Ken. "First, Lieutenant Kobayashi, welcome to VF-88." Ken nodded his thanks. Burgess looked at his pilots. "Okay, we know the mission. So I want to go over the details Lieutenant Kobayashi needs to know.

"First, however, this morning we received a crucial piece of information from Sergeant Takayama, who works with Lieutenant Kobayashi. Last night, a Jap Army base, Miyakonojo, on Kyushu, radioed the Imperial War Ministry. The signal, in code, included the identity of the officer who will be attending this August five meeting. It also stated he would be flying a Nakajima *Hayate*. His destination is Chofu Army Air Base. Captain Paschal, you might want to let Lieutenant Elgin know he made a good call on Chofu.

"Lieutenant Kobayashi, our designation for this plane is 'Frank.' Your plane, for example, is designated 'Tojo.' Sergeant Takayama is now waiting for another radio signal as to when the Jap will take off. As soon as we have that time fighters from carriers will launch, locate, and ambush his plane. We've projected a probable course. To be on the safe side our carrier pilots have been instructed to shoot down any 'Franks' they encounter.

"Second, we're on the outside edge of a typhoon. So there have been some limitations imposed on us. Nevertheless, we've taken steps to insure the success of this mission. As soon as Sergeant Takayama receives that second piece of information, in spite of the weather, eight divisions of Hellcats from the *Yorktown* and other Third Fleet carriers will patrol the air corridor that Lieutenant Kobayashi will take to Kyushu. Their task will be to clear the corridor of any Jap planes or ships at sea and to redirect unauthorized American planes that find themselves where they have been ordered to stay out of, insuring that those planes do not shoot down Lieutenant Kobayashi. Third, because Lieutenant Kobayashi might encounter rough weather, a PBM will tail him, within visual range, until he makes landfall. Finally, four destroyers are already in place, equidistant apart, who will offer further protection to Lieutenant Kobayashi.

"When we receive Sergeant Takayama's signal Lieutenant Kobayashi will take off in the *Shoki*. As we speak his plane is being transferred to the flight deck. Keeping in mind the weather, we have a low ceiling. Therefore, after takeoff, Lieutenant Kobayashi will climb to and maintain an altitude of angels six. As a reminder, Lieutenant, angels six is 6,000 feet. Thirty minutes later, three divisions of Hellcats will takeoff from the *Yorktown* and climb to angels eight, designated Divisions One, Two, and Three. The divisions' call signs are Flatiron One, Flatiron Two, and Flatiron Three, respectively. Lieutenant Kobayashi has no call sign since he's a Jap pilot for this mission and his plane lacks communications equipment anyway.

"Upon approach to Honshu, Division One, Flatiron One, will maintain an altitude of angels fifteen. Flatiron Two and Three will climb to angels twenty. When Lieutenant Kobayashi approaches Atsugi Flatiron One will engage him. I will lead Flatiron One and command all three divisions.

"Lieutenant Kobayashi, Division One's ammo will be blank cartridges. What we've done is removed the rounds and sealed the shells. When fired only muzzle flashes will be coming at you. It's going to give the impression to the Japs on the ground of a red-hot dogfight. Furthermore—"

"Lieutenant Burgess," interrupted one of the pilots in the back. "We've talked about that and we think it's a bad idea."

Burgess trusted his pilots. He always let his men express their ideas without fear of being raked over the coals.

"Go ahead, Ray."

Ensign Raymond Wright, Division Three Flight leader, stood. Ken looked at Wright's baby face and wondered if he had yet started to shave. "Sir, we know we're going to have to make this dogfight look as real as it gets. But if Lieutenant Kobayashi goes to the deck and you're above him, shooting down while in pursuit, then the Japs on the ground aren't going to see any rounds hit the deck. It doesn't make sense. It's like we've always been told: 'They're not stupid.' We think we have a better idea than giving Division One blanks."

"Let's hear it."

"Sir, Division One splits into two two-plane sections, each section on either side of Lieutenant Kobayashi. The wingman of each section, furthest from Lieutenant Kobayashi's plane, will fire live ammo. That way, if Division One wingmen fire down, their rounds are going to hit the deck. The Japs will see those rounds hitting the ground on their base. Section leaders, closest to Lieutenant Kobayashi, will fire blanks. But both section leaders should have just the first half of their ammo as blanks, just in case things get hot and the Japs get planes into the air. As wingmen they'll be further from his plane, so they can avoid hitting him. The Japs won't know the difference but they will see the blank's flashes."

Burgess didn't waste time. "Ray, go to the flight deck and have the plane captains load Division One's planes per your proposal. Like you said, 'just in case.' Then get back here on the double. Okay, any other comments or questions?" There were none. Burgess could tell that his pilots were satisfied.

"Okay, let's continue. Divisions Two and Three will fly cover at angels twenty and if the Japs at Atsugi launch fighters to assist Lieutenant Kobayashi Divisions Two and Three will engage and protect Division One until Division One is able to disengage.

"Lieutenant Kobayashi's *Shoki* will be armed with live Jap ammo. The logic for this decision is obvious. If the Japs perform maintenance we don't want them seeing blanks. Lieutenant Kobayashi is an experienced pilot although he has had only about one hundred hours in the *Shoki*. Is that about right, Lieutenant?"

Ken nodded, feeling part of a team. "I flew a crop duster back home. I didn't find that much difference between that and a fighter."

One of the pilots in the back raised his hand. "So we got us an ace here; at least five grasshoppers dusted?" A pencil was thrown at him during the jeering.

Commander Brady, Executive Officer of the *Yorktown*, stood, the signal for Lieutenant Burgess to sit down. "Thank you, gentlemen. There is one more point. This mission is critical. If Lieutenant Kobayashi succeeds, and we pray that he will, he may be instrumental in saving thousands, if not tens of thousands, of American lives. It is of the utmost importance that nothing jeopardizes this mission. Accordingly, this is a voluntary mission. Every pilot in this room has agreed that should the Japs shoot down any VF-88 planes over Japan the others are to make sure the pilot or pilots are not taken alive. Lieutenant Burgess and the other pilots have agreed to this. Are there any questions?"

Ken stood. "Commander Brady, am I to understand that you regard this as a suicide mission for VF-88?"

"Lieutenant Kobayashi, I am led to understand that Admiral Halsey regards what you're doing is a suicide mission."

Ken, numb, looked at Lieutenant Burgess. Burgess smiled and winked. Ken turned and looked at the eleven pilots. Their faces were impassive. *Can we do any less*, they seemed to be saying.

Commander Brady broke the tension. "Since Divisions Two and Three will be flying a support role what I'd like is for Lieutenant Kobayashi to get together with Division One and go over their tactics for Atsugi, particularly in light of the ammo modifications for Division One. When that's complete, say in about 30 minutes, I want everyone on the flight deck. The *Shoki* should be in position now. Thank you very much. In the meantime, we wait to hear from Sergeant Takayama. There's hot java in the back. Help yourselves."

19

For over two hours Commander Blouin continued the hunt. The expanding box search had varied with the *Ingersoll* never repeating the same distance before turning 90° port or starboard. Depth charges had been varied too, ranging from 100 feet to as much as 300 feet. Blouin was determined to destroy the Japanese sub.

The sonar operator, Seaman 1/C Pete Halfkenny, rotated the sonar projector, waiting for that magic rubber bullet to come back slightly distorted, waiting for the Doppler Effect.

No one on the *Ingersoll* lost patience or determination. In the past, there had been searches that had lasted more than 30 hours and some had been fruitless. But Blouin knew the Imperial Japanese Navy was beaten and he wanted this kill, maybe the final one. So the course changes occurred, depth charges were launched and Halfkenny listened on his sonar. On two more occasions he found the bubbles of a pill several moments after a depth charge explosion and reported his findings to Commander Blouin.

"Pete, I think I know what he's doing. After the next pattern wait ten minutes then go passive. No pings. Let me know if you pick anything up. But give it ten minutes."

The next pattern was rolled, fired, and rolled and when the last explosion ripped the surface Pete Halfkenny put his earphones back on and waited ten minutes. Then he turned the hydrophone knob. He listened for two minutes. *There! Screws! Barely, but there.* "Bridge. Sonar. Got him!"

"Pete, where is he?"

"Skipper, he's just left our last ashcan drop."

"CIC. Bridge. What was our position when the last charge was rolled?"

Less than a minute later CIC gave Blouin the position.

Blouin went to the helm voice tube and immediately ordered a course change, returning to the last depth charge position.

"Depth charge party. Bridge. Set fantail depth for two zero zero feet. Set K gun depth for two five zero feet. Stand by to fire." All depth charge parties made the appropriate depth changes on the "ashcans," a term often used instead of depth charge. Blouin waited for one moment. "Fantail, roll two!" Blouin looked at his watch and waited 30 seconds. "K guns. Fire all depth charges!" He waited another 30 seconds. "Fantail, roll two!"

In order, stern, port and starboard, then again stern, depth charge stations rolled or fired their ashcans. They splashed into the waters and descended. Successive explosions violently ripped apart the surface.

Blouin waited two minutes. "Depth charge party. Bridge. All stations. Set depth for two five zero feet. Stand by to launch." Blouin waited two minutes. "Depth charge party. Bridge. All stations. Launch all depth charges!" Again, the water was rent with explosions.

"Sonar. Bridge. Inform me as soon as you hear something."

In the sonar shack Halfkenny patiently waited one minute then put on his earphones and listened.

*   *   *

The strategy of evasion had worked for almost two hours. Koyama Heichô listened to the screws of the destroyer as it maneuvered on the surface and, when close enough, the *I-402* entered the agitated waters caused by the last depth charge explosion and hid there for several minutes, waiting for the next depth charge pattern and headed for the last depth charge explosion to remain protected in its agitated waters. After that, just before the disturbed waters calmed, another Pillenwerfer was launched if the destroyer was close, allowing the *I-402* to escape at flank speed. But Iwata knew he could hold that speed for only several minutes. The batteries would soon be exhausted. The air in the *I-402* was becoming musty again. The men were becoming edgy.

The *I-402* leveled off at a depth of 60 meters. Commander Iwata knew he would soon have to carry out other evasive tactics. He also knew the American captain would soon revise his own strategies.

Koyama Heichô heard a click in his earphones.

To ensure that a depth charge detonated at the predetermined depth a hydrostatic fuse was set before the depth charge was launched. When the depth charge reached the preset depth the hydrostatic fuse snapped shut, sending into the water a loud, distinctive click which submariners knew and dreaded. If the depth charge was close to the sub the crew could distinctly hear the click. All they could do was brace themselves for the explosion. And hope. Seconds later their wait was over.

Whenever Leading Seaman Koyama Tsutomu heard the click, he removed his earphones, knowing if the explosion was close enough his ears could be damaged. But this time it did not matter. Iwata's strategy of evasion finally failed.

Two explosions rocked the *I-402*. Then four more, in quick succession. Then two more. Men were tossed about. Supplies fell. Several bulbs broke. Some pipes burst and seawater sprayed in. Men ran to get supplies that would stop or slow down the water. Valves were closed. Near Iwata, a gauge glass fractured.

Ensign Oda appeared before Iwata, trembling, his hands opening and closing. "Chûsa! Okada Shô-i kôhosei and I are prepared! Please order the *kaiten* released! We can help you escape!"

"Oda Shô-i! You want us to surface to launch *kaiten*? Are you a fool? There is an American destroyer waiting for us on the surface! Return to your post!"

Oda's face reflected his humiliation and anguish. He looked around and knew everyone thought him a fool and he knew his request to surface had confirmed their opinion. His shoulders slumped but he recovered, a new expression visible. Iwata didn't like what he saw.

Another pattern of depth charges rocked the boat. Iwata knew the Americans were zeroing in on his boat. He reacted immediately. He looked at the depth meter. "Mori Shôsa! Make your depth one five zero meters!"

Mori's head snapped around, eyes wide, staring at Iwata. Mori knew the *I-402*'s maximum tested depth was 90 meters plus 50 percent, totaling 135 meters. The boat was too big, had too many variables such as the *kaiten*, which could explode on the deck, sending out sounds that the American destroyer's sonar would readily pick up. Not that it would matter. The *kaiten*'s explosion would destroy the *I-402*. And, he thought, what of the watertight hangar housing the metal barrels containing the aviation fuel? At 150 meters the hangar might breach or the barrels could rupture, destabilizing the *I-402*'s buoyancy and rendering her uncontrollable.

Iwata saw his XO's doubt and hesitation. And knew his reasons.

"Do you have an alternative?" hissed Iwata in Mori's ear. "The American captain has or will soon work out my strategy. He is a fox, that one. So, do we die from a depth charge or do we perhaps die while trying to save our lives and our boat?

Choose! Now!"

Mori issued orders. "Make your depth 150 meters! Ahead one third! Five degrees down bubble!" At 5° down bubble and 3 knots the rate of decline would be controllable, and not too detectable.

The diving officer echoed the orders. Nothing happened.

Unseen, Sakamoto Hei sôchô, Chief Warrant Officer of the *I-402*, moved to the helmsman and clutched his shoulder. The helmsman did not move. Sakamoto tightened his grip and the helmsman, while wincing, slowly eased the controls forward. The *I-402* commenced its perilous dive.

When Iwata turned from Mori he saw that Oda Shô-i had left the conning tower.

20

It was now afternoon. For a handful of men on the *Yorktown*'s flight deck time hung heavily. They were waiting for a message.

The *Shôki* was parked alone, wheel chocks holding her in place, three quarters distance from the bow, more than 200 feet from the stern. That gave Ken a span of over 650 feet for takeoff.

Divisions One, Two, and Three had been positioned aft, ready to take off after Ken launched. Behind the three divisions other planes had been moved further aft, if needed, or stored below in the hangar deck.

By now almost everyone on the flight deck knew what was going to happen; not the mission, just that a Jap plane was going to take off from their carrier. Most were mystified, asking each other what was the scuttlebutt. Those few who knew just shrugged their shoulders.

Ken, Roger Paschal, and Lieutenant Bill Patterson walked across the flight deck to the *Shôki*. In his left hand Ken carried his *katana*. It seemed like a long walk to Ken. He thought the *Shôki* looked isolated, as if the other planes were not allowed to be in or near the same location. Ken understood they were giving him enough length for take off. He also knew that the other planes were aft of the *Shôki* in case he crashed onto the flight deck while taking off with a fuel-laden plane. The Air Officer, Commander Macpherson, was not taking any chances. But those reasoned facts didn't shake Ken's feeling of remoteness.

Standing near the *Shôki* were Jim Reichheld and a flight deck crewman, otherwise known as an Airedale, Seaman 1/C Charlie Greene. He wore a yellow shirt and blue dungarees and a protective cloth cap and goggles. There was an oil rag in his right hand. Though he liked his job he really wanted to be a Machinist's Mate. He had plans when the war was over. Reichheld was smiling as Ken, Paschal, and Patterson approached.

"Gentlemen, I'd like you to meet the *Shôki*'s Plane Captain, Seaman First Class Greene."

Ken extended his hand. Greene, baffled, looked at Patterson for direction. Ken smiled and waited patiently. He was beginning to enjoy this. Then he saw that Patterson was about to lay into Greene so he caught Patterson's attention and shook his head. Patterson nodded.

"It's okay, Greene. He's one of us."

Confused, Greene transferred the oil rag to his left hand and wiped his right hand on his dungarees then reluctantly shook hands with the enemy; his expression was puzzled and wary.

"Seaman Greene here has been taking care of your plane," said Reichheld. "He's done a right fine job."

Ken looked at Greene who seemed still ill at ease. "Seaman Greene, you didn't put anything in my fuel tanks except gas, did you?"

"What do you mean?"

Greene looked at Patterson, confused and a bit anxious. He didn't like officers much. They had too much power over his life. And this guy in a Jap uniform didn't set him at ease either. When he had been assigned to the *Shôki* he had taken a lot of ribbing from his fellow Airedales, which just added to his suspicious personality. Now a Jap was questioning his work. He did not like it one bit.

"Lieutenant Patterson, I did what I was told to do. I took good care of this plane, just like it was one of ours. I don't like being insulted by anyone, especially a Jap. Sir."

Paschal started to laugh. "W-W-Well, if anything, that's certainly an endorsement of your m-m-m-mission, K-K-Ken. Seaman G-G-G-Greene, this 'Jap' here is actually L-L-L-Lieutenant Kobayashi, United S-S-S-States Army and a g-g-genuine American. I s-s-suspect he was j-j-just p-p-p-pulling your l-l-leg."

Patterson saw that Ken was smiling. He was relieved but taking no chances. "Seaman Greene," said Patterson, "let's all do a walk-around, shall we?"

Though tense and still a bit ruffled, Greene led them around the plane. The wheel chocks were in tight. Greene pointed to the uncovered pilot tube on the forward right wing, which gave the true air speed. Greene assured Ken the fuel tanks were topped off. "We used that Jap fuel they sent with the plane 'cause we didn't know if this engine could handle our higher octane. So if there's a problem it ain't my fault."

There were no leaks and the canopy had been wiped clean, inside and out. Then Lieutenant Burgess came running toward them.

"Got some news. It's from Sergeant Takayama." He unfolded a yellow sheet of paper. "'At 0900 hours decoded a radio transmission from Miyakonojo to Ichigaya. Lieutenant Colonel Shinaji Masataka. Departure time 1100 hours. At 1220 hours fighters from USS *Randolph* first identified then shot down a 'Frank' over the Shimonoseki Strait, about five miles northeast of Yukuhashi, in the Suo Sea. No parachute was seen and the plane splashed. *Randolph*'s planes loitered for one hour, looking for survivors. There were none. All planes returned to the *Randolph*.'

"Upon receipt of this action from the *Randolph* Sergeant Takayama informed us that two hours later, on a destroyer ten miles southeast of Kyushu, he sent an open message to the Imperial War Ministry of the loss of that plane and Lieutenant Colonel Shinaji. He also informed the Ministry that another officer, a Major Kobayashi, would shortly take off to attend the briefing at Ichigaya. He also sent the same message to Chofu. In both instances it was garbled. The Navy had a sub fifteen miles off the coast of Yokohama. Her skipper reported to Taka that his message, though garbled, was received and understood. So we know the Japs got it.

"Furthermore, when the Jap plane was downed the base from which it flew, and other bases from Miyazaki on the east coast to Makurazaki on the west coast, were hit by carrier-based fighter-bombers and fighters from Iwo Jima, with particular attention to the headquarters, barracks, and any identifiable communications facilities. At Miyakonojo the runway was left intact, which Lieutenant Kobayashi will ostensibly take off from. For the next ten days, every day at random times, those bases will be bombed by carrier planes, particularly communications facilities and their runways. Lieutenant Kobayashi, your mission is on."

"What's the pilot's name again?" asked Ken.

Burgess looked at the paper. "Lieutenant Colonel Shinaji Masataka."

Ken nodded and shook hands. "Then I guess I'm all set. Bill, thank you for your hospitality and the help of your crew. Thank you, Seaman Greene. Mr. Reichheld, it's been a genuine pleasure. Thanks for all your help, especially your modifications."

Reichheld took Ken's hand and held onto it as he looked at Ken. The grin was gone. "Like I said, I know what you're doin'. I hope the Good Lord watches over you. I wish you well."

Ken did not know what to say. He was overwhelmed with the extremes of fear and respect shown to him since he had started this mission on the *Missouri*. At that moment a sailor appeared, carrying Ken's flight suit. Ken thanked him and put it on. He put his officer's cap inside it.

Roger Paschal waited a discrete moment then pulled Ken aside. "I want you t-t-to k-k-know that everyone on the t-t-t-team thinks you are incredibly b-b-brave. Even Sergeant T-T-T-Tall B-B-B-Bear B-B-B-Bliss. Sergeant T-T-Takayama will m-m-make sure your assigned r-r-radio f-f-frequency is m-m-m-monitored around the c-c-clock. I k-k-k-know you'll c-c-come b-b-back b-b-b-but if n-n-n-not I'll w-w-write t-t-to your f-f-f-family and l-l-let them k-k-know what you d-d-d-did. And I k-k-k-know Admiral H-H-Halsey will d-d-do the same. He admires you. I f-f-found this for you. You decide whether you want to wear it."

Paschal handed Ken a small white cloth. Unfolding it, Ken's eyes widened. It was a *hachimaki*, to be worn around the head. It was lettered with Japanese characters, *Shichi Sho Ho Koku*, "Seven Lives to Serve Country." In other words, "Born seven times to serve the homeland."

"You understand I m-m-mean your h-h-homeland in the States. K-K-K-Ken, one m-m-m-more thought I had. It's v-v-v-vital. W-W-While there, *think* J-J-J-Japanese. In Japan, if you l-l-look and act the p-p-p-p-part, you've already w-w-w-won half the b-b-b-battle. I d-d-d-don't k-k-k-know what else t-t-to s-s-say except G-G-G-God speed."

"Listen. I know many people have put a lot of effort into this to make it work. Can you pass on my thanks, especially the pilots who are going to catch me over Atsugi?"

"Sure. It w-w-will b-b-be a p-p-p-pleasure."

At that moment the *Yorktown* and her escorts completed their turn into the wind.

Ken and Paschal shook hands then saluted. At the *Yorktown*'s island Commander Brady, the carrier's XO, stepped forward. "Ship's company! Ten-hut!" A crack like a rifle shot echoed across the flight deck as every one who heard Brady's order stood to attention. "Salute!" Like a well-oiled machine every man saluted. Ken turned and faced the *Yorktown*'s island, returning Brady's salute. Both men locked eyes.

Except for the *Yorktown*'s movement through the water, there was absolute silence on the deck for several seconds.

The incongruity was unspoken. Several times American ships had been the targets of *kamikaze* planes and now the *Yorktown*'s officers and crew were saluting a man in a Japanese flight suit.

Brady lowered his hand and everyone else saluting followed. But none moved as Ken Kobayashi and Roger Paschal walked to the port wing. Ken climbed onto the *Shôki*'s wing, followed by his Plane Captain, Seaman 1/C Greene. He saw that his flight bag had already been pushed in between the seat and cockpit wall and that Greene had already placed his flight helmet, goggles and gloves on the seat, the latter important as fighter cockpits were not heated. Ken put them on and climbed into the cockpit and adjusted himself in the seat, wishing he had a parachute. He knew that American fighter pilots wore an inflatable Mae West floatation vest and when they were strapped to their seat they were by design strapped to a parachute. Additionally, American planes were equipped with a one-man life raft and a survival kit which included a water purifying device. Ken wondered if Japanese pilots knew what they did not have.

Paschal handed Ken's *katana* to Greene who gave it to Ken. He laid it on the floor of the cockpit, between his flight bag and his seat. He looked for Paschal. Seeing him he removed his goggles and wrapped the *hachimaki* around his helmet. He saluted Paschal who smartly returned it. Ken fitted his goggles over the white cloth.

Greene strapped Ken in and gave him a thumbs-up then stepped back and automatically saluted. Ken returned the salute. Greene, surprised at what he had done, jumped off the wing. Commander Macpherson appeared, holding a flag in his hand, taking the role of Flight Deck Officer who would tell Ken when to take off. Ken looked at the instruments, refamiliarizing himself with them.

Paschal and Reichheld stepped back. Greene moved to the starboard side of the plane. Unexpectedly, Ken's stomach felt queasy. Again he asked himself if he knew what he was doing. Though nervous, Ken gave a thumbs-up gesture, letting Macpherson know he was ready. Macpherson signaled Ken to start his engine. Ken first adjusted the propeller to a low pitch, flat to the wind, ensuring little bite when the blades turned. As he reached for the starter switch he noticed another Airedale standing near the engine's port side, carrying a fire extinguisher. This was standard procedure in case the engine caught fire; with the holes in his engine there was a greater risk. The roar of the engine kicking over surprised Ken. When he had flown the plane before, it was from a runway. Brownish smoke shot out and he hastily checked the cockpit light switch. It was down. He swore at himself and hoped no one noticed his momentary alarm. After a few seconds of protest the engine ran smoothly, hitting on all cylinders. The exhaust turned gray. His instrument scan showed his oil pressure was right on forty kilograms, the cylinder head temperature gauge barely at 37° Centigrade. Knowing he would have to sit for about five minutes while the temperature rose to optimum he looked at his fuel gauge and regretted his joke at Greene's expense. It read full.

Ken instinctively reached up and back to slide the canopy forward. Immediately Macpherson gestured, crossing and recrossing his hands above his head. Ken froze. Then he remembered that he had been instructed that right after takeoff from a carrier there was the risk of ditching into the water. If the canopy was closed it might jam on impact and he would not be able to escape. He gave a thumbs-up to Macpherson.

When the cylinder head temperature read normal Ken opened the cowl flaps and placed the wing flaps in full down.

He was careful to open the throttle slowly. He could feel the strain of the *Shôki*, wanting to leap forward but held in place by the wheel chocks. Ken looked around. Every pair of eyes was on him or the *Shôki*. Even the pilots who would take off after him were watching. He wondered what they were thinking then dismissed it. He focused his attention on Macpherson.

Then Macpherson gave hand signals: run up the engine and step on the brakes extra hard.

Ken brought the engine up to 2,000 RPMs. Then, as part of his preflight checklist, he checked the integrity of the two magnetos, alternators with permanent magnets used to generate electricity for the plane's ignition system. He cut one magneto and the engine's RPMs dropped to 1,950. He turned it back on and revved the engine then cut the other and again the engine's RPMs dropped to 1,950. Satisfied, he turned it on and the engine returned to 2,000 RPMs. Again, Ken gave a thumbs-up to Macpherson. He was ready. He looked to his left and saw the Airedale with the fire extinguisher examining the exhaust manifold near the cowl flaps, looking for fire. Ken was not relieved.

In his final act as Plane Captain Greene removed the wheel chocks. Ken could feel the *Shôki* move a fraction, struggling to take off. Ken was practically standing on the brakes, keeping his plane positioned at a three-point attitude, stick back and his tail wheel still on the flight deck. Ken saw Macpherson gesture to Greene and the Airedale with the fire extinguisher to move away. Macpherson looked up at Ken. He now assumed command of flight operations. Ken pulled his goggles over his eyes.

From the safety of both port and starboard catwalks scores of sailors watched. An informal mixture of Airedales, officers, and pilots watched from the flight deck, clustered next to the island. Still more watched from the island's superstructure.

For several seconds Macpherson listened to the engine then gestured and Ken shoved the throttle forward to the firewall, putting the engine at maximum. Ken heard and felt the *Shôki*'s engine growling with fury. Macpherson faced the bow, watching it go up and down with the waves. He looked at his watch; the *Yorktown*'s bow rose and fell every six seconds. He estimated the *Shôki* would take about ten seconds to reach the bow. He wanted to make certain Ken got high in the air as fast as possible. Ken watched Macpherson. He felt the propeller torque wanting to pull the plane forward and to the left.

With the *Yorktown* already turned into the wind and Macpherson feeling the rise and fall of the ship he concentrated on the *Shôki*. When the bow reached bottom he gave Ken the go-ahead by violently dropping his flag arm and falling prone to the deck.

Ken released the brakes. Like a tiger, the *Shôki* lunged forward. As expected, the plane pulled to the left but he corrected. Approaching the *Yorktown*'s island the tail wheel lifted off the deck. Passing the *Yorktown*'s island he was moving at 30 knots. Everything on the deck was becoming a blur, though looking straight ahead he thought he saw several men on either side, in the catwalks, waving. The headwind speed was close to 30 knots and the *Yorktown*'s speed was 30 knots. Ken was taking off into a 60-knot wind.

Seconds before the *Yorktown*'s bow reached its apex the *Shôki* eased straight off the deck. Then it disappeared.

Uncertain, sailors, flight deck personnel, pilots, and everyone at the island raced to the bow, expecting the worst. Even experienced carrier pilots had gone into the drink on takeoff.

Then the *Yorktown*'s bow dropped and like a Phoenix the *Shôki* appeared, its powerful engine pulling it up.

Men yelled, whistled, and applauded as the plane gained altitude.

When Ken felt he had enough speed he pulled the stick back and the *Shôki* readily climbed, returning to Japan.

21

Halfkenny ignored the ambient noise outside the sonar shack. He listened intently after the ashcans had erupted. Screws. That's what he waited for, the revealing sound of movement.

"Bridge! Sonar!"

Blouin bent to the sonar voice tube. "Go ahead, Pete."

"Sir, I've picked up screws but they're fading. I think he's going deeper."

"Pete, he might be going under a thermocline."

"I can't be certain, sir, but I don't think so. I can still hear it so he doesn't appear to have found one. Skipper! I'm picking up some popping sounds!"

"Pete, stay with it. He may be breaking up, but I want to make certain."

*   *   *

Chief Petty Officer Sasaki Sadamitsu ran from the torpedo room, racing to the conning tower. Tears streamed down his face. He knocked down men who tried to stop him as he made his way to the conning tower.

Out of breath he stopped and stood at attention, just over a meter from Iwata. Iwata looked at Sasaki, perplexed. Sasaki was a seasoned veteran. Nothing had ever distressed him.

"Sasaki Jôtô heisô! Why have you left your station?"

Sasaki stood at attention, a terrible moan coming from the bowels of his soul. Everyone on the conning tower felt a chill. Iwata felt his skin tighten.

"Sasaki Jôtô heisô! Report!"

Sasaki just stood and wept, his body racked with emotion.

For the second time in his career Iwata raised his hand and struck a man across the face. He felt no sting of conscience; the welfare of his boat and crew were at stake.

"Sasaki Jôtô heisô! Report!"

"Chûsa! Oda Shô-i! Okada Shô-i kôhosei! Forward torpedo room!" Then, in front of his captain, Sasaki, still at attention, vomited. Partially digested rice oozed down his naked chest.

"Mori Shôsa! You have the con!"

Iwata slid down the conning tower ladder and ran forward toward the torpedo room. Sasaki was running behind him. When he entered the torpedo room he stopped short. His skin prickled. Blood, in two sites, was visible. Other crewmen simply stared, too shocked to even notice their captain. In a second Iwata took it all in.

Iwata walked over to Oda Shô-i, who was facedown on the deck. Two pools of blood, one beneath both his abdomen and neck, were expanding. His knees were beneath him. Iwata rolled Oda's body over. Oda was dressed in full service uniform. A small knife was jammed into Oda's neck, his left hand still on it. Another knife was deep in his abdomen, pulled from left to right. Oda Shô-i wore a *hachimaki* around his head. Iwata saw that both knives had come from the galley. He knew neither was especially sharp. It was, he realized, a painful death. Oda's contorted face revealed his agony.

He walked over to Okada Shô-i kôhosei, the 17-year-old midshipman, so ready to die in the *kaiten*. Okada's body, fully dressed in a seaman's uniform, was crumpled at the foot of a bulkhead, the back of his head bashed in at several places. Iwata turned the boy's body over and touched his young face. Around his waist was a *sen-nin bari haramaki*, a thousand-persons-stitches-stomach-wrapper. Mothers, grandmothers, sisters, daughters or wives of men in the military would stand with a cloth on the sidewalk or village street and ask 1,000 passers-by to make one stitch for luck and protection. She would then send the *sen-nin bari haramaki* to her loved one and he would wear it around his stomach, the stitches signifying the hopes and prayers of 1,000 people accompanying it. Iwata saw a small packet next to Okada. He turned and looked at Oda's body and saw a similar packet. He knew that pieces of their fingernails and a lock of hair were in each man's packet, their only mortal remains to be sent to their families. Tears filled Iwata's eyes. All his energy was drained. He looked at Sasaki.

"Sasaki Jôtô heisô! Report!"

Sasaki too was drained. He went to Oda's body and went down on one knee. He laid Oda's body flat on the deck. He could not bring himself to touch the galley knives. He stood, as if guarding Oda's body.

Sasaki spoke softly. "Oda Shô-i felt frustration and humiliation that he could not help you evade the American destroyer. To atone for this failure he gave his life for *Tennô-Heika*. Okada Shô-i kôhosei also felt shame but not being an officer he felt he could not die as honorably as Oda Shô-i. So he slammed the back of his head against the bulkhead. It took several times before he lost consciousness. He bled to death."

Iwata laid Okada's body flat and covered his head with a nearby cloth. He stood and walked to Sasaki. He stood very close.

"Sasaki," he whispered hoarsely, "I have known you a long time. Why did you not stop this foolishness?"

Sasaki stood at attention, struggling to contain his anger.

"Chûsa! Oda Shô-i was my superior! He ordered us not to interfere! I understood his shame!"

"And what of Okada Shô-i kôhosei? Do you think he was mature enough to make this decision?"

"Chûsa! I understood his shame also!"

"What was their shame, Sasaki? That we cannot defeat the Americans? That we lack the proper equipment to fight? That all we have left to give is our lives? It is a waste! Do you not see that? We cannot defeat them!"

Iwata leaned against a bulkhead, his eyes closed. *Foolish*, he thought. *Perhaps Mori was right. My arrogance has led to these needless deaths.*

Another pattern of depth charges exploded. Two of the men in the torpedo room cringed. Embarrassed, they quickly stood straight. Being well-trained they looked around, searching for leaks. Another explosion, this one close. Too close. All were thrown to the deck. The *I-402*'s stern pitched up several meters and to green, to starboard. A depth charge had exploded less than 30 meters from red, the port stern.

Throughout the boat bulbs broke and leaks erupted. More glass gauge faces broke. Crockery in the galley fell off shelves and smashed on the deck. Supplies, tightly packed throughout the boat, fell onto the deck. Several rice sacks that fell ruptured, spilling their precious contents. In the torpedo room several rivets popped out. The hull, Iwata knew, would soon lose structural integrity.

He sprang to the voice-powered phone. "Mori Shôsa! Damage report!"

"Chûsa! Depth charge on red stern! Engine room reports flooding and repeated banging from overhead!"

The kaiten*!* Iwata thought.

Iwata was in a dilemma. He knew the destroyer would pick up the banging, caused by their forward motion. But he had to maintain forward motion or else the boat would lose its trim due to the water flooding the stern. At 150 meters the boat, taking on water, could sink.

Iwata, gambling on a possible solution, acted quickly.

"Mori Shôsa! Ahead slow! Order the damage control party to the engine room!" He hung up the voice-powered phone.

"Sasaki Jôtô heisô! After I leave secure this compartment! No one leaves or enters!"

Iwata entered the passageway and started to run aft, to the engine room. When he saw crewmen ahead he yelled, "Make way!"

Reaching the engine room he stopped to catch his breath and make a quick survey. He looked up and immediately understood. The depth charge explosion had lifted one end of a *kaiten*'s wooden platform.

He saw that the brass washers were now conical and were six inches down from the overhead. Two showers of seawater gushed into the engine room.

By 1945 the steel in Japan was of poor quality, primarily due to the U.S. Navy's blockade. The steel bolts were stretched six inches and thinned from two inches to one and three-quarter inches.

Five hundred pounds of water per minute rushed through each opening. The damage control crew, standing in over one foot of water, was trying to divert it to the bilges, gutters on either side of the engine room, to be pumped out to the sea.

"You and you!" yelled Iwata. "Get four boards! You," he pointed at another crewman, "get wood plugs, rags and two chains!"

While he waited he looked at his engine room crew. The room, despite the water, was still hot. Each man was dressed solely in a *fundoshi*, their skin glistening with sweat. The smell of oil was heavier in the engine room than in other compartments.

Within two minutes the crewmen had returned. "You four! Hold up the boards and divert the water to the bilges! You two! Wrap the rags around the wooden plugs!"

With the water deflected to the sides of the sub's walls Iwata grabbed a chain, stood on a pipe and started to wrap the chain around one bolt.

Suddenly the *I-402* was rocked by another explosion. The washers were slammed against the overhead then slammed down. Iwata fell off the pipe, eyes wide as water doused him. Had the explosion occurred seconds later he would have lost several fingers from both hands. He got back up on the pipe and wrapped one end of the chain to the bolt, above the washer, then jumped off the pipe.

"You! Remove this deck plate!" Underneath the deck plate were longitudinal steel "T" bars and ribs. Iwata secured the chain to one of the "T" bars. He repeated the same steps with the other bolt and secured the chain to another "T" bar.

He grabbed one of the wood plugs, wrapped a rag around it and jammed it into the overhead where the bolt exited. Other damage control crewmen repeated Iwata's steps in both openings. Soon the water flow was reduced to manageable drips, allowed to float to the bilges.

Another depth charge explosion rocked the *I-402*. *He truly has a bone in his teeth*, thought Iwata, thinking of the American destroyer captain. But the chains held the bolts and the wood plugs did not fall out.

"Maintain a watch on the chains!" ordered Iwata as he left the engine room, running back to the forward torpedo room.

When he arrived he picked up the voice-powered phone.

"Mori Shôsa! Discharge oil!" Discharging oil from the bilge was an old trick, often used to convince the hunter that the submarine was damaged. It never worked. "Mori Shôsa! I am going to impulse tube seven from the torpedo room." He hung up the phone.

"Sasaki Jôtô heisô! Make number seven tube ready to receive debris," Iwata ordered, pointing to wooden cases.

The crewmen packed torpedo tube seven with debris and supplies, anything that would float. Tubes one through six, already loaded with torpedoes, were useless.

When more explosions tore through the water Iwata ordered Sasaki to impulse number seven tube with air, launching the debris with air. Then they waited. Iwata knew it might not work but the crew expected some action.

Exhausted from the tension, Iwata saw the fatigue and fear in his crew. He picked up the voice-powered phone and buzzed the conning tower.

"Mori Shôsa! Iwata! Status!"

"Chûsa! Repair crews are in action! Depth is 150 meters at 0° bubble! Speed is two knots! Maintaining speed and course!"

"Mori Shôsa! Is Watanabe Tai-i charting thermoclines?"

"*Ha!*" replied Mori.

Another time, thought Iwata, and he would have smiled. Now he had to save his boat.

"Are we still below the thermocline?"

"Chûsa! Watanabe Tai-i reports we are!"

Good, he thought, as he replaced the phone. *Good. We stay deep and hidden.*

"Sasaki Jôtô heisô! Except for yourself clear the torpedo room! Seal the hatch!"

Confused, Chief Petty Officer Sasaki Sadamitsu ordered the torpedo room cleared. Hesitant at first, the crew moved sharply when Iwata glared at them. As the last sailor exited Sasaki sealed the hatch.

Iwata looked at the bodies on the deck. Then, hardening himself, he went to a bulkhead and grabbed an axe. He stepped to Oda's body. Sasaki saw grim tension on his captain's face.

"Sasaki Jôtô heisô! What I do next must remain in this

room! No one else on this boat must know what happens! Do you understand? You may report it when and if we get to home-port! Is that understood?"

Beyond confusion, Sasaki simply nodded once.

Iwata bent over Oda's body and pulled out the knives and tossed them aside in disgust. He picked up the packet with Oda's hair and fingernail pieces and put it in his right breast pocket. He momentarily looked at Sasaki then down at Oda's body. He lifted the axe and violently drove it into Oda's abdomen, right at the self-inflicted wound. He did it again. And again. Then he changed the angle and struck several times, following the length of the original cut. He stopped, breathing heavily. He then moved Oda's head to the side and precisely struck at the neck wound, creating a large gash.

He looked at Sasaki and saw him trembling, horror across his face. Before Sasaki could utter a word Iwata went to Okada's body. He knelt down and gently touched Okada's face, looking at him as if he was asleep. He picked up Okada's packet and placed it in his left breast pocket and removed the cloth that he used to cover Okada's head. Then he stood and with the side of the axe he smashed Okada's head, carefully avoiding his face, and then crushed Okada's right shoulder. Then he attacked Okada's right leg. Sinew and bone were visible.

"Sasaki Jôtô heisô! Open torpedo tube seven! Sasaki! Now!"

Numb with terror, Sasaki opened torpedo tube seven.

Iwata picked up the voice-powered phone and pressed the conning tower button. Mori answered.

"Mori Shôsa! Iwata! Status!"

"Chûsa! Depth is 150 meters at 0° bubble! Speed is two knots!"

Iwata needed to gamble if his boat and crew were to survive. He knew he owed them that. "Mori Shôsa! All stop! Ultra quiet!"

"Chûsa! We are still flooded in the engine room! We will lose trim if we stop engines!"

"Mori Shôsa! I gave a direct order! I will return to the con directly! Carry out my orders!"

Mori hung up the phone. Iwata breathed deeply several times then looked at Sasaki, who shuddered when he looked into his captain's eyes.

"Sasaki Jôtô heisô! Help me load these bodies!"

With particular tenderness the bodies were loaded into tube seven. Iwata nodded and Sasaki sealed the tube. "Now we wait, Sasaki."

The wait was not long. More depth charges erupted but were too far away to damage the *I-402*. Iwata had the moment he needed. They would be masked from the destroyer's sonar for several minutes.

Iwata grabbed the voice-powered phone. "Conning. Forward Torpedo room! This is the captain! I am going to impulse tube seven from the torpedo room." He replaced the phone.

"Sasaki. Flood and impulse tube seven."

*　　　*　　　*

"Bridge. Sonar."

"Go ahead, Pete."

"Sir, I'm picking up some new sounds. I never heard it before."

"Pete, pipe it into the speaker." Blouin moved to the bridge speaker and listened for several seconds. He looked at Tom Maher. "Mister Maher, what do you think?"

Maher moved to the speaker and listened. "Sounds like he's launched a torpedo but it's not a torpedo."

Blouin looked over the water. "Yeah, like he's shooting blind. Or he no longer controls his boat's firing control. Son of a bitch! We took a bite out of him." Blouin went to the sonar voice tube. "Pete. You got a location?"

"Sorry, Captain. I think he might be under a thermocline."

"Mister Maher, change course 90 degrees starboard. Let's see if we can shake him loose."

As the *Ingersoll* turned 90° starboard Seaman, First Class, Pat Murphy was still the port bridge lookout. And he was still hungry. However, he had had four cups of coffee and though the coffee had not lessened his hunger he had to go to the head awfully bad. He scanned the waters. While moving his binoculars from right to left he saw something about 1,500 yards from the *Ingersoll*'s port side. Like the last time, he ignored the bridge phone and turned to the open bridge doorway. "Mister Maher! There's debris in the water!"

Both Blouin and Maher ran to Murphy's lookout station. "Where," asked Blouin while automatically scanning the water.

"Over there, sir," Murphy said while pointing.

Blouin scanned the waters and located the debris. He went to the helm voice tube. "Helm. Come left, steer course 290 degrees."

Within minutes the *Ingersoll* reached the debris field and reduced speed to 5 knots so sailors could hook the debris and pull it aboard. Maher went aft to examine the debris. He picked up the phone and buzzed the bridge.

"Sir, it's wooden cases and supplies and some junk."

"Tom, the starboard lookout just reported an oil slick about 2,000 yards. I think he's playing a game. Let's resume the search. Return to the bridge."

When Maher reached the bridge the phone buzzed. He picked it up and listened then hung up. "Captain, the fantail reports debris 4,000 yards off the starboard stern."

"Helm, all-ahead two thirds. Right standard rudder, steady on course 330 degrees."

As the *Ingersoll* approached the new field Blouin ordered speed reduced to less than five knots. It was easy to make out the two bodies floating on the surface, less than one hundred feet away. Rather than using grappling hooks to retrieve the bodies Blouin ordered two swimmers from amidships into the water with ropes to secure the bodies. These bodies were not debris, and would be handled with respect. Both Blouin and Maher made their way to the amidships main deck.

While the destroyer circled, each swimmer reached a body and looped the torso then grabbed onto knots forward of the loops and all were hauled aboard.

As Blouin and Maher reached the amidships main deck sailors were laying out the bodies for inspection. Blouin saw how placidly the sailors positioned the bodies. There was no sense of triumph. They were no longer enemies.

Blouin ordered speed back to standard, 15 knots. Both he and Maher stood silent for a few seconds.

One of the dead men wore an officer's uniform, the other a seaman's uniform. Both bodies displayed minor bite wounds from fish.

Maher bent down and examined the pockets of the dead officer. He found a small leather folder in the breast pocket. He removed it and shook off the excess water then handed it to Blouin.

Blouin opened it and found what he hoped he would not. He examined the snapshots and sighed. A man, a woman and two young children, one an infant.

Blouin turned and looked at the body in the seaman's uniform. He stared at the face. A boy, he thought, just a kid. Thin and small of stature. *He should be in high school*, thought Blouin. *Christ, it's over. Don't they know it yet?* He examined their injuries, consistent, he felt, with wounds from explosions.

"Tom, maintain ASW Condition One. I'll radio the *Yorktown* that we probably sunk a pigboat and recovered two bodies. We'll join up in a while. In the meantime, assemble a burial detail and prepare these bodies. When they're cleaned up and wrapped in canvas go to my inport cabin. You'll find a Jap flag in the top left drawer in my desk. The least we can do is let them rejoin their crew honorably." Several of the *Ingersoll*'s crew looked at their skipper with disbelief, some with anger.

Captain Blouin's decision was not without precedent. On April 11, 1945, a "*Zero*" *kamikaze* suicide pilot, flying through fierce antiaircraft fire, crashed into the USS *Missouri*, hitting the hull below the main deck. Damage was minimal with no American casualties. The pilot's body was found among the wreckage. When asked if the body should be pitched overboard Captain William Callaghan, acknowledging the pilot's courage, instead ordered a burial at sea. The next day a Marine honor guard fired a salute and his body was committed to the deep.

Blouin stood silently for a moment, looking at the body of the boy. *Damn! The bastards are sending their* kids *to war to get killed*. He started to return to the bridge, stopped and gazed silently out at the ocean for several seconds, then turned to Maher.

"Tom, tell the sailmaker to forget the last stitch."

Blouin closed his eyes briefly then headed for the bridge. *A boy, just a boy*, he thought as he walked away, *younger than my son*.

A sailor drew near Maher. "Sir, what did the skipper mean? We don't have no sailmaker on board, do we?"

Maher watched Blouin walk away then looked at the sailor.

"No, we don't. Sailors are a superstitious lot. It was felt you couldn't always be certain if a man was really dead so when men were buried at sea, the ship's sailmaker would wrap the body in canvas and stitch it up. On his last stitch, he would push his needle through the man's nose. If the man was still alive it was felt he was sure to scream or move. No one wanted to bury a living man. I guess the captain wants to make sure we don't hurt these men anymore."

*   *   *

Iwata returned to the con. He saw that Mori was agitated. "Mori Shôsa! Report!"

"Chûsa! Damage control reports that flooding in the engine room is contained! We are losing trim! Bubble is ten degrees up!"

Iwata ignored the affront. "Mori Shôsa, order all available crewmen to the bow. We will stabilize the old way. Let the damage control party deal with the leak!"

Mori Shôsa ordered all available crewmen to all forward compartments. Slowly, ever so slowly, the *I-402* reached 0° bubble. Iwata looked at the clock. Enough time had passed for the bodies to reach the surface. Would, he wondered, two bodies be enough to convince the Americans? With the debris and the oil slick it might. There were only two ways to find out. The first was to wait to see if more depth charges were released. Koyama was the second. He descended to the sonar station. One place was good as another to die.

"Koyama Heichô! Report!"

"Chûsa! The destroyer slowed speed to five knots for several minutes then increased speed to fifteen knots! Then they changed course, then reduced speed to five knots! Their speed is now fifteen knots! Course unchanged!"

"Have they used active sonar?"

Koyama hesitated for just seconds. He had not expected the question. Puzzled, he turned to face Iwata. "No, Chûsa. They have not pinged for several minutes. Chûsa! Why have they not tried to locate us?"

Iwata ruffled Koyama's head. "When a dog barks the fox

knows he is there. The Americans are using their nose and not their bark. Soon they will go away. Listen and wait to see if I am correct."

Koyama Heichô closed his eyes and rotated the hydrophone knob. His eyebrows went up slowly. The American destroyer's screws were receding. He looked at Iwata who smiled and walked away. He mounted the conning ladder and ascended.

"Mori, the Americans are leaving. In thirty minutes make your speed six knots and depth thirty meters. Tonight we surface and jettison the *kaiten*. When repairs are completed resume course for Formosa. When we arrive we will make permanent repairs." He touched his left breast pocket, thinking of Okada.

"I have two letters to write and a report about a traitor. You have the conn. If you need me I will be in my cabin."

22

When Ken's plane dropped below the *Yorktown*'s bow he pulled back on the stick. The *Shôki* responded with its powerful engine like a spirited stallion. As he turned toward Kyûshû he looked over his shoulder and saw the flight deck of the *Yorktown* quickly recede. In less than a minute he reached 2,000 feet and decided to stay at that altitude for a few minutes, to make certain the bullet holes in the plane did not interfere with his flying. Reichheld was right; she flew like he hoped she would. Feeling the cold he reached up and back and slid the canopy closed.

He climbed to his designated altitude of angels six, 6,000 feet. He looked through the glass canopy as the engine's resonance permeated the cockpit. Ken loved flying. He remembered when he and his brother Tom flew a crop dusting plane over their and others' farms. The sense of control was overwhelming, the sense of freedom boundless. He loved being in the air, above where birds seemed to glide on invisible platforms.

There were no boundaries save the earth below and the limitations of the *Shôki*. For several minutes he forgot his mission, instead reveling in the sense of freedom. Then his mission intruded and the reasons for it.

He wondered about the man whose place he was taking and his own feelings of that man's death. Enemy or not he was a man who may have had a sweetheart, maybe a wife and kids. He was fighting for his country and his way of life. *Just like me*, thought Ken. *Are we any different? Did he believe in his cause as deeply as I do? Do I? I fight for a country that imprisoned my family and me. What do I believe? Did he dedicate his life to his family or his Emperor and country?*

He shook his head, purging the disturbing thoughts. He increased his air speed to 200 knots, an economical speed for the *Shôki*. He was not, he thought, anxious to rush to his death.

Occasionally, the *Shôki* was buffeted by winds from the receding typhoon, but Ken thought she was ignoring any transient turbulence. Then he smiled, realizing he referred to the *Shôki* as "she," something the Japanese did not do. He knew he would have to watch that.

He flew for thirty minutes without distraction. He was on course at 6,000 feet. Then they came at him, one on either side and two behind him. His first instinct was to push the throttle but instead he looked at them, first his left then right. They were less than 200 feet from him. They were Hellcats. The pilot on his right brought his Hellcat closer to the *Shôki*. Twenty-five feet from Ken's right wing the pilot raised his goggles. Ken recognized him. Then Lieutenant Bob Stanton saluted Ken.

Ken turned away for a second. When he looked back Stanton's right hand was still saluting. Ken nodded and returned the salute. Stanton dropped his hand and banked his Hellcat away and the division backed off. Ken knew Stanton did not have to do what he did. It's a strange war, he thought. When he looked over his shoulder he saw that Stanton's division had climbed to 8,000 feet and was several hundred feet behind him. Nevertheless, he acknowledged, they were there and he was grateful.

Then the coffee from the *Gatling* and the *Yorktown* caught up with him. *Holy water time*, he told himself. With his bladder complaining and cursing himself for not having used the head before taking off he fervently hoped that Japanese planes had the tube. He groped under the seat with his hand and audibly sighed as he pulled a rubber tube up. A small funnel was attached to the end of the tube. With the flat of his other hand he slapped the funnel opening to clear the tube of any blockage, including spiders. It was difficult but he unfastened his flight suit then his uniform pants and pulled his penis out and placed it over the rim of the funnel. He smiled ruefully, wondering if Greene had found any spiders. Too late now, he acknowledged, as warm urine rapidly flowed into the funnel. Underneath the fuselage urine dissipated in the atmosphere.

Fifty miles further another division took up a protective position. When Ken looked down he saw a destroyer paralleling his course. He confirmed his direction and speed.

Other than the new Hellcat divisions escorting Ken the flight was uneventful. The Hellcats stayed at a safe distance, insuring a sense of solitude but close enough in case any plane might interfere with Ken's flight. Soon he would sight Kyûshû and he knew there would be no turning back. Twenty miles from the coast he dropped to 1,000 feet and reduced speed to 125 knots. The escorting Hellcats peeled away to return to the *Yorktown* and the PBM returned to Okinawa; Ken was on his own.

As he approached Japan he slipped his hand into his shirt pocket and gently touched the wrapping. He tried to crush the question but could not. Sadly, he wondered if Kyoko were married. Then, painfully, he wondered if she were alive.

Approaching Nobeoka, on the eastern coast of Kyûshû, Ken dropped to five hundred feet and reduced his speed to 100 knots. Drawing near he remembered Captain Paschal asking, *"Koketsu ni ittekureruka?"* He asked himself if he was indeed ready to enter the cave of the tiger.

At the coast he saw fishermen first running from their boats then returning when they saw the *Shôki*'s red "meatballs" painted on the wings. They waved as he flew over them.

Now over Japan he scanned the skies for enemy planes then remembered he was piloting one. He was safe, as far as the Japanese were concerned and as long as he stayed within the air corridor laid out by the American Navy. He had another six hours before American planes were allowed to resume their attacks within his air corridor.

He looked down at the mostly mountainous landscape and saw the destruction wrought by America's awesome military supremacy. He could see that bombs had smashed the national highway and coastal railroad at Nobeoka; the ground was scarred with craters. Buildings were leveled, burned, or simply pulverized. Railroad tracks were torn apart. Several rail cars, like broken toys, were cast about. Workers, men and women, repairing the tracks looked up at him, just in case. There were other marks on the ground, numerous rectangular mounds. Turning away, he knew there were bodies under those mounds. Ken tried to put the images out of his mind. He had a job to do and he remembered what America had been saying for almost four years: "They asked for it."

He banked slightly, and climbed to 2,000 feet and increased speed to 150 knots, heading toward Takamori, about 35 miles northwest of Nobeoka. As he flew he surveyed the landscape. No matter where he looked the terrain was disfigured.

When he looked down at the rice fields he noticed two things: bomb craters and how little rice there seemed to be. *Starve your enemy and he can't fight*, he thought. But he noted that farmers still labored, working around the craters. He saw some farmers working on the hillsides and remembered when Kyoko and he had visited the countryside that rice farmers had planted rice seedlings in tiny paddies on terraces, accessible only by ladders. Now, he saw them looking up at his plane then going back to work. He wondered how Americans would have dealt with daily bombings on their farms or villages or cities. Looking down at the mountains he saw focused zones of destruction. From his briefings he knew that coal was mined in the mountains of northern Kyûshû. *Shut down your enemy's energy source and he can't manufacture*, he mused.

Once over Takamori, serviced by a secondary road, he was equally opposite the western and eastern coasts of Kyûshû. Now his course was to the north, toward Moji, fed by a national highway and a rail line. Like Nobeoka and Takamori, the Americans had attacked Moji, an opportune military and economic target having both a national highway and rail line.

He proceeded due north, heading for the coast, his final landmark being Hachiya. Just south of Hachiya a bridge lay in ruins, having been attacked several times by bombers.

Sixteen nautical miles to the east of Hachiya lay Usa. Ken remembered a story told to him by an Army Air Force pilot a few months back. Usa, before the war, exported products to the United States, and these products had been labeled in English "Made in USA." The pilot told him that every time Usa had been bombed many of the bombs had been labeled "Really Made in USA!"

Being near the coast, Hachiya had not fared any better than other targets. Japan, he thought, was literally being decimated. Again, he dismissed his feelings; he had his mission. Before him lay Shimonoseki Strait, the body of water separating Kyûshû from Honshû, Japan's main island.

At its closest points, Moji on Kyûshû and Shimonoseki on Honshû, just a quarter of a mile separated the two islands. Beneath the waters of the strait a train tunnel serviced both islands. Though the strait itself was shallow it was deep enough to allow ships—including warships—passage.

But the waters of Shimonoseki Strait were not safe for any shipping; American B-29s had been dropping thousands of mines in the Strait. And all around Japan, in every strait and every entrance to Japan's harbors, tens of thousands of mines lay waiting for any vessels.

As he passed Hachiya he came over the Suô Sea and saw several coastal craft circling to his left. This was the spot where the Hellcats from the *Randolph* had earlier shot down the "Frank." He knew they were searching for survivors. He reduced his altitude to 500 feet and speed to 100 knots then banked left toward the site and loitered for a few moments, hoping the man had died immediately.

Then, puzzled, he wondered why he felt that way. That man was the enemy. *He was* my *enemy,* he told himself angrily. *He's Japanese, I'm an American!* He banked hard to the right, heading toward Ube, on the southern coast of Honshû.

As he approached the coast he started to climb, quickly reaching 5,000 feet, and accelerated to 150 knots. At that altitude he saw other planes in the sky. And two were flying toward him, one on either side. They were Imperial Japanese Navy planes and as they passed one of the pilots saluted him. Ken was surprised. Based on the radio intercepts, captured documents and interviews with Japanese prisoners, he knew the Imperial Japanese Navy and Army got along like *mizu* and *abura*, water and oil. Relieved, he continued on his course.

Over Ube he changed his course to east-northeast. He was 411 nautical miles from Atsugi, a straight course with no planned deviations. He increased his speed to 175 knots and climbed to 10,000 feet. For the first time since taking off from the *Yorktown* he felt relaxed. At 175 knots he had about two hours of flying, ample time to wonder what he was going to do and say once he landed at Atsugi, especially when they started to interrogate him. However, he had to admit, after passing the two Imperial Japanese Navy planes, that this was the best way to get into Japan; the "Kobayashi Group" had, he acknowledged, been right.

It was a relaxing flight especially since only a few Japanese planes crossed his path. So far everything was proceeding according to plan; no American planes were visible to him. The only discordant note was the horrific destruction he could see.

Then he arrived over Kure, 106 nautical miles from Ube. Kure was one of Japan's major naval bases, in Honshû's Inland Sea. It was here that the super battleship *Yamato*, the world's largest, was built. On April 7, 1945, during the invasion of Okinawa, American carrier-based planes had sunk the *Yamato* in less than two hours. As Ken flew over Kure's docks he spotted two battleships, both dead in the water. One was the *Haruna*, which had had its stern blown off by a bomb from a B-29 on June 22, 1945. On July 28 planes from American carriers had sunk her. American carrier planes sank the other battleship, the *Hyuga*, just six days before Ken took off from the *Yorktown*. From his altitude he could plainly see how effective America's air power was. Countless tons of bombs had been dropped, destroying most of the base, numerous ships, and surrounding industrial sites and obliterating a vast section of the city itself. He flew on, his mind closed to the devastation behind him.

Further east, 214 nautical miles, lay Kôbe and just 21 nautical miles further on was Ôsaka. Both were on the eastern end of the Inland Sea and both were constant targets for the Army Air Force's bombers and the Navy's carrier-based planes. And both cities had felt the fury of General Curtis LeMay's firebombing strategy. Ken knew that Ôsaka, Japan's second-largest city, held Japan's largest army arsenal and the Maruzen oil refinery as well as aircraft factories and, of course, military barracks. But as he flew over the cities he was troubled that the bombing strategy included the destruction of the cities themselves. Flying over Kôbe and Ôsaka the effects of the firebombings were unmistakable. Vast sectors of the cities were completely devoid of structures; just rubble and bomb craters now occupied most of Ôsaka's landscape. He thought of the civilians who had nothing to do with the war, especially the children.

Ken knew that America had earlier run out of primary Japanese industrial, military, and civilian urban targets for its bombers and carrier-based planes and that secondary, tertiary and even quaternary targets—military, industrial, and civilian—had already been burned to the ground. When he looked down he saw that the few individual buildings left standing were reinforced—concrete or metal—but that explosions or flames had gutted most of them.

From briefings Ken knew that about 90 percent of Japan's buildings, both residential and non-residential, were made of wood and plaster. They were perfect targets for LeMay's incendiary bombs.

Factories, before they had been leveled or gutted, were surrounded by masses of closely-packed flimsy wooden workshops, the homes of the workers themselves, where families would produce small components for the factories. When the incendiary bombs exploded, no amount of fire-fighting effort saved them. Worse, by this time Japan's water supplies were inadequate for large-scale fire-fighting.

What were most visible to Ken were the city blocks and streets, both now containing mostly rubble. He wondered if the civilians or even the military and governmental leadership knew what was in store for Japan after Pearl Harbor. Probably not, he thought. No one, he concluded while looking down, could have predicted the wrath of an enraged America.

His next landmark, 32 nautical miles distance, was Kyôto, the former imperial capital of Japan. He had been there several times while he was a student at Tôkyô Imperial University, once with Kyoko.

The last emperor to live there was Meiji, who, in the late nineteenth century, had brought Japan into the modern world. Kyôto was a beautiful, ancient city, unchanged, for the most part, by the rest of the country's modernization.

When Ken looked down he was gratified to see Kyôto was still untouched by the war's destruction. Then he saw the new factories and new housing for workers and it saddened him. He knew that with the factories Kyôto was now a legitimate military target for bombers and wondered why Kyôto had not yet been bombed.

Ken did not know that on June 1, 1945 Secretary of War Henry L. Stimson had met with General Henry "Hap" Arnold, commander of the Army Air Force, to discuss the strategy of B-29s in Japan. At that meeting General Arnold was forbidden from bombing Kyôto without Stimson's permission. Stimson knew that Kyôto was revered by the Japanese as a cultural and religious center and feared that bombing Kyôto would enrage the Japanese so much that Japan would be driven into Russia's arms after the war. Unknown to General Arnold there was another reason.

While serving as Governor General of the Philippines, 16 years earlier, Stimson had visited Kyôto and come away with a deep sense of its antiquity and its place in Japan's culture and religion.

Ironically, the Los Alamos Target Committee, on May 10-11, 1945, chose Kyôto for the first atomic bomb precisely because it had not yet been bombed and because civilian workers and war industries had been moved there, making Kyôto a legitimate target.

The other choices for the atomic bomb were, in order, Hiroshima, Yokohama, Kokura Arsenal, and Niigata. The possibility of bombing the Emperor's palace was discussed but because it had little strategic value it was dismissed. Besides, rational minds knew that Emperor Hirohito had to survive in order to surrender.

Ken reduced his speed and surveyed the city and recalled their trip. Kyoko and he had stayed at a *ryokan*, an inn, and she had practically dragged him around Kyôto, proud of its rich heritage. And he remembered their third night because that was when they made love for the first time. As he recalled those hours of tenderness the pain of the longing besieged him. Again, he wondered whether Kyoko was still alive. After lingering for several minutes more he went back on course, to Nagoya, 47 nautical miles east of Kyôto.

When he arrived over Nagoya he was shaken. Nagoya was Japan's fourth-largest city and third-largest manufacturing center, with most of the industry dedicated to the war effort. From air reconnaissance photographs he recognized the giant Mitsubishi airframe plant and the Mitsubishi aircraft engine plant. Or what was left of them. Both were almost completely demolished and the workers' home factories surrounding them had simply disappeared. The workers who did not heed the air raid sirens were killed, most incinerated by the fires.

As he flew over Nagoya he estimated that as much as fifty percent of the city had been burned to the ground. As were the memories he had when he and Kyoko and his brother, Tom, had visited Nagoya to meet Kyoko's grandparents. As he flew from Nagoya he was still shaken. Most of Kyoko's extended family had lived in Nagoya. He wondered if she might have been there during a raid. He tried to dismiss these thoughts but failed.

As he flew closer to Tôkyô he was struck by how few planes there were in the air. Surely, he reasoned, there should have been planes patrolling the skies of the empire's capital city and nerve center.

Less than a hundred miles from Nagoya he easily spotted another memory with Kyoko, Fuji-*san*, Mount Fuji, a sacred symbol of Japan. They had taken the Tôkaidô rail line from Tôkyô to the city of Fuji and then made their way to the base of Fuji-*san* to join hundreds climbing to the dormant volcanic peak. He remembered her laughter when she told him that until the Meiji Restoration women were not allowed to climb Fuji-*san*. He decided to fly over rather than go around. He remembered that the mountain's height was over 12,000 feet so he started to climb to 15,000 feet. He wanted to see as much as possible. And he did.

As he flew toward the gently sloping peak he sighted two immense displays of awesome devastation. On either side of him, one more than 100 miles to the northwest, the other about 75 miles to the east, billowing clouds of thick smoke ascended into the sky. He knew right away what it was but not where.

In the early morning hours of the previous day 784 B-29s from the Twentieth Air Force bombed several targets throughout Japan. 627 B-29s carried out firebomb raids on four Japanese cities: Hachiôji, Toyama, Nagaoka, and Mito. At the same time another 120 B-29s bombed Kawasaki's petroleum facilities. In other parts of Japan another 37 B-29s dropped mines in Shimonoseki Strait, in Nakaumi Lagoon, at Hamada, Sakai, Yonago, Najin and Seishin. The raids, in their totality, were the Twentieth Air Force's largest single-day effort of World War II.

Kawasaki, to the east, had been bombed numerous times before. But Toyama, northwest of Ken's position, had not experienced the wrath of *B-san*, the name given to the B-29 by the Japanese. But Toyama was a center of aluminum production and when the B-29s were finished the aluminum production facilities, which were still burning, as well as 95 percent of Toyama were gone, except for the smoke and ash that Ken saw at 15,000 feet. The memory with Kyoko was lost, intermixed with the smoke and ash. He flew over Fuji-*san* and started to descend to 5,000 feet. Atsugi and the Hellcats were waiting for him, just over four nautical miles.

23

Atsugi Naval Air Base was Tôkyô's last strategic line of aviation defense. And by August 1945 it was failing.

The Imperial Japanese Navy built Atsugi in 1938 as Emperor Hirohito's Naval Air Base. The 302nd Naval Air Group, the Emperor's pilots, trained some of the best pilots in Japan before and during World War II. The 302nd was augmented by the 1st and 2nd Sagamino Naval Air Groups.

With 220 buildings and 489 *chô*—1,200 acres—Atsugi Airdrome, as it was also called, was the largest aviation base in Japan and only the best pilots were stationed there. At the beginning of the war with America, operations were on a limited scale.

As the Americans relentlessly came closer to Japan, Atsugi Naval Air Base was officially activated on April 1, 1943, commissioned to defend the Kantô Plain, which included the Imperial Palace, Tôkyô, and Yokohama, with an initial force of 60 aircraft. But that was soon to change.

In Rabaul, in the spring of 1943, Imperial Japanese Navy Commander Kozono Yasuna was given command of the 251st *Kôkutai*. American B-24 Liberator bombers were constantly raiding Japanese installations in the region. Kozono, an intelligent and skilled combat pilot, was frustrated at not being able to stop the B-24s' night raids. He had an idea and suggested that the *Gekkô*, a three-seat fighter, might make a good night fighter that could shoot down the long-ranging B-24s during their night raids. Under Kozono's direction ground crews at Rabaul removed all the equipment from the *Gekkô*'s observer's cockpit position and mounted two fixed 20 mm cannon which fired obliquely upward at an angle of 30°. Two comparable cannons were installed in the ventral fuselage behind the wing firing 30° downward.

In May of 1943 two B-24s were intercepted and destroyed by the modified *Gekkôs*. Persuaded by these results the Imperial Naval Staff adopted Kozono's modifications and the *Gekko* J1N1 was designated as a night fighter.

By February 1944 the Atsugi Naval Air Group received the latest *Zero* and *Gekkô* fighters, bringing Atsugi's alert air strength to 72 carrier fighters, 24 night fighters, and 12 reconnaissance planes. In October 1944 the Imperial Naval Staff promoted Kozono to captain and gave him command of Atsugi.

Kozono was an inspirational and disciplined commander. His air group at Atsugi was the first to receive the order to defend mainland Japan "to the end." He was utterly devoted to *Tennô-Heika* and took those orders literally.

But Atsugi had more to offer. Besides the *Gekkô* and *Zero* fighters Atsugi also had other planes—*Raiden* and *Suisei*. In addition to the main runway Atsugi has special runways, one for the *Shûsui*, a rocket-powered fighter plane, and the *Renzan*, a four-engine bomber designed to attack mainland America. However, they were only in trial production.

Atsugi was ringed with antiaircraft guns and several radar stations and had about 7,000 personnel. It had sufficient food and ammunition stored to fight the war for another two years. Moreover, like many air bases in Japan, it had kept hidden over 1,000 *kamikaze* planes for the expected American invasion of mainland Japan.

But everything was to change because America had a new

weapon, something the skilled pilots at Atsugi and other Japanese air bases could not counter.

On July 7, 1944, 14 B-29s from Chengdu, China bombed cities on Kyûshû. But Chengdu was too far from Japan to carry out effective raids. Events far away from China would remove those limitations.

One month earlier, June 15, the American Marines invaded Saipan. On July 23 the Marines took Tinian. On August 10 Guam, which had been lost to the Japanese in December 1941, was retaken. The Marianas campaign was complete and soon the B-29s would have new bases, closer to Japan.

On November 24, 1944, 111 B-29s flew from the Marianas to Tôkyô, arriving over the city around noon. But from 30,000 feet, using a strategy called high-altitude precision bombing, the raid was marginal. At that altitude the bombs were scattered by winds often over 100 miles an hour. Some fires were started but no factories were hit. Within two hours the fires were put out and debris was being cleared away. Several more raids were carried out, using the same strategy, but for the most part were ineffective. Then Major General Curtis LeMay suggested a different bombing strategy, proposing that instead of trying to hit specific military or industrial targets the cities of Japan themselves become the targets.

Several, including Admiral Nimitz and General Hap Arnold, opposed LeMay's proposal, preferring that the B-29s strike directly at military and industrial targets. So the high-altitude precision bombing continued. Between November 24, 1944 and March 4, 1945, there were 22 B-29 raids on Japanese industry but just one factory had been destroyed. The cost was high—102 B-29s and their crews were lost. Everyone agreed that the strategy was not working.

Then LeMay further defined his proposal, advocating a strategy of accurate low-level incendiary attacks on Japanese cities. When the results of the previous raids were reviewed in detail his proposal was accepted.

On the night of March 9-10, 1945, 334 B-29s, from Guam, Saipan, and Tinian took off for Tôkyô, each bomber loaded with more than seven tons of high explosive and incendiary bombs containing magnesium and jellied gasoline. Every bomber had been stripped of its defensive weapons—except the tail gun—so it could carry the added payload. Over their targets the B-29s flew at just 500 feet. Their target was Tôkyô's Kôtô industrial area between the Sumida and Ara rivers, over nine square miles of industry and housing.

Within thirty minutes after the bombs were dropped the fires that engulfed Kôtô were totally out of control with flames reaching hundreds of feet into the air. Night had turned to an orange day.

Before flames reached them houses made of wood and paper burst into flame from the ambient heat. The subsequent firestorm replaced oxygen with lethal gases, suffocating thousands. People who ran into the streets heard the terrible roar of walls of fire approaching them so they turned in other directions, only to run into other walls of fire. The superheated air ignited people's clothing even though they were not adjacent to the flames. Those who breathed the superheated air died as their lungs burned.

The firestorms made the air so hot that people wearing *monpe*, baggy field pants, found the heat going through the material and burning their flesh, causing the *monpe* to stick to their scorched skin. Old women wearing thick quilted coats removed the padded hoods due to the heat. It was a tragic mistake. Their hair, then skin, erupted in flames.

For too many there was no escape. Heavy smoke, driven by the frenzied winds, raced about the streets of Tôkyô, suffocating thousands more. Those who ran into reinforced buildings, thinking they would be safe, soon became trapped in spontaneous infernos.

The Meiji Theater, a large ferroconcrete structure, was jammed with people who were confident the building was air-raid-proof. They were right, except for the roof. A terrible rumble preceded the conflagration as the roof collapsed on the hundreds who had sought shelter. Those who did not die immediately were literally baking as they tried to exit but were blocked by bodies already jamming all the doors. Then the entire inner structure erupted in flames, burning to death the few that remained alive.

The entire Susaki district of Chiba was destroyed and with it most of Tôkyô's famous *geisha* houses and many of the city's most famous *geisha*.

Others thought they could escape the flames by going to open areas—parks, playgrounds, or schoolyards—but the flames were driven by winds up to 80 miles an hour and eagerly embraced the open spaces as well as the people huddled in them. In so many instances people literally burst into flames, their clothing an enticement for the heat; no one could help them.

The firestorms did more than simply consume everything in their paths. The rising heat was so powerful that vacuums were created as the flames rose. Horrified onlookers watched as a family raced ahead of the flames, a father leading his family to safety in a park. He held a child in one arm and clutched his wife's hand with his free hand. She held an infant in her other arm. He was yelling something to her but she could not hear, so loud were the predatory flames. While running she looked back, having felt the heat close behind her. She fell. Her baby dropped from her arm. The baby rolled back and was sucked into the embrace of the fires. The mother froze for one second, immeasurable horror on her face, then ran after her child. Before she reached the flames that had already consumed her baby she was a running pyre. Others grabbed the father, his child still in his arm, when he started to run after his wife. It was all for naught. In minutes everyone in the park was consumed within the expanding inferno.

The B-29 bomber crews, flying at just 500 feet, were not unaffected. Blood-red mists and the stench of burning flesh wafted up and nauseated the bomber pilots, forcing them to grab oxygen masks to keep from vomiting.

Elsewhere, people ran through walls of fire to reach the Sumida River. There were selfless deeds that night. People had had no time to dress properly and the superheated concrete bridges on which they ran melted the flesh on their bare feet to the bone. Soon the bridges were clogged with burned bodies. Those who were dying threw their children into the river hoping others would save them. Those in the river tried, risking their own lives.

The banks of the river quickly became crammed with people, unable to enter the already packed river. But the horror did not stop at the banks. Those in the river, especially closest to shore, whose bodies were not covered by water, were burned to death. And those who were further from the banks simply suffocated from the smoke that hung over the river. They were lucky. In some areas of the banks the firestorms raised the river's temperature. Many were boiled or steamed to death. That night there were tens of thousands of bodies in the Sumida River, boiled, burned, or suffocated to death.

The raid had gone on for more than two and one-half hours.

The next morning almost 16 square miles of Tôkyô were unrecognizable. All that was left was to count the dead.

The Tôkyô Fire Department, never able to cope, did the tallying as they started to recover charred masses that had once been human beings. The Tôkyô Fire Department estimated that the raid killed 97,000 people, burned or injured over 125,000 and left 1,200,000 without homes.

General Curtis LeMay was going to burn Japan to its knees. And everyone in Tôkyô feared this was just the beginning.

The B-29s were bringing America's full fury to the heart of the Japanese Empire and the proud and skilled pilots of Atsugi, the Emperor's pilots, had been unable to stop them.

Atsugi was about 32 miles from Tôkyô and had not suffered from LeMay's B-29 firebombing strategy. But that did not mean that Atsugi was safe. Fear of the B-29 drove Atsugi underground. Thousands of officers and enlisted men, assisted by civilian workers, labored night and day for six months carving out underground runways and enormous caverns that would house hangars, barracks, a massive underground repair plant, and extensive underground quarters for flight personnel. It also had an underground generator to supply energy needs. When the work was completed Atsugi had twelve caverns. It was not enough and didn't protect Atsugi from the Americans.

On April 19, 1945, fighters from Iwo Jima had carried out 106 sorties against the Atsugi-Yokosuka area, shooting down 24 planes in dogfights and destroying 14 planes on the ground.

On May 17 American fighters from Iwo Jima flew 41 strike sorties against Atsugi. The attack was so sudden that American pilots destroyed parked aircraft. Buildings above ground were bombed or strafed.

But the greatest humiliation for Captain Kozono and Japan's military transpired on May 25, 1945. During a B-29 raid on Tôkyô 27 buildings within the Imperial Palace compound, including the main palace, pavilions of the Dowager Empress and the Crown Prince, as well as of Empress Nagako, burned to the ground. Yet the Imperial Palace had not been bombed directly. Instead, flaming debris from burning buildings near the palace had been carried by the wind across the moat and over the wall, setting the dry brushwood within the palace grounds aflame. Fires quickly spread to the buildings.

Nearly 10,000 soldiers, government workers and fire fighters, augmented by 40 fire engines, tried to control the flames for fourteen hours. Soldiers were ordered to save as many valuables—art objects and paintings—as possible, which they succeeded in doing. Twenty-eight palace staff died, including a dozen palace firemen in the administration building's forecourt who, owing complete fealty to Emperor Hirohito, died at their posts because no one had ordered them to evacuate.

The next day Emperor Hirohito and Empress Nagako moved through the ashes and thanked those who had fought so hard to save the palace. Later, Hirohito expressed his peculiar joy at the palace having been struck by the B-29s. "We have been bombed at last! At least now the people will realize that I am sharing their ordeal with no special protection from the gods." It was untrue as the Imperial Palace was off limits to American attacks, something Hirohito already knew from neutral governments.

Japan's Minister of War, General Anami Korechika, ashamed at his failure to protect the Emperor and the Imperial Palace, offered to resign, but Hirohito declined.

During this and subsequent B-29 raids over Tôkyô and the Kantô Plain Kozono's pilots at Atsugi had fiercely defended the skies and though they could not stop the B-29s, half the damage done to the bombers while over Tôkyô and the Kantô Plain had been inflicted by Kozono's pilots. But Kozono felt he had failed *Tennô-Heika*, and his shame was immeasurable. Even more he wanted the Americans to invade.

24

In the eastern sky, six miles east of Atsugi, a division of four American fighter planes flew at 15,000 feet in a random pattern, hidden by the clouds. A couple of times one of the planes had left the group, surveyed the sky west of Atsugi, and then rejoined the other planes in the clouds.

Three miles further to the east and at 20,000 feet two other divisions of American fighter planes were flying a random pattern in the clouds.

It seemed an arrogant thing to do, loitering over Japanese territory. But these pilots weren't too worried. They knew that yesterday scores of carrier-based planes had struck Atsugi and knocked out the base's radar installations. Atsugi would be blind for several days.

Atsugi, however, was on constant alert and men with powerful binoculars had spotted the single plane as it traveled west. Several Japanese pilots wanted to investigate but were cautioned that the plane they saw was probably a decoy; that other American fighter planes were undoubtedly waiting for Japanese planes to engage. They were also reminded it was imperative that Japan conserve its planes for the impending American invasion. Some of the antiaircraft guns around Atsugi opened up but the range and lack of effective radar hampered accuracy.

The lone plane appeared again then disappeared back in the clouds before Atsugi's antiaircraft guns could be brought to bear.

* * *

Ken reduced his air speed. At four miles and closing he could see Atsugi. As he approached the base he scanned the sky but saw nothing. He wondered when they would come. He looked down and was not surprised at what he saw, just disappointed to see how shabby it looked. This was not the Japan he had known four years earlier. The Japanese had always paid close attention to every detail. Now that had changed.

Buildings that had been bombed were left in disrepair. Wooden hangars had collapsed on planes. Planes that had been strafed or bombed were left in place, rusting carcasses. Several runways were pitted with bomb craters. The main runway, however, looked like it had been recently repaired and would be safe to land on. Flying over the base he looked down to his right and saw several men looking up and pointing to the left of him. Ken looked to his left.

He saw the tracers blaze past his canopy on the left followed by two planes, moving fast because they were plunging at him, a high side pass. He knew it was going to happen but it still rattled him. The flyby of the Hellcats was so close that their thunderous engines made him cringe more than the tracers had.

Instinctively, he banked to the right then resumed course as tracers crossed his intended path. Two more Hellcats, diving, streaked by before him at incredible speed, firing as they headed for the deck. Captivated, he watched the tracers and bullets as they kicked up the dirt. Men on the ground started to run, no longer paying attention to their mundane work.

Ken reacted on instinct, heading for the ground. At 200 feet he leveled off and searched for the Hellcats. Planned or not, he was shaken by both passes. He knew they had no intent to injure him but they intended the Japanese to know they were playing for keeps. He flew several hundred feet and saw tracers streaking past him. He looked over his right shoulder. The First Section was coming at him again, a flat side pass. The First Section's wingman, shooting live ammunition, kept his rounds close to the *Shôki* and hoped Ken didn't make a sudden turn into them. Scores of .50 caliber bullets hit several men on the ground as they were preparing an antiaircraft gun, tearing apart their bodies before they fell.

Ken shoved the throttle forward to the firewall and pulled his stick back hard, climbing vertically. The two Hellcats, caught off guard, flew straight for several hundred yards before pulling their sticks back to follow. Japanese pilots started to run to their planes in underground hangars while antiaircraft crews tried to track the Hellcats.

As Ken reached 5,000 feet four *Zeros* took off from underground hangars and reached 200 feet, but just. Several more were exiting the underground hangars, anxious to get into the fight. None of them made it. The two other Hellcat divisions came out of the sky with blazing Browning machine guns. Division Three went after the four *Zeros* in the air and blew them apart. Division Two simply ripped into the *Zeros* that had just exited the hangars. Then Division Three split into two sections and began to make passes at other planes still exiting from the hangars. Division Two also split into two sections and went after gun positions and buildings. So sudden and swift were their tactics that the Japanese never had a chance to muster any immediate opposition. Both divisions went at Atsugi from four separate directions, destroying opportune targets. Curiously, the Hellcats avoided the base headquarters and buildings adjacent to it.

Both sections of Division One were now climbing after Ken, the outer wingmen firing live ammunition while the section leaders fired their blanks, guesstimating the number of rounds dished out before their blanks were depleted.

It took Ken three minutes to reach 10,000 feet. Then he looped back and started to dive, as if preparing to come up behind Division One and start firing. Instead, canopies facing each other, he flew by Division One, heading straight for the deck. Diving faster than 400 knots it took Ken one minute to descend to 5,000 feet. He started to throttle back.

When Division One descended to 5,000 feet all four planes started to fire at Ken, now at 3,000 feet. Hundreds of rounds passed Ken's plane, biting into the dirt. Ken toggled the cockpit light switch. In seconds smoke started to come out of his engine. *Show time*, he thought.

Soldiers and pilots on the ground thought he was going to crash into the ground. Then, at 2,000 feet, he slowly pulled the stick back as far as it would go. Had he pulled back quickly he would have blacked out. Two hundred feet above the ground he leveled off and throttled back more, then turned, heading directly for Division One, which had just leveled off. They were at opposite ends of the main runway, two miles apart. Everyone on the ground stopped to watch the crippled *Shôki*, smoke streaming from the engine's cowling. One mile from Burgess' division Ken nudged his stick over to the right and moved his rudder to the right as well, starting a corkscrew turn. Then he opened up with his guns, two 20 mm cannon in the fuselage and two 37 mm cannon in the wings. As he turned while approaching Division One the rounds spiraled out, wider and wider.

"Fuck!" said Lieutenant Burgess, Division One's leader, then grinned. "This is Flatiron One! Break off! I say again, break off!" he ordered into his radio.

Immediately the four planes dispersed and climbed. Ken passed through the opening and turned, now coming behind Division One. Two minutes had passed since smoke from his engine first appeared.

Burgess had already looped and knew what Ken had done. The rounds had not targeted his division. Ken was barnstorming for the Japanese on the ground. It wasn't in the plan, Burgess thought, but it was inspired.

Burgess' division grouped together into two sections, banked, and headed straight for Ken. With everyone on the ground watching, enthralled with pride, Ken opened up again and repeated the corkscrew maneuver. Again, the rounds spiraled ever wider as he turned and Division One, guns blazing, dispersed.

On the ground, hundreds of men cheered and waved their caps. Others applauded or waved their arms, all marveling at the courage of their Army comrade.

"This is Flatiron One. Show's over. Let's go home." Then he thought to himself, *Good luck, fellow.*

Ken watched the three Hellcat divisions form up. He looked down, ready to line up on the runway. Then his hand froze, the stick unmoved. He guessed he had another minute of smoke left so he throttled up the engine and went after the Hellcats, guns blazing.

Division Three was bringing up the rear. Ensign Ray Wright was the first to spot the tracers. "Flatiron One! Bogey on our tail! Lieutenant, doesn't he know we're breaking off?"

Burgess looked over his shoulder and saw Ken gaining on his planes and wondered what the hell he was doing. Ken's tracers weren't coming that close to his planes. *Show's over, kid. You're smoking. Land the damn plane.* Then he spotted, behind Ken, antiaircraft crews readying their guns, waiting for the Hellcats to cross their path. He understood that Ken was putting his plane between the Japanese antiaircraft guns and the

Hellcats. It was a risk; more than one plane was lost by friendly fire on both sides.

"This is Flatiron One. Let's head for the ceiling. The Japs are going to flame our tails with their flak."

The three divisions followed Burgess as he climbed to 5,000 feet then changed course then climbed to 10,000 feet, changed course again and headed for 15,000 feet, knowing the antiaircraft crews could not adjust the flaks' timing fuse quickly enough to match the Hellcats' altitude and course changes.

Two antiaircraft explosions shook Ken's plane. Fragments of metal peppered the *Shôki*. He immediately checked that he still controlled his plane. Then the smoke coming from his engine became darker.

The Japanese gun crews saw this and immediately ceased their firing, fearing they had hit the *Shôki*. Burgess saw it too and prayed that Ken would break off and land his damn plane.

Ken, hoping the Hellcats were safe and knowing he had less than two minutes left, broke off and headed for the main runway.

Below, hundreds of men were running to burning or collapsed buildings to rescue anyone who might still be alive. No one bothered to see if any of the *Zeros*' pilots had survived; the planes had exploded.

Ken flew the *Shôki* a quarter of a mile to the side of the runway, searching for any bomb craters or ruts, and was relieved to see it was clear. He checked the wind sock for wind direction. He was flying downwind. He looked back at the control tower, which the Hellcats had ignored on purpose, and saw a green light. With dark smoke still coming from his engine he throttled back to about 100 knots, just enough speed to keep him aloft, lowered his landing gear and flaps, and slid his canopy open. He then opened his cowl flaps, allowing air to go across the engine, which also gave him increased drag.

He passed the end of the runway and flew a half-mile before he turned 180°, heading into the wind and onto Atsugi's runway.

He was edgy. He lined up the *Shôki* and remembered his first solo landing when he and his brother Tom took flying lessons. Everything that could go wrong went through his mind, including being arrested by the *Kempeitai*, Japan's dreaded Military Police. He closed his eyes for a few seconds, picturing his family, Kyoko, and his brother Tom.

Just one chance to land, he thought. He nudged his stick forward just a bit and controlled his descent with his throttle, "flying it down," as his instructor had often told him. His air speed was less than 80 knots.

Japanese ground crews not helping the injured or fighting fires stopped their work and ran toward the runway. Several fire trucks headed for the runway.

When Ken was ready to touch down he pulled the throttle almost fully back. First his left wheel touched down then his right wheel. As he approached the control tower he turned and taxied toward the flight line, while watching the engine's cowling. The smoke started to thin. He backed his throttle all the way, waited a few seconds, then toggled the light switch closed and cut his engine. He lifted his goggles and released his safety harness. Then the Japanese were upon him.

Pilots and ground crews swarmed over and around the *Shôki*. Several pilots jumped on the wings and pulled Ken out of his cockpit. Panicked, he struggled, then stopped. Hundreds were yelling "*Banzai! Banzai!*"

He looked around and saw everyone cheering. When he stood on the starboard wing two pilots hoisted him on their shoulders, awkwardly turning a circle so everyone could see Ken. Hundreds yelled "*Banzai! Banzai!*" as he was displayed. He was lowered to the wing, then to the ground, where again he was hoisted on other pilots' shoulders. He was carried through the jubilant crowd as it swelled. Several reached up to grab his hand. He knew he had landed safely on Japanese soil.

The festive mood was interrupted by the arrival of a convertible car, horn honking, as it slowly moved into the crowd. Few paid attention to the car; Ken was Atsugi's hero of the moment. The driver, impatient, stopped the car, stood, and yelled "*Ooi! Ooi!*"—Hey! Hey!

Those near the car turned and, seeing the passenger, stood at attention. Captain Kozono Yasuna stepped out of the car and made his way through the crowd. Those he passed stood at attention, several apologizing. Kozono, his face taut, walked up to Ken. Everyone around the two men stood silent, at attention.

Ken immediately snapped to attention and saluted Kozono.

Kozono's mouth was bowed down as he returned the salute.

"Captain, I am Major Kobayashi!"

Kozono nodded several times. "Shôsa! I command this base. We rarely have Army pilots visit us here. Where was your destination?"

Now or never, thought Ken. "Captain, I was flying to Chôfu Army Air Base before my flight was rudely interrupted," he answered as he removed his flight helmet and gloves. Soot from the smoke covered his face.

Kozono's eyes bored into Ken's. Slowly, his mouth changed to a grin as he offered his hand to Ken. With an inner sigh of relief Ken took Kozono's hand.

"Noteworthy flying, Major! Noteworthy! Where did you come from?"

"Captain, I flew from Miyakonojô."

"Let us see how much damage was done to your plane."

They walked around the *Shôki*. Kozono looked at the bullet holes in the cowling. When they reached the tail Ken noticed that Kozono seemed to ignore the damage Atsugi's gunners had done to the *Shôki*. Kozono led them back to the engine and he inspected the bullet holes with interest.

"You were fortunate, Major! Your plane will be repaired here. Since you are an honored guest I will have my own flight crew make repairs immediately. Your plane will be ready perhaps in two days." He looked at the sun then his watch. "It is getting late. I would be pleased if you would have dinner here and you can stay here tonight. Tomorrow I will arrange for you a ride to the train. It is not far from here, less than ten minutes from the base. The train will take you to Chôfu."

Ken had not planned to stay overnight. However, he knew from here on out he was improvising as he went along. He could not think of a reason to turn down Kozono's proposal. Also, he thought, it was getting late and here was a chance to be around the Japanese military, giving him an opportunity to see how they think and behave. Besides, to them he was a genuine hero who had bested four American fighters as well as being a stranger; they would not be on their guard.

"You are most generous, Captain. I would be honored to have dinner with you."

"Good!" Kozono looked around and spotted a sailor. "Morita Nitô hei! Get up to the cockpit and gather Major Kobayashi's possessions!"

Ordinary Seaman Morita saluted and quickly made his way to the *Shôki*. He climbed on the wing and looked in the cockpit. He saw Ken's bag and sword. "Captain! The major's *katana* is here!"

Ken knew the sailor was hesitant to touch an officer's sword. And he saw fear on Morita's face as he looked at Kozono. He moved quickly, knowing how officers treated their subordinates. But he would have to do it right. He knew, based on his interrogations of captured Japanese soldiers and sailors, that officers in the Imperial Japanese Army were particularly known for their brutality and disdain for the ordinary soldier.

"Nitô hei! Do not touch my sword! Take my bag out and get off the wing!"

Morita moved swiftly and jumped off the wing with Ken's flight bag in his hand. Ken climbed on the wing and retrieved his *katana*. Kozono's eyes widened when he saw the sword's *tsuba*, the decorated hand guard.

Holding his sword Ken jumped off the wing and followed Kozono to his car. Kozono got in the rear and Ken hesitated, wondering if he should get in the rear as well or in the front, next to the driver. Kozono gestured for him to get in the rear. Meanwhile, Ordinary Seaman Morita had placed Ken's flight bag in the trunk. Kozono gestured for Morita to get in the left front passenger seat. At Kozono's order the driver headed back to headquarters, three quarters of a mile away.

While still near the runway Kozono ordered the driver to stop. He got out and walked over to one of the *Zeros* that had never gotten off the runway. It was still smoking. The body in the cockpit was unrecognizable. Kozono bowed his head for a moment then returned to his car, his face grim. As they drove on Kozono stood in the car several times, surveying the destruction done by the American planes.

While Kozono was seated Ken noticed him glancing at his sword more than once. When Kozono turned to stare at a burning building Ken looked at Kozono's sword and saw that it was of average quality, probably made just before or during the war in a factory.

As they drove over the grounds Ken looked around. Several buildings were still burning. But he also saw that several buildings that had clearly been bombed in previous raids had been left in disrepair. The grounds were scruffy; underbrush had grown wild everywhere. Planes that had been damaged beyond repair were left to crumble where they were. To Ken it was sad. Again, this was not the Japan he had known.

When they arrived at the base's headquarters Ken was

even more disappointed. Many windows were cracked; some were missing. Paint was peeling. Everything looked shabby. It was as if no one cared anymore.

The driver parked in front of the main entrance and got out. He opened the door for Kozono. Morita jumped out and got Ken's flight bag. Without a word spoken Morita knew he had been assigned to this Army major. Kozono led Ken into the building. Morita stayed outside, the bag held in his hand. He dared not put it down.

When Kozono entered the main room of the base headquarters everyone stood at attention, awaiting orders. Kozono ignored them. Ken looked around. Civilian workers were wearing *kokumin-fuku*—national wear—the drab semi-military khaki uniform worn by male workers throughout Japan.

Posters urging military and civilian workers and soldiers, sailors and pilots to strive ever harder to defeat the enemy hung on the walls. Some were curling at the corners. The theme was of constant effort to defeat the enemy. Ken noticed that the Americans were not depicted as American posters portrayed the Japanese.

He knew that American factories portrayed Japanese soldiers and political leaders as bucktoothed caricatures, with tightly slanted eyes behind enormous, thick round glasses, ready to rape white women or bayonet Allied POWs. He recalled, while at Manzanar, reading America's comic books. The comics' heroes were always defeating caricatured Japanese soldiers, who were portrayed as if they were incapable of any act of decency.

Other posters he saw on the wall depicted Japanese soldiers, sailors or pilots as heroic figures fighting and defeating an enemy, often unseen.

He looked around. Fans were mounted on walls but were not working. It was hot in the room. Evidently electricity was in short supply, he guessed. Then he saw on another wall two large posters, one showing a distorted Churchill being used for bayonet practice by Japanese soldiers. The other poster portrayed a distorted Roosevelt on a cross with bayonets pointing at him. The poster of Roosevelt provoked conflicting memories. Before the war Ken remembered President Roosevelt working hard to invigorate an economically desperate America. Then he remembered an official government document, Executive Order 9066 signed by the same president, nailed to doors and poles on sidewalks, on post office walls and published in newspapers, which forever changed his life, his family's lives and the lives of tens of thousands of loyal Americans of Japanese lineage. Still, seeing the poster saddened him. Ken was twelve when Roosevelt was elected president and, like so many Americans, the only president he knew. When Roosevelt had died Ken was saddened. He remembered hardened soldiers and officers crying when they heard the news.

Kozono saw him looking at the poster.

"If only they were here now. I would cut off their heads with my sword. Roosevelt was a coward, just like Truman, sending their bombers but not their soldiers. If they did we would drive them back into the sea, just like we did the Mongols."

Ken, with those same conflicting feelings, wanted to remind Kozono that twelve American pilots had just attacked Atsugi, Japan's largest air base, destroyed several buildings and several Japanese planes. They were also prepared to sacrifice their lives for the success of his mission. He kept his counsel.

"Major, it's hot. Take off your flight suit. I must contact Chôfu and let them know you will not arrive."

While Kozono went to the communications center Ken removed his suit and put it on a chair, with his helmet, goggles and gloves. He crossed his fingers and waited to see if Bliss' bombing plans had been carried out. If Taka's messages to the Imperial War Ministry and Chôfu were not perceived as genuine he knew he was dead. If Kozono was able to get through.

Moments later Kozono returned. "Our telephone lines have been damaged and Chôfu is not responding to our radio signals. We will try later."

Ken hid his relief. The "Kobayashi Group" had planned well.

When Kozono saw Ken's arm-of-service color he was intrigued.

"An engineering officer reporting to Chôfu. You must be building something important on Kyûshû that would interest Chôfu. No, I think you are reporting to the War Ministry."

Ken was taken aback and Kozono saw it. He laughed.

"Be at ease, Major Kobayashi! I know of the August five meeting at Ichigaya. One of my staff officers will be attending. You must be hungry. Let us have dinner with some of my pilots. I am certain they want to honor you. We will speak no more of the meeting."

They left the building. Outside, Ordinary Seaman Morita was still holding Ken's flight bag.

"Morita Nitô hei! Go inside and get Major Kobayashi's flight equipment and bring them to the officers' quarters. Wait outside there until further orders!"

"*Ha!*" replied Morita. He released Ken's flight bag and ran inside. Seconds later he reappeared, stopped, and saluted Kozono and Ken, then ran to the officers' quarters, carrying Ken's possessions.

*   *   *

When Ken entered the officer's dining facilities he expected the spartan setting. Japan's best pilots, the code of *Bushidô* in their hearts, sat at simple long tables and benches. Naked bulbs dangled from the ceiling. Flies buzzed aimlessly, waiting for food to be laid out. The floor was dirty. The walls were drab and covered with propaganda posters. There were posters of American planes and bombers being shot down by either Japanese fighters or antiaircraft fire. Crude drawings showed American ships burning and sinking while Japanese planes circled overhead.

As he sat at Captain Kozono's table he saw a rat walking, not rushing, under a table. No one else seemed to notice or care. He shuddered as he wondered what the kitchen was like.

Ken was the center of attention with pilots coming up to him and praising his flying and courage. Civilian workers, dressed in the drab *kokumin-fuku*, brought food. His eyes widened. The quality and quantity of food was in stark contrast to his surroundings. The slices of raw fish on the plates in front of him were visibly fresh. He wondered how many fishing boats had risked being sunk to get such fresh fish. The rice was steaming. And the *sake* flowed but it was of poor quality and many would have hangovers in the morning. He knew the Japanese were eating a subsistence diet but the military were obviously not suffering.

During the dinner no one asked why he landed at Atsugi; it was evident. And no one asked him to where he had been flying. He was toasted numerous times and was careful how much *sake* he drank. He wanted to observe his hosts. Several pilots replayed Ken's dogfight maneuvers, using their hands to show how they would have fought the Americans. As the evening proceeded he heard the name Mutô uttered several times. One pilot came up to him, clearly drunk from too much rice wine.

"Kobayashi Shôsa! Do you think you flew as well as Mutô Tokumu sôchô today?"

Ken was ignorant of Mutô but all of Japan knew of his exploit.

On February 16, 1945, Warrant Officer Mutô Kinsuke of the 343rd *Kôkutai* was flying his N1K2-J *Shiden-Kai*, the Violet Lightning, over Yokohama. A dozen Hellcats came straight for Mutô, each American pilot anxious to score a kill, particularly against the Violet Lightning, regarded by American pilots as one of the best all-round Japanese fighter planes in the Pacific. In one of the most remarkable aerial encounters of World War II Mutô single-handedly engaged in a blistering dogfight with the dozen Hellcats. It was an uneven contest and when it was over Mutô had shot down four Hellcats before the rest were forced to break off and escape to their carrier.

Ken looked at the faces arrayed around him, each eagerly awaiting his response. He smiled and shrugged his shoulders.

Everyone laughed and raised their cups, to him and Mutô.

Two hours passed. It was evident to Ken that these men did not want to end the evening and that he was the reason. There were few reasons to celebrate anymore but Ken's spunky arrival seemed to have lifted the spirits of everyone in the room. However, it was getting late and Ken yawned a few times. Kozono, seeing Ken's fatigue, stood with a *sake* cup in his hand.

"Kobayashi Shôsa! Today we saw you defeat the enemy even though you were outnumbered. But I think there is deception here. You are wearing the uniform of an Imperial Japanese Army officer, which I believe is false."

Ken froze. The smiles that were on the men in front of him faded. Some men stood, their faces serious as they looked at Kozono. Others stared at Ken, their faces either impassive or curious.

Kozono continued. "What Kobayashi Shôsa did today was not possible."

Ken looked at Kozono, wondering if he had been uncovered. He looked for the nearest exit but dismissed the idea; he knew he would be dead before he ran ten steps.

"Kobayashi Shôsa! I believe you are not in the Imperial Japanese Army! I believe you are a spy! What I saw today forces me to conclude that, in fact, you are in the Imperial Japanese Navy, for only the best pilots are in the Imperial Japanese Navy! *Kanpai!*"

Everyone stood laughing, *sake* cup in hand. "*Kanpai! Kanpai! Kanpai!*" echoed every voice in the room as they vigorously toasted Ken.

Ken's stomach flip-flopped. What Kozono saw as disbelief on Ken's face was actually near emotional collapse. Since he landed at Atsugi he had been waiting for the shoe to drop, to be arrested, tortured and killed.

Kozono raised his hand for silence. His pilots quieted down.

"Kobayashi Shôsa! Today we saw a true warrior of Japan! Today we saw a *samurai!*"

More cheers resounded. Ken stood and turned to Kozono.

"Captain. Perhaps I should have joined the Imperial Japanese Navy. The food and *sake* are superior!"

Everyone in the room, especially Captain Kozono, rocked with laughter. "Kobayashi Shôsa! I will try to arrange a transfer for you. Atsugi can use more pilots like you. Now, it is time for you to retire. You have an important journey tomorrow."

*　　*　　*

Morita Nitô hei was still standing at attention outside the officers' quarters. Ordinary Seaman Morita led Ken to his room. Ken walked in and looked around. A flickering bare bulb hung from a wooden beam. The room was austere, a small four-*tatami* room, measured by two rows, each consisting of two *tatami* mats laid side by side. Each *chûkyô-ma tatami* measured 90cm by 180cm. In the middle of the four *tatami* was a *natsugake* or summer-use *futon*.

Against the wall was a lacquered two-draw bureau, marred by scratches. Morita Nitô hei had already placed Ken's flight bag next to the bureau. The top draw was open and he could see that his *yukata* and *obi* and his clean clothing were in it. He removed his boots, careful not to damage the *tatami*. He went to the bureau and opened the bottom draw and saw his flight suit, helmet, goggles, and gloves were in it. The *hachimaki* that he had worn on his flight helmet was neatly folded on top of the bureau.

On a wall were wooden pegs for hanging clothes. The wall opposite the door had a window which faced one of the bombed radar towers.

Ken could tell the room had been cleaned. He looked at Ordinary Seaman Morita, who was standing in the doorway. "Morita Nitô hei, did you clean this room?"

"*Ha!*" replied Morita. "I felt I should do it while you were eating dinner! I hope the Shôsa is not disturbed!"

"No, Morita Nitô hei. You have done well. I wish to take a hot bath before I retire."

"*Ha!* I have prepared the *ofuro* for the Shôsa!" He pointed down the corridor.

"Morita Nitô hei! Wake me at 0500 hours!"

"*Ha!*" Morita saluted and left.

Ken removed his socks, clothes and *fundoshi* and put on the *yukata* and wrapped the *obi* about his waist. He left his room.

Having first washed then rinsed, Ken climbed into the wooden *ofuro*, the tub. Pipes going through the wall into an outside wood burner fed the *ofuro*. One inlet came out the bottom of the tub for cold water; the other went into the top for hot water so the water would circulate. The hot water pipe was directly over the fire in the burner. Morita had already added more wood to the fire outside the building. Ken spent almost an hour immersed in the almost steaming water.

Clean and relaxed he dried off then put on his *yukata* and *obi* and returned to his room. He saw that Ordinary Seaman Morita had prepared the *futon*. The *kakebuton* had been pulled back. Ken noticed that the bottom portion of the *futon*, the *shikibuton*, was worn but had been cleaned. At the head of the *futon* Morita had placed a *makura*, a pillow filled with *sobagara* husks. He remembered how comfortable the pillow was when he was at Tôkyô Imperial University. He closed the door. He found the light switch but it was broken. Just before he unscrewed the bulb he saw that Morita had washed and hung to dry his *fundoshi*. He unscrewed the bulb. Ambient light from outside softly illuminated his room. He removed his *yukata*. He lay on the *shikibuton* and pulled the *kakebuton* over him. It was 12:50 A.M. He closed his eyes and as he fell asleep he had a strange sense of being home.

25

August 4, 1945

At precisely 0500 hours Morita Nitô hei knocked on the door of Ken's room. The door opened. Ken was dressed in his uniform.

"Morita Nitô hei! Exactly on time! Have arrangements been made to take me to the train station?"

Ordinary Seaman Morita, caught off guard, snapped to attention and saluted. "*Ha!* Kozono Taisa has informed me that you are to be taken to Yamato Station!"

"I am going to eat my morning meal. I will be back here within the hour. Pack my belongings in my flight bag."

"*Ha!*" said Ordinary Seaman Morita as he saluted.

Ken ignored both salutes, a display of contempt for Morita. He left his room and proceeded to the dining facilities. The room was already occupied by scores of officers. Several stood and greeted Ken. He was invited to sit at a table. His morning meal was simple: hot bean-paste soup, pickled vegetables and rice and green tea.

The conversations around him were subdued. Another day meant the possibility of more American fighters and fighter-bombers attacking Tôkyô and Yokohama, their areas of responsibility. Some men talked about the massive firebombing raids by the B-29s over Hachiôji, Toyama, Nagaoka, and Mito as well as Kawasaki's petroleum facilities, and Ken knew they were talking about the smoke he had seen as he crested Fuji-*san*. A pilot sitting near Ken pointed at another pilot, sitting at a different table.

"His family is in Toyama. He has spent the last two days trying to find out their fate. He regrets not being here last night to honor your victory."

When someone spoke to him Ken's answers were brief. Otherwise he ate in silence, occasionally glancing at the man whose family was doubtless dead. As Ken was finishing his meal Captain Kozono entered the dining facility. Everyone stood to attention. He gestured for them to return to their food. He made his way to Ken's table and sat down.

"Good morning, Kobayashi Shôsa!" He spoke louder. "I have entrusted Morita Nitô hei to take you to Yamato Station. He is stupid but he takes orders well. Make sure you tell him to return to Atsugi when he takes you to the station! Otherwise he may try to drive my car back to his home!"

Several men broke out in laughter. Ken, not knowing the meaning, just smiled.

"He comes to us from a stupid homeland!" More laughter.

Ken, from the time he first saw how Kozono treated Morita, knew he was the object of mockery, and he was not interested in participating in another man's denigration. "Thank you, Captain. Do you know when my plane will be repaired?"

Kozono's smile disappeared. He seemed displeased that Ken did not appreciate his humor. "It will be repaired within two days. You can leave your flight belongings in your room. They will be here when you need them; Morita Nitô hei will attend to it."

Ken stood. "Captain, I am grateful for your hospitality. It was an honor to stay at Atsugi. With your permission I will now prepare to leave."

Kozono stood, putting aside his feelings. "Kobayashi Shôsa! You are always welcome to return to Atsugi. You affirmed Japan's honor yesterday. Your plane will be ready when you return."

Both men shook hands then saluted. Everyone in the room stood and saluted Ken and he faced each one while holding his hand in salute. Then he brought his hand down, turned, and left. He walked back to his room where he found Ordinary Seaman Morita waiting for him outside the room, Ken's flight bag at his side.

"Morita Nitô hei! Captain Kozono informs me that you are to drive me to Yamato Station. Have you packed all my belongings?"

"*Ha!* I am ready to drive you to the train station."

"Good. Lead the way to the car."

Morita saluted and they left the officers' quarters. Kozono's car was parked in front. Morita opened the passenger door, expecting Ken to get in the rear. Ken got in the front passenger seat. Morita ran to the rear and put Ken's bag in the trunk then got behind the wheel. He started the engine and headed toward the main gate. He stopped at the guard post and was passed through. Morita turned the car left and headed toward Yamato Station, three kilometers distance.

They drove in silence. Ken knew this was the Japanese way. Japanese men did not customarily prattle like Westerners but kept their thoughts to themselves. Also, and more importantly, Ken was an officer. Morita could not address him unless spoken to first or he needed to ask a question. Ken could see that Morita was nervous driving Kozono's car. He wanted to put Morita at ease. It had just the opposite effect.

The temperature was 25° Centigrade, comfortable for the hour, but Ken knew it would get hotter.

"Morita Nitô hei! Is this your first time driving Captain Kozono's car?"

"*Ha!* Shôsa! I am grateful that Captain Kozono has given me this responsibility!" he replied while briefly looking at Ken. That's when a front tire hit the rut in the road, causing the car to lurch to the side.

"Fuck," said Morita. In English. American English.

Ken, startled, looked at Morita and saw the color drain from Morita's face. Morita glanced at Ken out of the corner of his left eye. When he saw Ken looking at him he immediately looked ahead, at the road. Morita's knuckles turned white as he gripped the steering wheel. Ken knew he had to react to Morita's outburst.

"Morita Nitô hei! I recognize that word. Where are you from?"

Morita did not respond. Ken knew a Japanese soldier or sailor would risk a beating if he did not immediately answer a superior's question, especially an officer's question. Ken repeated his question. Morita's mouth grimaced as he drove, the car accelerating. Ken looked about and saw there were no other vehicles on the road.

"Morita Nitô hei! Stop the car immediately!"

Morita pulled to the side and stopped. His tightly-gripped fingers rolled back and forth on the steering wheel. His breathing was shallow. Ken saw Morita was about to lose control. He took another approach.

"Morita-*san*, where are you from?" he asked quietly, without menace in his voice.

Morita, still holding tight to the wheel, slowly faced Ken.

"Shôsa! I am disgraced! I am not from Japan! Please forgive my dishonor!"

"Morita-*san*. I was in America once, before the war. I speak a little English. I have heard this word spoken before, sometimes for a similar reason. There is no one else here. Please explain."

Morita, unable to control himself, started to cry. Ken

had seen this before in Japanese men. Japanese men normally masked their feelings, not wanting to show loss of control in front of others. If not resolved, eventually those feelings could erupt to the surface. Sometimes a man would just break down and cry or he might, in very rare instances, strike out violently. Ken was looking at a young man, perhaps three to four years younger than himself, releasing pent-up emotions he dared not before.

"Shôsa! I am from America! I am an American!"

Ken could only imagine what Morita had been through once the war between American and Japan had started, based on his questioning of captured Japanese soldiers.

"Morita-*san*, are you *kibei*?" He felt at ease asking the question since he and his brother Tom had been *kibei*, Japanese Americans studying in Japan. The word *kibei* literally translated to "returning to America."

"No, Shôsa," replied Morita, his shoulders heaving as he tried to regain some control. "After I graduated from high school I came to Japan to live with relatives and study my ancestral homeland. I came in Showa Sixteen, June. I planned to stay only six months but in August all ships between Japan and America stopped. I could not leave Japan. In Showa Seventeen, May, I was told I would be drafted into the Army." Ken's mind automatically converted the dates. Morita came to Japan in June 1941 and was called by the military in May 1942.

Morita continued. "I told them I was an American citizen. They laughed and told me I was not, that I was a Japanese citizen. I did not understand. Then they told me."

Before 1924 the Japanese government regarded any child born of Japanese parents who had emigrated to another country to be a citizen of Japan. It was called the law of *jus sanguinis*, practiced by many nations. In 1924 the law in Japan was changed, mostly due to pressure from Japanese Americans. The law was rewritten so that children born after 1924 would no longer be considered Japanese citizens unless requested by Japanese parents living abroad. However, there was a caveat. Japanese parents who had a child born before 1924 needed to submit a form to the Japanese government, revoking their child's *de rigueur* Japanese citizenship. If the form was not submitted the Japanese government regarded the child a Japanese citizen. Consequently, Japanese Americans, born before 1924, who were in Japan when war broke out were subject to Japanese military service.

"Morita-*san*, where in America are you from?"

Morita started to regain control. This was the first time anyone in the military had shown him any empathy. He was surprised and his guard came down slowly.

"Shôsa, I am from San Francisco. It is in northern California."

"Yes, I was there once. It is a beautiful city. Is your family there now?"

"Shôsa, I do not know. In Showa Seventeen, March, I read in the newspapers that Japanese Americans were arrested and forced into camps."

"Yes, I read that too. It is regrettable. I assume you joined the Navy. Why?"

"Shôsa, I had heard stories about how the Army treats soldiers. And I had heard how some Japanese Americans, who were drafted, were treated. So I joined the Navy in Showa Seventeen, May."

"You have been in the Navy for over three years yet you are an Ordinary Seaman. Why have you not been promoted?"

"Because I am an American."

Ken didn't buy it. He knew the Japanese had treated some Japanese Americans very well because of their knowledge of America. Besides, Morita seemed to be a special target for insults form Kozono. "Is that the only reason?"

Morita looked straight ahead, silent for several minutes.

His eyes were moving left and right, as if searching for the right words.

"Shôsa, six months ago I was a Leading Seaman. At night a B-29 approaching Atsugi was rammed by one of our pilots. One of the Americans was able to get out and he parachuted near the base. He was taken prisoner and because he was not an officer the sailors were allowed to beat him. I refused. I was called a traitor. Captain Kozono ordered me to strike the American. I refused. I was immediately reduced in rank. Later that night the American was bound, blindfolded, then beheaded by an officer who wanted to bloody his *katana*. There was a celebration afterward. I was ordered to appear and I was bound and blindfolded, like the American. I thought they were going to kill me. But they just pretended they were going to cut off my head. It went on for several hours.

"The next day I requested a transfer to a ship; I wanted to die but I wanted to do so with honor. Captain Kozono refused my request. So I am here. And here I will die."

"What do you mean, Morita-*san*?"

Morita looked at Ken, weighing whether he could be frank. He decided he no longer cared. "When the Americans come I will die. The American B-29s will bomb Atsugi and I will probably die. Or I will die by American soldiers shooting at me. Or Captain Kozono will order me killed because I will not kill American prisoners. And if I am taken prisoner by the Americans I will die because they will execute me as a traitor."

"You seem certain the Americans will invade."

"Major, for the first two years of the war I believed everything. We were told that America was losing, that Japan had one glorious victory after another. We were told the American Navy was all but destroyed. I believed it. Then, in June of last year, the B-29s bombed the Imperial Iron and Steel Works at Yawata. Then in November B-29s bombed Tôkyô. Now most of

Tôkyô has been destroyed.

"I know America. Nothing Japan does can stop them. Almost every night the B-29s bomb Japan wherever they choose. During the day their fighter planes strike wherever they desire. Their ships fire at will. Their submarines have encircled Japan, stopping shipping. Japan is starving and we no longer can import oil. They cannot be stopped. They have conquered Iwô Jima and Okinawa. Yet every battle Japan has lost is announced as a victory. We are told that we are luring them closer so we can destroy them when they invade Japan. We cannot stop them. They will invade Japan. I will die. *Shikataganai*."

Ken, sapped at Morita's fatalism, sat still. This lowly sailor, who never fired a shot at the enemy, had a complete grasp of Japan's tactical situation. Ken was torn. He wanted to tell a fellow American who he was and why he was in Japan but knew he could not. Unable to respond, he gestured that Morita resume driving to Yamato Station.

When they arrived Ken waited for Morita to get his bag. Morita placed Ken's bag next to him. Then he stood at attention and saluted.

Ken, feeling guilt at not having returned Morita's previous salutes, came to attention and returned Morita's salute. As he picked up his bag he started to turn to enter the station but stopped.

"Morita Nitô hei. You are right. *Shikataganai*." It cannot be helped.

Morita nodded once. Ken turned and entered the station.

Inside, the station was crowded, mostly with women, waiting for their train to arrive. Almost all were carrying bags full of vegetables. They looked tired and hungry. He guessed they were taking food back to their homes, to Tôkyô. Scattered throughout, groups of soldiers or sailors stood silent. There were some officers as well but they were detached from the rest.

Posters, many faded, were plastered on the walls, sacrifice

their common theme. Others displayed heroic Japanese soldiers or sailors crushing American or British forces. One caught his attention: "*The sooner the Americans come, the better... One hundred million die proudly.*"

Ken looked at the schedule then went to the ticket window and asked the clerk, an old man, for a ticket to Shinjuku Station, on the Odakyû Line, short for the Odawara-Kyûkô Line. It was the 7:30 A.M. express, no stops, a 40-kilometer ride taking about 65 minutes. Ken placed his coins on the counter but the clerk didn't touch them. He seemed confused.

"What is it, old man? Is the amount incorrect?"

"No, Major. The coins are correct. But you don't have to pay. I just need your travel voucher. You do not need a ticket. You are in the Imperial Army."

Ken knew he had blundered, not taking for granted that the Japanese military would not have to pay a fare. And he had no travel voucher, an error of the "Kobayashi Group."

"I forgot to get a voucher so I will pay." The old man shrugged and gave Ken a ticket for Shinjuku. Ken stepped back and as he turned he saw a policeman looking at him. Ken walked away from the ticket window and saw an old man selling newspapers. He moved towards the newspaper stand and almost collided with a woman. He tried to get out of her way by moving to his right but she moved to her left. They gently bumped into one another. Ken apologized while the woman mumbled something which he was certain was an insult. He smiled then saw the policeman still looking at him. And he realized his second error. Americans move to the right to avoid each other; the Japanese move to the left, something he had forgotten from his time at *Tôdai*. He remembered what Captain Paschal had told him before he took off from the *Yorktown*. "W-W-While there, *think* J-J-J-Japanese. In Japan, if you l-l-look and act the p-p-p-p-part, you've already w-w-w-won half the b-b-b-battle."

Ken continued to the newspaper hawker. Several papers were available, including the *Nichinichi*, the *Asahi*, and the *Nippon Times*. He was familiar with all three but chose the *Nippon Times*, a paper he had read when he was at the university.

The *Nippon Times* had always been a curiosity to him. It was written in English and covered Japan and the world, with many stories coming from international wire services. Ken was curious how the *Nippon Times* was now reporting the world news. He paid the man 35 *sen* and folded the paper under his arm, intending to read it on the train. Then he saw the policeman approach him. Ken looked at his uniform; he was a major in the *Tokkô*, the Special High Police. The *Tokkô* were comparable to Nazi Germany's Gestapo. Ken braced himself.

"*Ohayôgozaimasu*, Shôsa."

Ken stared at the cop for one full minute. Ken was taller by several inches and he looked down at the cop purposefully. He was gambling. "Good morning, Shôsa. May I help you?"

"Actually, Major, I thought perhaps that I could help you. Have you not been on a train for a while?"

"That is not correct, Major. Why are you concerned?"

"Because I saw you pay for your ticket. We who serve *Tennô-Heika* do not have to pay."

"That is true. However, I believe that all of us must sacrifice. I choose to pay the fare."

"Where are you traveling to, Major?"

"Does my destination concern the police?"

"Normally, no. But I am curious. And I am with the Special High Police."

Ken looked around. Everyone who heard them had stopped talking and was looking at him and the policeman. He knew about the Special High Police, the *Tokubetsu Kôtô Keisatsu*, *Tokkô* for short.

The secretive *Tokkô* was established in 1911. Its initial purpose was to suppress "dangerous thoughts," such as anti-emperor or anti-government movements. Their main targets were communists, socialists, anarchists, leftists, labor unions and Koreans living in Japan. With the war their power had grown and their interests seemed boundless.

Like any organization with authority, the *Tokkô* sought avenues to expand its power, which brought it into direct conflict with the regular police. By the 1930s a *Tokkô* detective could command regular police officers and detectives, resulting in rivalry and fear of the *Tokkô*. The war enhanced their power further. Even senior military officers, including the most powerful in Japan, could not ignore the *Tokkô*. Ken knew, from when he had attended Tôkyô Imperial University, that he could not ignore a question from the *Tokkô*.

"I have been ordered to report to the War Ministry."

The *Tokkô* officer was pleased. He felt he had humbled another Imperial Army officer. "Major, I see you are an engineering officer. Are you going to build something at the War Ministry?"

Ken noted that everyone within earshot was paying attention to their exchange. "Beyond what I have told you, I am not authorized to speak more of it. However, if you insist, I can speak about this with your superiors. Then you can explain to your superiors why you are speaking publicly about military matters."

The *Tokkô* officer's face reddened. "I am traveling to Tôkyô myself. Perhaps we will speak of this again." Stiffly, he walked away. Ken looked at some senior Imperial Army officers. One noted Ken's *tsuba* and knew that Ken came from true *samurai* lineage. He discreetly nodded his approval then turned back to his companions. From the reports he had read Ken knew that there was no love lost between the *Tokkô* and the Imperial Japanese Army.

At precisely 7:30 A.M. the train from Odawara arrived and Ken boarded with the crowd. He entered the third car and, knowing the trip would easily be over an hour, quickly found an aisle seat. The seats were comfortable with green fabric, although some areas were frayed from neglect or lack of material to make repairs. Seating was arranged so that two passengers sat next to each other, facing another pair. Across the center aisle, seats were arranged the same way. Overhead wooden shelves held luggage or packages. Passengers could raise or lower the windows and almost all the windows were open even though it was still early morning. The other passengers next to and opposite him stood until he took his seat.

The car soon filled. The last passenger to enter was the *Tokkô* cop who stared at Ken as he walked by. Ken stared back, not yielding, and the cop knew it. There were no seats left and Ken watched as the cop went into the second car.

Exactly on time, the Odawara-Kyûkô Line train pulled out and Ken settled in for the ride, the next stop Shinjuku Station. He unfolded the paper and started to read the stories. He felt he was reading the *New York Times*. There were no headlines "above the fold" as there were in the *Times*. Laid out at the top center was

Nippon Times

Below it was

NO. 16,661 (THE 20TH YEAR OF SHOWA)   TOKYO, SATURDAY, AUGUST 4, 1945   PRICE 35 SEN

laid out like the *New York Times*, eight columns wide.

Next were the subheads, summarizing headlines, followed by the articles. It was as if the war was of little importance to the editors. Instead, most of the articles seemed written for American readers. Disbelief was his initial reaction.

The first article was:

COMMUNIQUE IS RELEASED ON
POTSDAM CONFERENCE

'Big Three' Fail to Produce Anything
with Direct Bearing on War in Pacific

The "Big Three" communique agreed upon at the Potsdam Conference was announced simultaneously in Washington, London and Moscow on August 2 at 9:30 p.m. GMT (Tokyo time, August 3, 6:30 a.m.) according to a Domei dispatch from Stockholm.

Contrary to all predictions made by the Anglo-Americans, the "Big Three" conference at Potsdam appears to have failed to produce anything that has direct bearing upon the war in the Pacific, according to Domei.

According to a United Press newscast, the communique, summing up the series of conferences between President Truman, Premier Stalin and Prime Minister Attlee and also former Prime Minister Churchill and drafted and signed by the three men, conspicuously failed to make any reference to the Pacific or the war against Japan.

Ken put the newspaper down. He looked out the window and saw the countryside as a blur. He recalled what Admiral Halsey had told him before he left the *Missouri*, that the United States, Great Britain, and China had issued the Potsdam Declaration, demanding that Japan unconditionally surrender, or face "prompt and utter destruction."

He looked forward and saw an old woman, a grandmother he thought, looking at him. She had a smile on her face which only accentuated her wrinkles. He smiled back. She leaned forward and touched his hand, so uncharacteristic, he thought.

"I know what you are thinking. You will help defeat the Americans. You are young and strong. I have two grandsons in the Army. I have not heard from them for a long time. The last I heard they were in the Philippines defending the Empire. Nevertheless, I know they are well and serve *Tennô-Heika* with all their heart. But you are here to help defend Japan. With strong, young men like you the hairy barbarians will be destroyed."

Ken's face smiled but his soul wept for her. Most of the Japanese forces were wiped out in the Philippines, through combat, starvation or disease. Very few had survived to surrender. *This old woman will not see her grandsons again*, he thought. *Nor would she receive their ashes.* He nodded his assurances to her then wondered if in touching him she was touching her grandsons. He went back to the *Nippon Times*.

Another story reported that the

U.S. SENATE ADJOURNS; TO RECONVENE OCTOBER 8

Barkley Asks Vacation-Bound Colleagues to Consider Number of Problems

The United States Senate Thursday night adjourned the session in which the United Nations Charter and the Bretton Woods Monetary Agreement were accepted for the United States, according to a Washington dispatch to Lisbon. The Senate will reconvene on October 8.

Senator Allen Barkley, Kentucky Democrat and Majority Leader of the upper chamber, told his vacation-bound colleagues before they adjourned that they would see 12 urgent domestic legislative tasks when they return.

Ken's attention was caught by two subheads to the right; the first was in the third last column.

ENEMY'S AIR ACTIVITIES OVER
JAPAN INTENSIFIED

8,000 Deck Planes and
12,000 Land-Based Machines
Appear During Month of July

Since the first part of July, the enemy air operations over Japan proper has become particularly intensified, and mobilizing the army and navy air forces at the Marianas and on Yiojima and Okinawa and the newly organized task forces, the enemy has persistently raided our aircraft production facilities, transportation systems, and urban areas. During July, the enemy planes that attacked Japan proper totaled 8,000 deck planes and 12,000 land-based planes, including 4,000 B-29s, making a total of 20,000 or an average of 600 planes a day.

In column eight, the last on the right, a story reported specific raids on Japan from American air bases on Iwô Jima. He could not help but think that if America had been bombed it would have been the headline in the States. He read the column and near the end a word jumped out at him.

105 YIOJIMA-BASED P-51'S
ATTACK JAPAN ON FRIDAY

Hit Chiba, Ibaraki, Tochigi and Keihan Areas;
Toyama City Raided on Wednesday

About 105 Yiojima-based P-51 fighters, coming in two waves, raided the Chiba, Ibaraki, Tochigi and Keihan areas on Friday morning.

The first wave of 60 P-51's, led by three superforts, appeared over the mainland at about 9:50 a.m. These raiders attacked military facilities.

The second wave of some 45 P-51's also led by three superforts appeared at about 10:15 a.m. The enemy planes closed their attack at about 11:30 a.m.

The article continued, listing other targets the P-51s attacked. It also reported a lone B-29 operating over Tôkyô, from 11:18 P.M. to after midnight, and listed the areas of Tôkyô the B-29 flew over. He reread the column and, his knowledge of Japan's geography sure, he recalled why he recognized the word.

> The Tokai Army District Headquarters made the following announcement at 2 p.m. Thursday.
> Approximately 70 B-29's, in a two-hour raid on Wednesday night subjected Toyama City and environs to incendiary attacks, causing fires to break out in various parts. However by dawn the fires were brought under control.

The smoke he had spotted in the northwest sky as he flew over Fuji-*san* had to have been coming from Toyama. And since he saw the smoke on Friday morning the fires had not been brought under control as reported. *Damn, the control of the population is absolute*, he thought. He looked for more articles about Japan's position but found little. There was an article about Russian forces occupying Urfahr in Austria on the north bank of the Danube, opposite the American-occupied Linz; both Russian and American military police were controlling traffic over the Danube Bridge.

Near the bottom of the page, in the sixth column, were two articles that made him shake his head.

Big Iye Air Base Set

> The Americans have completed an airfield on Iye Island of the Okinawa group to be used as a base for large aircraft says a frontline report. Already B-24's have been transferred from the Philippines area for a large-scale air offensive against Japan.

Plank Commands P.I. Area

> General Douglas MacArthur's Headquarters announced the appointment of Briga-

dier General Edward Plank as the commander of the Philippine area on July 31,
according to a Manila dispatch from Lisbon
received by Domei on August 1.

He turned the page and quickly scanned the articles. He returned to one.

VITAL ROLE OF SHIPPING

U.S. Landing Operations and Marine Transportation Power

(By A SPECIAL CORRESPONDENT)
Ships will play a vital role in the planned
American landing operation on the mainland of Japan because, in addition to the
war of attrition now going on in the vast
Pacific war theater, the battle of supply
is growing in severity. Modern warfare is
dominated by the necessity of producing
and supplying vast quantities of war materials, so that it can be said that the maintenance and strengthening of supply routes
may well decide the outcome of the war.

It went on to explain how, in the war with Germany, the British and then America had suffered massive shipping losses at the outset of the war, more than they were building. Then in the first half of 1943 the Americans had turned the tide and were producing more ships than the Germans could sink. It went on to point out

However, after the first half of 1942 the
American shipbuilding capacity was placed
on a full operational basis, while the perfection of the convoy system reduced Germany's power to destroy Allied shipping,
so that the difference between tonnage
sunk and tonnage built was reversed. In
other words, the tonnage of ships built by
the Anglo-American nations surpassed the
tonnage of ships sunk and their shipping
policy was stabilized at least for the time
being.
    As stated above, the enemy has approxi-
mately 53,000,000 tons of ships at present.

It is doubtful, however, whether this will be sufficient for the planned landing operations on our mainland.

He scanned the page, hoping to find any article that would show that someone in Japan had a rational thought. Down at the bottom he found a story.

PRESS COMMENTS

Friday, August 3
SET TO SMASH INVADERS

YOMIURI HOCHI—Japanese Anti-Air Raid Units, in their intercepting operations against the enemy planes which raided the mainland during July, shot down or damaged 1,021. Compared with the number of raiding planes, the above figure may not be one in which we can show great pride, but it should be remembered that these battle results were achieved with a fraction of our defense power. Japan at present is steadily increasing her fighting power in anticipation of an enemy landing on the mainland, at the same time conserving her strength for the big battle to come.

This does not mean the conservation of fighting power in a passive or indifferent way. Actually, it means storing up of fighting power in a very positive manner. The Imperial Headquarters, on August 1, announced: "The Army and Navy Forces are steadily strengthening their fighting preparations against an enemy invasion." This gives added confidence to the entire nation.

At the bottom right of the page something caught his eye.

Try Again

"So your wife has chosen your new secretary for you. Is she a blonde?"
"No, he's a brunette."

He stopped reading and looked out the window again. They passed rice fields, most of which were bare. Thinking about the articles he had just read he remembered *Alice's Adventures in Wonderland*. He recalled part of the conversation between Alice and the Caterpillar.

"Who are *you*?" said the Caterpillar.
This was not an encouraging opening for a conversation. Alice replied, rather shyly, "I—I hardly know, sir, just at present—at least I know who I was when I got up this morning, but I think I must have been changed several times since then."
"What do you mean by that?" said the Caterpillar sternly. "Explain yourself!"
"I can't explain *myself*, I'm afraid, sir," said Alice, "because I'm not myself, you see."

Dismayed, Ken folded the newspaper and put it on his lap. He laid his head back and closed his eyes. The train was drawn by an electric-powered engine and was quiet. The metal wheels rolling over the tracks had a calming effect. Within minutes he was asleep, his body gently rocked by the swaying of the train.

He was awoken by the train slowing. He looked at his watch. Just over thirty minutes had passed; not enough time to reach Shinjuku Station in Tôkyô. He looked out the window and saw they were approaching Noborito Station. They came to a stop and the doors at either end of the car opened. The train was supposed to be an express line to Shinjuku Station with no stops.

Two men entered the opposite end from where Ken was sitting. Both were Imperial Japanese Army colonels. Ken's immediate thought was that the *Tokkô* cop had arranged for the train to stop for reinforcements.

He watched the men walk down the center aisle toward his end. Their attitude was aloof as they looked for empty seats. They looked at Ken's uniform and saw that he was a Combat

Engineer officer and passed him. Finding no empty seats they entered the second car. Ken was alarmed; that's where the *Tokkô* went. A few minutes later the *Tokkô* cop reentered the third car. Ken tensed and put aside the newspaper. The cop passed Ken then stopped and looked at him. His face reflected anger and humiliation. He turned and looked at the people sitting in the seats and moved on. Five rows from Ken he stopped and looked at a soldier, an Army private, sitting in a window seat on the other side of the train from Ken.

"Stand up, fool! Don't you know to relinquish your seat to a superior?"

Ken watched as the private, startled, struggled to stand. The old woman sitting next to the private stood and backed into the aisle.

"Honorable Major, please take my seat. I do not mind standing."

The *Tokkô* cop ignored her; he wanted to humiliate an Army soldier, just as he had been humiliated. He reached over and slapped the soldier in the head. "*Bakayarô!* Give me your seat!"

The train started to move out of the station.

Then Ken saw the crutches as the soldier reached for them, leaning against the wall. The soldier lifted himself off the seat. Ken could see he had lost a leg. He guessed the soldier was a teenager. Ken pieced together the puzzle. Obviously one of the colonels had taken the *Tokkô*'s seat.

Do I become involved, Ken asked himself. *Do I call attention to myself?* Ken got up and moved toward the *Tokkô*. *Think Japanese*, he thought.

"Private, remain seated. Major, this soldier needs his seat. This woman has offered you her seat instead."

"Major, this is none of your concern. This fool has failed in his duty."

"Major, let this soldier keep his seat. He has not failed in his duty. You can see he has lost his leg serving *Tennô-Heika* and the Empire."

"Major, I want this window seat. I can breathe the clean outside air rather than the smell of peasants. He can find another seat."

Ken stared at the *Tokkô*. There was nothing on his uniform to indicate that the man had ever served outside of Japan. He was, guessed Ken, a paper pusher. "There are no other seats in this car, Major. Perhaps you could look in the other cars."

The major ignored Ken and reached again to strike the private, who cringed while trying to stand. Ken, angered, grabbed the major, turning him so they faced each other, and slapped him in the face. It was hard and loud. Everyone else in the car feared what might happen next. Both men had pistols and swords.

With his right hand, the major instinctively reached for his *katana* but before he could step back to pull it out Ken grabbed the major's right hand with his left and with his right fist punched the *Tokkô* cop squarely in the nose. Those close enough heard the crunch of bone splintering. Blood spurted out and flowed onto the major's jacket. Shocked and enraged, he broke free of Ken's grip, stepped back and grabbed the hilt of his sword. Before he could pull it Ken's sword was already out of its scabbard, its tip at the major's throat. The major froze.

"Major!" said Ken. "You are offensive and rude! You have disturbed everyone in this car! This soldier you slapped has served *Tennô-Heika* and sacrificed for it. You, on the other hand, have grown craven behind a desk! Either leave this car and search elsewhere for a seat or die where you stand! A fool becomes wise when he dies!"

Everyone in the car waited. These men were of equal rank. Everyone knew a superior could strike a subordinate with impunity but two equals could bring serious injury or death to both and others if they chose to fight. Ken watched the man struggle with his emotions. Both held their position. The major looked to his left. The young soldier was still standing. Then the major looked back at Ken, whose sword had not moved. He looked at the people who were sitting opposite Ken. Their faces were blank. Then he saw the *tsuba* on Ken's sword and knew Ken was of *samurai* lineage.

Slowly, he removed his hand from his *katana* and stood straight, lifting his chin a bit higher.

"*Ha!*" I understand! What he understood was that Ken's *katana* was truly *samurai* whereas his had been stamped at a factory like so many swords for officers. He felt humiliation.

Ken slowly reseated his sword then stepped back. Satisfied the *Tokkô* cop would not try anything else he moved to the side and the major acknowledged the unstated command. He proceeded to the end of the car, opened the door, and without looking back passed into the next car.

Ken watched him exit and close the door behind him. As the *Tokkô* cop passed into the car Ken turned his back and told the soldier to sit down and urged the old woman to take her seat. When he looked at the soldier he saw he was crying. Ken knew the boy's thoughts. He should have died for *Tennô-Heika* rather than surviving. He left the boy alone.

Ken returned to his seat and sat down. The old woman with two grandsons had picked up his newspaper and handed it to him. He thanked her.

She leaned forward and spoke softly to Ken. "One of my grandsons is no older than that boy. Perhaps when they return to defend our homeland they will serve under you. You are a good man, Major."

He smiled but he was saddened by her hopes. He looked out the window and pictured what the American invasion would be like. He turned and looked at the boy who had been crying. He had regained control but was looking down, at a leg no longer there.

Ken closed his eyes again. After about fifteen minutes he opened them and looked out and saw young men and women cutting down trees.

Their cuts were close to the ground. When they were done they went to cut other trees. Others came and dug around the stump. After they pushed away enough soil they put rope around the stump and started to pull the rope. With great effort they were able to pull the stump from the ground, roots intact.

Ken was curious. He knew firewood was something the Japanese needed but stumps and roots, laden with moisture, were of no value. Maybe, he thought, they were clearing the field to grow food and wanted to clear the stumps as well as rocks. He dismissed the thought and closed his eyes again.

The train slowed down as they approached the outskirts of Tôkyô. The old woman was looking out the window, up at the sky. She seemed nervous. He saw others doing the same. He turned around and saw most of the passengers doing the same and grasped they were looking for American fighters, which often attacked trains. Ken looked out the window but he ignored the skies. He surveyed the scarred landscape. He looked out the other side of the train and saw the same. Enormous areas were simply desolate, devoid of anything recognizable but as piles of rubble. In the distance he saw they were approaching a large office building. As the train closed the gap he looked into the structure. He saw the building was nothing more than a shell, empty of any floors or walls. Fire had shattered the windows and burned away the wooden window frames, allowing fire and smoke to paint dark patches of soot on the outside walls. He had seen scores of reconnaissance photographs of Japan but he was not prepared for what he was riding through.

Where wooden houses once stood now metal pipes, some twisted by powerful heat, projected from the ground mimicking skeletal arms and hands grasping for air above the flames. Metal tubs were blackened and warped. Metal cookware, disfigured by heat, lay scattered. Rubble, not consumed by the ravenous flames, had been pushed back from the streets onto now-empty lots so as not to block movement by foot or vehicle.

Horse carcasses were left where they had fallen; some consumed by flames while others were picked at by scavenging dogs or rats. He noted, though, that some carcasses had precise cuts on their flanks.

The closer the train drew to Shinjuku Station the more barren became the land. America's B-29s had decimated a great city and Ken was saddened because his memories were all that he had left of a once-great metropolis.

While looking out the window color drained from his face; he was shocked at what he didn't see. The train was passing a large open area on the right that was no longer recognizable, but he knew what it had been, a place of tranquility Kyoko and he had often visited.

Meiji *Jingû*, the magnificent Shintô shrine and park dedicated to the divine souls of Emperor Meiji and his consort, Empress Shôken, was gone.

When Ken and Kyoko could steal some time for privacy they often came to the shrine and walked through its forested areas or the iris garden that *Meiji Tennô* particularly liked.

Gone were the magnificent buildings that had been built by over 100,000 volunteers and completed in 1920. The massive wooden *torii*—Shintô shrine archways—had been consumed by firestorms created by the B-29s, as had the trees. It was now an unwelcoming and empty field.

Ken was stunned and no longer saw the landscape as the train came closer to Shinjuku Station.

The train, however, could not pull into Shinjuku Station because it no longer existed. A B-29 raid had destroyed it. Heat from the firestorm had warped the tracks. Moving people and goods was more important than a building so only the tracks had been replaced.

Ken looked at his watch; it was 0835 hours. He stood and reached for his flight bag but stopped. He turned and walked to the soldier who had lost his leg.

"Private, do you have a bag with you?"

The boy tried to stand but fell back. Ken let the old woman leave her seat then reached and helped the boy stand.

"Yes, Major. It is above. Please do not trouble yourself. I can reach it."

Ken stood back and watched the boy struggle while he tried to pull down his bag. He failed several times, almost falling twice.

Ken, frustrated for the boy, reached up and grabbed the bag. It was a *furoshiki*, a square of cotton fabric tied to hold all his personal belongings. The colors and patterns had faded from use; the material was tattered. He placed it on the seat.

"Private, do you have family meeting you here?"

"Yes, Major. They should be here at the station."

"Come. I'll carry your bag for you."

"Please, Major, please let me try. My family cannot see me unable to care for myself."

Ken stepped back and watched the boy bend. He removed his hand and gripped the top of the crutch under his armpit then tried to pick up the *furoshiki*. He lost his balance and recovered. He repeated his attempt. This time he fell into Ken's arms and started to weep.

Ken stood him up. "Brace up, Private! Brace up! You have family waiting for you. They will understand. I will carry your bag! Follow me!"

Ken picked up the *furoshiki* and grabbed his own bag then moved toward the door, all the while watching the boy out of the corner of his eye. The other passengers moved to the other door and filed out, not daring to impede the major who could draw his *katana* so quickly.

Unsteadily, the private moved toward the door. When he reached the stairs he stopped and leaned one crutch against the door. With his free hand he grabbed the side of the doorway, then slowly hopped down the stairs on his solitary leg and one crutch. When he reached the ground he turned and retrieved the other crutch and positioned it into his armpit and stood as tall as he could, looking into the crowd. Ken stood behind him and waited for the boy's family to meet him. From the crowd a woman came forward, tears running down her face. From her age Ken assumed she was the boy's mother. She stopped in front of the boy then buried her face in his chest and sobbed. Behind her an old man stood, tightly gripping a handkerchief to his mouth.

Ken went to the man and handed him the boy's *furoshiki*. The old man took the bag and bowed. Ken returned the bow, but not as deeply as the old man. Ken turned and looked at the boy and his mother, both crying, and knew that the same scene was being repeated across the United States and other nations. He shook his head and walked away.

He was disoriented at first. With Shinjuku Station gone it took him a few moments to find the bus and trolley stops that would take him to Tsukiji, where he would try to find a *ryokan*—an inn—and rent a room. He saw several lines of waiting people and walked over. He asked a man if he was waiting for a bus or trolley.

"The buses are few and far between due to gasoline rationing, Honorable Major. The trolleys are more dependable. Where are you going, Honorable Major?"

"Tsukiji."

"Ah. Over there; that line there. A trolley should arrive soon."

"Thank you." Ken walked to the end of the line. Immediately, people urged that he make his way to the front of the line. At first he declined. Then Ken remembered what Captain

Paschal had told him. He moved to the front.

While waiting for the trolley a bus pulled up, heavy smoke belching from the rear. Initially, Ken thought it was on fire. Then he saw an attendant shoveling charcoal at the bus' rear. Ken walked to the bus' rear and raised his brows. Mounted to the rear of the bus was a stove and the attendant was shoveling charcoal into it. Ken saw that the bus' engine was being powered by fumes from burned charcoal. *The military is hogging the gasoline*, he thought.

Ken walked back to his position in the line for the trolley. At 9:00 AM a trolley arrived and stopped in front of him. He entered and took a window seat. The driver rang the trolley's bell and then left Shinjuku Station.

As the trolley drove toward Tsukiji, Ken surveyed the immeasurable destruction of Tôkyô. In areas where B-29s had dropped bombs not a single wooden structure stood. Many of the ferroconcrete buildings, not directly hit by bombs, had survived the explosions but not the fires. They were empty shells, like scattered hollow weeds left standing after a tornado had struck. As the trolley moved further east the environment became repetitive, so complete was the devastation. Yet, here and there were areas left untouched. He could only marvel at how successfully the American Air Force had left selected areas of Tôkyô untouched.

The trolley made numerous stops as it wended its way through the city. Looking out the window Ken saw people walking. Others were riding or guiding horse-drawn carts. Still others were pulling carts. He noticed how slow everyone moved. Their faces were pallid, eyes sunken. Women not wearing *monpe*, the drab national baggy pants, wore Western clothing. But their clothing, like them, looked worn-out. Some people wore *kimono* which also showed signs of disrepair. He turned away, knowing the people of Tôkyô were eating less every day. *How could they be expected*, he wondered, *to maintain their clothing when they barely maintain themselves?*

Soon they were approaching the Imperial Palace on the left. On his right, just before the palace, he recognized one building he had visited several times while at *Tôdai*, the white stone and concrete United States Embassy. It was situated just southwest of the Imperial Palace, just over a mile from the outer perimeter of the palace. Though closed, the embassy and surrounding area, including the American ambassador's residence, had not been bombed. Nothing had changed.

He sensed a change in the passengers. As the trolley approached the palace it slowed. Passengers stopped talking and stood. Uncertain, Ken followed suit. Everyone, except the driver, faced the Imperial Palace. Then, to his surprise, everyone bowed. Again, he emulated their behavior. The older passengers bowed lowest. Everyone held their suppliant position until the trolley passed the palace then sat down.

As the trolley drew closer to Tsukiji the landscape showed less destruction. When the trolley came to Tsukiji Station, the end of the line, he approached the driver.

"How much is the fare?"

"Honorable Major, there is no charge for His Majesty's Imperial forces."

Ken, out of habit, carried his bag in his left hand as he left the trolley, in case he had to give or return a salute. When the trolley pulled away to turn and make its way back to Shinjuku Station it revealed Tsukiji, a different world. Colonel Mashbir was right. Nothing had been touched. He put his bag down and turned, facing west, and looked at what was left of Tôkyô. He looked at his watch; it was 10:40 AM.

The devastation was ironic, he thought. The West had helped to build Tôkyô and now the West had all but destroyed it.

Tôkyô, when it was Edo, was a city of one or two-storied buildings mostly constructed of wood, and repeatedly plagued by fires. When a particularly devastating fire swept through Tôkyô in 1872, the government took the opportunity to both improve the appearance of the city and try to lessen the number of fires by passing an ordinance requiring most structures to be built of brick and stone. And that required help from the West. By the 1870s, Western-style buildings—made of concrete or bricks—sprang up throughout the city.

He remembered a course he took at Tôkyô Imperial University which examined the transition of Edo to modern Tôkyô, designed primarily by two British architects. One was Thomas James Waters, known for designing the first examples of Western-style architecture in Japan. Waters arrived in Japan at the end of the Edo period, commissioned to design a factory for the fabrication and storage of weapons and ammunition. Pleased with his work, the Meiji government then hired him as chief engineer to design the Ôsaka Mint Bureau in 1868. The redbrick building was completed in 1871. Waters' next task was perhaps his most inspiring. Following a conflagration in the Ginza-Tsukiji area in 1872, the Tôkyô administration decided to lessen the chance of impending fires by utilizing brick. By 1877, the main access road of Ginza was lined with European-style brick buildings designed by Waters, the government's first implementation of urban planning.

The other British architect was Josiah Conder, who designed over 50 major Western-style buildings in Tôkyô, ranging from Gothic to Renaissance to Tudor to Moorish. For the Meiji government, however, eager to echo the European style, Conder's style proved too wide-ranging, and Conder eventually set up his own firm, although he continued to advise the government.

Conder became the Imperial College of Engineering's principal instructor, giving lessons and lectures. His courses covered diverse topics from ancient Egyptian through Indian to existing European architecture, and emphasized construc-

tion techniques using wood, brick and stone. He remained in
Japan until his death in 1920, devoting his career to modern-
izing Japan's architectural expertise.

Richard P. Bridges, an American, produced one of the
earliest examples of quasi-Western architecture when he designed the Tsukiji Hotel, built in Tsukiji's foreign settlement in
1868. He later worked on the Shimbashi and Yokohama Station
buildings.

Now, most of their work was gone, eradicated by the
Great Kantô Earthquake of 1923. What was left of their work
and what was rebuilt after the 1923 earthquake was reduced
to rubble by America's B-29s. As Ken had witnessed, most
ferroconcrete buildings left standing were empty shells, their
interiors consumed by the voracious flames.

He now turned back and looked at a different world. He
stepped to the east, leaving desolation behind him.

St. Luke's Hospital dominated the skyline of Tsukiji. He
looked up and saw the bell tower of the main building. Atop
the tower was the crucifix, the landmark for all American pilots that this area was not to be attacked. He walked closer to
the seven-story building, remembering its history.

St. Luke's Hospital was started in 1902 under the guidance
of Rudolf Bolling Teusler, a young and energetic missionary
physician from Virginia, anxious to carry Episcopal Christian
healing and teaching to Japan. The hospital started in a modest
wooden cottage in the old foreign settlement of Tsukiji. It had
space for about ten patients and little or no medical equipment.
Over the years the hospital grew. In March 1923 foundations
for new buildings were started and completed just three weeks
before the Great Kantô Earthquake of September 1, 1923 struck.
The quake and ensuing fires destroyed all the buildings but not
the newly-finished foundations. Teusler was undeterred. The
United States reacted quickly. General John J. Pershing, the
acting Secretary of War, ordered that a complete field hospital

be immediately shipped from Manila to Tôkyô. By October 15 it was ready for patient care. By early summer of 1924 barracks were constructed with beds for about 225 patients. Other buildings were soon erected. Tragically, a fire on January 13, 1925 destroyed most of the new buildings. Yet, by May 1925 almost all of the buildings had been replaced with donations from American churches. By 1933 the main building, crowned with a crucifix, was completed. And it was here, Ken recalled, that the seeds of the Tôkyô Doolittle raid of 1942 were sown.

In 1934 several American baseball players, including Babe Ruth, Lefty Gomez, and Lou Gehrig went to Japan to participate in a 17-game exhibition tour against a Japanese all-star team. A last-minute addition to the team was a third-string catcher named Moe Berg.

Morris "Moe" Berg was an enigma. He graduated *magna cum laude* from Princeton where he majored in modern languages and played baseball. He received a law degree from Columbia Law School then studied philosophy at the Sorbonne. While a student at Princeton he and a teammate, also a linguist, would often speak to each other in Latin on the baseball field. Yet as a professional baseball player Berg was less than average. He was slow on foot and a second-rate hitter. In 1933, batting 65 times, he hit a paltry .185 and played in just 40 games. He had six career home runs. One teammate commented, "He can speak twelve languages but can't hit in any of them." Yet no one denied he was brilliant. Casey Stengel once described Berg as "the strangest fellah who ever put on a uniform."

In 1934 that would prove to be true. While in Tôkyô Moe Berg read in a Japanese newspaper that the daughter of America's ambassador to Japan, 22-year-old Elsie Lyon, was a patient at St. Luke's Hospital, having just given birth.

For one day Moe Berg tried to become Japanese. He dressed in a *kimono* and put on a pair of *tabi*, which have a split in the sock for the large toe so that they may comfortably be worn with *geta*. He then put on *geta*, traditional wooden thong sandals with two parallel slats of wood running left to right across the bottom which kept the feet several inches above the ground. He combed his thick black hair back and parted it in the middle. He left his room and carried a bouquet of flowers as he headed to St. Luke's Hospital. Moe Berg was going to visit the ambassador's daughter.

When Berg arrived at the hospital he asked in Japanese for Mrs. Lyon's room. He took the elevator to the fifth floor. When he got there he stepped off and threw the flowers in a wastebasket and got back on the elevator, heading for the seventh floor. There was a piazza there, a perfect setting to relax or have lunch. He did neither. He opened a door and climbed a cramped spiral stairway and reached the bell tower. He had, as he had been told, a sweeping view of Tôkyô.

Berg reached into his *kimono* and removed a 16 mm Bell and Howell movie camera. For over twenty seconds he panned Tôkyô, including the shipyards, military facilities, and industrial centers that were spread throughout the capital. When finished he returned the camera to his *kimono* and descended to the first floor and left the hospital, no one the wiser. Ken had been told that Colonel Jimmy Doolittle had studied Moe Berg's film before his Tôkyô bombing raid of 1942.

Ken tried to picture an American baseball player in *kimono* and *geta* on top of St. Luke's filming the city. He smiled and walked away.

It took him little time to locate a *ryokan*. He headed for the Tsukiji Catholic Church, a building he enjoyed studying whenever he had been in Tsukiji. Like most buildings in Tôkyô, the original, built in 1878, was consumed by fire in the Great Kantô Earthquake. When the new church was proposed several designs were put forth. But the benefactor insisted on a pantheon style, complete with Doric columns under the pediment. In 1927 the benefactor had his wish. However, there was a paradox in the construction. All of Tôkyô wanted brick and cement, including the Catholic community in Tsukiji. But there was not enough brick and cement for every project. So the church, though destroyed by fire, was constructed of wood. However, in keeping with the design for a pantheonic building, the exterior was mortared, even the Doric columns. Ken smiled, recalling the building's history. Across the street was what he really sought, a *ryokan*.

It was a simple two-story affair made of dark wood. It was sandwiched between two other homes, also made of wood. In the front were two sliding doors made of hardwood with panes of glass. He knocked on the door and waited. Shortly he heard the shuffling of hesitant feet. It was just after noon.

A wizened woman opened the door. Her gray hair was pulled back into a bun. She was dressed in the drab *monpe* and smock. She wore slippers. But her eyes captured his interest. They were penetrating; nothing, he felt, eluded her scrutiny. When she saw Ken she bowed more than once. Even in Tsukiji the military was feared.

"Oba-*san*, I need a room for a few days, perhaps a week. Do you have one available?"

She was flattered that in spite of how she was dressed and looked he treated her politely when he called her aunt. Most Imperial Army officers were rude. That he wanted a room, however, caused her some unease. She knew that an officer would expect to be fed breakfast as well as housed. That would cost her money. And, of course, he would want to take hot baths and wood cost money too. More than she had.

"Yes, Honorable Officer. Just one, but someone came by earlier looking for a room. They said they would be back today. I told him I would hold it for him."

From her expression Ken could almost read her mind and smiled inwardly. *She is a sharp one*, he thought. He reached into his pocket and took out folded *yen* notes. From her reaction it was more money than she had seen in years. He remembered that in 1941, before the war, the *Yen*-Dollar exchange rate was ¥1 to about 23 cents.

"How much for the room, Oba-*san*, for a week," he asked as he started to unfold ¥10 notes. He did so slowly, knowing she was adding up her costs as well as her profit. Not once did she take her eyes off the money. When he reached ¥50 her head tilted a little but her eyes never left his hands. He knew that factory girls were earning ¥2 a day. He had to be careful; salary in the Japanese military was parsimonious. Too much largesse might raise her curiosity. But he also knew that inflation had devalued the *Yen*. He unfolded five more ¥10 notes but she didn't move. He knew that a four and a half *tatami* room, with breakfast, could cost between ¥10 to ¥15 a night. *I want the room*, he thought. *Besides, it's not my money.*

"Oba-*san*, what size room do you have?"

Oh, that I had a ten tatami *room*, she yearned. "Six *tatami* is all I have available."

"Ah, that large. The other rooms are rented, Oba-*san*?"

"Yes, Honorable Officer. But the tenants are away on business. And they have already paid in advance so I cannot rent out their rooms."

"Are they six *tatami* rooms also?"

Trapped, she thought. "No, Honorable Officer. They are four and a half *tatami*, smaller and not as nice as the one that is available. But that one is promised to someone else. *Sumimasen*." I'm sorry.

Ken counted out five more ¥10 notes. Her eyes widened. "Oba-*san*, rented or promised?"

The old lady bent out from the door and looked both ways down the street. She saw nothing and pulled back.

"It was promised but he has not yet returned. And he is not an officer like you. I feel an obligation to rent it to you. I am poor and everything is so expensive, especially food. I will have to charge ¥25 per night, and at that I will be sacrificing. But it is for the war."

Ken gave her ¥250, far more than enough for the week he asked for, including breakfasts.

"Come in, please, come in. I would carry your bag but my back is old and sore all the time. Please forgive me. Come in. Come in. Here are slippers for you. Those boots you wear would scratch my floors terribly."

Inside her entryway were several pairs of slippers. He removed his boots and put on slippers. He followed her to the second level. She seemed to glide to a room and smoothly lowered herself to her knees and effortlessly opened the *fusuma*, a wooden sliding door frame decorated with *washi*, handmade rice paper, on both sides. She gestured with her hand for him to enter. The room was clean and neat. The six *tatami* were in two rows, three *tatami* laid side by side. Ken put his bag down, removed his slippers—knowing that even slippers could damage *tatami*—and then walked into the room.

Curious, he looked at the *tatami* mats. Unlike the *tatami* at Atsugi he could tell these were of high quality. He picked up a corner of one. They were like the ones his mother had in her tearoom. He could feel the two separate layers, a straw core, and the soft reed cover edged with *goza* cloth, which formed the visible pattern. He stood and looked around the room. In the middle of the six *tatami* was a *futon*, above the *futon* a shaded lamp suspended from the ceiling. The windows faced the front of the building. Two four-draw lacquered bureaus were on opposite ends of the room. One had a shaded lamp while the other held a simple vase, lending a restrained balance. Opposite the windows was a closet.

Oba-*san*, curious, watched him. No previous tenant had ever done that before. She was pleased that her establishment satisfied his requirements.

She escorted him to the *yoku-jô*, the tub room. It contained a *yokusô*, a wooden tub. Ken was not surprised that the room was spotless. She then showed him the *datsui-jo*, the changing room where he would strip before going to the *yoku-jô*. Without a word exchanged, she knew he was pleased. They went downstairs to the entranceway. Ken removed the slippers and put on his boots.

"Oba-*san*, could you serve dinner."

"Honorable Officer, I had not included that in my cost!"

"That is quite all right. I will pay for it. What time could you serve dinner?"

"Honorable Officer, is six o'clock acceptable to you?"

"Yes, that is acceptable. Will anyone else be here for dinner, Oba-*san*?"

"Regrettably, no, Honorable Officer."

"Do you have *sake*, Oba-*san*?

"I am deeply sorry, Honorable Officer. I have none." *Does this foolish officer know how little* sake *there is in Tôkyô and how expensive it is? Besides, what little I have I share with my friends.*

Ken nodded. "I understand. It is very expensive. I would appreciate it if you could unpack my bag. I am going for a walk. Perhaps I can find some *sake* while I am out. Please prepare dinner for two. Since we are near the fish market could you shop for fresh fish, rice, and vegetables? And also shop for tomorrow's breakfast?"

Dismayed, she calculated the cost for dinner for two. *For two? It is true he pays well but I did not expect this.*

Ken guessed what she was thinking. "Oba-*san*, I have come from Kyûshû and have not been in Tôkyô for a long time. I do not wish to eat alone. I was hoping you would have dinner with me. Of course, I will give you extra money for the food. I am certain that you yourself would not normally shop at the fish market. But I would depend solely on your good taste. Will ¥50 pay for the food?"

Oba-*san* was, for the first time in her adult life, speechless. But she was not stupid.

"It will help, Honorable Officer. And I will help pay the difference because you are in the Imperial Army. We must all make sacrifices. Even old women like me. Yes, I will personally go shopping and I will be honored to prepare dinner and eat with you. I will make a dinner like your own mother's cooking!"

She saw the sadness in his face and truly regretted what she had said.

"Yes, Oba-*san*, I look forward to that. Army food is never the same as a mother's."

He left the *ryokan* and headed toward Ginza, to so many memories of Kyoko. And of his brother, Tom.

*   *   *

The train ride from Atsugi to Shinjuku Station and the trolley to Tsukiji had offered Ken a detached view of Tôkyô, keeping him apart from the surroundings. Walking to Ginza, however, gave him another perspective. The dust that rose when he walked the streets drove home a starker reality. He stopped often to look at particular settings. He had never seen or embraced such utter bleakness. No reconnaissance photos Ken had seen in readying him for his mission could prepare him for what he saw. Here and there large buildings made of marble or stone stood. Ken knew these buildings had purposefully not been bombed by B-29s because the Americans were going to use them during the occupation. But for so much of Tôkyô, looking anywhere but at Tsukiji, the city was unrecognizable both in spirit and in fact. Before his mission he had studied aerial reconnaissance photographs and knew that fifty percent of Tôkyô had been destroyed.

Coming closer to Ginza Ken saw men and women, teenagers and kids carefully sifting through the debris of buildings, looking for anything salvageable. Most would go to the war effort but some would be kept or sold on the black market. Others, working in already-cleared lots, were trying to make the earth produce food. For some there was meager success. For most, despite their dedication, the earth lay fallow.

He came across several ramshackle huts of corrugated metal held together with rope. These were the new dwellings of those who had lost their homes and who refused to leave Tôkyô. There were some children around, but most had been evacuated to the countryside, just as London had done during the Blitz.

He stopped and watched these people. They were shabby and dirty. Not just the dirt one normally acquires from sweat and working with the soil. These people, he felt, had lost their sense of pride of cleanliness he so often associated with the Japanese. When he looked at their faces and saw through the sweat and dirt he saw exhaustion from too little food, constant fear of American bombers and fighters, and homelessness. Their will had been drained. Above all else he saw hopelessness.

He moved away, heading for the center of Ginza. No matter where he looked he saw the same scene played out. Dazed people trying to exist in a city that no longer existed.

When he reached Ginza he was shaken. It was as if he were looking at photographs of the 1923 earthquake, which had finished off the last of Ginza's original brick buildings. Except for a few sections, Ginza was gone. Miraculously, some of the department stores appeared unscathed. Ken remembered Ginza as not only a glamorous shopping area, what some had called Japan's Fifth Avenue, but as a spot of Bohemian life where he and Tom spent many an evening in decadent splendor, frequenting the bars, dance halls, cabarets, and cafés and lots of girls. It was where he had met Kyoko.

He walked to the 8-*chôme* section of Ginza to look at

one of the department stores and found that the bombing and fires had not touched it. Several of the sidewalks in front of the store were disfigured with deep holes. At first he thought they were incomplete construction sites, running the length of the sidewalk. When he stepped closer he saw they were trenches, hastily dug bomb shelters. However, they were shallow and had no covering, offering little protection from bombers or fighters. And no protection from jellied gasoline bombs. The Japanese military, believing that Japan would never be bombed, had never developed underground air raid shelters for civilians. Rather, civilians were advised to dig their own shelters at their homes; a trench or pit in the soil and a flimsy cover. He walked further and found what he hoped for.

An old man had a pushcart with various items for sale. Ken went over and spoke with him. The man was wary at first; Ken was in a uniform. Soon he relaxed. After all, Ken was not a police officer, even though there was one on the opposite corner.

They chatted about the weather, the old man's family, and his offerings on the pushcart. And how Ken would like to buy a bottle of *sake*. The old man looked at the cop. He had a feel for these things. Besides, the military were always looking for *sake*. And women.

"What kind of *sake* would you be interested in, Honorable Major?"

"I had not thought of it. Would you know where I might be able to buy some?"

The old man looked around then lifted some articles of clothing. Underneath were several 1.88 liter bottles of *sake*.

Ken smiled. He asked the price.

"*Sake* is very expensive, Honorable Major. And there is so little for a poor person like me to buy it. A bottle will cost ¥9. And at that I am losing money."

Ah, the spirit of profit still lives, even here among the ruins of Ginza, thought Ken.

"I will need two bottles."

The old man said nothing to imply this would present a problem. Ken removed his money and unfolded four ¥5 notes.

"Honorable Major, you will need something to carry them in. I have *furoshiki* here."

"I agree." Ken watched the old man pick a *furoshiki* and deftly wrap the two bottles in the cloth so they would not strike against one another. "How much for the *furoshiki*, old man?"

"These are of good quality, Honorable Major. ¥2."

Exactly my change, thought Ken, smiling. "Agreed."

Ken took the weighted *furoshiki* and walked further west. Pieces of masonry crunched under his boots. No one bothered to look at him as he moved past them. The day was hotter. He held up his hand and looked at the sun. Sweat had collected on his face. His armpits were moist. He moved about aimlessly, wondering how this could have happened; what lunatic had started this madness. How would it end? Then he thought of his mission and the scores of thousands of Americans who would be killed or wounded trying to stop the madness. And the incalculable number of Japanese who would die trying to stop the Americans.

As he continued he tried to locate places he and his brother or Kyoko had frequented. It was impossible. Save the department stores nothing really existed anymore.

After a while he noticed the shadows had changed. He looked at the time. It was nearing 5:00 P.M. He hurried back to Tsukiji and Oba-*san's ryokan*.

When he knocked a different woman opened the door. It was still Oba-*san* but her hair had been washed, combed and styled. And she was dressed in a *kimono*, a very fine one, he noticed. The wrinkles seemed less obvious; she had applied makeup to her face.

"*Dôzo, dôzo*, Honorable Major." Please, please. "Come in.

I hope your day was pleasant. Ah, I can see the sun has not treated you well. Please. Come upstairs. I have prepared the *yokusô* for you. The water is hot. Dinner will be ready when you are ready."

Ken placed the *furoshiki* on the floor. She picked it up and from the weight and shape of its contents knew what it contained. He removed his boots and put on a pair of slippers then walked up to his room. He removed his slippers before entering. A *yukata* was on one of the bureaus. He saw that she had unpacked his bag. He found his clothing neatly placed in the bureau. He placed his jacket, cap, *katana*, and holster on the bureau.

Then he remembered. He touched his shirt pocket, remembering the two items he had taken with him before he left the *Missouri*. He carefully reached in and pulled out the *omamori*, the rectangular paper amulet given to him by his mother, and the packet containing the red string that Kyoko had given him in 1941 before he returned to the States. He placed them in his flight bag.

He removed a clean *fundoshi*. He took the *yukata* and *fundoshi* to the changing room, just off the *yoku-jô*. He removed his slippers and clothing then went into the *yoku-jô*.

In the *yoku-jô* were a *koshikake*, a low stool, about 20cm tall, and a small hand-basin which contained a bar of soap, a pumice stone, and some scrub cloths and sponges. There was no sink or toilet, which were in a separate room. There was a cold-water tap in the wall. On a shelf was a folded towel. Ken removed the contents of the hand-basin and used it to scoop water from the *yokusô* and drenched himself several times with hot water while he sat on the stool. He left some water in the hand-basin. Then he scrubbed himself clean, missing nothing of his body. When his soapy hand rubbed his genitals the response was immediate. He looked at his engorged penis and for a second debated. *No*, he decided. *Anyway, soap stings.*

He sat there a moment, letting the soap lay on his skin. Then he dipped his hand in the basin to remove any soap and threw the water out. Next he dipped the basin in the *yokusô* and rinsed himself. He did this several times. He stood and scooped water from the basin with his hand and made sure there was no soap behind his scrotum or between his buttocks. Then he put his foot in the *yokusô*. The water was hot. He knew it could reach 50° Centigrade, like at home. He expected it. He knew the trick was to immerse himself in the water and be still. The surface of the water was hotter than below it. He closed his eyes. The sensation was remarkable. Soon all the day's tension drained from his body, replaced by a sense of stillness.

Unexpectedly, he heard a knock on the door. He realized he had dozed off. "*Hai!*"

"Please excuse me, Honorable Major," she said through the door. "Dinner is ready when you are."

She left. Ken regretfully exited the *yokusô* and filled the hand-basin with cold water. Standing near the drain in the floor he emptied the cold water on his head, letting it flow down his body. Then he dried off and went to the changing room.

Dressed, he returned to his room. Oba-*san* was kneeling outside the door. With a bow she asked that he follow her to the next room, a four-*tatami* room. He followed her to the adjacent room. She descended to her knees and bowed, gesturing for him to enter. He entered and was awed at what he saw. She gestured for him to sit at the table in the middle of the room. He lowered himself at the table, and sat back on his heels. When he was seated she sat down on the other side of the table and bowed. The *sake* was hot and waiting. The food was elegantly laid out, ready for his visual and gustatory appreciation.

Oba-*san* poured *sake* from the *tokkuri*, a ceramic bottle, into his *ochoko*, a small ceramic *sake* cup. He drank it. The temperature was perfect for him, 40°C, but just as at Atsugi the quality was poor. She picked up the *tokkuri* and refilled his *ochoko* and he drank again, feigning to relish the taste. He then poured *sake* for her.

Somehow, she had found food that should have been available only in peacetime. He knew the black market was where she got the food but the quality and quantity was abundant given Tôkyô's plight.

The food included *sunomono*, pickled clams with cucumber, *yasai no takiawase*, cooked vegetables, and assorted *sashimi* including yellowtail, mackerel, and albacore. A bowl of *gohan*, boiled rice, was still steaming. When he looked at it he could tell the rice had been cooked with extra water to inflate it, which he politely overlooked. Finally, there was *sumashi-jiru*, a flavorful broth of chicken stock with ginger.

He looked at what was spread before him. Her placement made it clear the food was there for him.

The dinner started quietly. They ate slowly, with Oba-*san*, in deference to her guest, eating very little. Ken wanted to know her thoughts about Tôkyô, the people, and her sense of the present. She might be able to tell him what he wanted to know. So he asked questions and let her talk. She felt comfortable after drinking more *sake*. They spoke about why she lived alone.

"My husband died two months ago from tuberculosis. The doctors told us there was no treatment for him. Our son died on Iwô Jima. There were no ashes to bury, no clipped nails or hair to receive. I believe our son's death ended my husband's life. My son was a scholar; he was going to be a writer. Instead he was made a soldier and died."

Ken heard the sadness in her voice. The *sake* allowed her to freely express her feelings.

"We have little to eat, Honorable Major. Many people now eat acorns, mugwort, and chickweed, even thistle. We women have become creative in using anything that grows for food." She drank more *sake*. "Our rations are less than before the war with America. But we are winning. Have we burned any American cities, Honorable Major?"

Ken did not respond, knowing it did not matter.

"So much of the rice we are given is unhusked, so many people are sick from eating it. We eat stray cats and dogs, if we can find one. Even rats if we can catch them. Nothing is available. For a while, I am told, soybean oil was used for oil for cars and trucks. It did not work. How long has it been since you were in Tôkyô, Honorable Major?"

"A long time, Oba-*san*, a long time."

She nodded her head. "There are few cars or trucks now. Charcoal or fuel bricks power those few that move. Do you know what fuel bricks are, Honorable Major?"

"No, Oba-*san*."

"You make them at home, by mixing garbage, coal dust and oil residue. Then you bake it solid." She smiled when she said that. "You use precious wood to make precious fuel. Then you burn it in your car. But it doesn't really work. Did you see any cars moving today, Honorable Major?"

She was sapping his emotional energy. Perhaps at this point an Imperial Army officer would have struck or even killed her. But she seemed not to care.

"No, Oba-*san*, I did not."

"Please forgive my rudeness, Honorable Major. Would you like to smoke a cigarette?"

"No, Oba-*san*. I never enjoyed the pleasure."

"That is good, Honorable Major. I could not light it for you. Last year we housewives were limited to just four matches a day. Do not worry! I have flint to start a cooking fire. But it is difficult to light a cigarette with flint." She started to laugh. "But that is silly of me. We were limited to just six cigarettes a day. So it is good you do not smoke, Honorable Major. My cigarettes are not very good; I make them. I use dried persimmon leaves or I shred and dry eggplant. I roll them in the pages I tear from my books. I have so few books left, Honorable Major. And now there is very little eggplant.

"So, when the Americans come we will have little to greet them with except our lives. But we are one hundred million *samurai*, prepared to die for *Tennô-Heika*." She stopped, realizing she had violated propriety. "I have offended you, Honorable Major. Please accept my deepest apologies."

"No, Oba-*san*, I know that His Imperial Majesty's subjects make enormous sacrifices every day."

She drank more *sake* and then looked up at the ceiling. Ken saw she was tired and had drunk too much.

"*B-san* seems to have little interest in Tsukiji, so I will die alone. Or when the Americans invade they will rape and kill me. Honorable Major, why do they burn our cities? Why don't they fight our gallant soldiers instead?"

Ken sat across from the enemy, just as he had at Atsugi. But this woman was not the enemy. He had no answer for her, or for himself.

They ate in silence for several minutes. Then, feeling guilt at having saddened the setting, Oba-*san* decided to ask Ken a question, one that every soldier is asked by an older woman.

"Honorable Major, do you have a wife or sweetheart?"

Ken placed his chopsticks down. "My mother always asked me that question. I had a sweetheart. But we lost touch. The war has disrupted so many lives."

Oba-*san* understood that the subject was too painful for him. She smiled and poured more *sake*. They ate in silence for several moments. Her next question caught him off guard.

"Honorable Major. Do you know anything about American soldiers? I have heard that when American Marines invade they kill all the men, then rape the women and eat the children. I have heard that they are hairy giants who cannot be defeated. Is this true?"

He felt uncomfortable with her question. He was certain

that every Japanese citizen felt the same fear. "I know that what we hear and read is not always completely true. I am sure that the Americans feel that Japanese soldiers have behaved not necessarily in a positive manner. I am not sure we can say that American soldiers will do what you fear."

"Honorable Major, I have seen posters that urge the Americans to invade Japan so that we can kill them. Are they coming?"

It was a question he dreaded but knew he had to answer. "Yes, Oba-*san*, the Americans will invade."

"At night I am unable to sleep. Before the war I saw some American movies. They are big people. They must be very strong. If they invade they will kill many of us, perhaps more than we will kill of them. My friends and I often talk about the invasion. We are all afraid."

Ken looked at his watch; it was almost 2200 hours. "Oba-*san*, the dinner was beyond my expectations. I am grateful. Please excuse me, but it is late and I must rise early tomorrow. Thank you for your hospitality."

She understood and bowed. "Do you wish that I wake you, Honorable Major?"

"Yes, please. Is six o'clock too early for you, Oba-*san*?"

She smiled. "At six o'clock I will awaken you. I will have breakfast ready for you."

She bowed and they bid each other good night.

✻   ✻   ✻

Ken fell asleep within minutes of lying down. One hour later he awoke with a start. He heard an increasing rumble and ran outside, wearing a *yukata* and *geta*. Men and women, many with children, were already in the streets, looking up at the sky. Oba-*san* also was there.

A single B-29 was skirting Tsukiji from the northeast. It

was heading west, flying low at just over 5,000 feet. As it got closer Ken heard the deep rumbling from its four massive engines. Searchlights darted back and forth, combing the dark skies for what was heard but not seen. Japanese antiaircraft guns saturated the sky with flak. Then two or three searchlights found the B-29 and held it in their crossbeams for several seconds. Several people pointed at *B-san*. The flak missed and the B-29 never deviated from its course. Except for pictures, Ken had never seen a B-29 but, looking up in that brief instant, he appreciated the enormous size of the plane. He knew the B-29's wingspan was over 140 feet and its length was just less than 100 feet, making the B-29 the largest bomber in the war.

As it flew other searchlights held it briefly and everyone watching followed the B-29 on its unwavering journey heading west. Past the Imperial Palace it changed course, heading toward the northwest, whether to evade the searchlights and flak or seeking out a target Ken did not know. Searchlights continued to crisscross the sky, at times locating the B-29 as it passed Shinjuku Station.

Scant moments later there was a huge bright light in the sky, about 100 feet above the ground. At first, Ken thought the plane had been hit by flak and exploded.

A woman on his left shouted, "*Hora! Edo no hana!*" Look! The Flowers of Edo!

He looked at her, recalling the expression from a course he had taken at Tôkyô Imperial University, "From Edo to Tôkyô," tracing Edo's transition to Tôkyô. Most of the buildings in Edo were made of wood, bamboo, straw and paper, a veritable tinderbox.

During the Edo Period, rival fire brigades would often engage in fistfights, competing as to which brigade would terminate the fire. Soon, another expression came into being: "*Kaji to Kenka wa Edo no hana*"—"Fires and fistfights are the flowers of Edo!" As the instructor explained, both fights and fires—like flowers—were always blooming during the Edo period. What Ken did not know was that the expression, *Edo no hana*, came back in 1945 from a woman firefighter in Tôkyô, where the B-29s were dropping incendiary bombs. When one of the bombs exploded she was heard to exclaim *"Edo no Hana,"* as the opening of the incendiary bomb was, to her, like a flower opening.

Scant seconds later, Ken and those around him heard an explosion. Buildings below the B-29 burst into flames. As the B-29 progressed there was another explosion in the sky. More fires on the ground started. Fires followed still another explosion. He realized that the B-29 was a "pathfinder." The B-29 executed a 270° turn and started to drop more incendiary bombs. Ken couldn't see it but the B-29 pathfinder was creating an "X" in the middle of the target.

Soon, while the fires burned, more B-29s would come, using the burning "X" as a guide to where they should drop their bombs. Ken and the crowd around him waited in silence. Moments later they heard the approaching rumble. This time it was farther north of Tsukiji and at a higher altitude. Once over the fires a B-29 dropped thousands of pounds of incendiary bombs. Massive infernos soon started. Soon another B-29 came, this time at a lower altitude and closer to Tsukiji. It too loosed thousands of pounds of incendiary bombs over the target first ignited by the pathfinder. The pattern continued for almost two hours, one B-29 after another came, at different altitudes and vectors, each separated by about two minutes, insuring the Japanese antiaircraft crews could not predict where any B-29 would be. But the target was the same. Ken knew that the tactic was different from that in Europe, where bombers had flown in massed formation for protection against German interceptors. B-29 crews no longer feared Japanese interceptors. Few Japanese planes rose to challenge *B-san*.

As the fires grew, consuming what was left from prior raids, Ken could only watch and wonder how many people were able to get out before being incinerated.

He turned and went back to his room, hoping to get back to sleep. He knew the next day would be long. He also knew he might die.

26

August 5, 1945

Ken awoke with a start. He heard more plane engines overhead, lots more. They were coming from the coast, heading inland. He knew they were American fighters and fighter-bombers and that Tôkyô was going to get hit during daylight hours.

"*Ohayôgozaimasu*, Honorable Major. Breakfast is ready for you," Oba-*san* said as she knocked on Ken's door at precisely 6:00 A.M.

Ken was already awake, thinking about what he had seen hours earlier. He got up, donned his *yukata*, and went to the toilet. When he returned to his room to dress he found that his uniform had been cleaned. Oba-*san* had done it while he was in the soaking tub last evening, and hung it outside to dry overnight. She had returned it to his room while he was in the toilet. Dressed, he went downstairs.

"Good morning, Oba-*san*." He looked at what she had prepared. "After last evening I am not certain I can eat more."

Oba-*san* had prepared boiled rice, *miso* soup, pickles, dried fish, and *ocha*, green tea. After eating he thanked her and returned to his room. He put on his holster and *katana* and was ready to leave the room when he stopped and took his *omamori* from the flight bag and put it in his shirt pocket. He went downstairs. Oba-*san* was at the door, smiling and pointing to his boots. She had cleaned them too. *Just like my mother*, he thought. He put them on, thanked her and left.

The meeting was not until 10:00 A.M. The night before, he had decided to walk to Ichigaya, about three miles distance as the crow flies. Wryly, he thought, there was little left to interfere with a straight line.

Soon Ken reached the Ginza. Black-market vendors were already out with their wares. *If anyone in Japan benefits from the war, they will*, he thought. A woman approached a cart. She carried a *furoshiki*. She bowed to the man who owned the cart. He bowed only his head. Her demeanor conveyed fatigue, her body showed malnourishment, and her eyes reflected hopelessness. She placed her *furoshiki* on the cart and untied it. Ken saw several items. The cart owner picked them up. Some were metal, tarnished, but Ken had no doubt they were of value. Family heirlooms could not fill an empty belly. The cart owner's attitude was dismissive. She pleaded, pointing to her possessions. Ken saw the cart owner feign reluctant acquiescence. He lifted some cloth and transferred her possessions to the cart and replaced the cloth. He then shifted other material. Ken saw that underneath were different kinds of foods, enough perhaps for twenty people. The cart owner placed a few turnips, unhusked rice, and small pieces of fish onto her *furoshiki*. She protested and he shrugged his shoulders. He started to return her possessions but she quickly wrapped the *furoshiki* and walked away. Her family, depending on how many she was feeding, would eat at least one meal this day.

He passed through Ginza, closing his mind to what he saw.

He came across numerous camps where people had built crude shacks from discarded wood or metal. Those fortunate enough had roofs made from tin. It was early morning and some were squatting before metal bowls, preparing meager breakfasts. They fed the cooking fires with scraps of wood that had perhaps once belonged to their home. Some of the shacks housed children, poorly dressed and unwashed. Their childrens' eyes focused on just one thing: the food being readied by the adults.

Then he came to Hibiya Park on the south side of the Imperial Palace. Hibiya Park was not particularly large, just over 16 *chô*—41 acres—twenty times smaller than New York's Central Park. It was built on land that had been a military parade ground. When it was converted to a park it was Japan's first based on Western design. Ken knew it was rebuilt after the Great Kantô Earthquake. Looking around he knew it would have to be rebuilt again. As he continued he saw hundreds of people farming the land, trying to grow vegetables.

Further into the park he saw several hundred teenage girls, broken into groups of 30 or so, holding sharpened bamboo poles. They were being trained by army officers to lunge and stab at straw dummies made up to look like American soldiers. *And we'll counter with bombs from ships and planes, tanks, and soldiers with flamethrowers, grenades, machineguns and rifles*, he thought. He watched for a while. Most of the girls were grim but some of them were giggling, not fully grasping what was being asked of them. And a few of the officers were smiling at the girls.

A few feet from him he saw a pile of pamphlets and walked over and picked one up. The cover showed a crude drawing depicting two soldiers struggling. A Japanese soldier was on top of an American soldier. The Japanese soldier held a bayonet in his right hand and was poised to thrust it into the American's neck. It was entitled "The People's Handbook of Resistance Combat."

Ken flipped the pages. He came across a page that gave guidance on how to deal with poison gas and flamethrowers. Another page gave instructions on how to spread obstacles including carts, large rocks and logs over open fields where

American planes might land.

Another page read, "Take advantage of the enemy's un-guarded moment—If the enemy is alone stab him in the back. If followed, snipe at officer or machine gunner. If they are in a bunch, use hand grenade. At any rate, never be discovered before attacking."

The illustrations were rudimentary, showing how easy it would be to do any of the above.

Further on, illustrations depicted how to deal with an American in "close combat, hand-to-hand fight." The first dealt with the use of a sword or spear and advised, "Neither swing vertically nor horizontally, but always thrust at tall Yankees in their belly." The second showed, "With sickle, hatchet, heavy kitchen knife, or fireman's hook, attack from behind, approxi-mately one meter distance." The third advised, "Scuffle; make full use of judo and karate. Kick the testicles. Strike the pit of the stomach."

Another section showed how to attack an American tank with mines, Molotov cocktails or a "thrust-mine," the latter re-quiring someone carrying a thrust-mine attached to a bamboo pole to run up to a tank and detonate the mine against the tank. It would, of course, kill the person carrying the thrust-mine. He put the pamphlet down and moved further west.

He came across two Imperial Army sergeants. One of them yelled "Now!" A boy, no more than seven, jumped out of a camouflaged hole in the ground. He had a rucksack on his back and a string in his hand. The other end of the string was attached to the rucksack. One of the sergeants pointed at a wooden mockup of an American tank, a Sherman. The boy ran toward the phony tank and rolled under it. A second later Ken heard a muffled firecracker go off. Soon smoke drifted from underneath the tank. The boy, smiling, started to come out, but he was ordered to stay where he was.

The other sergeant yelled, pointing toward a cluster of

dummies dressed as American soldiers. Another boy came from behind a tree. The boy, with a rucksack on his back and string in his left hand, walked toward the dummies, smiling and waving with his right hand. When the boy reached them he held out his hand and said something Ken could not hear. Then the boy scampered to the middle of the dummies and pulled the string. A firecracker exploded and a puff of smoke came from his rucksack.

Another boy was ordered to raise his head from a hole. The sergeant pointed toward a truck. The boy repeated what the first had done with the mock tank. The exercises were repeated several times until all the boys had their turn. The sergeants called all the boys back to them. About 30 boys surrounded them. All were yelling and laughing. Some pretended to pull their strings. The first boy who had walked up to the dummies was singled out for praise. One of the sergeants spoke.

"When you see American vehicles, run under them! When you see American soldiers on foot go up to them and ask for something. What is that word we taught you?"

"*Chokoreeto* !" all the boys yelled.

"And when the Americans give you *chokoreeto* what do you do?"

"Pull the string!" they yelled with laughter.

Then the boys cheered, "Banzai! Banzai!"

Ken's heart sank. He pictured these and thousands of other boys hiding in holes or behind trees on Kyûshû and Honshû, prepared to jump out and run amongst Americans. But when American soldiers established a beachhead and advanced into Kyûshû they would know about the boys. And when the boys ran toward American soldiers they would have no time to ask for chocolate.

When he had interviewed Japanese prisoners he was told that every Japanese soldier had to kill ten Americans before his death. Now the children were being trained to do the same. He knew American soldiers would not readily kill children. But he also knew that when American soldiers learned that children were being used as human bombs they would have to shoot the children to save themselves.

Ken shook with rage and was about to strike the sergeant closest to him when a little boy ran up and stopped him. With a rucksack on his back the boy stood ramrod straight. Then he saluted Ken, holding his small hand to his forehead, awaiting a return salute. The others stood motionless, watching an Imperial Army officer and the boy. It took all of Ken's determination to compose himself. He stood at attention and returned the boy's salute. The boy dropped his hand and smiled, then turned and skipped back to his companions.

The sergeants training the boys, subordinate to Ken, also saluted. He looked at the group of boys for several seconds, his eyes welling up. He faced the sergeants and returned their salutes. He walked away, a bit slower. He wondered if the boys had been told there would be more than a firecracker in their rucksacks.

Soon he came upon two groups. One group of about 200 was turning the soil. The other group, old men and women in their sixties, was training to repel American soldiers with bamboo sticks. Another group of old men were drilling with 19th century rifles. Ken wondered how many would explode when fired. As he walked between the two groups he remembered an ironic passage in the bible: "*...they shall beat their swords into plowshares, and their spears into pruning hooks; nation shall not lift up sword against nation, neither shall they learn war any more.*"

He walked out of the park and soon came near the Imperial Palace, the surrounding walls unscathed. Angered by what he had seen in the park he ignored the castle still venerated by so many. He wondered what kind of leader would allow his nation's children to die for a lost cause. He closed his mind to his anger and focused solely on his mission.

Within sight of Ichigaya he came across an odd collection of two rows of scores of small buses. The rows, parked on both sidewalks, were separated by the small street. About twenty buses were on each sidewalk. Their fronts faced each other, perpendicular to the street between them. What was odd was that their engine casings and the engines had been neatly removed. The paint on most of the buses had long since rusted away. In each row the buses were neatly parked side by side, less than ten feet of space between them. None of them had tires and their axles had been removed. He thought it strange; Japan needed every scrap of metal it could find. Why, he wondered, were these buses neatly parked here?

Then, as he drew closer, he grasped their purpose. People were mingling about them. There were also people inside the buses. Several windows had pieces of cloth shutting out the outside. Metal pipes pierced through the roofs and dark smoke drifted from some of the pipes. Some buses had laundry lines tied between them. They were the shelters of people who were homeless. Between the Imperial Palace and the Imperial War Ministry, two centers of power that held the fate of tens of millions, were the victims of their power.

During his walk from Tsukiji he felt unrelenting shock at the intensity of destruction of Tôkyô. And where there were children and old people, all suffering from lack of food, he felt despair. He wrestled with his feelings about America. He had seen the combat films of hardened American Marines on Okinawa, after so much death on both sides, still capable of tenderness for the civilians, particularly the children. Yet Americans were capable of destroying entire cities and killing tens of thousands, including children. *It's got to end, damn it, it's got to end.* Then he stopped walking and looked around. *The Japanese did it too, but it still has to end.*

*   *   *

Japan's Imperial War Ministry on Ichigaya Heights was a squat, rectangular, three-story tan building made of poured concrete. A quasi-medieval main entrance offered the sole distinguishing portion. Above and behind the main entrance a tower added an additional three stories over the entire complex. A crescent driveway went behind the main entrance, allowing cars to deliver important personages who would alight and enter the building behind the main entrance.

The Imperial War Ministry had once been the military academy so Ken was unsurprised that it looked like a large school building. When he reached the outer gate he joined a line. There were more than 50 officers, mostly army colonels and navy captains, waiting to enter, and the guards were hard pressed as they checked everyone's identification. As Ken neared the gate he saw how closely each officer's identification was inspected and compared to a list. But the Imperial War Ministry had its own protocol and no one seemed disturbed at the close scrutiny. Then came Ken's turn. He looked nonchalant as he handed over his papers. The lieutenant made a show of closely examining Ken's papers. Ken looked at the lieutenant but peripherally he was watching the soldiers with the rifles.

"Shôsa! Your name is not on the list. Can you explain, please?"

"Another officer was coming but his plane was shot down. I am his replacement."

The lieutenant nodded and looked for some papers on the desk. "Ha! Here you are! Kobayashi Shôsa! Please excuse my ignorance, Shôsa! Regrettably, your name as replacement is not alone."

The lieutenant saluted as he gave Ken his papers. Ken returned the salute and started to enter the Imperial War Ministry when a sergeant with a rifle moved in front of him. Several voices behind him yelled.

Taka's message, he thought, *didn't get through! So close! Damn, so close!*

Then the sergeant did a most unusual thing. He positioned his rifle straight up in front of his body, presenting arms, saluting with his rifle. Ken saw those who had already passed through inspection snap to attention. Ken turned and saw a car approaching. It was a general staff car, presumably conveying a high-ranking officer. Ken too stood to attention. As the car passed it slowed and the rear window rolled down. Everyone saluted the passenger. Ken recognized him as clearly as he would have recognized General Douglas MacArthur.

Japan's Minister of War, General Anami Korechika, returned the salutes as his car drove into the Imperial War Ministry.

Ken could feel the electricity of excitement. Many of the men around him, from throughout the ever-shrinking Japanese Empire, had never seen such a high-ranking officer. To many of them General Anami was a direct link to Emperor Hirohito, and as such the closest they would ever come to *Tennô-Heika.*

As Anami's car went out of view behind the main entrance the officers, usually reserved, expressed their gratitude at having seen the man who controlled their destinies. Ken passed through and joined others as they entered the building. He looked around, as did others who had never been to Ichigaya.

In the foyer the floor was dark hardwood as were the doors. Facing them were two sets of wood stairs both of which led to double doors opening onto the second floor.

The eight steps on the left were not as imposing as those on the right. The 14 steps—wider than those on the left—seemed to Ken to be cleaner and were not scuffed.

No one approached the steps on the right. He heard someone say the stairway belonged to Emperor Hirohito and only he, or members of the Royal Family, could mount them.

Two Imperial Army lieutenants, with white gloves on, motioned everyone to move to the stairs on the left. In ones and twos everyone proceeded to the second floor. They were led down a corridor. They passed a communications room on their left and a conference room on their right. They went through a set of doors that brought them into a spacious room.

Ken estimated it was about 30 meters in length and close to 20 meters wide. From back to front about 200 chairs occupied most of the floor space. Both sides of the room had windows. At the front of the room was a stage, the floor painted black. There was a fireplace on either side of the stage. At the rear of the stage were large burgundy drapes surrounding a set of closed gray curtains. Ken assumed there was a projection screen behind the curtains. Overhead, wooden beams crisscrossed the ceiling which was dotted with hexagonal lights.

Ken and the others were guided to unoccupied seats, which were filling up fast. There was little conversation and most of that was muted. These sober men knew their destinies had already been mapped out.

On the stage several officers sat at a table facing the audience. In the middle of the table sat Lieutenant General Arisue Seizô, Imperial Japanese Army Chief of Intelligence. Senior officers of the Imperial Army, Navy, and Army Air Force flanked him. To the right and left of the table were large wooden easels, covered by cloth.

When the last of the men entered and took their seats the doors were closed. When Ken heard the doors closed he looked around and noted that all the seats were occupied.

Lieutenant General Arisue rose and everyone in the room stood to attention. Arisue walked to the right side of the table and took a few steps forward.

"Good morning. Please be seated." He waited a few seconds.

"For many of you the trip was long and, in some cases,

dangerous. Today we will review the final plans for the Decisive Battle. The Americans have done what we expected of them. They have intensified their air and naval operations against Japan. I need not belabor what we all know. Most of Tôkyô and other major cities have been destroyed.

"Last March the Imperial General Staff completed an outline for our defense operations, code name *Ketsu-Gô*. *Ketsu-Gô* One concerns the Fifth Area Army's defense of Hokkaidô, the Kuriles, and southern Karafuto. *Ketsu-Gô* Two involves the Eleventh Area Army's defense of northern Honshû. *Ketsu-Gô* Three relates to the Twelfth Area Army's defense of central Honshû. *Ketsu-Gô* Four and Five deal with the defense of south-central and southern Honshû by the Thirteenth and Fifteenth Area Armies. *Ketsu-Gô* Six is the defense of Kyûshû by the Sixteenth Area Army, and *Ketsu-Gô* Seven provides for the defense of Korea by the Seventeenth Area Army.

"Last March many possibilities faced us, including the Americans invading Formosa, Korea, or the eastern coast of China or Okinawa. They chose Okinawa, which was a great victory for Japan because it allowed us to better see the tactics the Americans will employ for the Decisive Battle. The Imperial General Staff felt that we faced two options. The first was that the American Navy would encircle Japan and try to force us to surrender through blockade and bombardment, the latter by both the American Navy and Air Forces. The second option was that the Americans would invade Japan.

"Recently, the Potsdam Proclamation, released by Washington and London, called on Japan to surrender unconditionally—"

"Never!" several voices rose from the audience.

"One Hundred Million will die for the Emperor and Nation!" yelled others.

Arisue watched as they voiced their firm belief. Then he continued.

"The American people are impatient and wish this war to end soon. But blockading and bombing Japan will never force us to surrender!

"We now know, from past American strategies, and from their recent reconnaissance flights, that the Americans intend to invade Japan and we believe we know where. Based on that information we have invoked *Ketsu-Gô* Six, the defense of Kyûshû, and *Ketsu-Gô* Three, the defense of central Honshû.

"We have endeavored to prepare for both. Our strategy is direct. We intend to kill as many Americans as possible before they touch our sacred soil. We have seen this gallant tactic before, particularly on Iwô Jima and Okinawa. But Japan is our sacred homeland, not an isolated island like Okinawa or Iwô Jima.

"During the battle for Okinawa *kamikaze* pilots valiantly sacrificed their lives for His Imperial Majesty, showing us the way to cripple the American invasion fleet.

"If we kill enough Americans before they reach Japan's soil perhaps they will realize they cannot defeat us and agree to a negotiated settlement with comparatively advantageous conditions for Japan.

"We have resources for a protracted battle and the will and determination of one hundred million of His Imperial Majesty's subjects to aid us in this decisive battle—"

Half the officers in the audience immediately jumped to their feet and shouted, "Banzai! Banzai!" Ken joined them as did the rest of the audience.

General Arisue let them go on. He knew their sentiments might change shortly.

"I have asked Hori Eizô Shôsa to give the details of our defense. He works in my command. Some of you may know of him."

Several in the audience smiled or softly laughed. In fact many did know of Major Hori's reputation. Throughout

America's military operations in the Pacific, Major Hori had accurately predicted each invasion commanded by General Douglas MacArthur, including roughly how many men would be used and the approximate date of each invasion. The laughter stemmed from the fact that Major Hori was dubbed "MacArthur's staff officer" because of his uncanny accuracy.

That skill came to the attention of senior staff officers after America had taken Saipan in June 1944. Tôkyô feared that after Saipan fell MacArthur would bypass the Philippines and invade Japan—a scenario for which Japan was unprepared. Hori felt otherwise, believing that, strategy aside, MacArthur's promise to return to the Philippines was paramount. He painstakingly reviewed MacArthur's past campaigns and presented his conclusions to his superiors. Major Hori was able to convince skeptics that MacArthur instead would invade the Philippines. MacArthur proved him right.

Major Hori Eizô stood as Lieutenant General Arisue returned to his seat. He bowed toward Lieutenant General Arisue, who in turn nodded.

Hori was a pleasant-looking man. He was small of stature and there was the hint of a smile about his lips. His eyes, however, were sharp. Ken didn't know why but the thought came into his mind that Hori was a skilled *Go* player, one of the oldest strategy games in existence, far more challenging than chess.

"Good morning. Arisue Chûjô has instructed me to give you a presentation of where American forces will next strike."

Major Hori walked to a set of easels on the right side of the table. He removed the cloth coverings from each easel. On the first easel was a large map of Japan. Ken was stunned.

It showed both invasion beachheads that America had named Olympic and Coronet. And the map was accurate.

"On or about November first," said Major Hori, "American forces will invade the southern coast of Kyûshû, at these beaches."

Ken had a sense of déjà vu as Major Hori pointed to the very same Kyûshû beachheads that Colonel Hobart Hanford had identified in his briefing in Manila.

"Thus, *Ketsu-Gô* Six will be detailed this morning. My conclusion is based on four factors. First, there have been abundant reports of American air movements over Kyûshû, whether air raids or reconnaissance. Before any invasion the Americans gather as much information as possible, particularly from air reconnaissance.

"The second is geography and oceanography. Only these beaches contain the terrain suitable for the type of invasion the Americans will employ. Furthermore, these beaches will accommodate any size American warship, including battleships and aircraft carriers.

"Third, there are numerous air bases in southern Kyûshû which the Americans would want to utilize, for both fighters and bombers.

"Fourth, following the pattern of previous American invasions, if the Americans secure these landings it will give them a launch point from which they will invade their final objective, Tôkyô and the Kantô Plain—"

Many men shot out of their seats, some with their hand on their *katana*. They started to shout, "Badoglio! Badoglio! Badoglio!—"

Ken, startled, did not understand their shouted outbursts.

"SILENCE!" General Arisue slammed his hand down on the table then stood. "There are no Badoglios here! Hori Shôsa was ordered by me to give us his forthright assessment of American objectives! Hori Shôsa is as loyal to *Tennô-Heika* as every other man in this room! Sit down and listen! We need to know this information in order to be better prepared!"

Those who had stood took their seats but Ken could see on their faces their unease at Major Hori's fourth point.

Ken, hearing General Arisue say "Badoglio," kept repeating the word in his mind. Then it came to him.

In July 1943, as Italy's military situation became more perilous, Benito Mussolini was removed from power. Italy's King Emmanuel III named General Pietro Badoglio premier. On September 3, 1943, with the Allies having already secured Sicily and ready to invade Italy, General Badoglio arranged an armistice with the Allies. On October 13, 1943, Italy declared war against Germany. To Japan's military, General Badoglio was the ultimate symbol of treason. To call someone "Badoglio" could result in a fight to the death.

Ken now understood why so many in the audience became angry. Major Hori had declared that America might succeed in taking southern Kyûshû and use it as a staging area, like Sicily, to invade the Kantô Plain, including Tôkyô and Yokohama.

For the next two hours Major Hori gave such an accurate portrayal of America's invasion of Kyûshû that Ken felt that Hori and Hanford could have compared notes.

Major Hori did not use flow charts. His approach was simpler. The maps were all he needed. Ken absorbed all he could, his eyes going from the maps to Major Hori.

Major Hori told his now-silent audience that Japanese reconnaissance planes, from mid-October, would patrol out as far as 300 miles from Japan, searching for the American invasion fleet, hoping for at least a 24-hour warning before the American fleet reached its offshore anchorage and that Japanese fleet submarines would patrol even further out.

When the invasion fleet reached its offshore anchorages, where troop transport ships would send men over the sides onto beach invasion ships—Higgins boats—the remaining Japanese fleet submarines, already on patrol and informed of the American fleet's location, would attack the American invasion force from behind, attempting to cut off lines of communications. In addition to launching conventional torpedoes they would also launch *kaiten,* manned torpedoes. Though Major Hori conceded the *kaiten* had been fairly ineffective in the open sea, he told his audience that in the limited waters around Japan the *kaiten* might prove effective.

"While the invasion force is still at sea, hundreds of *kamikaze* of the Imperial Army and Navy will deliver a decisive blow against the American invasion force by initially destroying as many aircraft carriers and fire support warships as possible. Our goal is to distract these vital ships from their principal mission of supporting the landing ships. By sinking enemy carriers we significantly reduce their air forces.

"The battle of Okinawa has been carefully analyzed. During the battle individual *kamikaze* attacked American warships. We know that numerous enemy ships were sunk and hundreds damaged, but the American invasion fleet was not deterred. For *Ketsu-Gô* Six that strategy will change. Several *kamikaze* will attack individual targets from different directions, thus enhancing the chance that one or more *kamikaze* will be able to strike their target. To enhance success the Imperial Navy is converting two thousand training biplanes into *kamikaze.* The pilots are being trained for night attacks. Some may question the wisdom of this but radar does not disclose the wood and cloth structure of biplanes.

"American fighters and fighter-bombers from Okinawa and Iwô Jima will undoubtedly provide air cover for the invasion. When the time and location of the invasion is confirmed 100 transport planes will carry 1,200 airborne soldiers to Okinawa, to attack and disrupt American air bases.

"We have estimated that there will be over 1,000 transport ships carrying American soldiers and marines. Each troop transport ship can carry about 3,500 soldiers and Marines or supplies or a combination of both. Furthermore, we estimate there will be about 1,000 beach invasion ships, what the Americans call landing ships, troop or tank. These vessels will carry either men or supplies, including tanks, trucks, artillery, food, water, and so forth, directly to the beach and offload them.

"As the enemy fleet draws closer to Japan their troop transport ships will become the principal target for *kamikaze* attacks, before the troops transfer from the troop transport ships onto Higgins boats. After troops transfer onto Higgins boats and approach the beachheads *kamikaze* will attack them as well.

"We will be able to carry out these attacks night and day for ten full days or until all planes for *Ketsu-Gô* Six are expended.

"We will overwhelm American air defenses with waves of 300 to 400 planes sent out at one-hour intervals. Conventional fighters will distract American naval anti-aircraft guns and carrier-based fighters, thus allowing our *kamikaze* to attack the troop transport ships.

"To counter the American invasion force Japan has the following resources.

"First, combined air forces of the Imperial Army and Navy now total over 10,000 planes. 1,000 regular planes and 1,600 *kamikaze* will be employed in the defense of Kyûshû. From Korea, Manchuria, and even Northern China, 200 combat and 500 *kamikaze* planes will be rushed in if required. Another 500 to 1,000 *kamikaze* are expected to be fitted out in the homeland by the end of August.

"The Imperial Navy, cooperating with the Air General Army, will contribute 5,225 Navy planes—over 1,000 fighters, over 4,000 anti-convoy and anti-task force bombers, and the rest reconnaissance aircraft.

"An additional 600 planes from Formosa are also assigned to strike at American bases in the Ryûkyûs, when the Kyûshû battle begins. 7,500 planes will defend Kyûshû at the outset, and 2,500 planes will defend the Kantô district.

"The Air General Army will direct operations covering Kyûshû from headquarters near Ôsaka; the Navy, from the

Nara area.

"I noted that we now have 10,000 planes. However, between now and November, we will continue production of planes, especially *kamikaze*. In all, therefore, against the expected invasions, there may be over 12,700 planes."

Ken was appalled. Colonel Hanford had said at the Manila briefing that Japan had at best 5,000 planes.

Major Hori continued. "Once the battle for Kyûshû begins air operations will continue day and night, particularly against troop transport ships.

"When American fighter planes attack as independent units we will not counterattack, except when the situation is absolutely necessary or particularly advantageous. We must save our planes for the invasion fleet.

"When the invasion fleet is at its anchorage our destroyers, 19 in all, will fall upon them, at night, in concert with *kamikaze* attacks. Until then, they will be hidden in the western Inland Sea. Each destroyer will carry, in addition to shells and standard torpedoes, two *kaiten*. The *kaiten* are to be used principally against the large warships which will support the landings with naval gunfire. Each *kaiten* will carry a 1,542-kilogram warhead, enough to sink their largest ships.

"The *kôryû*, a five-man midget submarine, will be utilized with either two torpedoes or an explosive charge with which to ram an enemy ship. The Navy will have 540 *kôryû* in service for the invasion. Furthermore, the *kairyû*, an enhanced midget submarine with two men, will also be armed with either two torpedoes or an explosive charge. The Navy will have 740 *kairyû* for the invasion. Both will be used to attack troop transport ships.

"Over 2,000 *shin-yô* will attack troop transport ships at night. Each *shin-yô* carries in its bow 250 kilograms of explosives and has a speed of 30 knots."

Ken, troubled, shifted in his chair. *Shin-yô*, or "ocean

shaker" seemed a most appropriate name for a wooden suicide attack boat, he thought.

Ken remembered Hanford's briefing in which Admiral R. L. Conolly's ships were given the mission of eliminating suicide boats and sub pens, both the midget and large sub pens at Ô Shima, Ôdôtsu, and Birô Jima. But, as Hanford pointed out, the U.S. Navy had estimated the Japanese had about 50 submarines as well as an unknown quantity of midget subs and suicide boats. Ken was alarmed that there would be at least 2,000 suicide attack boats. Made of wood and with a low profile, they would make impossible targets for American radar to locate. Operating at night would mask their approach, except by sound or searchlights. And U.S. Navy doctrine prohibited using lights at night. In either case it would be almost impossible to stop a *shin-yô* from reaching its target.

Major Hori spoke of another weapon the Japanese had introduced during the battle for Okinawa, the *Ôka*, or *Cherry Blossom*, a piloted, rocket-propelled bomb transported near its target by a bomber then released. When the rocket engine was ignited it could reach speeds up to 600 miles per hour. It carried a 2,700-pound explosive and once launched it could not be stopped.

As Major Hori turned to a map that depicted the defense of the beaches of Kyûshû, Ken's eyes bore into his. As if he felt them, Hori looked at Ken for a few seconds, a questioning expression in his eyes. Then he walked to the map.

The map displayed the locations of numerous havens for the Navy's *shin-yô*, *kaiten* facilities, and ports for *kôryû* and *kairyû* midget subs.

"Farthest offshore, electronically detonated mines, just below the surface, will await the invasion ships. Further in, conventional mines will await.

"Closer to shore we will have *fukuryû* lying in wait. The Crouching Dragons will be concealed in two types of underwater lairs. One type has been constructed with reinforced concrete and watertight steel doors. The sunken ships offshore are the other type of shelter. Compartments in the ships have been sealed off and converted to watertight shelters. Both concrete shelters and sunken ships have sufficient oxygen tanks. When ordered to action, each Crouching Dragon will wear a diving suit and oxygen tank. As many as eighteen *fukuryû* can be stationed in each underwater lair nine meters below the surface. The outermost rank of *fukuryû* will release anchored mines or transport mines to detonate landing craft that pass overhead.

"Those landing craft that pass the outermost rank of *fukuryû* will face three more ranks of *fukuryû*. Each Crouching Dragon will be separated by about 18 meters. Each *fukuryû* will carry an explosive charge, mounted on a pole with a contact fuse, a form of the Army's lunge mine. He will swim up to a landing craft and detonate the charge. In all, there will be 4,000 *fukuryû* awaiting orders."

American commanders had never conceived this tactic. Ken acknowledged it was ingenious. And deadly because America was ignorant of it.

Major Hori went to another easel.

"Like Kagoshima Bay, Ariake Bay is an important landing zone for the Americans. This map illustrates our defensive and offensive forces in Ariake Bay should the Americans reach the shore. The same defensive capabilities await the Americans in Kagoshima Bay and the other invasion sites."

Ken listened as Major Hori told his audience that every square meter of beach of every beachhead had been plotted. No matter where an American soldier or Marine stood the Japanese defenders would know exactly where to fire their artillery, machine guns, or mortars. No matter where an American crouched or hid his position would be known. No matter how deep he dug his foxhole for protection he could not hide from mortar fire. No matter where a tank landed it would be fired on by accurate artillery.

No matter, thought Ken, *no matter*.

"In preparation for enemy tanks our combat engineers will construct defenses that start at the shore and reach inland. All coastal roads will be destroyed. This will force American tanks into terrain which will make them vulnerable to ground units using lunge mines.

"On every invasion beach, Americans will encounter coastal batteries, anti-landing barriers, bunkers, reinforced pillboxes and underground fortresses connected by tunnels. As American troops come ashore, they will be struck down by artillery, mortar, and machine guns while they struggle through concrete debris and barbed wire laid out to channel them into ever more precise fire from our guns.

"On the beaches the American soldiers will encounter mines, booby traps, and trip-wire mines. Beyond will be thousands of machine gun positions and hundreds of sniper units. Suicide units concealed in 'spider holes' will attack American troops as they move inland. During the landings our soldiers will be sent to sever American phone and communication lines. English-speaking officers in American uniforms will interrupt American radio communications to halt or misdirect American artillery and naval gunfire, order troop withdrawals, and spread confusion among American troops. We know this will work because the Germans did the same during what the Americans press called the 'Battle of the Bulge.' Other infiltration teams carrying explosive charges will blow up American tanks, artillery units, and supplies as they come ashore.

"Should the Americans establish beachheads our infantry will attack them at the shore, insuring that American naval gunfire will be hampered for fear of killing their soldiers. And their planes will not drop bombs or fire their machine guns at our troops for the same reason.

"Further inland our heavy guns will devastate the Higgins boats before they reach the beaches. Many of the artillery guns have been or will be mounted on railroad tracks in deep caves, protected by concrete and steel."

Major Hori moved to another easel holding a map.

Hori detailed the military units that would defend Kyûshû. Ken remembered Colonel Hanford's projected Japanese military strength. According to Major Hori's figures Hanford's numbers were a serious underestimate.

In previous landings American soldiers or Marines had always outnumbered the Japanese by two to one and sometimes three to one. The 14 American divisions landing on the beachheads of Kyûshû—approximately 436,000 soldiers and Marines—would be facing 560,000 Japanese troops, tenacious soldiers who were training on Kyûshû's terrain and defending their homeland.

Major Hori went to another easel.

"By November 1, when the Americans are expected to invade, 900,000 soldiers will be assigned to defend Kyûshû."

Ken, stunned, leaned forward in his chair. He remembered General Willoughby's message he had read while on the *Missouri*, that Japanese reinforcements to Kyûshû were accelerating. But if Major Hori was correct the American invasion force would be severely outnumbered. Coupled with Japan's plans to attack the troop transports at sea with *kamikaze* and other suicide tactics Japan might be able to delay or even prevent the establishment of beachheads. But if the Americans did establish beachheads and move inland the augmented Japanese Sixteenth Area Army would create even greater casualties, for both sides.

Major Hori spent two hours detailing how Japanese ground forces would engage American forces.

The basic strategy was that if the Americans started to move inland the Sixteenth Area Army would take command of all naval ground forces in its command area and would assume operational control of air forces supporting ground actions.

These soldiers were the core of the Japanese Home Army. They were well fed and well equipped. They were linked throughout Kyûshû by direct underground communications. They knew the terrain, had months to build up arms and ammunition, and had improvised an efficient system of transportation and resupply practically invisible from the air. Many of the soldiers knew they were the elite of the Imperial Japanese Army and were inspired with a zealous fighting spirit that persuaded them that they could crush the American invaders.

A key strategy of the Sixteenth Army called for troop reinforcement of areas under attack by transferring units from other areas. That, Major Hori conceded, would not be easily accomplished since American air raids had severely damaged Japan's transportation system. Therefore, troop reinforcement schedules had to be based on movement by foot. If the battle at the beach was in doubt the strategy would shift to interior combat and resistance would begin. Guard units and Civilian Defense Corps recruits, with the Army in command, would be used as interior opposition troops.

Their task would be to reduce American forces by guerrilla warfare, surveillance, deception, disruption of supplies, and blocking supply movements as American soldiers moved inland.

Major Hori outlined the utilization of the National Volunteer Combat Force. Ken recalled seeing the civilians training in Hibiya Park, including the children. Major Hori told his audience that the National Volunteer Combat Force had undergone extensive training in beach defense and guerilla tactics. The civilians would be armed with sharpened bamboo sticks, single-shot rifles, lunge mines, satchel charges, Molotov cocktails, and one-shot black powder mortars. Others would be armed with swords, long bows, and axes.

These civilian units would be employed in nighttime attacks, hit-and-run tactics, delaying actions, and massive suicide charges at any perceived weak American positions. And as the Americans moved further inland the children would be used.

"Each member of His Majesty's twenty-eight million strong National Volunteer Combat Force has read or has had explained to them 'The People's Handbook of Resistance Combat.' Should the Americans move inland each member of the National Volunteer Combat Force, under the direction of the Sixteenth Area Army, will know what to do when they encounter Americans."

Hori paused for a moment and surveyed his audience. He had been talking a long time but not one man had strayed from his presentation. He knew that they understood what was at stake. Japan had never been defeated. The very survival of Japan depended on crushing the Americans on the beaches of Kyûshû. He understood that if the Americans took southern Kyûshû the war was lost.

Major Hori faced Lieutenant General Arisue, who nodded. Hori returned to his chair.

Lieutenant General Arisue stood. "Sakamoto Jirô Taisa, Combat Engineering, will now review engineering preparations for the expected invasion. Sakamoto Taisa."

Colonel Sakamoto stood and bowed toward Lieutenant General Arisue then walked to the left of the table and uncovered several maps of southern Kyûshû. Like Major Hori's maps they were detailed but were drawn by civil engineers. There were no arrows showing troop movement or unit designations. Instead, these maps showed roads, trenches, cave entrances, revetments, barriers, ravines, mountains, wooded areas, and other structures, natural or manmade, that would hinder movement.

Colonel Sakamoto then proceeded to detail how the topography of southern Kyûshû had been altered to hinder—or channel—enemy troop movement. Ken, a mechanical engineer, did his best to absorb the additional information. He was uncertain that American air reconnaissance would show all of what the Japanese had accomplished. Iwô Jima and Okinawa had shown how masterful the Japanese could be at defensive positions and obstacles, particularly honeycombed tunnels.

Then Colonel Sakamoto called the engineering officers in the audience to come forward and give progress reports for the areas of southern Kyûshû they were representing. Each officer in the audience stood as he was called and walked to the stage to give precise reports, complete with charts and maps. Then Ken was called. He stood and walked on to the stage, his hands empty.

"Sakamoto Taisa! I regret to report that Masataka Chûsa was killed when American planes shot down his plane. I was dispatched more to listen than to contribute."

Ken then walked over to Colonel Sakamoto's third map, remembering the last set of air reconnaissance photographs he received while on the *Missouri*. "However, I can report that the trenches designated here, here and here have not yet been started. Moreover, this bridge, which will allow reinforcement by our soldiers, as outlined by Hori Shôsa, has not been completed. Please excuse me."

Colonel Sakamoto was clearly embarrassed and Ken knew he was the cause of it. He had to help Sakamoto recover face.

"However, Taisa, I know that the work has been planned but often interrupted by American bombing. I am certain that these projects will be completed within the month, more than enough time for the American invasion."

Colonel Sakamoto seemed mollified. Ken nodded once and Sakamoto returned the nod. Ken went back to his seat, all the while silently thanking the air reconnaissance unit that delivered the daily reconnaissance photographs to the *Missouri*.

Colonel Sakamoto had other officers come to the stage

and make reports. This time, however, he asked each man the actual status of preparations. It was here that some engineering officers acknowledged that actual progress did not match projections. Ken noticed that Lieutenant General Arisue did not look pleased.

Lieutenant General Arisue stood, a signal that Colonel Sakamoto's briefing was over. Arisue walked to the front of the table. "It is imperative, knowing what we do about the impending invasion of Kyûshû, that all defensive plans be completed. No matter what our brave soldiers and sailors and pilots do to attack the Americans, if our defenses do not match their zeal, their sacrifice, we will fail. And if we fail at Kyûshû then the Americans will invade the Kantô Plain."

Lieutenant General Arisue turned and nodded at Major Hori. Hori stood and walked to an easel with a map of the Kantô Plain.

"If the Americans secure their objectives on Kyûshû they will prepare to attack the Kantô Plain—"

"Never!"

"We will crush them on the beaches!"

"One hundred million will die first!"

Ken looked at those who had stood and shouted their frustration at Hori's statement. *Can't they see what is coming?* he thought. *Do they really want millions to die for their pride?*

Major Hori was angered with the blind fanaticism he saw. He knew that the Americans, after suffering appalling casualties on Kyûshû, would bring to bear all their industrial and military might before they invaded the Kantô Plain. And he knew it would be limitless, especially the firebombs from the B-29s.

He once told a friend in early 1944, after too much *sake*, that had the United States been at war only with Japan, it would probably have ended by the end of 1943 with an overwhelming American victory. His friend, being a friend, told him never to say those words to anyone else, ever.

Major Hori stood still for several seconds, thinking that Japan would suffer immeasurable death and destruction, far more than Germany had undergone. He knew that America's war with Japan was driven by revenge for Pearl Harbor and that nothing short of Japan's unconditional surrender would stop them. And he knew America would win. But he was Japanese and a patriot; he too would die for *Tennô-Heika*.

"My conclusion is that should the Americans invade the Kantô Plain they will do so next March, possibly the beginning of the month. If they do these are the forces they will face on the Kantô Plain."

The last easel held a map labeled:

PLAN FOR DECISIVE GROUND BATTLE ON KANTÔ, JULY 1945

Ignoring the previous outburst, Major Hori detailed what he believed would be the landing beaches, America's strategies, the amount of men that would come ashore and the total Allied forces involved. There was utter silence as the level of American materiél and manpower—after Kyûshû—was grasped.

Major Hori related what would be left of Japan's military strength to defend Tôkyô and Yokohama, inadvertently comparing the military forces on both sides. On the map Japan's forces were overwhelming, particularly if the civilian militia was counted, but he knew that the Americans, having overwhelming matériel superiority, would be relentless and thorough in attempting to destroy Japan's Kantô Plain defenses and forces before invading.

Ken watched and listened as Major Hori detailed how the battle for the Kantô Plain would be fought. The tactics used for defending Kyûshû would be used here as well. Over 2,500 *kamikaze* planes would attack troop transport ships and carriers. Newly-built Imperial Navy *shin-yô* would attack American ships. What fleet submarines were left would attack. What *kaiten* were left would leave their lairs and attack troop transport ships and Higgins boats. More *fukuryû* would be trained and prepared to sacrifice their lives destroying Higgins boats as they approached the shore. Hori went on but Ken's attention started to drift, not from fatigue or disinterest but despair. He knew the Americans would secure the beaches and reach the Kantô Plain.

The Kantô Plain, however, was not the same terrain as Kyûshû, the latter being mountainous and deeply scarred by numerous narrow and steep streambeds, so crucial to Kyûshû's defense.

The Americans and Japanese knew the Kantô Plain's terrain was flat to slightly rolling and contained the largest tract of low-lying ground in the country. The Americans would utilize their infantry and mechanized divisions in vast sweeping movements, destroying Japanese units as they rolled over them. And America's armored divisions, hardened combat veterans that would come from the battlefields of Europe, driving thousands of tanks, including the new M26 Pershing, would crush whatever or whoever lay in their paths.

Facing those American divisions and tanks would be the rest of Japan's armed forces, equally hardened and determined soldiers, sailors, and pilots, all prepared to die for their emperor. Behind them would come millions of civilians in massive "*Banzai*" charges. And Ken remembered that thousands of children would try to run under the tanks and trucks and amongst American soldiers. *How long would the battle last*, he wondered. *How many would die?*

Major Hori turned and bowed to Lieutenant General Arisue and returned to his seat. Arisue nodded and stood.

"Are there any questions?"

The room was quiet for several moments, as if to pose a question was to question Japan's ultimate victory. Then Ken stood. He knew he was not supposed to call attention to himself. He had done his best to keep a low profile at Atsugi. It would be here, he was certain, that he would be exposed. But he had to know.

"Hori Shôsa! Thank you for your excellent presentation. The Americans have a saying: 'Timing is everything.' How confident are you on the dates for the American invasions?"

In the back an Army colonel jumped up. "There will be only one American invasion! We will destroy them on Kyûshû and at sea! There will not be a second invasion!" Others stood and cheered.

Lieutenant General Arisue gestured for everyone to sit. "Hori Shôsa. It is a fair question. Please respond."

Major Hori stood, nodded toward Lieutenant General Arisue and walked to the front of the stage.

"I agree. It is a fair question. All our estimates should be questioned, especially by those who will be at the front, such as this officer," said Hori, as he pointed at Ken. It was a rebuke to the officer in the back.

"I have studied the career of MacArthur *Gensui*, from his command during World War One to the present. He is brilliant but he is also very arrogant. He believes he cannot be defeated and is therefore unimaginative in his strategy. And that makes him vulnerable. Please excuse what I say next. I have accurately predicted every invasion he has made, including locale, date, time, and the number of soldiers and Marines he would use. It is not difficult. As I stated earlier, my conclusions are based on four factors. For me it is as simple as using an abacus."

As before, Major Hori turned and nodded to Lieutenant General Arisue and returned to his seat. Arisue walked in front of the table to the center of the stage.

"Does that satisfy your concern, Shôsa?"

Ken nodded and sat down. Arisue looked out at the audience.

"Our goal is to kill as many Americans as possible while they are at sea and more when they try to come ashore and even more if they do come ashore and still more if they move inland."

He paused and tried to look at each man in front of him. "If our strategy holds we will kill more Americans than they can tolerate, forcing them to reconsider their demand for unconditional surrender." He picked up a piece of paper. "We all know the bravery and sacrifice of our forces on Okinawa. General Ushijima's chief of staff, General Chô Isamu, wrote this message, to be transmitted to the Imperial War Ministry, moments before his ultimate atonement to His Imperial Majesty: 'Our strategy, tactics, and techniques were all used to the utmost. We fought valiantly, but it was as nothing before the matériel strength of the enemy.'

"We must match our flesh and blood and *Yamato Damashii*—our Divine Race spirit—against the matériel wealth of our enemy. Japan has never been defeated. No foreign army has occupied our sacred soil. We cannot fail His Imperial Majesty. We must remember what all *samurai* have known: 'Death is lighter than a feather, but duty is weightier than a mountain.' If necessary, one hundred million must and will die to maintain the honor of His Imperial Majesty!"

Ken followed as every man in the room stood and cheered their accord. The cheering went on for several moments. Finally, Arisue raised his hand. The audience sat down.

"There are some issues which must be addressed. Because of the American blockade of Japan importation of fuel ceased in May. The Imperial Army has over forty-nine million liters of aviation fuel with almost forty-million liters reserved for our *kamikaze* attacks on the American fleet.

"Half of the training planes and ten percent of transports have been converted to run on alcohol. Oil from pine tree roots is in production but no deliveries have yet been received."

Ken suddenly remembered, while on the train ride from Atsugi to Shinjuku Station in Tôkyô, seeing young men and women cutting down trees and pulling up the stumps with their roots intact. The Japanese, he realized, were so low on fuel that they were converting pine tree oil to aviation fuel.

Arisue looked at another piece of paper in front of him. He hesitated for a few moments.

"After the Americans invaded Saipan there was no doubt that, unless they were stopped in the Philippines or at Okinawa, Japan would be invaded; thus the plans for *Ketsu-Gô*. While we are engaged in this life-and-death struggle there can be no risk that Allied prisoners of war—American, Australian, British, Dutch, and others—will rise up and attempt to escape and aid in the invasion. Japan holds over 350,000 prisoners of war— military and civilian—throughout the Empire.

"Therefore, Deputy Minister of War Kawabara Naoichi issued this policy clarification to all commanders of prisoners of war camps, military or civilian:

"At such time as the situation became urgent and it be extremely important, the prisoners of war will be concentrated and confined in their present location and under heavy guard the preparation for the final disposition will be made.

"The time and method of this disposition are as follows:

"(1) The Time

"Although the basic aim is to act under superior orders, individual disposition may be made in the following circumstances:

"(a) When an uprising of large numbers cannot be suppressed without the use of firearms;

"(b) When escapees from the camp may turn into a hostile fighting force.

"(2) The Methods

"(a) Whether they are destroyed individually or in groups, or however it is done, with mass bombing, poisonous smoke, poisons, drowning, decapitation, or what, dispose of them as the situation dictates.

"(b) In any case, it is the aim not to allow the escape of a single one, to annihilate them all and not to leave any traces."

Ken was numb; he felt the blood drain from his head. He knew the Japanese were masters of often saying one thing and meaning another. There was, however, no ambiguity here. He understood what Arisue had just read. All Allied POWs— military and civilian, including women and children—were to be put to death—by whatever means available—when the Americans invaded Japan, whether prisoners tried to escape or not.

Ken looked at the men at the table. Not one face expressed concern over what Arisue had just read.

Lieutenant General Arisue looked to his left and right and everyone at the table stood. In turn the entire audience stood; the meeting was over.

As they exited Arisue looked at them. He knew many would be dead by the end of November. There was one other set of papers in front of him. He wondered if he should call them back but changed his mind. He picked them up and read them as he did when he first received them.

The American B-29s had destroyed so much of industrial Japan that the few homes that were left had been turned into mini-factories. But the workers' production was down. The civilians of Japan were slowly starving. In July the daily ration of rice was reduced to 294 grams. Arisue knew that in Tôkyô and other major cities, what was left of them, few people received the full allotment, and even that was mixed with edible weeds that, before the war, had been fed to chickens. The supply of fish was half of what had been available before the war with

America. And, he knew, the future was bleaker. Arisue had been told that the next rice crop would be the worst in over forty-five years. By November 1, when the Americans were expected, existing stocks of rice would last at most four days of the reduced July ration. With the Americans controlling the ocean, the quantity of fish would be reduced further. Medical supplies and drugs for civilians had already been reduced by half. Civilians who traveled to the farms for food were forced to barter using family heirlooms as farmers refused to accept the inflated *yen*. Even soldiers were not above corruption. Food for the military was being stolen by soldiers and sold on the black market to wealthy civilians. Japan, Arisue acknowledged, was rotting at the core. And when November 1 arrived it would disintegrate.

Arisue looked up from the papers. The room was almost empty. *No*, he thought. *Let them have their moment of glory.*

* * *

Ken filed out with the rest. Few exchanges were heard. Then he heard someone call his name. He looked in the direction where the voice came from. Several men approached him. He thought he recognized one of them.

"Kobayashi Shôsa! I have told these men about your exploits over Atsugi! They do not believe it! Help me defend my integrity!"

Then Ken remembered that one of Captain Kozono's officers would be attending the briefing. He smiled and spent several minutes describing the dogfight over Atsugi. Several men's chests swelled from pride, picturing one Japanese pilot defeating several American pilots!

"It will be the same when the Americans foolishly try to invade Kyûshû! There will be other pilots like you, Kobayashi Shôsa! With men like you we will push the barbarians back into the sea!"

There were more compliments as the group broke up. Ken left the building and retraced his steps back to Tsukiji.

The sun was still hot as he walked through Hibiya Park. He saw more people trying to produce food from the soil. More groups were training, preparing to die for a war whose fortunes had been reversed three years earlier, at Coral Sea and Midway, and later, defeated, on so many islands and atolls, at so many naval battles, and at Iwô Jima and Okinawa.

✻ ✻ ✻

Oba-*san* greeted Ken when he knocked on the door. She could see he was troubled.

"Honorable Major, I have prepared the *yokusô* for you. Dinner will be ready when you are."

"Thank you, Oba-*san*."

The hot waters of the *yokusô* did not pacify his mind. While immersed he kept thinking about Hori's presentation.

They ate in silence. She could see that he was preoccupied and knew that if he wanted to speak he would. *Geisha* or inn owner it was the same. Know your guest and honor his needs.

Ken thanked her for the dinner, almost as opulent as last evening's. She bowed deeply, acknowledging his gratitude and his parting.

He returned to his room, removed his slippers, and went to his *futon*. He removed his *yukata* and laid it at the foot of the *futon*. He turned off the light then lay down and stared at the ceiling, wondering if the Japanese military would really kill all Allied POWs.

Then he remembered reading a report about the Palawan Massacre that occurred on Palawan Island off the Philippines on December 14, 1944. Two and a half years earlier, about 400 American prisoners had been transferred from the Cabanatuan

POW camp to Palawan to lengthen the Japanese airfield on the island. The Americans were housed in old quarters in Puerto Princessa. Time, brutality, disease and starvation had taken their toll. The Americans were mere shadows of their former selves. Most of them had little clothing left to wear. There were no medicines to combat the diseases that wasted them further. Then, in October 1944, MacArthur returned to the Philippines.

By December 1944, of the 400 who originally came, some 150 were left. The Japanese, fearing advancing U.S. forces would liberate the American POWs, herded the remaining Americans into three air raid trenches. Japanese soldiers poured gasoline on the American POWs and into the trenches and tossed in flaming torches followed by hand grenades.

Ken tried to imagine what the men experienced as the Japanese soldiers doused them with gasoline.

Japanese soldiers cheered as the American POWs were engulfed in flames. Several POWs survived the explosions and ran from the trenches. The Japanese were ready, having already set up a deadly machinegun crossfire. Most of the POWs were cut down. Others were bayoneted, decapitated, or clubbed to death.

Some escaped by running over a small cliff that ran parallel to the trenches, but were hunted down. Most were shot, bayoneted or clubbed to death. Those that were still alive were buried by the Japanese. Of the 150 American POWs at the Palawan Prison camp, only 11 soldiers, sailors and Marines survived the carnage.

Ken was certain that the Japanese would carry out the order to kill all prisoners of war, including civilians.

He knew he had to return to Atsugi soon and fly to Iwô Jima or Okinawa. General Willoughby had to be told the actual Japanese force levels on Kyûshû, both now and those projected for November.

Ken thought about the terrible slaughter that would befall America's forces. America's projected casualties were based on an estimate of 280,000 Japanese soldiers on Kyûshû. According to Major Hori there were now 560,000 Japanese troops deployed there, and by November 1, when America would invade, 900,000 Japanese soldiers, Army and Navy ground troops, pilots and auxiliary personnel would be on Kyûshû, all of them anxious to kill as many Americans as possible.

He could not fall asleep. He looked in the direction of the door, waiting for the *Kempeitai* to burst in and arrest him, keeping him from completing his mission. And there would be no time to grab a sharp knife, what he had promised Admiral Halsey.

But there was another thought that would not go away. He had pulled it off. He had gotten the details of Japan's defense plans. If he got off Japan he just might save thousands, even tens of thousands of American lives. If he got out of Japan.

He knew he had to get to a radio at Atsugi soon. *American forces have no idea what awaits them. I've got to get out of here,* he thought.

He hoped his plane at Atsugi was repaired. There, he reasoned, was the safest place to send a message, ostensibly to Miyakonojô.

Perhaps tomorrow, August 6th, he would leave Tôkyô and return to Atsugi, send a quick radio message, and fly to Iwô Jima or Okinawa and make his report.

27

August 5, 1945

Before midnight, three planes took off from the island of Tinian, each one headed for a separate Japanese city. One flew to Kokura, another to Nagasaki, and the third to Hiroshima.

28

Just after midnight, on the island of Tinian, three B-29s were lined up and prepared for takeoff. One was loaded with cameras. The second contained several scientific instruments. The third B-29, named the *Enola Gay*, carried a new type of bomb.

The *Enola Gay* was one of 15 new B-29s that had been requisitioned for this mission. Each one had been stripped of all gun turrets and armor plating except for the tail gunner position. New fuel-injected engines, new reversible-pitch propellers, and faster-acting pneumatic bomb bay doors had been installed. The bomb bay had been reconfigured to suspend a single 10,000-pound object from a single point. These B-29s would fly higher, faster, and above the range of Japanese anti-aircraft fire.

The new bomb had taken three years to develop, test and build and cost the United States $2,000,000,000. It was called "Little Boy," though there was nothing little about it. Little Boy was ten feet long, 28 inches wide, and weighed almost 9,000 pounds. The bomb looked like an elongated trash can with four fins attached within a square base.

Earlier, the *Enola Gay* had been parked so that her bomb bay doors were directly over a trench that held a pneumatic lift which supported Little Boy. Carefully, ever so carefully, the pneumatic lift slowly elevated Little Boy into the *Enola Gay's* bomb bay.

Numerous klieg lights illuminated the three B-29s and the surrounding area. Military film crews and photographers captured all they could of the historic moment. Tape recorders were rolling to capture almost every word spoken.

A truck carrying the *Enola Gay's* crew pulled up near the bomber. The crew jumped off and was immediately surrounded by photographers, film crews and men thrusting microphones at them. The flashing lights besieged the crew.

Navy Captain William S. Parsons, chief of the Ordinance Division of the "Manhattan Project," was shoved against the *Enola Gay's* landing gear wheel by an eager photographer who yelled, "Smile, you're going to be famous!"

The carnival-like atmosphere disturbed Parsons and he did not smile. He and the rest of the *Enola Gay's* crew forced their way through the boisterous, backslapping crowd. Before mounting the plane's nose ladder Parsons took an MP's sidearm as he had forgotten his own.

The crews, scientists, and cameramen of the two other B-29s climbed into their planes.

The commander of the *Enola Gay*, Lieutenant Colonel Paul Warfield Tibbets, Jr., settled into the pilot's seat. He and his co-pilot, Captain Robert A. Lewis, went through their pre-flight checklist. The rest of the crew checked their equipment.

Lt. Morris R. Jeppson, the bomb electronics test officer, and Parson's assistant, went to his console to check his newly-installed equipment.

After everyone had checked in with Tibbets he leaned out his pilot's window and yelled, "Okay, fellows, cut those lights."

On the ground, men moved back from the B-29s, taking their equipment with them. Some of them stopped talking, gradually realizing the historic moments they were watching or recording. All three planes' engines started.

Tibbets waited until he was certain his plane's four engines were working properly. He released his brakes and started taxiing, increasing his ground speed. Because of the weight of the bomb he waited until he was near the end of the runway before lifting off the ground, at 2:45 A.M., Tinian time. The other B-29s followed.

The three B-29s gained altitude in the inky darkness, heading west, toward Japan.

Fifteen minutes passed when Captain Parsons and his assistant, Lieutenant Jeppson, entered the bomb bay.

Parsons was considered one of the Navy's finest gunnery engineers and was brought into the project by General Leslie Groves, director of the Manhattan Project. Parsons had directed the design and assembly of the bomb and knew every component, inside and out. Now he had just one more task that he was best suited for. He had to arm the world's first atomic bomb that would be used in war.

Little Boy could have been armed on the ground, before takeoff. However, Parsons knew that B-29s sometimes crashed while taking off. If the *Enola Gay* crashed with the bomb armed there was a chance it could explode, killing everyone on the ground within a three-to-four mile radius.

It was icy cold and noisy in the bomb bay and both men knew they would be in there for perhaps thirty minutes. If all went well. There was one minor problem. Parsons had never armed an atomic bomb.

The day before, Parsons spent uncounted hours practicing. Now that practice had to come to fruition. Though his fingers were bleeding from the previous day's practice and now numb with cold, the last task, inserting the detonating charge, was completed within 15 minutes. Parsons and Jeppson left the bomb bay.

Later, Jeppson returned to Little Boy's nose and removed three green plugs and replaced them with three red plugs. The electrical circuit was closed.

At 6:25 A.M., Japan time, Colonel Tibbets received a coded message from a plane that had flown over Hiroshima, one of the three B-29s that had taken off before midnight on August 5. The message was that the sky was blue over Hiroshima. Tibbets switched on the intercom. "It's Hiroshima!"

At 7:41 A.M. the *Enola Gay* leveled off at 32,700 feet.

When the *Enola Gay* reached Japan's coast Colonel Tibbets announced over the intercom, "This is for history, so watch your language. We're carrying the first atomic bomb." Everyone knew their words were being recorded.

At 7:47 A.M. the bomb's electronic fuses were tested; they worked.

At 8:04 the *Enola Gay* changed to a westward course.

At 8:09 the crew of the *Enola Gay* sighted Hiroshima.

The target was the T-shaped Aioi Bridge, located in the center of Hiroshima.

At 8:15 A.M. the *Enola Gay*'s pneumatic bomb bay doors opened.

At 8:15:17 A.M. Little Boy was released from the *Enola Gay*, from an altitude of 31,500 feet.

In less than one minute, at an altitude of 1,900 feet and in one fifteen-hundredth of a microsecond, Little Boy changed the world forever.

29

Ken awoke and looked around the room. Something was amiss. Then he realized that there were no planes flying over Tsukiji, heading inland. He wondered why.

Oba-*san* had breakfast waiting for him. Like a good hostess she sat on her heels on the floor a few feet away, ready to respond to any of Ken's desires.

As he ate he thought about his return to Atsugi Naval Air Base. Getting an encoded radio message to the U.S. Navy would be problematic; how would he justify dismissing the radio operator? Then another thought came to the surface. He knew that when he returned to Atsugi Captain Kozono would hound him with questions regarding the Ichigaya briefing. Furthermore, some officers at Atsugi might think it strange that an officer from southern Kyûshû would give up a chance to spend some time in Tôkyô even if fifty percent of the city was destroyed. Somewhere there would be women who would want to spend time with an officer, especially one with money. Then his eyes closed a bit and he smiled, which Oba-*san* thought odd. He knew he was being pulled by memories. He needed to see some areas of Tôkyô even if the buildings no longer existed. The memories of Kyoko were pulling at him and he would not resist.

Ken thanked Oba-*san* for breakfast, returned to his room

and while dressing he laid out his plans for the day. Before leaving he asked Oba-*san* if she could prepare dinner. She looked down and Ken smiled. "Of course, Oba-*san*, I would hope that you would join me. Here is money for food and more *sake*."

She counted the *yen* notes and was delighted. It would be another feast.

As he left the *ryokan* he saw some middle-aged woman across the street. Upon seeing him they bowed. He acknowledged their gesture with a single nod. As he walked away he did not notice the looks of appreciation on their faces. Nor was he privy to their thoughts of envy directed at his hostess and not just because he was a lodger.

His pace was steadfast, having promised himself that he would not be distracted by the destruction around him as he approached his objective. Within thirty minutes he arrived at the Imperial Palace on his left. He saw pedestrians stop and bow. Even a policeman bowed. He did the same. As he continued he saw people walking, mostly men, on their way to work. Many women held umbrellas aloft to protect them from the sun. From Japanese propaganda posters he had seen Ken knew that the Japanese liked to portray themselves as lighter in skin color than other Asian peoples. Only the lower classes in Japan, especially farmers, had darker skin. No woman in Tôkyô would allow her skin to darken.

Despite his earlier resolve he could not keep the images of a destroyed city from his mind. In so many areas there were no homes left, just barren blocks of earth etched with the outlines of once-standing homes. He was uncomfortable and imagined people looking at him, knowing he was an American. There were few children about, most having been evacuated to the countryside. But those that were about clearly were malnourished and their clothes bedraggled. They displayed no animation, just lethargy. And there was nothing immediate that he could do. He walked on.

Soon he reached his first goal, *Tôdai*, Tôkyô Imperial University, where he and his brother Tom had studied and matured for four years. He was pleased. It had not been bombed nor had the adjacent areas. Clearly, the American government had decided to leave this area untouched. Japan, after defeat, would need its best citizens to rebuild both the nation and a new form of government.

As he approached the Hongô Campus he smiled. The Akamon, or Red Gate, had not changed. All the wood was painted a deep vermillion. Atop the gate was an upward curving roof seen on pagodas. On either side of the center entrance were two doors with massive metal hinges and decorative metal bolts. When Ken moved closer he saw the metal eaves still retained the Maeda family *mon*, the family crest. He approached the center entrance.

The Red Gate was built in 1827 to welcome Tokugawa Yasuhime, who was marrying into the Maeda family. She was the daughter of Tokugawa Ienari, the eleventh *Shôgun*, and the marriage would further cement the alliance. Lord Maeda was an influential *daimyô*, a feudal lord, and ally to the Shôgunate.

In 1868 the Shôgunate was overthrown by allies of the Emperor Meiji. Soon Emperor Meiji moved to Tôkyô. Lands were confiscated from *daimyô* who had opposed him, including Lord Maeda.

In 1872, anxious to modernize his heretofore isolated nation, Emperor Meiji ordered a school system established, the First University Medical School. In 1874 it was renamed Tôkyô *Igakkô*, Tôkyô Medical School. In 1877 three more schools were established: law, science and literature. Emperor Meiji was determined that Japan would become equal to the Western world.

Students, dressed in school uniforms like Tom and Ken had worn, were entering or leaving the campus, carrying books or satchels. That surprised Ken; he was certain that *Tôdai* would have been evacuated. He decided to enter the campus and walk around. He entered a different world. The Hongô Campus seemed undisturbed by the war. Nothing had changed; bustling students going to their classes, groundskeepers cleaning the pathways and austere professors ignoring all else as if only their thoughts were of any consequence. Ken froze then turned to face the Akamon. He realized that a faculty member might recognize him. And if so there would be but two outcomes. He would be mistaken for his brother Tom or, because he had returned to America in April 1941, they would know he was a spy.

He exited the campus and waited for classes to begin. Soon the pathways cleared and he reentered the campus, heading for the spot he had spent hours studying, thinking and, time permitting, alone with Kyoko. Sanshirô Pond.

Long before Edo was renamed Tôkyô the first *Shôgun* of the Edo Period, Tokugawa Ieyasu, gave the pond and the surrounding garden to Lord Maeda Toshitsune in 1615 after Maeda had helped Tokugawa take Ôsaka Castle.

Lord Maeda made certain the garden was scrupulously nurtured since it was a gift from the *Shôgun*. More than 250 years later the Sanshirô Pond would become the center of *Tôdai*, giving students and faculty a place of isolation surrounded by uncounted forms of flora, carefully tended by gardeners.

But before he could reach Sanshirô Pond he heard harsh voices yelling, cursing. He had never heard voices like this at *Tôdai*. Curious, he decided to investigate. Near the Medical Library scores of students were assembled. All the students had a rifle with fixed bayonet. As he approached, his knees weakened. He saw that the rifles were pre-World War One. It was bad enough to have seen how desperate Japan was becoming by having kids train with explosives in rucksacks or teenage girls training with sharpened bamboo poles or old men with ancient rifles. Now they were taking young men, the brightest minds in Japan, potential future leaders, and training them to die for an outmoded *Bushidô* ethic with hand-me-down rifles. Ken watched seventeen-year-old boys in quasi-military uniforms charging dummies, plunging bayonets into the fake torsos. They were cheering; they had no idea what they would face. Then he heard gunfire, both rifle and machine gun. He rounded the library and stopped.

Four boys were in a shallow foxhole. One was firing a machine gun in short bursts while another fed ammunition. Two other boys were firing rifles. It was standard military tactics; the riflemen supported the machine gunner against flanking enemy infantry. The students were firing live ammunition, not blanks. Ken was sickened that his beloved *Tôdai* was being used as a military training base. He wondered how students at Princeton, Stanford or Harvard would react if guns with live ammunition were fired on their campuses.

Standing above the students was an Imperial Army sergeant, barking orders while constantly yelling, "*Bakayarô!*"—stupid boy, an egregious insult the sergeant clearly enjoyed using on *Tôdai* students, his social and intellectual superiors. When they saw Ken, the sergeant snapped to attention. The boys jumped out of the ditch and also stood at attention. As Ken approached the sergeant saluted. Unsure, the boys also saluted. Ken stood in front of the boys and returned their salute while ignoring the sergeant. He turned to look at the targets, backed by earthen mounds three meters in height, high enough to stop wayward students from being killed. He then faced the sergeant. "*Gunsô!* Your field glasses!"

"*Ha!*" The sergeant fumbled for his binoculars, which were in a cloth case hanging from his neck by a web strap. He handed them to Ken. The black paint had worn away exposing the brass.

"Brass! The enemy can see these in sunlight! *Bakayarô!*" The students turned away and smiled.

Ken turned to look at the targets. The students had not come close. He took a rifle from a student, an Arisaka Type 38 model from 1905, and, while still standing, placed the butt of the stock into his shoulder and fired one round, then handed the rifle back to the student. Another student looked through his binoculars; Ken had hit the target dead center. The students were silent. Not even the sergeant had hit near the center, even while prone and his rifle supported by the earth.

"Perhaps," said Ken to the students, "you are better suited to studying than shooting. There is no shame in that."

Neither the students nor the sergeant replied. Ken walked away, heading to the Sanshirô Pond.

When he reached the pond, memories of Kyoko washed over and enveloped him. The pathways were clear; students were either in class or learning to kill Americans. At one spot there were four large flat rocks in a line, from the edge of the pond and moving toward the middle. He sat down on the outermost one, the one they had often shared.

They had often carried rice balls to break up and feed the *koi*, the multicolored carp that inhabited the pond. The *koi*, seeing humans approach, would always gather in large numbers awaiting the food to be tossed to them. Gyrating about and lunging for the food on the water's surface resulted in a merger of the variegated colors, as if a rainbow had been dipped in the pond and started to dissolve into colorful confusion. The *koi* were never satiated; there were just too many. Kyoko would always laugh and Ken would savor her laughter.

This time he had no food to feed the gathering fish. The fish were patient; someone always fed them. He envied their certainty. Overhead, birds flew from tree to tree, oblivious to Ken's presence. A strong warm breeze caused the branches to sway back and forth.

Their last time at Sanshirô Pond, in March 1941, was different. Both were serious. Kyoko was now studying at Tôkyô

Women's Medical Professional School. In another year she would graduate and be a doctor. Ken would graduate in one week from *Tôdai* and both knew he would return to the United States. Not for the first time they discussed marriage. To both of them it would be a perfect blend: a Japanese girl who was familiar and comfortable with American culture and a Japanese-American boy familiar and comfortable with Japanese culture. And on their last time at Sanshirô Pond he again raised the issue of marriage. Though she yearned to marry him one implacable barrier stood between them: her father, Susumu.

Masamune Susumu was a highly-respected surgeon, practicing at St. Luke's Hospital in Tôkyô, and because of his research well-known to American doctors. In 1932 he had been invited to practice surgery and conduct research at Columbia University's College of Physicians and Surgeons in New York. It was a distinct honor to Columbia because Japanese doctors, when overseas, typically practiced and taught in Berlin. He and his family had stayed for four years. While there Kyoko, having already studied English, had attended high school and, outside of their apartment, had quickly embraced American culture. She loved Manhattan; the bright lights, the movies, the restaurants and baseball, particularly because the New York Yankees had played in Tôkyô in 1934. And she loved the Macy's Thanksgiving Day Parade, the lights and gaiety of Christmas and New Year's Eve, all of which her father's American colleagues had invited the Masamune family to celebrate. But her father, in practicing surgery in New York, had seen a darker side of America, its crime and violence, unheard of in Japan.

Back in Japan, with Ken seeing his daughter, Dr. Masamune had tolerated his headstrong daughter's relationship with Kenji. After all, he reasoned, Kenji was an intelligent and cultured *kibei*, a student at *Tôdai*, but he frowned on their growing closeness. However, he knew that after graduation Kenji would return to America and that would be the end of it. But Kyoko had other thoughts. Her love for Ken had deepened far beyond what either expected. On their last day at Sanshirô Pond Ken again asked Kyoko to marry him. With tears she declined, not telling Ken why. But he knew why and he would not ask Kyoko to choose between him and her family.

After a while they walked back to her school, the ache each felt for the other unbearable. Kyoko's pain was even greater knowing that he would leave soon and perhaps find a new girl in America. That was not in Ken's mind.

Ken's memories were interrupted. Students were coming to the pond. He looked at his watch; he had been there for almost two hours thinking about Kyoko. He knew he had to see for himself. He made his way to the Red Gate and exited the campus.

Then another memory arose, the *geshuku* where Tom and he had lived for four years.

Around the Hongô Campus many enterprising housewives rented out a room to students, collecting a lucrative remuneration as *Tôdai* students generally came from wealthy families. In turn the students lived with a family, were given two meals a day, breakfast and dinner and, for Ken and Tom, an opportunity to further immerse themselves in Japan's culture. Since a Japanese woman ran the household while her husband worked she collected the rent. Some would also offer to do laundry for an extra fee. In the case of Ken and Tom, some of the benefits to the Takahashi family included their three kids learning English and occasionally inviting friends over to observe the two exotic *kibei* from America.

Ken and Tom always referred to the woman as *Okami-san*, proprietress, though she would smile and ask the boys to call her by her name, Atsuko. They could not as it seemed being too familiar to them. However, they called Atsuko's husband by his surname, Takahashi-*san*, and Atsuko's three kids by their first names, which they preferred because now they had two older and very smart brothers. At dinners both Ken and Tom would regale the Takahashi family with stories of America and try to explain American politics, often eliciting laughter or looks of confusion. American movie stars, some of with whom Mr. and Mrs. Takahashi were familiar, was always a delightful subject. American baseball was something the kids enjoyed hearing about but could not understand why Japanese Americans were not allowed to play with or against white teams. Explaining football was a lost cause and Ken and Tom stopped trying after a few attempts.

Ken and Tom shared a large eight-*tatami* room which was comfortable for them and gave them privacy so they could study. A plus was that they could listen to American radio stations broadcasting from Hawaii without disturbing the Takahashi family.

It was just a ten-minute walk to the Takahashi home and Ken decided to take a look. An occasional cart, hand- or horse-pulled, crossed his path. When he arrived at the Takahashi home he saw a *Tôdai* student leaving, heading to the Hongô Campus. And just as she had done when Ken and Tom lived there, *Okami-san* waved after him, urging that he study hard. Ken's eyes watered; *Okami-san* had been like a surrogate mother to Tom and him. On more than one occasion Ken had spoken with her about his relationship with Kyoko; though she was certain nothing would come of it, *Okami-san* had always encouraged him. He lingered for a moment. When he and Tom had moved in in 1937 *Okami-san* was thirty years old. Now, 1945, she looked not thirty-eight but in her mid-fifties. Even though the area had not been bombed the war had taken its toll. Her hair was now gray, her clothing showed wear. She had lost weight. Ken wondered if her children had been evacuated.

Unexpectedly, she turned in Ken's direction and after a moment cocked her head to the side, one eyebrow raised. She put her hand over her eyebrows to block the sun. He wanted to run to her and tell her who he was and that peace would soon return. Instead, he turned and walked away, wiping his eyes.

Ken resumed his path, heading in almost a straight line, walking about two and one-half miles. This time his pace was slower, impeded by piles of rubble in some places but mostly by his thoughts. In about forty-five minutes he reached Tôkyô Women's Medical Professional School. Or what was left of it. He stood transfixed recalling the times he had come to the school to meet with Kyoko when classes were over for the weekend. Each time they met it was like their first date, without her parents' knowledge. Now the memories had been shattered by B-29s.

He slowly entered the campus and saw that so much had been destroyed. Inpatient and outpatient wards, laboratories, and the school buildings were demolished. Remarkably, the main hospital building, housing inpatients and outpatients, the attached clinical lecture hall and the school dormitory were unscathed. He saw a groundskeeper and approached him.

"*Konnichiwa*." Good day. The old man squinted at Ken, straining to see the author of the voice. He moved closer.

"Ah! Honorable Officer! Good day!"

"Tell me, old man, when did this happen," asked Ken as he pointed in the direction of the bombed buildings.

"April thirteenth, Honorable Officer. Terrible. Terrible," he replied while shaking his head.

"Are there any students still here?"

"Yes! Oh yes! Most have left but the senior students are still here helping the doctors care for patients."

"Which building?"

"Ah! I will show you, Honorable Officer. Please follow me."

The old man turned and shuffled off, carrying what was left of a straw broom. He moved slowly, and Ken felt constrained walking at such a slow pace, but the old man was doing him a favor. Soon they reached the main hospital building and the old man opened the door for Ken and bowed, bidding Ken to enter. Before entering Ken saw that one of the glass doors was cracked and left unrepaired.

"*Arigatô*," said Ken. Thank you.

"*Dôitashimashite*," said the old man. You are welcome.

Ken walked over to what seemed a receptionist desk. An old man sat behind the desk. When he saw Ken he stood and bowed. Ken replied with a nod.

Ken inhaled deeply and stepped forward, taking a gamble. "*Konnichiwa*. I am Major Kobayashi. I am looking for a doctor. She studied at the medical school."

"*Hai!* What is her name, please?"

"Masamune Kyoko."

"Sorry, I do not know that name." He looked at Ken and saw the urgency in his eyes. "Let me look in our files. Perhaps she was here at another time."

While he was gone Ken looked around. Many people were in the waiting area. All looked drained. There were several youngsters with their mother or grandmother. Most of the kids were coughing, some producing sputum. He knew about tuberculosis and suspected that the kids were suffering from it. He looked at the boys and it struck him hard. They were almost emaciated, unlike the boys he had seen practicing with explosive-laden rucksacks. He grasped that the boys who would die asking for chocolate from Americans were being fed by the military. They wanted the boys to be healthy in order to kill themselves. Those whose parents did not offer their sons for sacrifice were denied an adequate diet.

The receptionist returned in a few minutes. "Honorable Major, there is no doctor here by that name."

Ken thought for a minute, wondering if Kyoko had married and fearing the answer. "Is there a woman doctor here with a first name of Kyoko?"

The receptionist smiled. "I thought of that, Honorable Major. There is no doctor with the name Kyoko. So sorry."

Ken thanked the man and turned to leave. He lingered a moment to look at the kids waiting to see a doctor. He grimaced; this was not his concern. He left the building and the grounds, deciding to return to the *ryokan* in Tsukiji.

Shortly he saw the U.S. Embassy. He walked toward it. He could not help but admire the skill of the American bomber pilots in avoiding the area, especially after the B-29s changed to night bombing runs. There was a policeman on either side of the main entrance. Seeing Ken they snapped to attention and saluted him. *Think Japanese*, he thought. *Think arrogant Imperial Japanese Army officer.* He nodded once.

Soon he came within sight of Ichigaya Heights and stopped for a moment, trying to fathom how otherwise educated men, leaders of their armed forces, could demand that an entire population sacrifice itself for just one man, Emperor Hirohito. *I've got to get back*, he thought. *I've seen and heard enough.*

Continuing he came to the collection of buses he had seen two days before and stopped. There was still laundry hanging. He looked closely and saw that some of the clothes belonged to kids. Here and there women gathered in small groups. Some children were clutching their mothers' clothing. One woman held a young girl and Ken saw the child wearily reach for her mother's breast. The woman gently brushed aside her daughter's hand; she had no milk to offer. Ken looked at his watch. It was nearing 4:00 P.M. He pressed on, keeping his eyes mostly on the ground; he didn't want to see any more deprivation. Soon he reached the *ryokan*.

Oba-*san* greeted him as he removed his boots, handing him his slippers. She could tell he was tense and preoccupied.

"Honorable Major, I have the *yokusô* ready. Stay as long as you like. Dinner will be ready when you are."

"Thank you, Oba-*san*."

He undressed in his room. While he was gone she had washed his *fundoshi*. He grabbed it and the *yukata*. He went to the *datsui-jo*, the changing room, and removed his undergarments. As before, he washed his body with soap before entering the *yokusô*, the wooden tub. He immersed himself completely, even his head. He held his breath for almost two minutes before coming up for air. He put a wash cloth behind his head and leaned back, closing his eyes. All he pictured was the smiling face of Kyoko and wondered if she had left Tôkyô, had married or was dead. Nothing else entered his mind and that is how he consumed his time. After a while he climbed out of the tub and dried himself then went to the changing room and put on the fresh *fundoshi* and *yukata*. He went downstairs. Dinner was awaiting him as was *sake*.

"Honorable Major, was your day enjoyable?"

"Yes, Oba-*san*, enjoyable and informative. It has been a long time since I last saw Tôkyô. So much is gone, so much."

She heard and saw his sadness and poured more *sake*. Without thinking he drank it. Even the poorer quality did not deter him as he held out his cup for more. Oba-*san* knew that the day had not gone well and was prepared to be as gracious a host as possible. She refilled his cup and he emptied it. Then she did something out of the ordinary for her; she picked up his chopsticks and plucked a piece of fish and fed him. Without thinking he accepted it. But it was *sake* that he desired most. Their dinner was eaten in silence. She knew she would have to put him to bed and hoped she was strong enough.

His last conscious thought was that he would leave tomorrow for Atsugi, send a coded radio message to Sergeant Tetsuo Takayama and fly to Iwô Jima.

30

August 6, 1945

President Harry S. Truman was aboard the U.S. Navy cruiser USS *Augusta*, sailing for the United States. The Potsdam Conference had ended and Truman had taken his measure of Soviet Premier Josef Stalin. While walking the deck he was handed a decoded top secret radio message that had been sent from Secretary of War Henry L. Stimson. The message had been written before Truman had left for the Potsdam Conference. After reading it Truman smiled.

In Washington, D.C., at 11:00 A.M. Eastern Standard Time, Acting White House Press Secretary Eben A. Ayers handed out to the White House press corps a shocking press release.

```
THE WHITE HOUSE
Washington, D.C.
IMMEDIATE RELEASE
STATEMENT BY THE PRESIDENT OF THE UNITED STATES

Aug. 6, 1945

Sixteen hours ago an American airplane dropped
one bomb on Hiroshima and destroyed its use-
fulness to the enemy. That bomb had more power
than 20,000 tons of T.N.T. It had more than two
thousand times the blast power of the British
"Grand Slam" which is the largest bomb ever yet
used in the history of warfare.
```

The Japanese began the war from the air at Pearl Harbor. They have been repaid many fold. And the end is not yet. With this bomb we have now added a new and revolutionary increase in destruction to supplement the growing power of our armed forces. In their present form these bombs are now in production and even more powerful forms are in development.

It is an atomic bomb. It is a harnessing of the basic power of the universe. The force from which the sun draws its power has been loosed against those who brought war to the Far East. Before 1939, it was the accepted belief of scientists that it was theoretically possible to release atomic energy. But no one knew any practical method for doing it. By 1942, however, we knew that the Germans were working feverishly to find a way to add atomic energy to the other engines of war with which they hoped to enslave the world. But they failed. We may be grateful to Providence that the Germans got the V-1s and V-2s late and in limited quantities and even more grateful that they did not get the atomic bomb at all.

The battle of the laboratories held fateful risks for us as well as the battles of the air, land and sea, and we have now won the battle of the laboratories as we have won the other battles.

Beginning in 1940, before Pearl Harbor, scientific knowledge useful in war was pooled between the United States and Great Britain, and many priceless helps to our victories have come from that arrangement. Under that general policy the research on the atomic bomb was begun. With American and British scientists working together we entered the race of discovery against the Germans.

The United States had available the large number of scientists of distinction in the many needed areas of knowledge. It had the tremendous industrial and financial resources necessary for the project and they could be devoted to it without undue impairment of other vital war work. In the United States the laboratory work and the production plants, on which a substantial start had already been made, would be out of reach of enemy bombing, while at that time Britain was exposed to constant air attack and was still threatened with the possibility of invasion. For these reasons Prime Minister Churchill and President Roosevelt agreed that it was wise to carry on the project here. We now have two great plants and many lesser works devoted to the production of atomic power. Employment during peak construction numbered 125,000 and over 65,000 individuals are even now engaged in operating the plants. Many have worked there for two and a half years. Few know what they have been producing. They see great quantities of material going in and they see nothing coming out of these plants, for the physical size of the explosive charge is exceedingly small. We have spent two billion dollars on the greatest scientific gamble in history—and won.

But the greatest marvel is not the size of the enterprise, its secrecy, nor its cost, but the achievement of scientific brains in putting together infinitely complex pieces of knowledge held by many men in different fields of science into a workable plan. And hardly less marvelous has been the capacity of industry to design, and of labor to operate, the machines and methods to do things never done before so that the brainchild of many minds came forth in physical shape and performed as it was supposed to do. Both science and industry worked under the direction of the United States Army, which achieved a unique success in managing so diverse a problem in the advancement of knowledge in an amazingly short time. It is doubtful if such another combination could be got together in the world. What has been done is

the greatest achievement of organized science
in history. It was done under high pressure and
without failure.

We are now prepared to obliterate more rapidly and completely every productive enterprise
the Japanese have above ground in any city. We
shall destroy their docks, their factories, and
their communications. Let there be no mistake;
we shall completely destroy Japan's power to
make war.

It was to spare the Japanese people from utter destruction that the ultimatum of July 26
was issued at Potsdam. Their leaders promptly
rejected that ultimatum. If they do not now accept our terms they may expect a rain of ruin
from the air, the like of which has never been
seen on this earth. Behind this air attack will
follow sea and land forces in such numbers and
power as they have not yet seen and with the
fighting skill of which they are already well
aware.

The Secretary of War, who has kept in personal
touch with all phases of the project, will immediately make public a statement giving further
details.

His statement will give facts concerning the
sites at Oak Ridge near Knoxville, Tennessee,
and at Richland near Pasco, Washington, and an
installation near Santa Fe, New Mexico. Although
the workers at the sites have been making materials to be used in producing the greatest destructive force in history they have not themselves been in danger beyond that of many other
occupations, for the utmost care has been taken
of their safety.

The fact that we can release atomic energy ush-
ers in a new era in man's understanding of nature's forces. Atomic energy may in the future
supplement the power that now comes from coal,

oil, and falling water, but at present it cannot be produced on a basis to compete with them commercially. Before that comes there must be a long period of intensive research.

It has never been the habit of the scientists of this country or the policy of this Government to withhold from the world scientific knowledge. Normally, therefore, everything about the work with atomic energy would be made public.

But under present circumstances it is not intended to divulge the technical processes of production or all the military applications, pending further examination of possible methods of protecting us and the rest of the world from the danger of sudden destruction.

I shall recommend that the United States consider promptly the establishment of an appropriate commission to control the production and use of atomic power within the United States. I shall give further consideration and make further recommendations to the Congress as to how atomic power can become a powerful and forceful influence towards the maintenance of world peace.

END TEXT

Before long, radio stations across America and in Hawaii began broadcasting the White House statement. Few Americans understood what it meant, especially the word "atomic." Many could not believe that the American government had spent two billion dollars to develop a single bomb. None could imagine that an entire city had been wiped off the face of the earth by one bomb. But most Americans were also thinking Pearl Harbor.

*　　　*　　　*

Earlier in the morning in Tôkyô, at 8:16 A.M., the *Nippon Hôsô Kyôkai*, the NHK or Japanese Broadcasting Company, noted that Hiroshima's radio station was not broadcasting.

The Ministry of War at Ichigaya in Tôkyô, where Ken had attended the briefing on August 5th, tried to reach the Army Control Center in Hiroshima without success. A young officer was dispatched by plane to investigate, a flight of three hours. One hundred miles from Hiroshima the officer and his pilot saw an immense cloud of smoke. As they approached Hiroshima they could see that what was left of the city was engulfed in flames. They landed south of Hiroshima and reported by radio to Ichigaya that Hiroshima no longer existed.

Then the Japanese Foreign Ministry informed Japan's Foreign Minister Tôgô Shigenori about the American radio broadcasts of an atomic bomb destroying Hiroshima. Tôgô demanded that the Army investigate.

Later that afternoon, *Kempeitai* Command Center employed its own communications network and soon received word that a small number of B-29s had completely destroyed Hiroshima. Soon word spread to other military and governmental organs. Something dreadful and ominous had happened and both the government and the military needed to find out.

31

August 7

Ken awoke with a hangover. He sat up and the pain in his head was immediate and pounding. He slowly lay back on the *futon*. *I'm not supposed to have a hangover, not with* sake, he thought. *That's what my dad told me.* He turned to his side and raised himself to his hands and knees; the world was spinning. He slowly raised himself to his knees then stood on unsteady legs. He went to the bathroom and straddled the squat toilet that lay on the floor. Squatting, he almost fell forward twice while he urinated and voided. His waste would slowly sink to the bottom of the well and later be suctioned out by workers who would then sell the feces to farmers for fertilizer.

Finished, he went to the *yoku-jô*, the tub room, and washed. He returned to his room and dressed, packing his bag and collecting all his belongings. He would tell Oba-*san* that she could keep the balance of his rental fee.

Knowing breakfast would be waiting he carried his *katana* rather than buckling it and headed to the stairs. When he reached the landing he froze. Three members of the *Kempeitai* stood in the entranceway, a captain, a lieutenant and a sergeant. Each had a white armband on his left arm with the characters, 兵 憲, law soldier. Their faces were impassive. Ken was ready to draw his sword. Oba-*san* was too frightened to move or say anything. Ken put down his bag and descended the stairs.

None of the *Kempeitai* had removed their boots, a display of rudeness. The *Kempeitai* captain stepped forward and bowed to Ken.

"*Ohayôgozaimasu*, Kobayashi Shôsa!" Good morning, Major Kobayashi.

"*Ohayôgozaimasu!*" replied Ken, waiting for the other shoe to drop.

"Please forgive this intrusion but there is a matter of the most extreme urgency. I have been instructed to escort you to Ichigaya immediately."

Ken noted that the hands of the three *Kempeitai* were relaxed, not near their pistols or swords. Ken's arms flexed. He knew that he could draw his *katana* faster than they could draw their pistols.

"Captain, please explain."

"So sorry, Major. I only know that General Arisue has ordered your presence. I do not know the reason."

Ken looked at the captain's eyes, searching for deception, but could find none. Something else was up. He knew that if his mission had been discovered the *Kempeitai* would have arrested him on the spot with guns drawn. *Why*, he wondered, *is General Arisue summoning me?* Ken nodded once.

"Oba-*san*, I will return later. Please put my bag back in my room."

Oba-*san* bowed deeply. The sergeant opened the door and stood aside as Ken, the captain and the lieutenant filed out. The sergeant exited and closed the door. Oba-*san* ran forward and opened it just a crack. Outside was a large car, a driver at the wheel, with a diesel engine running. *No charcoal for the* Kempeitai, she thought. The lieutenant opened the rear door and the captain gestured for Ken to enter first. The captain followed and the door was shut. The lieutenant and sergeant entered the front seats.

Nothing was said as they drove to Ichigaya Heights. At

one point, on the same direction Ken had taken yesterday in returning to Tsukiji from Kyoko's medical school, they came across a horse carcass lying in the street. Numerous cuts of flesh had been taken from the haunches. Though not normally meat eaters, Tôkyôites were scrounging for anything available to survive another day. In a short time they arrived at Ichigaya. The captain escorted Ken into the building.

This time there was but a handful of officers and some civilians clustered by themselves. When they saw the *Kempeitai* captain they stopped talking but were relieved when he left, his task completed. Ken was too. In a moment General Arisue and a civilian exited a room and approached the officers and civilians. Arisue saw Ken and acknowledged him. Ken looked at the civilian and thought him distinguished and professorial. Few words were exchanged; General Arisue led them all into a conference room with a large rectangular table and chairs. At each position on the table was a collection of documents.

"Please sit down," said Arisue. "We have important matters to discuss and little time. With me is Dr. Nishina Yoshio."

Ken looked at Dr. Nishina and he recalled the name. Then it hit him. Nishina was Japan's leading physicist and friend of renowned physicist Niels Bohr and a close friend of Albert Einstein as well. What Ken did not know was that Niels Bohr was one of the leading physicists contributing to the Manhattan Project, America's atomic bomb program. *What the hell is going on*, Ken wondered.

Among them, only General Arisue and the civilians knew that Dr. Nishina was director of *Rikagaku Kenkyûsho*, the Institute for Physical and Chemical Research. There, Dr. Nishina directed Japan's atomic program to develop *genshi bakudan*, an atomic bomb, beginning in 1941. Their proposed budget was ¥50,000, equal to $11,500, a number ridiculed by the Imperial Japanese Army as being ludicrous to develop such a weapon system. In 1945 the Army changed its decision when a physicist, Dr. Ôdan Masaharu, while conducting atomic research in Tôkyô, detonated a bomb that destroyed his laboratory and two adjacent buildings. The explosion also killed Dr. Ôdan. However, the Army was too late.

Dr. Nishina asked everyone to read the documents in front of them. The first was the White House press release. Next was the history of Japan's efforts to develop an atomic bomb. When Ken saw the proposed budgetary request for ¥50,000 he was dumbfounded, quickly converting *yen* to dollar. The last document was the preliminary report from the officer who had flown to Hiroshima yesterday. Dr. Nishina stood and for the next thirty minutes he explained what an atomic bomb was and what it theoretically could do. When finished he sat down. No one spoke. Some did not look up. Ken could not comprehend.

General Arisue stood. "Everyone here will fly with Dr. Nishina and me to Hiroshima this morning." He looked at Ken. "Kobayashi Shôsa will come with us. We will drive to Tokorozawa airfield. There, several Army technicians have been assembled and will accompany us. Are there any questions?"

Ken stood. *I have to get out of here*, he thought. "General, I have no experience in physics."

"I will explain why on the plane."

The officers, all experts in explosives ordnance, looked at Ken, an engineering officer, as if he had been honored to be chosen. Arisue stood, signaling the end of the meeting. Ken followed Arisue, Nishina and two civilians out. The rest followed.

The drive to Tokorozawa took less than an hour, located about thirty kilometers west of central Tôkyô. The airfield was Japan's oldest, opened in 1911. It was insignificant in comparison to Atsugi, having but one runway, but it had not escaped the ravages of American bombing and fighter plane attacks. But the Japanese were quick to repair it after each raid. Two planes were ready on the runway. Arisue, Ken and a few Army technicians entered one. Nishina, two of his colleagues and the rest of the Army technicians and ordnance officers boarded the other and both planes took off without incident. Shortly, however, Nishina's plane developed engine trouble and had to turn back. Recognizing the urgency Arisue decided to continue.

While in flight Arisue sat next to Ken. "Kobayashi Shôsa, I wanted you to come with us because if what we have read is true then it is certain that the Americans will use this bomb during their invasion of Kyûshû. If so then all our plans will be for naught. You know the terrain of Kyûshû, and showed during the conference that you are clear-headed. You must help decide if the landing beaches can be adapted to absorb this bomb."

Ken heard what Arisue said but was thinking about something else. How, he wondered, did Japan ever expect to develop an atomic bomb with an initial budget of $11,500 when the United States had spent two billion dollars? Didn't anyone in Japan realize the industrial might of America? He looked out the window as they flew over Hiroshima and thought, *Now they do.*

They landed at the same field that the junior officer had yesterday. They were greeted by the airfield commander. Half his face was burned but the side that had not faced the explosion was not. He told General Arisue that if skin was covered by cloth there would be protection from the blast. Arisue looked at the man and wondered if he was rational. Transportation was awaiting them and they wasted little time driving to Hiroshima.

Hiroshima, located toward the southern end of Honshû, was about 420 miles from Tôkyô by direct flight. The city was, in the eyes of U.S. military commanders, a legitimate target, comprising a port that was used for military embarkation, industrial and military targets, including military bases as well as the headquarters of the Fifth Division and Field Marshal Hata Shunroku's 2nd General Army Headquarters, responsible for the defense of all of southern Japan. Earlier in the war the population was over 380,000 but by August 1945, due to evacuations of non-essential residents, the population had dropped to about 250,000. When the United States began preparing its bombing strategy it purposefully left a handful of cities off limits in case the atomic bomb was to be used. They wanted to make certain they could measure the actual damage an undamaged city suffered. It was a cold and pragmatic calculation.

Arisue and Ken sat in the same car in the back seat, both silent with their own thoughts. Soon they reached the outskirts of the city or what was once a city. Smoke was still rising from fires. People not killed by the explosion were walking without a destination or just sitting, their faces blank. Even babies were not crying. Their driver had to maneuver around debris, dead horses and humans. The odor of burned flesh was nauseating and, despite the heat, the car's windows were rolled shut. As they approached the center of Hiroshima they saw additional bodies, many barely recognizable as such, scattered about. Not tens or scores but hundreds, tossed about as if dolls or parts of dolls. Most were simply charred remains. Ken saw a body laying face down and a smaller body near it. Both were charred except the larger body's back. He realized it was a woman and the smaller body was her child, which had been strapped to her back. The instantaneous heat of the explosion had charred the body of the child but its being tied to its mother's back had offered protection. Ken turned away.

Further from the city center the buildings had been congested. Both homes and workshops were made of wood. They no longer existed. The center of Hiroshima contained numerous concrete buildings, some of which still stood as mute skeletons, their wooden doors and window frames and interiors consumed by the flames. Except for a handful of concrete buildings every structure in Hiroshima was gone, either disintegrated from the explosion and shockwave or consumed by the firestorms. The closer to the center they approached fewer people were found alive. Some concrete structures, buttressed with steel, were misshapen. Not even in Tôkyô were such distortions seen.

The cars reached the center and Arisue ordered the driver to stop. The other cars followed suit. Everyone exited their vehicles. All of them covered their faces with cloth as the air was full of particles which made them cough.

"Kobayashi Shôsa," said Arisue, "take two technicians and walk around. Make notes of what you observe. One of the technicians has a camera; pictures must be taken."

Ken had no idea where to go so he chose a direction not taken by others. The two Army technicians followed him. They walked slowly. Here and there a survivor approached, asking for water. Ken and the technicians shared their water. Others just walked aimlessly, not understanding. Ken knew they never would.

Several times Ken stopped to listen. All he heard was a wind, the kind he had heard while riding a horse in the open land east of San Gabriel. It was a wind that carried hollowness, no buildings to impede its motion. The hair on his neck rose. He looked around. What was once a city of tens of thousands was now nothing. They walked for several hours, in a random pattern. If something caught their attention they would investigate. They came to a bridge and though the sun was now in the opposite direction they saw what appeared to be shadows of the uprights. Ken, an avid photographer in high school, was intrigued. Light creates shadows but the sun was now behind them. The shadows were pointing toward him. He realized that the heat from an atomic explosion that Dr. Nishina had spoken about had burned the shadows into the asphalt. The Army photographer took some pictures, a dispassionate chronicler. They eventually came to a bank building and decided to sit on the front steps to rest. It was the Sumitomo Bank, a concrete building. One of the technicians took off his face cloth and lit a cigarette. He inhaled deeply then exhaled. The smoke flowed over to Ken's face and he turned away. Something on the step to his left caught his attention. It was another shadow but there was nothing that would have caused it. Yet something had to cause the shadow. Slowly he grasped that someone had been sitting on the step at the moment the atomic bomb exploded and had been instantly vaporized. Yet for the fraction of a second that the person had been on the step when the bomb detonated, his body had blocked the light of the blast and left a shadow burned into the concrete. He wondered if the person's brain could react fast enough to know what was happening and thought not. He stood and slowly walked back to the bridge. He looked at the numerous shadows burned into the asphalt and imagined each a person. He dropped to his knees and began to cry, like a man who has found the body of his dead child, wondering how his adoptive homeland could inflict such evil upon his ancestral homeland. The emotional pressure built to such a degree that he screamed. The two technicians came running, then stopped, keeping their distance, understanding.

Ken cried for several minutes then recovered. *It must end*, he thought. *If one is dropped then others will be.* Then he remembered what General Arisue had said. The bombs might be used at Kyûshû during an invasion. Millions of Japanese military and civilians would be killed. *The madness must end.* With Ken in the lead they walked back to the cars. General Arisue was already there. With Hiroshima's public transit system wiped out he and Ken went to the Ujina Shipping Command in Hiroshima Bay by boat. Ken and Arisue compared notes and Arisue wrote an extensive report by candlelight. He offered three main conclusions: 1. a special bomb was used by the Americans; 2. burns could be minimized or prevented if people covered their bodies with cloth or by jumping into shallow holes in the ground; 3. a rumor heard was that the same type bomb would be used on Tôkyô on August 12.

Ken was stunned that Arisue believed people only needed to cover their bodies with cloth to minimize burns. *Didn't he see the charred bodies*, he wondered. *Was he trying to diminish the bomb's effects?* But he chose to say nothing. It was late and he could not contribute more. Otherwise, he would be drawn further into this new crisis.

Arisue gave his report to Ujina's commander and ordered that it be sent immediately to Ichigaya in Tôkyô. For Arisue and Ken it was a restless night.

32

August 8

In the morning there was hell to pay. General Arisue, after eating breakfast with Ken and Ujina's base commander, discovered that his dispatch was still on the commander's desk. He made two quick decisions. First, he ordered that the report be sent via radio.

"What if the Americans," asked the commander, "hear our broadcast?"

"*Bakayarô!* The Americans already know about the bomb! Send it!"

Arisue turned to Ken. "Kobayashi Shôsa! When this fool has finished sending the report I want you to fly it back to Tôkyô and take it to my office!"

"*Ha!*" replied Ken. *Then I can leave.*

Later that afternoon Dr. Nishina and his group arrived in Hiroshima. At first he surveyed the city from his plane and knew immediately that the Americans had indeed used an atomic bomb. After landing he minutely examined various materials, including melted roof tiles and concluded that the heat from the explosion had reached 2,000° Centigrade, a temperature not even approached in the firebombings of Tôkyô. When he met with General Arisue both agreed the Americans had indeed developed an atomic bomb and that Japan's survival was at risk.

*   *   *

In Moscow, Japanese ambassador Satô Naotake had been summoned to meet at 6:00 P.M. with Vyacheslav Mikhailovich Molotov, Chairman of the Council of People's Commissars and People's Commissar of Foreign Affairs of the Union of Soviet Socialist Republics. It was a meeting for which Satô had long been waiting. Later, the time was moved up to 5:00 P.M. at Molotov's request. At precisely 5:00 P.M. Ambassador Satô arrived. Satô welcomed Molotov back from his meeting at Potsdam. Molotov was not as effusive, cutting Satô off and waving him to a chair. Then Molotov read aloud a document: a Soviet declaration of war against the Empire of Japan.

*   *   *

Ken and his pilot returned to the plane and took off. In his tunic was General Arisue's report. He looked at his watch; it was 1600 hours. Barring American fighter planes they would arrive in Tôkyô in three hours, by 7:00 P.M., where he would deliver the report and return to Oba-*san*'s *ryokan* and make ready to fly from Atsugi to Iwô Jima or Okinawa.

When he returned to Tsukiji Oba-*san* quickly prepared dinner. It was simple yet tasteful. She wanted to ask questions about the *Kempeitai* but knew that would be risky so refrained. She noticed that Ken seemed anxious and he saw her looking at him.

"Oba-*san*, I will leave tomorrow. You may keep the balance of the rent; use it as you see fit. You have been a gracious host and I will recommend your establishment to different officers who may soon come to Tôkyô."

33

August 9

Around 7:50 A.M. an air raid alert shook the residents of Nagasaki, a major shipbuilding city with a large military port. The residents had long-dreaded the arrival of *B-san*. There was tangible relief when the "all clear" signal sounded at 8:30 A.M.

Then at 10:53 A.M. two B-29s were sighted but the military, assuming that the planes were solely on a reconnaissance mission, chose not to sound an air raid alert.

At 11:00 A.M. a B-29 named *The Great Artiste*, piloted by Captain Frederick C. Bock, released instruments attached to three parachutes.

Another B-29 named *Bock's Car*, piloted by Major Charles Sweeney, followed. At 11:01 A.M. the plane's bombardier, Captain Kermit Beahan, found a break in the clouds and informed Major Sweeney that he could see the target. A bomb, named "Fat Man," was released.

After forty-three seconds, at a height of about 1,650 feet, exactly halfway between the Mitsubishi Steel and Arms Works in the south and the Mitsubishi-Urakami Torpedo Works in the north, "Fat Man" exploded.

Days earlier, numerous survivors of the Hiroshima bombing had traveled to Nagasaki seeking safety.

St. Mary's Cathedral Church, the largest Christian church in Asia, was destroyed.

Northern Nagasaki ceased to exist.

34

Oba-*san* carried Ken's bag to the first floor. He objected but only mildly; it was her last act as hostess. At the door he removed his slippers and put on his boots and stood straight. She bowed, certain she would never see him again. He smiled at her while thinking of *Okami-san*. He picked up his bag and she opened the door for him. He stepped out, turned and bowed to her then walked away, knowing he would never see her again.

He walked down the narrow street and took a turn, heading toward Tsukiji Station. The street was empty. People would soon be leaving their homes for work, like him, heading to Tsukiji Station. He soon neared the Tsukiji Hongwanji Buddhist Temple, which he had visited several times while at *Tôdai*. He had found it interesting that when it was rebuilt after the 1923 Great Kanto Earthquake the ferroconcrete structure was designed with an Indian motif. He had always been fascinated that most worshipers at the temple were Buddhist despite living in the capital of a Shintôist culture. He recalled the grandeur of the Main Worship Hall with an image of Amida Buddha and considered going inside for a moment of reflection. As he approached the rear of the temple his thoughts were interrupted by movement to his right.

"Shôsa!"

Ken stopped. The voice was loud and sharp, like a rifle

shot. Emerging from a small alley was the one person he never expected to see: the *Tokkô* cop from the train, the man whose nose he had broken. The cop held his pistol, a Model 26 double-action revolver, in his right hand. His feet were spread apart as if in an American cowboy movie. His broken nose was bandaged. Ken smiled at the image in his mind: the town sheriff with a broken nose arresting the bad guy. The cop's face reddened, angry that Ken was smiling.

Ken said benignly. "Ah, Major, are you still angry with me?" He moved several steps closer to the cop.

"Stop there, Shôsa! I spoke with the *Kempeitai* yesterday. They told me about your trip to Hiroshima. I investigated further. There are no records of you at Imperial Army Headquarters." He moved closer to Ken. "Who are you?"

Ken knew he was in a tight spot. But he saw the cop's hand shaking. *I was right*, he thought, *just a paper pusher. Probably never fired a gun at anyone in his life.*

Ken closed his eyes for a moment and remembered all the years that Tom and he had studied *kendô*, the way of the sword, under the tutelage of their father, Katsuo. To avoid injury Katsuo Kobayashi and his sons used the *shinai*, a sword-like weapon made of four bamboo slats tied together by three leather strips. Like the *katana* it had a *tsuka* or hilt and a *tsuba* or hand guard between the blade and the hilt. It also had a leather *sakigawa* to cover the tips of the slats to prevent penetrating injuries. The design of the *shinai* mimicked the *katana* but the flexible bamboo slats insured that no bones were broken. But the training was the same as with the *katana*. Under their father's guidance they had mastered *kendô* and years later, while at *Tôdai*, they had proven their worth at several matches, often to the chagrin of the Japanese *shinpan* or umpire. But he was not facing his father, brother or another student and there were no *shinpan* to referee.

"Why do you question me, Major?"

"Why would an officer help a cripple who should have died honorably on the battlefield? Coming home with one less leg places a burden on others!"

"Perhaps," retorted Ken, "others on the battlefield saw it differently and chose to save his life. Have you ever been on a battlefield, Major?"

The cop's eyes widened as his lips bowed down. His fingers whitened as he gripped his pistol tighter. *I was right*, thought Ken, *a damn desk jockey.*

Ken casually looked to his left and right and saw no one else on the street. Then he looked into the eyes of the *Tokkô* cop and slowly blinked once. The cop looked into Ken's eyes, searching for something. Ken dropped his bag. The cop looked down as it hit the ground. He never saw Ken pull his *katana*. He did see his lower right arm hit the ground near the bag with his pistol locked in his lifeless fingers. Ken stepped aside quickly to avoid the spurts of blood from the severed arteries just below the elbow. The last thing the cop saw was Ken's *katana* as it arced toward the right side of his neck. His knees buckled then his body collapsed, lying next to his head. So swift and adept were the strokes no blood stained the blade.

Ken looked around again. The street was empty. He sheathed his *katana*, removed the pistol from the cop's lifeless hand and hurled it into the alley, followed by the arm and head. Then he dragged the body into the alley and covered all with trash.

He stood still for a moment, surprised that he was composed; the cop was the first man he had killed. But, given the behavior of the cop on the train, he had no misgivings. He returned to the street, reached for his bag, then froze. Kempeitai, he thought. *He spoke with the* Kempeitai. *They know.* He turned and looked down the alley.

"Fool! The *Kempeitai* are coming to arrest me but you thought you'd be a hero and arrest me first. You're not John

Wayne!" He then laughed nervously realizing he was speaking in English.

Ken grabbed his bag and made his way to Tsukiji Station. As he approached he saw that the area was crowded with people. Less than a third of a mile away was St. Luke's Hospital and undoubtedly many were going to it for work or medical, care. Others would take the trolley to the center of Tôkyô.

Like several major buildings in Tôkyô, St. Luke's Hospital had purposefully not been bombed. The U.S. Army knew that with the invasion the hospital would be needed for wounded American soldiers, Marines and pilots. Ken acknowledged the foresight and absolute confidence of U.S. military planners.

He slowed his pace, not wanting to attract attention. But as he neared the waiting trolley he knew it was too late. A military truck was racing toward him, full of *Kempeitai*. People scattered but they were not looking at the truck. Ken heard the roar of other engines. He looked over his shoulder. The hair on his neck prickled. Four carrier-based Marine F4U-4 Corsairs, the inverted gull-winged fighter plane that Japanese forces dreaded, were diving directly toward the station. Ken heard the "whistling death" scream from the planes' wings. Japanese continued to scatter, most running toward sidewalk shelters. The *Kempeitai* in the truck futilely fired their rifles at the Corsairs. One of the Corsair's pilots opened up with its six .50 caliber Browning machine guns, shredding the truck and the men in it. Two seconds later the truck exploded. Another Corsair headed toward running civilians.

Ken watched with horror as a woman, carrying a kid, ran toward a sidewalk shelter. She tripped and dropped the child. She quickly got to her feet and grabbed the kid by the hand and began dragging the child while heading to the shelter. She fell again and lost her grip on the kid. Ken did not hesitate. He ran toward her and pushed her into the trench then reached for the kid. At that instant a .50 caliber bullet hit the corner of the adjacent concrete building and broke into pieces. A piece of the bullet, deformed to about the diameter of a silver dollar, struck Ken in the back, a few inches below his right scapula, and sliced through muscle tissue. The force of the penetrating bullet fragment threw Ken forward. His forehead struck the ground but his torso covered the kid's body. Then the Corsairs flew off, seemingly seeking other targets. No one moved for several seconds, knowing that American planes often returned for a second or even third run. But no planes turned back; there was silence and collective relief. Then the woman crawled out of the trench and ran toward Ken, seeking her child. She pushed Ken aside and found her child, who was crying but otherwise uninjured; she picked up the child. She turned her attention to Ken, now unconscious. She saw the blood flowing from his wound. She turned to some of the men still in the trench.

"I am a doctor at Saint Luke's Hospital. Please carry this soldier to the hospital." The men hesitated. "Quickly!" Several men left the safety of the trench and lifted Ken, heading quickly toward St. Luke's. "You!" she said as she pointed to another man. "Pick up his bag and follow us!" One of the men carrying Ken lifted his scabbard to insure that it would not drag on the ground.

When they arrived at St. Luke's Ken was placed on a gurney, face down. The doctor handed her child to one of the nurses and told her to take Ken's bag. She then directed the gurney into an examining room.

Since St. Luke's Hospital was built and rebuilt with American missionary funding and American missionary doctors had practiced there the design was Western, exterior and interior. The room, like many city hospitals in America, was sterile and spartan. The walls were covered with white tiles, easy to wash and disinfect. Metal trays and glass-fronted metal cabinets held stainless steel vessels which contained all the paraphernalia or liquids, such as instruments, gauze or isopropyl alcohol that doctors and nurses would need to treat the sick and injured. Lights which would cast brightness onto patients were located in corners, to be pulled out as needed.

The doctor ordered a nurse to cut away Ken's tunic and shirt while she washed her hands and filled a pan with water and a bar of soap. She grabbed a clean towel, dipped it into the pan and rubbed it with the soap, then wiped the congealed blood from Ken's back. She was gratified that the blood from the wound flowed rather than pumped; no artery had been cut. But she knew that he needed surgery and, being a surgeon, she decided to perform it in the room.

Two more nurses appeared and helped the doctor prepare for surgery. All of them put on a cap and mask. One nurse poured diluted potassium permanganate, a topical antiseptic, over the doctor's hands to disinfect them. At the same time another nurse was washing Ken's back with the same solution. The disinfectant lent a vivid purple color to Ken's back. With all the movement and noise about him Ken began to moan; he was regaining consciousness. A nurse looked at the doctor, who nodded. The nurse got a wire mesh ether mask, put gauze between the two layers of the mask and poured ether on the gauze then put the ether mask over Ken's mouth and nose; Ken inhaled the fumes. In seconds he was deeply asleep. The other nurse rolled Ken on his left side for two reasons. One was to assure that he did not regurgitate stomach contents into his esophagus and aspirate them into his lungs; the second was to elevate his right shoulder to make it easier for the doctor to perform surgery on the wound. She would hold him in that position throughout the operation.

After the doctor dried her hands the other nurse gowned her over her street clothes and put rubber gloves on her hands. The doctor noted that the gloves had been repaired due to prior use. *We are at war,* she thought, not for the first time.

She took the scalpel from the nurse, stretched Ken's

skin, and made a clean incision above and below the entrance wound, enlarging it so she could have a clear view. Bleeders were tied off. She worked with practiced skill; this was not the first war-related injury she had treated. She then cut through connective tissue and muscle and exposed the ribs. She saw that one rib had been nicked by the bullet fragment and a piece of the rib had broken off. She explored for the bone piece, found and plucked it. To be certain it was the only piece broken off she placed it in the nick of the rib; it fit perfectly. She dropped it into a pan. She could not see the bullet fragment and knew it had bounced off the rib or migrated. Seeing Ken's lung expand she knew the fragment had not penetrated it. She examined the muscle tissue but could find no other wound track. Then she smiled. She lifted the inferior or lower portion of Ken's scapula and inserted her index finger under it and felt for the fragment. There! It moved, so it was not embedded in bone or tissue. With her index finger and thumb she grabbed the fragment and carefully removed it, dropping it into the pan. She inserted her index finger back under the scapula and felt for other tissue injuries. She felt none and when she withdrew her finger she saw little blood. She knew her patient would have some bone pain for perhaps a week but his rib would not miss the chipped piece. She took a final survey for any other sources of bleeding or foreign material such as cloth from his tunic, knowing it could lead to infection; she saw none. She began the easiest part, suturing tissue as she withdrew, starting with connective and muscle tissue then the skin. It was a quick procedure. At no time had she considered a blood transfusion given his size; she estimated that he had lost no more than half a liter.

"Clean the rest of his back and bandage the wound," she said to the nurse. The other nurse had already stopped the ether. "I'll be back directly."

The doctor removed her mask, cap and gown then left the room. At the desk she asked where her child was.

"Doctor Masamune, Takuma-*chan* is here," said an aide with a smile.

Dr. Masamune smiled and took her son from the aide. "I am sorry but I had to take care of someone. He saved you. Is that not wonderful?"

The boy nodded several times and grinned.

"Good. I'm going back to work but just for a few minutes. You stay here with Akane-*san*. I'll be right back!"

Dr. Masamune returned to the room. One of the nurses had removed Ken's boots, socks and pants. He was still face down. Dr. Masamune checked his vital signs and made certain that the bandaging was sufficient. All seemed well. Then she froze.

Her eyes had taken a thoughtful survey of his body and saw a scar on his lower back, just above his *fundoshi*. Kyoko stepped back a few feet and grabbed the edge of a table; it was hard for her to breathe. She looked at the nurses. Neither had seen her reaction. She waited a moment then walked back to Ken. She touched the scar, the same one she had seen and touched when they had first made love. Her breathing became rapid as the room spun around. *Brace up*, she thought, *brace up!* The scar, shaped like a shark's tooth, was about three inches long with the distal tip pointing toward his right kidney.

What is he doing here, Kyoko asked herself. *Why is he here?* She looked at the nurses again. She gathered herself and thought quickly.

"This patient is an officer. I will inform the Army that he is here. Cover him and move him to a private room."

The nurses did as ordered.

She watched them as they wheeled Ken out of the room. Her heart was still racing, her breathing shallow. *He is not Japanese; he's an American*, she thought. *What do I do?* And she was confronted with another, more powerful emotion: she knew she had not stopped loving him. She took several moments to compose herself before leaving the room.

She went to the admitting desk. "The soldier I brought in. Did he have any identification?"

"Yes, Dr. Masamune. The nurse just gave it to me."

"Give it to me. I have to contact the Army."

The woman gave Ken's identification to Kyoko. She stepped away and looked at it. She was stunned. It had a real name and age but it was an Imperial Japanese Army document. *How can this be*, she thought. "What room is he in?"

"He is on this floor; room twenty-two."

As she headed to room twenty-two the aide Akane approached her, still holding Takuma. "Doctor Masamune, Takuma-*chan* wants to be with you! He is such a good boy!"

Kyoko looked at her boy and feared for him; the *Tokkô* police were feared by all. "Akane-*san*, I want you to take Takuma to my parents' home. Tell them that I have to work today and possibly through tonight."

"*Hai.*"

"Please, go now." She hugged her boy then returned him to Akane. Kyoko, on the verge of tears, quickly walked away, heading instead to the pediatric ward to look at her patients, knowing that Kenji would not awaken for a few hours. When she entered the ward what she saw was the same: children malnourished, others suffering from tuberculosis or other respiratory ailments. Many had worms in their intestines and many more had skin ulcerations that would not heal. In almost all cases there were no medications for civilians, especially the elderly and young. The military had not hesitated to hoard what was available. Only her professionalism kept her emotions in check. But in the face of every child she saw Takuma. And her feelings about Kenji kept intruding. She tended to her patients for a time then looked at her watch and decided to go to Kenji's room. She avoided faces as she walked to room twenty-two.

She opened the door and closed it behind her. She stared

at his face. Her emotions, uncontrollable, were like a roller coaster, longing for him and fear that his presence might harm her family. She looked out the window and wrestled with her feelings. Then Ken moaned. She turned to look at him and saw his head move; he was waking. She looked at his face as he neared consciousness. She moved closer and waited.

Ken opened his eyes; everything was unfocused. He felt the urge to vomit but suppressed it, a normal reaction to ether. As his eyes focused he looked around, confused. It took a few minutes to remember what had happened. The last that he recalled was running toward a child.

Then he saw Kyoko and caught his breath. She was wearing a skirt and blouse. Her hair was long, like other women he had seen. And she had lost weight.

"Kyoko? Is that you?" he wondered aloud. "Where am I?"

She breathed deeply. "You are in a hospital," she said in English.

"Why?"

"You were injured while saving a child. American planes attacked not far from here."

"Yes, I remember. How is the kid?"

"A boy. He is fine. You probably saved his life. That is how you were injured."

Ken was regaining his full wits. He saw and felt her stiffness and he became wary. "And the woman? Is she okay?"

Kyoko stiffened. "Yes, you saved her as well."

He tried to lift himself up on his elbows but winced at the pain.

"You should stay flat," she said. "You just had surgery and we have no pain medicine."

He lay back. "Kyoko, why are you here?"

"I work here. I am a surgeon."

"What hospital is this?"

"Saint Luke's."

"Did you operate on me?"

"Yes. It was the least I could do. You pushed me into the shelter and saved my son's life as well."

That stung him. *So you did marry*, he thought. "Thank you for operating on me."

They both paused, gathering themselves.

"Kenji, why are *you* here?"

He expected the question and was unsure what would happen if he told her. He knew he could not lie; she would see right through that. She had always been able to do so. He inhaled deeply, which caused him to wince again.

"The United States is going to invade Japan in a few months. I came here to find out how Japan intends to defend itself against an invasion."

"Did you find out," she asked sarcastically.

"Yes. The Japanese military will defend Japan to the last man, woman and child. Perhaps even your child."

That stung her and he saw it. "Kyoko, I'm sorry. You didn't deserve that. What is your son's name?"

"Takuma."

"Interesting name. 'Explorer'?"

"Yes. After this damn war is over I hope that he will travel to different lands."

"To get away from Japan?"

"No. To get away from war. Are you a spy?"

"Technically, yes."

"What does that mean?"

"I want this war to end as soon as possible. We, I mean America, knows that the Japanese military has been training millions of civilians to fight Americans. Most of the civilians are armed with bamboo sticks. A few days ago I saw young boys being trained to run under American tanks and trucks with dynamite on their backs. It's insane. Japan has lost the war but the military won't stop fighting. I want it to end now. I don't want any more Americans or Japanese to die needlessly."

"What do you intend to do?"

"Get back to an American base and make my report."

"So more Japanese will die?"

"Have you looked in a mirror lately? I know Japan is on rations. Everyone is starving. You have lost weight."

"We all have to make sacrifices."

"Not everyone. The Imperial Japanese Army is doing just fine; I was at Atsugi. The food was plentiful."

"What did you mean when you said Japan has lost?"

"U.S. intelligence monitors all Japanese broadcasts. We know that the population has been told that every defeat is in fact a Japanese victory. Kyoko, the Japanese Navy no longer exists; it has been destroyed. The only ships in the Pacific are American, British and Australian. All the Japanese carriers and battleships have been sunk. It's over."

Kyoko became angry and scared. "I do not believe you! Why are you lying?"

Ken too became angry. "Have you heard about Hiroshima? Have you heard any American or British radio broadcasts?"

"No. And it is against the law to listen to foreign radio broadcasts. What about Hiroshima?"

"You don't know?"

"Know what? Two days ago it was announced that a few B-29s had dropped a new type of bomb. You are frightening me. Tell me!"

"Hiroshima was completely destroyed three days ago."

Kyoko stepped away from Ken's bed. "What do you mean?"

"The United States has developed a new bomb. Just one bomb destroyed the entire city. Perhaps tens of thousands were killed instantly."

"This is not possible! How do you know this?"

"I was there the day after. I saw concrete buildings reduced to rubble. Buildings made of wood disappeared. People were simply vaporized."

"How can this be? How can a city be destroyed by only one bomb?"

"It is called an atomic bomb. Japan tried to develop one but failed. The United States succeeded. Hiroshima is gone."

Kyoko heard the resignation in Ken's voice and sat down, tears streaming down her cheeks.

"When do you have to leave to make your report?"

"As soon as I can. I think the reason the American planes attacked today in Tsukiji was because they saw an army truck. They are looking for any target they can find; there are so few left."

"What will you do?"

"Get back to Atsugi and fly to Iwô Jima or Okinawa."

"You cannot fly to Okinawa. It is an Imperial Japanese Army base."

Ken sighed. "The United States conquered Okinawa in June."

Her eyes expressed astonishment but she seemed to ignore his statement. "How will you fly? Do you have a pilot?"

"I'll fly my plane."

"You will not be able to do that. Your shoulder will stiffen up even more. And your eye may soon swell shut. You will have to stay here for a few days."

"I can't. That truck that the American planes attacked was full of *Kempeitai* who were coming to arrest me. I have to leave as soon as possible."

"I am sorry. It is impossible for you to fly."

"I can't stay here. The *Kempeitai* will find me."

Kyoko walked toward the window and looked outside for several minutes.

"I read your letters," she said.

"What? What letters?"

"Those you wrote after you returned to America."

"I never heard from you."

"I know. My father did not post my letters to you and he kept your letters from me. I am sorry."

She had written to him several times before the war broke out but he had never replied. Or so she had thought. In 1944 her mother had given her the letters that Kyoko thought had been posted to Ken and Ken's letters to her. Her father had intercepted both and hid them.

What Kyoko had read in Ken's letters made her ache even more; he had avowed his continued love for her and promised he would return to Japan in early 1942. Then in September 1941 the letters from Ken had stopped. With the revelation from her mother in 1944 Kyoko understood why. Ken had assumed that she was not responding to his letters. For weeks she had not spoken to her father.

She turned. "I have to leave for a while but I'll be back. Stay in bed; don't try to get up."

"Kyoko, are you going to call the *Kempeitai*?"

Kyoko turned. The initial anger in her eyes was quickly superseded by the pain of his question. "No." She left, closing the door behind her.

As Ken lay in the bed he recalled his promise to Admiral Halsey to take his life if captured. He wondered how he could do it. Perhaps breaking the glass window and slicing his veins. When he tried to rise the pain in his shoulder forced him back. He decided to wait. He did not know why but his gut told him to trust Kyoko. Time passed slowly; the sun began to set. He closed his eyes and soon fell asleep.

Kyoko stopped in the corridor and knew she had to find a place of seclusion. She walked to the pharmacy room. With her key she unlocked the door and entered. She stood against the door for several moments then turned and locked it. She walked to a chair.

Despite her training and professional stoicism to the suffering surrounding her every day, Ken's sudden appearance melted that wall. All the pent-up feelings of loneliness and misperceived rejection by Kenji, her inability to express interest in other men and the nights of restless emotional and physical desire came crashing down upon her, and she cried as never before. She spent a half-hour in the room, letting out all her repressed emotions. The release was needed and beneficial. When she composed herself she went to the sink and washed her face and waited a bit longer until the puffiness of her eyes began to recede. She breathed deeply several times and left the pharmacy room. She knew she would have to deal with him. Then an idea formed in her head and she headed to a supply closet and grabbed some clothing and shoes.

She returned to Kenji's room and closed the door then leaned against it, as if barring intrusion. She looked at him, again asleep. She placed the clothing on the chair then walked closer to Ken. Still a doctor, she looked at his forehead; a lump and scratches but no more. She knew he would have a black eye by midday if not sooner. She stepped back, tears welling in her eyes. Confusion was her only comfort. *Why are you here*, she thought. *What are you doing in Japan?* She sat in another chair and looked out the window, recalling their relationship and the pain she felt when he had returned to America.

He was awoken by a hand on his left shoulder. He opened his eyes; it was Kyoko.

"I'm going to help you get up. I have some clothes for you."

He was surprised at her strength as she aided him to a sitting position, his legs dangling from the side of the bed. Suddenly the room tilted and she steadied him.

"It will pass in a moment. Just sit there."

"That was strange," he said.

"It is a combination of loss of blood and the ether and your blood pressure dropped. It will pass in a moment."

He looked at the chair and saw the *kokumin-fuku*—national wear—the drab semi-military khaki uniform worn by male workers.

He also saw his bag, holster with pistol in place, and *katana*. His boots were replaced by worn leather ankle shoes, and *tabi*, white socks. Kyoko also had a smaller bag with her.

"It's going to look strange if I wear these clothes and carry a *katana*, don't you think?"

For the first time he saw her smile.

"Trust me. I know what I am doing. Can you stand up?"

"Yes, I think so, if you steady me." She was careful as she put her arm under his left armpit and helped him to stand. Again he felt light-headed and she steadied him. His wooziness passed in a moment. He stood clad only in his *fundoshi*. She looked at his body. It was still hard and strong and her memories returned. He saw her face redden.

"So, what do you have in mind," he asked.

"You need to hide while you heal. I am going to take you to my place."

"Won't your parents object?"

"I have my own place. I rent a room in a home not far from here; it is small but it will do. No one knows about it, including my parents. It is about a kilometer from here. Do you think you can walk that far?"

"Sure. It's my shoulder, not my legs."

"Are you still dizzy?"

"No. I'll be fine. What do we do next? I can't leave my sword."

"I know." She got her bag and pulled out several rolls of white gauze tape. She got his *katana* and placed it against his outer right leg. "Here, hold this in place."

Ken did so as Kyoko tied the sword to his leg, starting at the calf and working her way up to his crotch. She fleetingly looked at the bulge in his *fundoshi* and closed her eyes a brief moment. She nervously licked her lips then tied the last strip.

"There. Too tight? Can you walk with that?"

"Let me try." She supported him while he took a few steps. "It's fine."

Kyoko got his pants and knelt down as he lifted his right leg with his hand on her shoulder. She pulled the right pant leg up over his foot.

"Good. Lower this leg and lift the other one."

He did so and she put the pants on and then drew them up to his waist and tied the rope that substituted for a belt. Her face neared his crotch and she paused a second, her hands shaking. *Too many memories*, she thought.

"Sit back on the bed." She got the socks and shoes and put them on him. "Stand up." She put the jacket on him. It was long enough to hide the bulge of the *katana*'s *tsuba*, the hand guard.

She put his holster in his bag then put his worker's cap on his head. "There, you look like every other worker in Japan."

"Now what do we do?"

"It is late. We leave here and go to the rear exit of the hospital then walk to my place. Are you sure you can walk?"

"I'll be fine. You lead the way."

"Let me look first. Sit down on the bed. I want to be certain we are not seen." Kyoko left the room and looked at both ends of the corridor; it was empty. She went back to Ken's room. "We can go."

Ken stood and waited a moment. He was still woozy. Kyoko grabbed his bag then grabbed his left arm, leading him out. When they entered the corridor it was still empty. They turned to the right, heading further away from the main entrance and reception desk. Though in pain, Ken walked at her pace but with an awkward limp due to the *katana* strapped to his leg. They soon reached the rear door and she opened it and they exited the building.

Kyoko stopped for a moment. "Walking will be painful for your shoulder. I would have put your arm in a sling but that might raise questions if someone approaches us. Can you keep your arm steady while we walk?"

"Sure," said Ken.

It was dark and few people were about. They did not speak as she led him. It was fortunate she knew the way as Tôkyô was in blackout. Only the moon illuminated their path. A few times Ken had to stop. His loss of blood and the pain were taking their toll. Soon, after just over a half-mile, they arrived. Ken stopped.

"Kyoko, wait. What about your husband?"

At first she was puzzled at the question then understood his thinking; she had a son. "I do not have a husband."

Ken, confused, did not speak. They entered the building and Kyoko removed her shoes then untied and removed Ken's. They put on slippers. To be safe she took his shoes and they went to her rented room. She turned on a dim light and looked at the one window, making certain it was covered. Ken looked around. The room was similar in size to his in Tsukiji, a six-*tatami* space. It was neat and clean. On one side of the room, opposite the window, was a *futon*. Kyoko put Ken's and her bag down. There was a wooden chair in a corner and she led Ken to it. "Do not sit yet." She removed his cap and jacket then untied the waist rope of his pants and pulled them down. Then, while Ken held his *katana* she removed the gauze tape from his leg. She took the sword from him and placed it in the corner behind the chair. She then helped him put his pants back on.

"Whose house is this," he asked.

"It is a married couple. He works and she stays home. Their children have been evacuated to the country."

"They won't mind my being here?"

"If you are quiet they will not know. Sit. Are you hungry?"

"Starving."

"Of course, you have not eaten all day." She busied herself preparing food for both of them. As she arranged the food Ken looked at the room again. On a small table was a radio. He smiled. It was a Philco radio, the one Tom and he had taken to Japan in 1937 because it had two shortwave bands and could pick up radio broadcasts from Hawaii. Two weeks before Ken left he had given it to Kyoko, telling her she could listen to American Jazz.

He remembered the argument he had had with Tom about Ken giving it to Kyoko. Ken ended the argument by pointing out that he had paid for the radio before they had left California and that, because Tom was going to stay in Japan, perhaps the Japanese government would give him a new one in gratitude.

Kyoko brought the food. It was not fresh but it was good. She handed Ken his food, allowing him to stay in his chair. Kyoko placed hers on a small table. Ken, ravenous, began to eat with his fingers, not waiting for *hashi*, or chopsticks.

"Kenji-*san, hashiwa dô desu ka.*" Kenji, would you like chopsticks?

He was embarrassed and smiled sheepishly. She handed him a pair of chopsticks and returned to the table. For the first time Kyoko smiled, though she hid her response with her hand. She watched him eat and was pleased that he had not lost his skill in using *hashi. And he is still handsome*, she thought.

They ate in silence, each occupied with their thoughts. He knew he could not get back to Atsugi, to his plane, and that he would have to get to a boat. But first he would have to find a radio transmitter to send a coded signal to the U.S. Navy.

Kyoko was concerned about her son and her parents. Should the *Kempeitai* or *Tokkô* find out that she had helped an American spy she and her family would be in danger. Yet she was torn. Her feelings for Kenji had never faded. Being with him now only enflamed them anew. She saw that he had finished eating and was fading. She put down her bowl and chopsticks and got up.

"Kenji-*san*, you need to sleep."

"Yes. Where?"

"The *futon*."

"Where will you sleep?"

"I have some blankets. I can sleep on one."

"I can sleep on the blanket."

"It is better for your back."

"Are you sure?"

"I know better. I am a doctor."

"I need to use a toilet."

"I will take you."

She led him to the common bathroom. He stopped at the door and looked at her, embarrassed. "It is all right," she said. "I am a doctor, remember?"

Sheepishly, he allowed her to help him to the toilet. He needed to urinate. She untied and lowered his pants then his *fundoshi* and he squatted over the horizontal toilet while he urinated. She tried to turn away but could not. She felt her skin flush as her vagina moistened.

Out of habit he shook his penis and could not help thinking, *Good to the last drop.* She watched. He stood and she pulled up his *fundoshi* and his pants and tied the knot. Nothing was said and she led him back to her room. She directed him to the *futon* and helped him lay down and spread a blanket over him. She got two blankets and a pillow for herself, laying one blanket down on a *tatami* not far from Ken. Then she turned her back to him and undressed to her underwear. When she turned to put out the light she saw that Ken was asleep. She lay on her blanket and pulled the other one over her. In the darkness she reached over and touched his arm.

35

The men assembled were nervous, despite their power. It was 11:30 P.M. Earlier they had been summoned to Emperor Hirohito's bomb shelter, about eighteen meters beneath the Fukiage Gardens, at the Imperial Palace. The room, about five and one-half meters by seven meters, was oppressively hot. There were two sets of tables on either side of the room, each covered by linen with a checkered pattern. At the head of the room was a smaller table covered with gold damask. A plain screen stood behind the table's single chair. Emperor Hirohito would sit at this table.

Six of the men in the room controlled Japan's future. They formed the *Gunji Sangikan Kaigi*, Supreme Council for the Direction of the War. Those in military uniforms, all high-collared, felt the heat more so. The civilians wore formal morning attire. All were sweating.

The members of the *Gunji Sangikan Kaigi* included Prime Minister Baron Suzuki Kantarô, a revered hero of the Russo-Japanese War of 1904-1905. He was named Prime Minister shortly after the Americans had conquered Okinawa. He was seventy-seven years old and very tired. He was deaf in one ear and often dozed off during meetings. And up until tonight he had been irritatingly indecisive during and after previous meetings that had been held after Hiroshima had been destroyed.

During those previous meetings Suzuki had either favored or opposed acceptance of the Potsdam Declaration of July 26, 1945, which demanded Japan's unconditional surrender. Tonight he favored acceptance.

Another was Foreign Minister Tôgô Shigenori. He was a towering intellect and did not suffer fools gladly. Many egos had been severely bruised by his tongue lashings. He had opposed war with America and throughout World War II he had doubted that Japan could win. In September 1942 he had been ousted by the military. In April 1945 he resumed his position. And like Suzuki he advocated acceptance of the Potsdam Declaration.

The third member of the Supreme Council was Navy Minister Admiral Yonai Mitsumasa. Admiral Yonai had been Prime Minister from January to July 1940. He had been forced to resign by the military because he had opposed an alliance with Nazi Germany and Italy. He too favored accepting the Potsdam Declaration.

The fourth was General Umezu Yoshijirô, Chief of the Army General Staff. General Umezu had been Vice Minister of War from 1936 to 1938. After that role he had been given command of the Kwangtung Army in China, from 1939 to 1944. Until Japan went on the defensive against the United States, the Kwangtung Army was the largest ground force in the Imperial Japanese Army. However, with U.S. forces approaching Japan, the Kwangtung Army was stripped of its best units and equipment, which were sent to fight American forces. In 1944 Umezu became Chief of the Army General Staff and a member of the *Gunji Sangikan Kaigi*. General Umezu opposed the Potsdam Declaration.

Fifth was Admiral Toyoda Soemu, Chief of the Navy General Staff. Two months before Japan attacked Pearl Harbor Admiral Toyoda was promoted to full admiral and was Commander-in-Chief of the Kure Naval District. He vehemently opposed war with the United States, which he believed Japan could not win. However, he too opposed the Potsdam Declaration.

The last and most powerful member of the *Gunji Sangikan Kaigi* was General Anami Korechika, Minister of War. In May 1943 General Anami was promoted to full general and in November was assigned to the Southern Theater, directing operations in New Guinea and Halmahera, both conquered by U.S. forces. He was recalled to Japan in December 1944 and joined the Supreme Council. In April 1945 he was appointed Minister of War. He was a true believer in the code of *Bushidô*. Despite the destruction of Hiroshima and Nagasaki General Anami opposed the Potsdam Declaration.

The Supreme Council had debated the Potsdam Declaration from the time they had received it through foreign neutral channels. During the prior meetings Prime Minister Suzuki would often waffle, one moment accepting the Potsdam Declaration; then, when General Anami whispered in his ear, he would oppose acceptance, which Foreign Minister Tôgô found infuriating.

The others attending included Chief Cabinet Secretary Sakomizu Hisatsune; Baron Hiranuma Kiichirô, former prime minister and now president of the Privy Council, an advisory group to the Emperor; Lt. General Yoshizumi Masao, chief of the Military Affairs Bureau, who would act as the army's secretary; Vice Admiral Hoshina Zenshirô, director of the Bureau of Naval affairs, who would act as the navy's secretary, and Lt. General Ikeda Sumihisa, director of the Cabinet Planning Bureau, delegated to respond to any detailed questions.

The seating arrangement was awkward and at the same time strategic. The three army representatives sat at the table which would be to Emperor Hirohito's left. They were flanked by Prime Minister Suzuki, closest to Emperor Hirohito, and Sakomizu at the other end. At the opposite table were Admiral

Yonai, Foreign Minister Tôgô, Admiral Toyoda, Vice Admiral Hoshina, and at the head of the table, to the right of Emperor Hirohito, was Baron Hiranuma.

In front of each man were three documents: the Potsdam Declaration, the position paper of the peace advocates and the position paper of the peace opponents. They sat in silence and waited.

At 11:50 P.M. a door at the front of the room opened and Emperor Hirohito, escorted by his military aide General Hasunuma Shigeru, entered. Everyone stood and bowed from the waist. Emperor Hirohito acknowledged their gesture with a slight nod and sat at the table in a straight-backed wooden chair. He was dressed in a military uniform. His audience was alarmed. He looked weary. His face was red and strands of hair hung down on his forehead.

He had been well-briefed earlier in the day by Suzuki and Tôgô on the purpose of the meeting. He had been asked to do something that he had been taught from boyhood an Emperor should not.

Suzuki began the meeting by asking Sakomizu to read the Potsdam Declaration. When this was done Suzuki began his presentation.

"Your Majesty, we are now beginning the second meeting today of the Supreme Council for the Direction of the War. At a lengthy session this morning, we diligently discussed the question of whether our government, under the strain of the present difficult situation, should accept the terms of the declaration you have just heard. After three hours of debate, we could come to no conclusion. Thereupon, the cabinet was called into session this afternoon, but after almost seven hours of debate on the same issue, was unable to reach unanimity. Since a decision cannot be postponed any longer, I have asked permission to discuss the issue before Your Majesty, even though I realize it is unthinkable to take such a step."

Suzuki then turned slightly toward Admiral Toyoda and General Umezu. He continued. "I wish to apologize for requesting Your Majesty to meet with us even though we are unable to inform you of any decision by the government. But I have done so because we have reached an apparently unbreakable deadlock."

He then went on to explain the division within the Supreme Council then turned to his foreign minister. "I would like to have Tôgô-*san* explain his views on the issue."

Tôgô stood, his sharp mind prepared. "It is both humiliating and terribly difficult for Japan to accept the Potsdam terms. However, present circumstances compel us." He then elaborated with details of the military state of affairs, cities destroyed, morale of the population, destruction of industries, the risk of a Soviet invasion and the atomic threat to the entire nation.

"It is with all of these inescapable factors in mind that I urgently recommend our immediate acceptance of the Potsdam terms. And I wish to point out the danger of making our acceptance contingent upon too many conditions. If we try to impose several conditions, the Allied nations may reject all of them. I strongly suggest, therefore, that we stipulate only one condition—the safety of our Royal House and the perpetuation of our imperial system."

General Anami seethed with anger. He realized a trap had been sprung and that he, Umezu and Toyoda were backed into a corner. He leaned toward Umezu on his left and whispered, "It begins to look as if there actually is a scheme afoot. Tôgô is presenting their plan. They have said nothing about presenting our plan. We cannot let them get away with that. Perhaps we should stop discussing surrender terms and insist on an all-out continuance of the war."

In fact, Anami, Toyoda and Umezu were prepared to accept the Potsdam Declaration based on four conditions:

Maintain the imperial system;

No Allied occupation of the Japanese Home Islands;
Japan will disarm its own military forces;
Japan will arrest and prosecute Japanese war criminals.

He knew Tôgô's statement, that Japan should not impose several conditions, meant that Anami's three terms should be ignored.

When Tôgô finished, Suzuki stood and asked Admiral Yonai to comment. Anami was becoming livid. He knew that Yonai supported Suzuki's position and that if Yonai stated it before the Emperor then Admiral Toyoda might hesitate to oppose Suzuki's plan in front of the Emperor.

Yonai stood and said, "I agree with the foreign minister."

Anami, unable to control himself, leaped to his feet. "I oppose absolutely the opinions presented by the foreign minister. I am convinced, in fact, that the only honorable course open to our government is to proceed resolutely with the prosecution of the war. If the people of Japan approach the decisive battle for our homeland with determination to show their full measure of patriotism, and to fight until none of us survives, then, Your Majesty, I am convinced that Japan can overcome the crisis facing her. I am confident we can drive back the invaders on their initial thrust and inflict unacceptable losses upon them because we shall be protecting our own sacred soil. What one of us would not fight fiercely for his own home?

"But even if the enemy repeats his thrusts and we cannot repel him, would it not be wondrous for this whole nation to be destroyed like a beautiful flower, leaving for the world's posterity only the great name of Japan and its brave, noble history? Would it not be glorious to be remembered as a people who refused to submit? Would it not be far better than surrendering ignominiously to our enemies?

"But if we are not to follow so stern a course, if we are to seek peace, let us insist that we seek it honorably."

He looked at Admiral Yonai and Prime Minister Suzuki,

both military men. "You speak of one condition, the condition that our Imperial House be preserved. But let me ask you: if the enemy refuses to grant that condition, would you agree that we go on fighting?"

Suzuki realized that Anami had moved his queen across the board. He nodded then said, "Yes. If the enemy refuses that condition, we shall continue the fight."

Anami looked at Yonai. "Yes," said Yonai.

The arguments went back and forth, both sides emotional.

Then Suzuki asked that Admiral Toyoda speak.

"I find myself still in support of General Anami and General Umezu," said Admiral Toyoda. "We can not predict that victory is certain in the final battle for our homeland; however, we cannot be certain that we will be defeated. If we negotiate with the enemy, our terms should reflect General Anami's four terms. And regarding demobilization, we must be particularly firm. Unless we disarm our own men, I cannot guarantee that the navy will agree to demobilization."

Suzuki realized that they were still deadlocked. Then Tôgô stood. "Every member of this council has spoken. Yet after two hours of debate and more hours of previous discussion we have not achieved agreement. We are hopelessly deadlocked. But Japan is in a terrible situation. We cannot afford further delay. Therefore, I propose to ask His Majesty for his opinion on the issue, and I hope we shall accept his opinion as our own."

Then Suzuki moved toward Emperor Hirohito's table. He bent from the waist at a ninety-degree angle and said, "I present myself humbly at the foot of the Throne, and I beseech Your Imperial Majesty's opinion as to which proposal we should adopt, the one stated by Foreign Minister Tôgô or the one proposed by General Anami."

The room was stunned into shocked silence. What Suzuki had asked had never been done in modern times. Even Tôgô and Sakomizu, who had known what Suzuki intended, were awestruck when he put forth his request.

Hirohito was swept with emotion. From childhood he had been taught that an Emperor should reign but never govern. In his twenty-year reign he had never once offered an official opinion on government policy. No prime minister had ever asked him to render an opinion. He was now prepared to do so but his white-gloved hands shook. He was about to begin when he saw that Suzuki was still standing.

"You may go back to your seat," he said softly.

Suzuki, deaf in one ear, cupped his other and said, "Pardon?"

Emperor Hirohito extended his gloved hand and in a kindly voice said, "Go back to your seat."

When Suzuki sat Emperor Hirohito stood. His audience stood and bowed then took their seats, at attention.

"I have given serious thought to the situation prevailing at home and abroad and have concluded that continuing the war can only mean destruction for the nation and a prolongation of bloodshed and cruelty in the world. I cannot bear to see my innocent people suffer any longer. Ending the war is the only way to restore world peace and to relieve the nation of the terrible distress with which it is burdened.

"I was told by those advocating a continuation of hostilities that by June new divisions would be placed in fortified positions at Kujûkuri Beach so that they would be ready for the invader when he sought to land. It is now August and the fortifications still have not been completed. Even the equipment for the divisions which are to fight there is insufficient and reportedly will not be adequate until after the middle of September. Furthermore, the promised increase in the production of aircraft has not progressed in accordance with expectations."

Anami, Umezu and Toyoda knew Emperor Hirohito's words were a public rebuke and were humiliated.

"There are those who say," Hirohito continued, "the key to national survival lies in a decisive battle in the homeland. The experiences of the past, however, show that there has always been a discrepancy between plans and performance. I do not believe that the discrepancy in the case of Kujûkuri Beach can be rectified. Since this is the shape of things, how can we repel the invaders?"

General Anami felt isolated and knew that his world was crumbling. Several of the men listening suppressed their sobbing though they could not hide the tears.

"I cannot help feeling sad when I think of the people who have served me so faithfully, the soldiers and sailors who have been killed or wounded in far-off battles, the families who have lost all their worldly goods—and often their lives as well—in the air raids at home. It goes without saying that it is unbearable for me to see the brave and loyal fighting men of Japan disarmed. It is equally unbearable that others who have rendered service should now be punished as instigators of the war. Nevertheless, the time has come when we must bear the unbearable.

"When I recall the feelings of my Imperial Grandsire, the Emperor Meiji, at the time of the Triple Intervention, I swallow my own tears and give my sanction to the proposal to accept the Allied proclamation on the basis outlined by the Foreign Minister."

Emperor Hirohito wiped tears from his eyes. Every man in the room was weeping openly. No one spoke. Emperor Hirohito turned and left the room. One of the men fell to the floor, weeping loudly. All had the same emotion: none feared for their lives or positions. Rather they were humiliated that they had failed their Emperor; that Hirohito would be the first Emperor in an unbroken line of 124 Emperors to capitulate to a foreign power.

When the door closed upon Emperor Hirohito's exit Prime Minister Suzuki stood. "His Majesty's decision should be made the decision of this conference as well."

No one spoke. To all it meant their silence was an assent to Emperor Hirohito's opinion. Japan would offer to surrender to the Allies with but one condition, that the Emperor not be "disturbed."

The conference ended at 2:30 A.M., August 10, 1945.

At 3:00 A.M. a meeting of the Cabinet was held, unanimously adopting a decision based on the Emperor's opinion. When the meeting ended Tôgô returned to his office at the Foreign Ministry and cabled the Swiss Foreign Ministry, asking Switzerland to inform the Allied governments that Japan would agree to the Potsdam Declaration.

Included in Tôgô's message was, "The Japanese Government are ready to accept the terms enumerated in the joint declaration which was issued at Potsdam on July 26, 1945, by the heads of the Governments of the United States, Great Britain, and China, and later subscribed by the Soviet Government, with the understanding that the said declaration does not comprise any demand which prejudices the prerogatives of His Majesty as a Sovereign Ruler."

36

Kyoko awoke with the sun. She put on a *yukata* and went to the toilet. When she returned she pulled back the blackout covering. She picked up the blankets and pillow and stored them. Then she looked at Ken. He was sleeping. His eye was bruised from when he hit his head saving her son but it was not swollen shut. She went closer and became alarmed. His breathing was shallow and his body was shaking as if shivering. She touched his skin. It was wet and hot. She knew he had a fever and also knew that his wound was infected and had already spread to his blood; it was septicemia.

"Kenji-*san*! Kenji-*san*!" She tapped his cheek several times until he responded.

"Wha... What is it?"

"You have an infection. It has spread to your blood."

"What are you talking about?"

"Your wound is infected and it has spread to your blood. I have to treat it."

"What do you have to do?"

"I need to return to the hospital and get medicine. You need to stay absolutely quiet while I am gone. No one must know you are here. Do you understand?"

"Sure. Just hit me on my head and I'll go back to sleep."

Kyoko smiled and shook her head. "I'll be back soon. Stay

in the room."

She removed her *yukata*, dressed and brushed her hair. She turned and saw that Ken had been watching her. She blushed. She grabbed her bag. At the entrance to the house she removed her slippers and put on her shoes and walked back to Saint Luke's Hospital, to the main entrance.

"Ah! Doctor Masamune!" said the receptionist. "Your patient is missing!"

"Really?"

"Yes. One of the nurses went to his room to check on him and he was gone. And so were his belongings. The *Kempeitai* were here earlier asking about him."

Kyoko became fearful and wondered if there were any *Kempeitai* around the hospital grounds. "What did you tell them?"

"There was nothing to tell. We knew nothing." The receptionist looked at Kyoko for a moment then continued, "They asked which doctor operated on him but we told them that no records were made as it was an emergency. But they did take his uniform."

Kyoko knew the receptionist and staff had lied to the *Kempeitai* and sighed with relief. "Perhaps he felt strong enough to return to his base. You know how dedicated soldiers are, *neh*?"

She left, heading to the ward to check on patients for about thirty minutes. Then she went to the room which contained medicines. She looked before she entered and locked the door behind her then began her search.

Kyoko knew the only drug that could treat septicemia was penicillin, in large doses. Penicillin was discovered quite serendipitously by Alexander Fleming, a Scottish bacteriologist, in 1928. However, not until 1939 were British scientists able to prove that penicillin could kill bacteria. But England was in a war of survival and England's scientists did not have the facilities to produce the drug in necessary quantities, so England turned to the United States for help. In 1941 a small sample was brought to the United States where a method of mass production was developed. By 1943 clinical trials were conducted and penicillin proved to be the most effective antibacterial at the time. With the American method of mass production the drug was available to Allied soldiers in time for the Normandy Invasion, saving thousands of Allied lives.

Obviously, neither Germany nor Japan had benefitted from U.S.-produced penicillin. However, Japan knew about the drug from pre-war medical journals. Japanese physicians, knowing of the importance of penicillin, went about trying to develop it. By 1944 scientists at the Imperial Japanese Army Medical School succeeded in developing *penishirin* and called it *hekiso*, due to its blue color. However, by this time Japan's ability to mass produce anything unrelated to war matériel was nigh nonexistent. But enough was produced to provide it to government and senior military leaders in Tôkyô. And given the fact that Saint Luke's Hospital had never been bombed by the Americans, civilian and military leaders were treated there and *hekiso* was in sufficient quantity.

Kyoko found what she needed and grabbed 20 bottles as well as half a dozen syringes with needles and put them in her bag. Additionally, she grabbed bandages and tape and placed them in her bag. Fearing she might encounter the *Kempeitai* she left through the rear door and retraced the path she and Ken had taken last night. Her pace was even, avoiding attention. She soon reached the house and went to her room. She found Ken's condition had worsened. The penicillin she had was formulated in anhydrous or pharmaceutical-grade oil rather than an aqueous solution, insuring it would remain in the body for at least twelve hours. With hurried precision she warmed the bottles by placing them between her thighs and squeezing tightly. Within minutes the viscous solution was sufficiently liquefied that she could draw from each bottle a sufficient quantity to equal two million units of penicillin. She went to Ken and gently turned him on his left side and injected him in the right buttock muscle. Though liquefied it still took over a minute to infuse the solution. Done, she gently rolled him onto his back and sat in the chair and waited.

Every hour she checked Ken's status. In about twelve hours, around 9:00 P.M., his shivering stopped and his fever receded. Quietly she left the house and went to buy fresh food; she knew he would be famished when he awoke. When she returned he was awake.

"It is good to see you are better," she said.

"I feel better, I think. What happened?"

"You developed an infection where you were shot and it spread to your blood. I gave you medication that stopped the infection."

"So you saved my life? I guess that makes us even."

"Not quite. You also saved my son's life."

"Yes, Takuma. Tell me about him."

Kyoko became uncomfortable. "Later, perhaps. You must be hungry. I have some fresh food for us."

"I am. I have money to pay you back. It's in my uniform."

Kyoko looked away for a moment. "The *Kempeitai* came to the hospital this morning, before I was there. They asked about you. No one knew anything except that you had had surgery and that you had left."

"That's good."

"No. They took your uniform."

"Damn!"

"It does not matter. There was blood on it and one of the nurses had to cut your tunic and shirt to remove it. You could not have worn them."

"I suppose you're right. But they know you operated on me. I have to leave before you get in trouble."

"They do not know who operated on you; the receptionist

lied. But you cannot leave now. The infection may return."

"What about you?"

"No one knows about this place, remember?"

"Sure. But what about your parents and your son?"

"My father is very powerful; he has treated many of Japan's political elite. He is more important alive than in prison." She walked the length of the room while in thought. Then, "Perhaps it might be wise if I visited my parents' home tomorrow, just in case. You will stay here."

"Are you sure it's wise to visit them? You may have to tell them about me."

"Only if they bring it up. I will tell them that I have been working at the hospital and sleeping there. That is what I have told them before. It is not unusual for doctors to sleep there. I will not be gone long. Eat as much food as you wish. Then get some sleep. In the morning I will get more on the way back from my parents."

Ken enjoyed the food and Kyoko enjoyed watching him.

"I see that you still have the radio," said Ken. "Can we listen to some music?"

She turned on the radio and chose an American station so he could listen to Jazz, always his favorite, but she kept it low. Soon Ken started to nod off. She checked his bandaging for blood and saw none. She pulled the blanket over him then got her blankets and pillow. Before she undressed she shut off the light then stripped to her underwear. She turned and heard his breathing. It was regular and she knew he was already asleep.

She knew tomorrow would be difficult.

37

August 11

As always, Kyoko arose with the sun. She put on her *yu-kata* and went to the toilet. When she returned she opened the blackout cloth. With the sun entering the room Ken awoke.

"Kenji-*san*, you need to bathe and I need to change the bandage."

"What about the woman?"

"Do not worry. She and her husband have left. He will be gone all day at work and she will shop for food. She will be gone for hours. Come, I will help you."

She helped him stand and put on his *yukata*, which she had found in his bag. They then went to the *yoku-jô*, the tub room. It was smaller than at Oba-*san's ryokan* but just as clean. It too had a *yokusô*, a wooden tub, and a *koshikake*, a low stool. Kyoko removed Ken's *yukata* then, to his embarrassment, his *fundoshi*, placing it aside. She would wash it later. She knew he had a clean one in his bag.

"Sit on the stool. Here," she said, handing him the hand-basin. "Wash your body except for your back. I will return to remove the bandage and wash your back."

Just like at Oba-*san's ryokan* the hand-basin contained a bar of soap, a pumice stone, and some scrub cloths and sponges. Here too was a cold-water tap in the wall. On a shelf were folded towels. Ken removed the contents of the hand-basin and used it to scoop water from the *yokusô* and sponged himself carefully, avoiding his back. He washed his head, chest and legs then stood and washed his genitals and between his buttocks. His shoulder still ached and hindered his movements. Again, being careful to avoid his back, he rinsed. A moment later Kyoko entered the room. Ken was careful to keep his back toward her.

"I am going to remove the bandage and wash your back," she said.

Delicately, she pulled the tape and removed the bandaging. The wound was swollen but there was no sign of bleeding; the suturing had held. She rubbed the soap against the sponge and began to wash his back, first focusing on the wound. Ken reacted when she gently pressed against it. "Sorry," she said.

"It's all right. How does it look?"

"The wound looks like it will heal well."

Ever so gently she glided the sponge over the incision one more time. Again, Ken moved his shoulder away a tad then relaxed. Kyoko moved away from the wound and moved to the rest of his back. It was still muscular but more so. She found herself scrubbing with an erotic intensity and her breathing became rapid as she washed his lower back. She stopped and put down the sponge and rinsed his back.

"Kenji-*san*, can you stand? Some soap has drained further down and I need to rinse it off."

Ken stood and she poured more water over his lower back to allow it to rinse his buttocks.

"Let me look at your forehead," she said as she moved to his front. She could not miss that he was fully aroused and for a moment she looked away; then, she looked into his eyes and swallowed. "The bruising has begun to recede," she said. "Let me dry your back." She reached for a towel and gently dried his back. As she approached his buttocks she stopped. "Can you finish?"

"Yes," he replied.

Ken dried his head, neck and front torso. But he found it difficult to dry his legs due to his shoulder wound.

"Let me help you," said Kyoko. She dried his buttocks and legs then moved to his front and dried his legs. As she bent to dry his shins her face neared his erect penis and she became dizzy. She stood, got his *yukata* and put it on him then tied it. It did not hide his response to her closeness.

"Thank you," he said. He was breathing rapidly.

"I must go and see my parents and my son. Come back to the room and I will bandage your back." She picked up the towel and his *fundoshi*.

Ken followed her and she removed his *yukata* and helped him put on his clean *fundoshi*. Struggling to remain professional she again examined his wound and bandaged it. With reluctance she dressed quickly. "I do not know how long I will be gone. There is food here when you get hungry. Whatever you do, do not make any noises while I am gone. Here, let me help you lie down."

For a while after Kyoko left, Ken could think of nothing else except that she seemed more beautiful than ever. Soon, his mind was racing about his mission. Deciding to listen to the radio, he got up and turned it on. He found the *Nippon Hôsô Kyôkai*, the NHK or Japanese Broadcasting Company, and listened to the music. Suddenly the program was interrupted with an announcer confirming that Nagasaki had been destroyed by America's new bomb. Ken's skin prickled. He knew the atomic bomb had been used again.

*　　　*　　　*

Kyoko walked to her parents' home, near *Tôdai*. Like most Japanese she had become inured to Tôkyô's destruction. Or so she thought. The few children she saw, lethargic due to illness or malnutrition, tugged at her heart, but there was nothing she could do.

Her parents' home was a little larger than those near it, reflecting his position at Saint Luke's Hospital, but was unpretentious otherwise.

When she entered she removed her shoes and put on slippers. Takuma heard her and came running, all the while yelling, "*Okâ-san! Okâ-san!*" Mommy! Mommy! She reached down and scooped him up, covering his face with kisses while he giggled.

She carried Takuma into the main room and sat down with him on her lap.

"Did you miss mommy?"

"Yes! Yes!" She smiled and hugged him tighter. Then her father entered the room.

"Ah, Kyoko-*chan*! It has been a few days."

Kyoko looked down for a second then stood. "Takuma-*san*, go to *Obaa-san*! She will give you something to eat."

"I do not want Grandma! I want to stay with you!"

She smiled, as did her father. She lowered Takuma to the floor. "Just for a little while. I need to speak with *Ojii-san*."

Takuma reluctantly went to find his grandmother.

"Kyoko-*chan*, where have you been? We have been worried about you."

"I have been busy at the hospital, *Otô-san*."

"Come; let us go to my study. We need to talk."

Kyoko dreaded this. Her father became a different person when they went to his study. He was overbearing enough but his study only heightened his intimidation. Whenever they entered it, she habitually looked at the number of books that lined the walls; she was certain there were more than 5,000. And she knew he had read all of them. The majority were Japanese, but many were American, British and German. Some were Greek or Latin, two other languages he had studied in school besides English and German. This was his domain, which he ruled like a *daimyô*, a feudal lord.

"Sit, Kyoko-*chan*. So, the hospital has been very busy?"

She knew he was mocking her. But it was parental, not hurtful. He had never belittled her; she was, like his wife, the center of his life and he loved them both. He could, she admitted to herself, read her like a book.

"No, *Otô-san*. I have been remiss in my obligations."

"I had some visitors yesterday. They were very polite but they had a keen interest in you."

Kyoko felt a chill. "Who were they?"

"Two *Tokkô*. Now, why would the *Tokkô* be interested in you?"

"I do not know, Father."

"I gather that there was an Army officer who had been injured and taken to Saint Luke's. Someone performed surgery on him. Might you know who the surgeon is?"

Tears began to flow down her cheeks. Her father arched an eyebrow. *So the game begins*, he thought.

"I am the surgeon."

"You state the obvious. But the *Tokkô* were uncertain. They asked me because I am the chief surgeon at the hospital. I told them I did not know but would investigate and would report if I found out. So now you have told me what I already knew. Who is the officer?"

Her tears flowed freely. He realized she was not trying to manipulate him as she had done when she was younger.

"Kobayashi."

His eyebrows knitted as he thought for a moment. "Tomoyuki? Why would he be at Saint Luke's? The Army has a fine hospital."

"No, Father. Kenji."

He stiffened in his leather chair, looking at Kyoko with shock. "Kenji? How? He is in America."

"No, Father. He is here, in Tôkyô."

"What is he doing here? Why—"

"*Otô-san*! He saved my life. He saved Takuma's life! He was shot in the back and I was there when it happened."

"Who shot him?"

"An American pilot..."

"I do not understand at all. Please explain."

Kyoko wiped the tears, gathering herself. "I had worked at the hospital overnight. Takuma had slept there while I worked. I was going to bring him here so I could return to work. We were at Tsukiji Station when an Army truck approached. Suddenly, several American planes attacked and destroyed the truck. Then they started to shoot civilians." She told him the rest of the story, her and Takuma's rescue by an Army officer, and that she had taken him to the hospital. Only after surgery did she realize it was Kenji.

"Where is he now," her father asked.

"He is safe."

"He is in your room?"

"What?"

"Kyoko-*chan*, I am your father. I have known about the room for quite some time. Your mother and I assumed you had a lover. Now, tell me why Kenji is in Tôkyô."

Kyoko knew it was not a request. She told him everything. When she finished she sat back and looked at the floor.

Her father absorbed the implications of her account. "Do you realize the risk to yourself, to Takuma and your family?"

She noted he had not addressed her by her name. "*Otô-san*, I did not know who he was until after the surgery!"

"Why did you not call the *Tokkô* when you knew?"

"I...I was in shock. *Otô-san*, I loved him."

"You mean you love him."

She looked at her father, wanting to be a little girl again. "Yes."

He stood and walked toward one of the bookshelves, reading the titles. He saw one, written by a doctor he had worked with at Columbia University's College of Physicians and Surgeons in New York City. He had respected the American surgeon but now he was an enemy, according to Japan, and perhaps even performing surgery on American soldiers who had killed Japanese soldiers.

"So, he is a spy."

"Yes. No. He wants to end the war. He wants to save lives. He wants to save Japanese lives. He told me about young boys being trained to wear dynamite on their backs to destroy American tanks and trucks. Do you not see? He wants to save those boys. He wants to save Takuma! He is Japanese too!"

"So, he is a traitor to his own people?"

"*Otô-san*, he has two loyalties. And he wants to save both nations from further destruction. Can you not see that?"

Dr. Masamune walked along the walled bookcase, letting his fingers touch every book's spine like a boy stroking a white picket fence with a stick. He liked his books; they had given him solace during the past few years. He knew the war was lost, that the Americans were closing the loop around Japan's neck. He saw how American bombers had destroyed his beloved Tôkyô with impunity. And he too had seen young and old being trained to repel American invaders as well as hearing gunfire on the campus of his beloved *Tôdai*. Like other educated Japanese he knew in 1941 that Japan could never have defeated America or equaled America's industrial might. Now an invasion was imminent and Japan would be unable to repel it. His shoulders sagged.

With his back to his daughter he asked, "What do you intend to do?"

"I do not know. I cannot betray him."

He turned to her. Not for the first time he noted that she had lost weight and looked wan. "No, I do not think you could. Do you wish to bring him here?"

"No!" At first alarmed, she calmed down. "Besides, I know he would not want to. As it is he fears endangering me."

"Why did you come here," he asked.

"I need you to take care of Takuma for a few days. By then Kenji will be strong enough to leave."

"Will you let him leave?"

"What do you mean?"

"You just told me you love him."

"He has to do what he must."

Dr. Masamune returned to his chair and was silent for several minutes. Then, "Your mother and I will care for Takuma. I fear we will not be able to care for you. What will you do now?"

"I need to return to the hospital and see some patients. After, I will go to my room and talk with Kenji."

"Go. I will explain to your mother as much as I think she can tolerate. You know that I love you."

Kyoko leaped from her chair and hugged her father then quickly left, not even saying goodbye to Takuma or her mother. Something else was driving her.

*   *   *

Kyoko returned from the hospital around 8:00 P.M. When she turned on the light she found Ken asleep. She noted that he had closed the blackout cloth on the window. She was exhausted and decided to bathe herself and take a hot soak to relax. She quietly disrobed and put on a *yukata* and went to the *yokusô*. After bathing she stepped into the *yokusô* and relaxed, letting the hot water release her tension. She thought it fortunate that she rarely encountered the owners of the house. But they were used to the hours she worked at St. Luke's. She stayed in the water for about thirty minutes then got out, toweled off and put on her *yukata*, and returned to her room. Ken was still asleep. She laid out the blankets and removed her *yukata* and got under the top blanket. She rolled on her right, facing Ken. Her eyes adjusted to the near-darkness. She could hear Ken breathing regularly and was pleased; the infection was gone. Ken was laying on his left side, something patients often did in their sleep to take pressure off the injured side.

While listening to Ken breathe she was conflicted; he was an enemy, a spy. She was obligated to tell the authorities. But she had never stopped loving him, and his being with her now only enhanced that love. She ached for his touch.

She was naked and recalled the last time they had lain together, in April 1941, before he returned to America. Slowly, she reached her hand across and touched his left forearm. Ken moved his arm but otherwise did not respond. She waited a moment then gently stroked his arm. Though asleep, he moved his arm closer, responding to her touch. To her his skin was electrifying; her body trembled. She had not had a man since Ken, and her body ached for the touch of a man, especially a man she loved.

"Kyoko," he said.

Panicked, she pulled her hand back. *If I pretend I'm not here he will fall asleep*, she thought. She was wrong.

"Kyoko, I know you are here. What time is it?"

"It is late. Go back to sleep."

"I know it's late. Where have you been?"

"I was at the hospital. I had some patients to see."

"You visited your parents today. How are they and Takuma?"

"They are fine. Takuma misses me but he is used to being with my parents."

"And your father?"

She was unresponsive for several minutes; he did not press her. Then, "He knows you are here," she replied.

Ken sighed. "Does he know why I am here?"

She nodded and then smiled, realizing he could not see her.

"Yes. I could not lie to him. Do not worry; he will not say anything."

"How do you know? I'm a spy."

"Because the *Tokkô* spoke with him yesterday, asking about a doctor operating on a soldier at Saint Luke's. He told them nothing."

Ken, trusting her, was relieved. He thought about her stroking his arm. They were silent for several minutes. There had been a thought in his mind since they arrived at her room. The darkness gave him the courage to ask.

"Kyoko, how old is Takuma?"

Kyoko froze. She never expected the question yet feared it.

"Why do you ask?"

"I'm curious. When was he born?"

Her body froze. "January 1942."

Ken was silent. Being an engineer the math was simple.

"Kyoko, when were you going to tell me?"

She started to cry. "I was afraid to."

"Afraid? Of what?"

"When I wrote to you I wanted to tell you, but I feared that you would not want to know you would be a father. We were not married. I thought you would look at me in a different way, that I was not a respectable girl. I feared you would reject me."

Ken thought about what she must have gone through, particularly the disapproval of her father and the ridicule of her classmates. He was amazed that she was allowed to continue her studies in medicine.

"Kyoko, why were you rubbing my arm?"

"I have missed you; I thought I had lost you."

"Kyoko, put on the light."

"I cannot."

"Why not?"

"I have no clothes on."

Ken laughed. "Put on your *yukata* then put on the light. Please. It's important."

Kyoko got up and put on her *yukata* then turned on the light.

Ken looked at her for a moment. Her hair was down and he could see her curves. "Please get my bag."

She did so. Ken said, "Open it up and take everything out."

Confused, she did as he asked. Sitting on the floor she removed each item carefully. When she removed his pistol she handled it as if it might infect her. Ken smiled. When she reached the bottom her hand froze. She turned to Ken. He smiled. She reached for the small item. It was folded blue paper. Gold-like string held the paper together. Though she knew what it was she carefully untied the knotted string and peeled back the paper, careful not to tear it. Inside, a small red string lay on white paper. When she looked at him, astonished, she smiled through her tears.

"Remember what you said to me when I started to board the boat in 1941?"

Kyoko looked at the red string. "Yes, I do." She closed her eyes. "'You are tied by an invisible red string to your future husband even before you are born.'" Her eyes welled up. "'Please keep this next to your heart and remember me.'"

"I have never forgotten you. Nor the red string. The day I met you I had decided that I was going to marry you. I haven't changed my mind. Or my heart. Come to me."

She looked at him for a long moment. He pulled back the blanket. She returned the small paper to his bag and stood and walked to the lamp. Then she changed her mind and untied her *yukata* and stood there for a moment. With his eyes he drank in her body. She was thinner; that was the war. But she was still the most beautiful woman he had seen and he longed for her even more.

She walked to the *futon*. Ken lay on his back and she lay beside him on his left. With her help he removed his *fundoshi*. She was more zealous than he, which made him thirst with anticipation.

He was hard and eager. She was moist and yearning. Conscious of his injury she mounted him and took hold of his engorged manhood and guided it into her, moaning deeply as each inch penetrated deeper. When she fully engulfed him she did not move. She placed his left hand on her breast. He lifted his right arm and placed his hand on her left breast. The pleasure journeyed down to her vagina like an electrical current. His fingers gently rolled her nipples, heightening her sense of pleasure. During Ken's absence her only pleasure had been her hand. From his two hands and his penis the sensation was overwhelming.

Ken also did not move but flexed his hardened organ; she squeezed back in response to each of his pulsations.

Their eyes locked. She longed to kiss him but feared leaning on him. As if reading her desire he placed his hands on her upper arms and pulled her down. She immediately placed her hands on the *futon* to support her weight. Their kiss was long and deep, as if they were trying to consume each other. He pushed her back and said, "Come to me."

"No, not now. Can we just stay like this for a moment?"

"No. Come to me. I want you."

She smiled as she lifted off his raging manhood and moved up, to the one place that often made her lightheaded and always lifted her to ever higher plateaus of ecstasy. She carefully placed her vulva over his mouth. She bent forward, her hands on either side of his head, and breathlessly waited.

Like a newborn to a nipple his tongue softly stroked and probed. Her body shuddered. Her taste was aromatic, as she had always been. Her moistness flowed over his tongue and he swallowed as if in urgent thirst. His tongue probed deeper, licking the walls of her vagina. He pulled it back then sucked her labia into his mouth while stroking them with his tongue. She sat up and put her hands behind his head and intertwined her fingers then lifted his head as if to pull him fully inside her. His licking became fervent, inducing spasms of intense pleasure. Soon her body tensed. She struggled to suppress her cries. Then he stopped. Far from disappointed, she moved back. He was still hard, if not more so, and she mounted him again. She bent forward and kissed him and licked her wetness around his mouth.

Slowly she moved her hips back and forth while Ken lay still. He liked it when she was in control. In moments her moans came more rapidly and her thrusting increased in rhythm. She bit her lower lip to keep the cries locked in her throat as her body rocked with continuous waves of pleasure, cresting, descending then cresting again, over and over. Then her eyes closed and the world disappeared while the pleasure her body experienced overtook all else. She stopped moving for a moment and looked into his eyes. She saw the spark and readied herself.

Ken's breathing increased. He could no longer keep himself from moving and he thrust up and down, slowly at first but soon faster. He swallowed, longing to taste her again yet needing to stay inside her, to be part of her. He lifted his hands up to touch her face but she grabbed them and intertwined her fingers with his as he began to moan. She took one of her hands and put it over his mouth, hoping the owners of the house would not hear. His body shook as he arched his back, the pain in his shoulder a vague memory. Then he stopped, the pleasure too intense to move.

Kyoko bent forward again and rested her head on his left shoulder and wept. He wrapped his arms around her. After a while she straightened her legs and lay on top of him. Soon, both fell asleep. He was still inside her.

38

August 12

The men assembled in the room read and reread the English language version of the translated radio broadcast from *Dômei*, Japan's official Radio News Service. Japan was offering to surrender.

These were serious men and each weighed every word carefully. With President Harry S. Truman were James F. Byrnes, Secretary of State; Henry L. Stimson, Secretary of War; James V. Forrestal, Secretary of the Navy, and Fleet Admiral William D. Leahy, Truman's personal Chief of Staff and the first U.S. military officer to ever hold a five-star rank in the U.S. Armed Forces.

Of principal concern to President Truman was whether Japan's offer to surrender was "unconditional" or "conditional." Within the document were the disquieting words, "...with the understanding that the said declaration does not comprise any demand which prejudices the prerogatives of His Majesty as a Sovereign Ruler."

Secretary Stimson reasoned that the presence of Emperor Hirohito on the throne was imperative, not only to the Japanese but to America, because only Hirohito could guarantee a peaceful occupation. All other leaders, military and civilian, would be subject to arrest and trial as war criminals, but the Emperor, as head of the Imperial State as well as the population, was crucial. If the American Army were to arrest Hirohito, the Imperial Japanese forces would fight to the last man. Admiral Leahy and Secretary Forrestal agreed.

Secretary of State Byrnes objected, pointing out that both President Roosevelt and Prime Minister Churchill had demanded that Japan must surrender "unconditionally." Furthermore, since both England and China had signed the Potsdam Declaration both of those governments needed to be consulted. No clear decision was reached except to wait until the Japanese sent their official written version.

*　　　*　　　*

The Swiss government delivered a written note to the U.S. Embassy in Switzerland. It was forwarded to the U.S. State Department. It was read by the same group of men. Secretary of State Byrnes issued a statement to The Associated Press:

"With regard to the Japanese Government's message accepting the terms of the Potsdam proclamation but containing the statement, 'with the understanding that the said declaration does not comprise any demand which prejudices the prerogatives of His Majesty as a sovereign ruler,' our position is as follows:

"From the moment of surrender the authority of the Emperor and the Japanese Government to rule the state shall be subject to the Supreme Commander of the Allied Powers who will take such steps as he deems proper to effectuate the surrender terms.

"The Emperor will be required to authorize and ensure the signature by the Government of Japan and the Japanese Imperial General Headquarters of the surrender terms necessary to carry out the provisions of the Potsdam Declaration, and shall issue his commands to all the Japanese military, naval and air authorities and to all the forces under their control wherever located to cease active operations and to surrender their arms, and to issue such other orders as the Supreme Commander may require to give effect to the surrender terms.

"Immediately upon the surrender the Japanese Government shall transport prisoners of war and civilian internees to places of safety, as directed, where they can quickly be placed aboard Allied transports.

"The ultimate form of government of Japan shall, in accordance with the Potsdam Declaration, be established by the freely expressed will of the Japanese people.

"The armed forces of the Allied Powers will remain in Japan until the purposes set forth in the Potsdam Declaration are achieved."

39

August 13

Three hours before dawn Ken and Kyoko awoke to thousands of explosions rocking Tôkyô, dropped by hundreds of B-29s. Though they knew that their section of the city was safe Ken held her tight as Kyoko moaned in terror and covered her ears. But Tôkyô was not alone. Hundreds of B-29s struck other cities and military sites, beating an already-dead horse. Hundreds of other U.S. carrier-based fighter-bombers and fighter planes bombed and strafed targets throughout Japan.

After two hours the bombing stopped in Tôkyô, followed by the wails of fire trucks.

"Will they ever stop," asked Kyoko.

"Soon, I think," said Ken.

Kyoko sat up. "You said the invasion was not imminent. What makes you think the bombing will stop soon? Will the Americans invade soon?"

"No. Kyoko, I don't think there will be an invasion."

Kyoko's face displayed confusion. "What do you mean?"

"I have to tell you some things. While you were away I listened to the radio. The Soviet Union has declared war on Japan. They have already invaded Manchukuo in China and the Kwantung Army is falling back. Japan has no allies or friends; she is completely alone. Also, America has used another atomic bomb. Nagasaki has been destroyed."

Kyoko, stunned, turned away. "Then Japan will surrender?"

"Perhaps. If not, I think America will continue to use atomic bombs until Japan surrenders. Or ceases to exist."

Kyoko was silent for several minutes, thinking of Takuma and her parents. "I am confused. Why does Japan continue to fight?"

"Because Japan has never been conquered and the generals cannot grasp the idea of surrender."

Kyoko stood and began to dress. "Where are you going," asked Ken.

"I need to go to the hospital then go to my parents and spend some time with Takuma and talk with my father."

"When will you be back?"

"I do not know. Later tonight."

*　　*　　*

"Your father is anxious to speak with you, Kyoko-*chan*," said Kyoko's mother with a smile. "You will eat with us, *neh*?"

"*Arigatô, Okâ-san.*" Thank you, Mother. Kyoko was confused. It had been months since her mother had smiled.

"*Okâ-san! Okâ-san!*" Takuma came running and Kyoko picked him up and squeezed him, grateful that he was all right.

"*Okâ-san!* I heard *B-san* this morning! He was angry!" Kyoko and her mother looked at each other, saying nothing.

"Takuma-*chan*, I am going to speak with *Ojii-san*. Then you and I can play for a while."

"But I want to play now!"

"Just for a few minutes."

Takuma walked away, his head tilted down, breaking Kyoko's heart. She walked to her father's study and found him in his leather chair. He was smoking a pipe. He had not done so for uncounted months, mostly because he was husbanding what little American pipe tobacco he had left. The last case of tins had been sent by an American physician from Columbia just before the U.S. had embargoed Japan. The enclosed note had simply read, "I don't know when I will be able to send more."

"Ah, Kyoko-*chan*! Come in. Sit down."

Kyoko's guard was up. Her father seemed almost happy.

"How is Kenji," he asked.

She flushed and he saw it. Inwardly he smiled. "He is healing. *Otô-san*, I need to speak with you, I need your guidance."

"This sounds serious. How can I help you?"

"Kenji said the bombing may soon stop. He also said the Americans may not invade. I do not understand."

Her father puffed on his pipe a few times. "Kenji is probably correct."

Kyoko froze, her body numb. "What do you mean?"

"Have you been listening to your radio?"

"Kenji has."

"I have been listening to the radio as well. Perhaps Kenji and I are hearing the same things."

"Did you hear that Nagasaki has been destroyed?"

"Yes. Sadly, it is true."

"*Otô-san*! Please! Tell me what you know!"

"It was announced on an American radio station that the United States has accepted Japan's offer of surrender."

"I...I do not understand," she said softly.

"Apparently our government and military have reached the conclusion that it cannot stop the American atomic bombings and that Japan could be utterly destroyed. The war is over." He looked at his pipe then smiled. "I like American tobacco."

"What will happen?"

"I do not know. However, I suggest that we listen to the radio this evening and tomorrow morning early. Now, eat with us and play with your son. One other thought, Kyoko-*chan*. Perhaps it would be wise if Takuma met his father."

Kyoko heard her father's words but was incredulous at his suggestion.

❋   ❋   ❋

Ken heard the outer door open and stiffened. It was late afternoon. He made sure his pistol was within reach. Then he heard the peels of laughter of a youngster and relaxed. Kyoko opened the door and Takuma ran in. When Takuma saw Ken he stopped. He was not frightened but perplexed. His mother had never had anyone in the room except him.

"*Konnichiwa*," said Ken to the boy.

Takuma, ever polite, said "Hello" back.

Ken was pleased to see the boy was not scared, just curious.

Kyoko knelt down next to Takuma. "Takuma-*chan*, this is the man who saved your life. Do you remember?"

Takuma nodded uncertainly. Kyoko knew it was a distant memory. "His name is Kobayashi Kenji."

Ken nodded and said, "*Hajimemashite*." I am pleased to meet you.

Takuma nodded in response but said nothing. Ken looked at Takuma and saw his own youthful face from photos. *I have a son*, he thought. *I am a father*. It took all his emotional strength to keep from standing and reaching for his son but knew he would frighten the boy. He would follow Kyoko's lead. He had a lump in his throat. Kyoko saw his emotions and decided to maintain a relaxed demeanor.

"Here," said Kyoko, "I brought some food. My father said to say 'Hello.' It was his idea to bring Takuma here."

Ken was surprised. "Why?"

"He said it would be wise if Takuma were to meet his

father."

Takuma turned to look at Kenji. "Are you my father?"

"Yes, Takuma-*chan*. I am."

"Where have you been? Have you been fighting for *Tennô-Heika* far away?"

Ken looked at Kyoko for help. She smiled and shrugged. "I have been far away. But I have not been fighting."

"Are you in the Army?"

"Yes. But I do not fight."

"What do you do?"

Ken looked at Kyoko again, pleading for help with his eyes.

"Are you hungry," she asked.

"Starving."

As Kyoko prepared the food she had brought she said, "My father told me that you are right."

"About what?"

As Ken and Kyoko spoke Takuma was walking around Ken, taking measure of him as a youngster would. Ken was delighted that the boy was not shy.

"He said there will be no American invasion."

Suddenly alert, Ken listened to Kyoko while watching Takuma circle him.

"Why did he say that?"

Kyoko stopped what she was doing and looked at Ken, her face serious yet displaying relief. "He heard on the radio that Japan has offered to surrender."

"What?"

"While we were eating he told me that, according to an American radio broadcast, the Japanese government had asked the Swiss government to transmit a message to the American government. It was an offer to surrender and the Americans have accepted Japan's offer. That is all he knows. But he did urge that we listen to the radio tonight and early in the morning."

"Did he say why?"

"No. But you know my father. Though he is sometimes unfathomable I have never known him to be wrong. Here, as you said, you are 'starving.'"

For the rest of the evening Ken entertained Takuma as Ken's father had entertained his kids. Takuma was delighted with Ken's ability, using the lamp, to create animal silhouettes on the wall.

Later, Kyoko and Ken agreed that she and Takuma would sleep on the *futon* and that Ken would sleep on a blanket. At 8:00 P.M. Ken turned on the radio and tuned to an American station, broadcasting from Hawaii. The station was repeating that Japan had offered to surrender and the U.S. had accepted. Ken then tuned to the NHK channel but heard no further news. At midnight Kyoko got two blankets for Ken. He turned off the radio and he lay on the blanket and she covered him with the other. Kyoko turned out the light and lay down next to Takuma, holding him, knowing that he would be safe now that the war was over.

40

August 14, 1945

As was her habit, Kyoko awoke with the sun and quietly woke Ken. They turned on the radio to the NHK, the Japan Broadcasting Company channel, and heard static. They decided to leave it on NHK. Kyoko woke Takuma and they ate breakfast in anxious silence.

*　　*　　*

At 7:15 A.M. NHK went back on the air. Ken and Kyoko sat with anticipation, both hoping that the American radio station was true.

The NHK announcer's voice was animated as he read his prepared text:

"We now have a special announcement. The Emperor will graciously promulgate a rescript." There was a momentary pause. Ken and Kyoko heard paper being shuffled.

"The Emperor at noon today will graciously broadcast, in person. This is a most gracious act. All the people are requested to listen respectfully to the Emperor." The announcer paused again.

Ken and Kyoko looked at each other. No commoner in Japan had ever heard the Emperor's voice, the Voice of the Crane.

"Electricity will be supplied to all districts that do not normally have the supply during the daytime. We especially request government offices, business offices, factories, railroad stations, and post offices to make use of all available receivers so that all citizens can listen to the Emperor's broadcast. The most gracious broadcast will be at noon. Moreover, in some parts the newspapers will be delivered after 1 P.M."

Kyoko gestured for Takuma to come to her. She held him as she softly wept.

After almost five agonizingly long hours the music on the radio stopped. There was silence for several seconds. Then a man's voice began speaking. The entire nation knew who it was.

"To Our good and loyal subjects:

"After pondering deeply the general trends of the world and the actual conditions obtaining to Our Empire today, We have decided to effect a settlement of the present situation by resorting to an extraordinary measure.

"We have ordered Our Government to communicate to the Governments of the United States, Great Britain, China and the Soviet Union that Our Empire accepts the provisions of their Joint Declaration.

"To strive for the common prosperity and happiness of all nations as well as the security and well-being of Our Subjects is the solemn obligation which has been handed down by Our Imperial Ancestors, and which We lay close to heart. Indeed, We declared war on America and Britain out of Our sincere desire to ensure Japan's self-preservation and the stabilization of East Asia, it being far from Our thought either to infringe upon the sovereignty of other nations or to embark upon territorial aggrandizement.

"But now the war has lasted for nearly four years. Despite the best that has been done by everyone—the gallant fighting of the military and naval forces, the diligence and assiduity of

Our servants of the State and the devoted service of Our one hundred million people, the war situation has developed not necessarily to Japan's advantage, while the general trends of the world have all turned against her interest.

"Moreover, the enemy has begun to employ a new and most cruel bomb, the power of which to do damage is indeed incalculable, taking the toll of many innocent lives. Should We continue to fight, it would not only result in an ultimate collapse and obliteration of the Japanese nation, but also lead to the total extinction of human civilization. Such being the case, how are We to save the millions of Our subjects; or to atone Ourselves before the hallowed spirits of Our Imperial Ancestors? This is the reason why We have ordered the Acceptance of the provisions of the Joint Declaration of the Powers.

"We cannot but express the deepest sense of regret to Our Allied nations of East Asia, who have consistently co-operated with the Empire towards the emancipation of East Asia.

"The thought of those officers and men as well as others who have fallen in the fields of battle, those who died at their posts of duty, or those who met with untimely death and all their bereaved families, pains Our heart day and night. The welfare of the wounded and the war sufferers, and of those who have lost their homes and livelihood, are the objects of Our profound solicitude.

"The hardships and sufferings to which Our nation is to be subjected hereafter will certainly be great. We are keenly aware of the inmost feelings of all ye, Our subjects. However, it is according to the dictate of time and fate that We have resolved to pave the way for a grand peace for all the generations to come by, enduring the unendurable and suffering the insufferable.

"Having been able to safeguard and maintain the structure of the Imperial State, We are always with ye, Our good and loyal subjects, relying upon your sincerity and integrity. Beware most strictly of any outbursts of emotion which may engender needless complications, or any fraternal contention and strife which may create confusion, lead ye astray and cause ye to lose the confidence of the world. Let the entire nation continue as one family from generation to generation, ever firm in its faith of the imperishableness of its divine land, and mindful of its heavy responsibilities, and the long road before it.

"Unite your total strength to be devoted to the construction of the future. Cultivate the ways of rectitude; foster nobility of spirit; and work with resolution so as ye may enhance the innate glory of the Imperial State and keep pace with the progress of the world."

Silence followed. For both Ken and Kyoko it was anticlimactic, but in different ways.

For several minutes neither spoke. Then Kyoko looked at Ken and whispered, "I do not understand what His Majesty said."

Ken collected himself. "It was difficult for me too, at first. He spoke in archaic court language, something that Japanese do not speak."

"I did not hear the word 'surrender.' Was my father wrong?"

"No. The Emperor was speaking in an indirect fashion."

Kyoko was becoming anxious. "What do you mean?"

"He said that Japan has agreed to the Potsdam Declaration."

"What is that," asked Kyoko.

"It was issued by the United States, Great Britain and China, demanding Japan's unconditional surrender." He touched her hand. "Kyoko, listen to me. The Emperor has announced that Japan has surrendered without saying it. The war is over. There will be no invasion."

"Is that all," Kyoko asked, angered.

"What more do you want?"

"I want peace! But it is as if the Emperor has simply turned off the light in a room."

"Actually, he has turned the lights back on, the first time in many years."

Kyoko looked down for several seconds. Then, "What will happen now? We have been told that American Marines will kill and eat our children and that women will be raped and murdered. Will that happen?"

Ken smiled. "No, they never did. I saw a film of American Marines caring for Okinawan civilians during the battle. There was a young girl shaking and a Marine was taking care of her, giving her food and water. There will be no more killings."

"What will happen now?"

"The American Army will occupy Japan just as the Allies now occupy Germany."

Kyoko looked frightened. "Will the Russians occupy Japan?"

"Knowing General MacArthur, not one Russian soldier will step foot on Japanese soil."

Kyoko stood and picked up Takuma, holding him tightly. Ken looked at both of them and choked up.

Kyoko turned to Ken. "What will you do now?"

"I'll report to American military personnel when they come to Japan. I'm still a soldier."

Kyoko was saddened by Ken's words, knowing that he would soon return to America. Ken was silent for several minutes. Then he walked to the window and looked outside. After a moment he turned to her and smiled. She smiled back but there was a hint of sadness in her eyes.

Then Ken began to laugh. Kyoko was confused. His laughter increased in intensity and she became frightened. "Kenji, what is it," she asked.

"Don't you get it? I risked my life coming here, I'm almost killed by an American pilot saving a woman and fall on a boy, protecting him from harm. And all of it was unnecessary. I didn't have to come here."

"I don't understand," she said.

"The damn bombs! They ended the war! My being here was unnecessary!"

"Then why are you laughing?"

"Don't you see the irony?"

"What irony?"

"In coming to Japan I didn't help the American war effort but instead found the woman I love! And I find out that I'm a father! That's the irony." He walked to her and grabbed her shoulders. "And now that I've found you and Takuma I want to marry you and take both of you back to America with me. Will you come?"

Kyoko heard his question but was dizzy with the speed of his proposal. Then reality came crashing around her.

"I cannot," she said.

Ken released her and stepped back. "Why not?"

"I am a doctor. Japan needs doctors. I must stay and help rebuild my country. Can you understand that?"

"Sure, but America will help rebuild. And there are plenty of doctors in the American military."

"And," she replied, "like you they will want to go home. I have to stay. Besides, no one in America will want a Japanese doctor."

"Where I live in California there are plenty of Japanese Americans. You'll have all the patients you want."

Kyoko smiled. "Kenji. I now know how much I love you, but I must stay here, where I am needed. Perhaps in a year or two..."

Ken closed his eyes momentarily then sat down. Takuma, understanding little, went over to him and crawled up on his lap.

"*Otô-san*, can I go to America with you?"

Ken's eyes moistened; Kyoko cried. *I'm a father*, thought

Ken. *Can I leave my son here?*

"Kyoko. Did you hear Takuma?"

Kyoko, unable to speak, nodded.

Ken reached out and held his son and Takuma wrapped his arms around Ken's neck.

"If you are going to stay then I will too."

"What?" asked Kyoko.

"I've found you and my son. I can't leave you now."

"But you are in the Army."

"The American Army will be disbanded, except for those who stay here for the occupation. The rest of the men will want to go home to their families. Besides, I'm an engineer. I can help rebuild Japan. After all, it is my ancestral homeland."

"What about your family?"

"I think they will understand. Besides, there are two other reasons for my staying."

"What are they?"

"I want to find my brother; my parents and sisters will understand. And the second reason is that I want to have more babies with my wife."

Kyoko ran to him and fell to her knees in front of the chair. He embraced her with one arm while he held Takuma with his right arm. For the first time in more than three years, Ken felt he was home.

エピローグ

EPILOGUE

August 6, 1945

The *I-402* entered the Port of Kaohsiung on the southwestern coast of the island of Formosa, a colony of Japan. Following the 1894 Sino-Japanese war, Li Hung-chang, the Ch'ing Dynasty's ambassador, had traveled to Japan to conclude peace terms. The outcome was the Treaty of Shimonoseki of 1895, in which Taiwan was ceded to Japan. The occupation was brutal and rebellions were crushed by the Imperial Japanese Army with unbridled ferocity.

*　　*　　*

Four hours after the American destroyer had broken off the search Iwata got under way at six knots, covering about 40 kilometers.

It was approaching 1700 hours.

"Mori! Surface!"

"Chûsa?"

"Surface! First, we must remove the *kaiten* and make repairs. We must reach Formosa quickly and inform the base commander of the traitor on the American carrier! He then can send a coded message to Tôkyô!"

"Chûsa! American planes will be able to sight us!"

At that point Iwata decided to violate the principal rule

of every submarine commander: Protect your boat from detection.

Enraged, he turned and grabbed Mori by the throat. "And if we do not inform Tôkyô then the traitor may give information that will enable the Americans to further destroy Japan. Do you have an alternative, Mori? No? Then surface! All ahead full!"

When the *I-402* breached the surface Mori, shaken, ordered the *kaiten* tossed overboard and repairs made. Within two hours he ordered speed increased to 18.5 knots.

From 1700 hours to 0430 hours the *I-402* remained on the surface, running at 18.5 knots. From 0430 hours to 1700 hours the *I-402* submerged running at 6.5 knots. For two days the weather favored them. The dissipating typhoon still caused heavy clouds and rain, offering cover from American planes.

The *I-402* covered the last 350 kilometers in 24 hours, reaching Kaohsiung Harbor on August 6th, at dusk.

* * *

A harbor pilot boarded the *I-402*. He was the same rank as Iwata but in his fifties. Both knew nothing need be said. The pilot guided the boat into a berth usually occupied by a cruiser. However, there were no Japanese cruisers in Kaohsiung Harbor. Nor were there any other Japanese warships present. America's Navy and Army Air Force had destroyed them.

When the *I-402* was secured camouflage netting was dragged out to cover the boat.

Iwata went on the dock and informed the harbormaster of his mission. Immediately, the harbormaster ordered the boat offloaded. Japanese soldiers gathered scores of men, all of whom were prisoners of war. Their treatment was brutal, with several being beaten when they stumbled.

Iwata recognized the tattered uniforms covering the

walking skeletons: Americans, British, Australians and New Zealanders. He was disgusted at their treatment but knew that nothing he said would change the abuse. With shame he averted his eyes and followed a sailor to the base commander's office.

Iwata was introduced to Captain Koizumi. They exchanged salutes.

"Chûsa, would you like a cigarette?"

"Taisa! Thank you, no. I fear that our cigarettes no longer agree with me."

Captain Koizumi smiled. "These are American cigarettes, sent by the Red Cross."

Iwata took a cigarette and Koizumi lighted it. Iwata inhaled and smiled, the taste of the American tobacco recalling memories of 1941, the last time he had had an American cigarette.

"Iwata, are you thirsty? I can offer you some tea."

"Taisa! Thank you but *ocha* will not satisfy me."

Koizumi smiled and nodded. "I have American whiskey. Would that satiate your thirst?"

"*Ha!* It has been a long time, Taisa!"

Iwata, closing his eyes, relished the taste of the Kentucky bourbon whiskey.

"Iwata, we are grateful for your courage in bringing the supplies we desperately need. We believe that the Americans will invade Formosa soon."

"Perhaps, Taisa. But I have another issue to discuss with you."

"Explain, Chûsa."

Iwata brought the glass to his lips and finished the bourbon. Being a good host, Koizumi refilled it.

"Taisa, I saw something that was deeply disturbing. A Japanese Army officer was being transferred from an American destroyer to an American carrier."

Koizumi sat straight up. "Are you certain?"

"My Executive Officer also saw him."

"Certainly he was a prisoner."

"No. He saluted the Americans during the transfer."

Koizumi refilled his glass and quickly drank from it. "Itô!" he hollered. In seconds, a sailor entered the office.

"*Ha!*"

"Send for Kobayashi Shôsa!"

"*Ha!*" replied Itô, who walked out to find Kobayashi.

"Kobayashi Shôsa," said Koizumi, "is the Imperial Army's Intelligence officer in Chôshû. It is about one hundred and thirty kilometers north. I am certain he will fly here. He is an excellent pilot. Perhaps he will help us understand this event. I will have food brought here for you."

Two hours passed. Iwata enjoyed the fresh food and the American cigarettes. Briefly, guilt washed over him, knowing that the cigarettes should have gone to the American prisoners of war. His thoughts were interrupted by a knock.

"Enter!" said Koizumi. Itô opened the door and stepped aside, allowing an Imperial Japanese Army officer, dressed in a flight suit, to enter. Koizumi and Iwata stood.

"Iwata Chûsa, this is Kobayashi Shôsa—"

Iwata yelled "BADOGLIO!" and threw himself at Major Kobayashi Tomoyuki, his hands reaching for Kobayashi's throat. "BADOGLIO!"

Tomoyuki fell backward, Iwata's hands squeezing his throat. Stunned, Koizumi leaped from behind his desk and grabbed Iwata. Itô, never seeing officers behave in such a manner, stood frozen.

"Iwata! Iwata!" Koizumi yelled as he wrapped his arm around Iwata's throat, trying to pull him off. In a move for survival Tomoyuki reached down and grabbed Iwata's scrotum and squeezed. Iwata screamed but would not let go. Finally, the combined efforts of Koizumi and testicular pain forced Iwata to release his grip. Koizumi pulled Iwata off and held him down and ordered Itô to call for guards.

"Itô!" rasped Tomoyuki, still prone as he rubbed his throat. "Ignore that order! Koizumi Taisa! Please release Iwata Chûsa."

Confused, Koizumi stood.

Iwata slowly stood, bent forward as if to attack again.

"Iwata! Report!" said Tomoyuki, now standing.

Breathing heavily, Iwata stared at Tomoyuki, anger and confusion on his face. "I saw you transferring from an American destroyer to a carrier! My Executive Officer saw you as well! You held your *katana*! You saluted the Americans!"

"Iwata Chûsa! I have been on Formosa for six months! How can you be so certain..."

No one spoke for several moments. Tomoyuki picked up his scabbard. "Did he have this *katana*?"

Iwata walked closer and examined the hilt of the sword. "*Ha!*"

Color drained from Kobayashi's face. In a flash, everything became clear to him. He knew of the briefing at Ichigaya on August fifth. He swallowed several times.

"Koizumi Taisa! Please have my plane fully fueled and ready at once!"

"Shôsa?"

Kobayashi ignored Koizumi. He remembered the first major disagreement with his brother, Kenji, in 1937, when Imperial Japanese Army forces carried out unimaginable atrocities in Nanking, China. Countless tens of thousands were murdered by Japanese troops in an uncontrolled rampage, with the tacit approval of their superiors. *Life* magazine had carried photographs of the atrocities even though the Japanese government denied the reports. Chinese civilians were shot, beheaded, burned, bayoneted, buried alive, or disemboweled. Tens of thousands of young girls and women were raped then murdered by Japanese soldiers on a rampage not seen in centuries.

The final schism between the brothers came in April 1941, their graduation from Tôkyô Imperial University, when Tom informed his brother that he was remaining in Japan.

Now the battle continues, thought Tomoyuki.

"Koizumi Taisa! There is an enemy spy in Tôkyô! Ichigaya must be informed!"

"Then we will send a message!" replied Koizumi.

"No! The Americans have continuously broken our codes. If such a message is sent the Americans will be alerted. I will fly to Tôkyô and arrest the spy myself!"

"The Americans will shoot you down!"

"Not if I fly this night and avoid their ships! The *Shiden* will make the journey to Chôfu!"

"Kobayashi! The range of the *Shiden* is sixteen hundred kilometers! Chôfu is over two thousand kilometers!"

"If we strip all armaments and add an external fuel tank I can reach Chôfu! Please prepare my plane. I know this spy."

"What do you mean?"

Tomoyuki walked to a mirror hanging on the wall and saw two images.

"Is it not obvious? He is my brother."

ABOUT THE AUTHOR

Michael Dana Kennedy is a Boston native. He graduated from Harvard University with a dual major in history and political science then attended Tufts University School of Medicine for two years. He spent the majority of his career in clinical research. In the late '80s he entered M.I.T., studying computer science. Kennedy founded two companies, both of which he sold. He then turned his attention to his life-long interest in history and began researching and writing his debut novel, *The Flowers of Edo*.